LOST IN HIS ARMS

Lord Wrotham's big, rough hand took hers, but instead of leading her back to the floor, he made his way to Elizabeth, speaking a word in her ear.

She laughed and nodded, then rearranged her sheets of music.

He pulled Charlotte onto the floor to stand in front of him. "I hope you will not be too scandalized by my request, my lady." His eyes said he hoped she was and a thrill ran from her head to her toes.

"I doubt you can shock me, my lord." She raised her chin and stared straight into his coal-black eyes.

"We shall see." He grasped her hands, the power in his a tangible thing. His touch spread delicious warmth throughout her body. They bowed and Elizabeth began a waltz.

Not exactly scandalous, yet a bold choice. The first figure moved easily, with little intimate contact. Then, in the second figure, his arms were supposed to embrace hers. Instead, they reached all the way around her back until they touched. He pulled her closer to him, his lips pressed against her ear, and whispered, "And now, my lady? A waltz can be a scandalous dance if your partner is of a mind to make it so." He pressed her tighter, almost indecently.

Yet she did not struggle. Could not. His big body against her—the hard strength of him leaving nothing for her to imagine—persuaded her that to fight him was futile. She would never be free. Never wanted to be . . .

To Woo A Wicked Widow

JENNA JAXON

LYRICAL PRESS
Kensington Publishing Corp.
www.kensingtonbooks.com

LYRICAL PRESS BOOKS are published by

Kensington Publishing Corp.
119 West 40th Street
New York, NY 10018

All Kensington titles, imprints, and distributed lines are available at special quantity discounts for bulk purchases for sales promotion, premiums, fund-raising, educational, or institutional use.

Special book excerpts or customized printings can also be created to fit specific needs. For details, write or phone the office of the Kensington Sales Manager: Attn.: Sales Department. Kensington Publishing Corp., 119 West 40th Street, New York, NY 10018. Phone: 1-800-221-2647.

Lyrical and the Lyrical logo Reg. U.S. Pat. & TM Off.

First Kensington Printing: April 2018
ISBN-13: 978-1-5161-0325-6
ISBN-10: 1-5161-0325-4

First Electronic Edition: April 2018
eISBN-13: 978-1-5161-0324-9
eISBN-10: 1-5161-0324-6

10 9 8 7 6 5 4 3 2 1

Printed in the United States of America

Chapter 1

Moonlight streamed into the mews, brightening the night and making Lady Charlotte Fownhope draw back into the shadows of the stable. She strained to hear sounds from her father, the Earl of Grafton's, town house, but only the clink of bridles came to her ears as Edward, her groom, led her chestnut mare and his horse into the light.

"You should have taught me to saddle her. Then I could have helped you." She came forward to take the reins.

"I'll always be here to do that for you, my lady." He smiled, his white teeth a flash in the swarthy, handsome face, then leaned down to kiss her.

His warm lips caressed her, calmed her even as the comforting scent of horses and leather that hung about him enveloped her. This was where she belonged, in Edward's arms. Not with Lord Ramsay, her father's choice for a husband.

A horse snorted and Charlotte jumped back. "We must

be off. Dinner will last only so long. With luck, no one will look in on me but my cousin Jane, so we will have until the morning before they know I am gone."

Edward nodded and cupped his hands to give her a leg up.

Once in the saddle, she gathered the reins and waited for him to mount, her stomach tightening with excitement. "You know the way?"

"Yes, we take the Great North Road as far as York, then over to Manchester and up to Gretna Green." He slid into the saddle. "We'll be on horseback the first two days. They won't expect that. They'll be looking for a carriage." He reached over and grasped her hands. "You'll be all right on horseback for so long?"

She nodded, prompted to sit up straighter. If she had to spend a week in the saddle to be with Edward, she would do it. "Let's go."

They walked the horses out of the light, into the darkness of the underpass, keeping quiet until they were at the end of the row of stables. Charlotte resisted the urge to look over her shoulder to see if they had been pursued. They had been careful. They would succeed. She drew her black cloak around her shoulders against the now-chill wind.

At a nod from Edward, she tapped her horse and Bella started into a quick trot. The clop, clop of the hooves on the cobbled streets soothed her. After months of planning, they were on their way at last.

Several hours later, Charlotte and Edward slowed for another tollgate. They had passed through four already, and after the first, Charlotte had turned the bag of coins over to him to take care of the fees. A twinge in her hip, an ache in her thigh muscle told her that her body had begun to feel the strain of constant motion in the saddle.

When they finally stopped for the night, she doubted she would want to climb back on Bella tomorrow.

Slowed to a walk, her mare nickered, and from somewhere behind the toll gate another one answered. Charlotte patted her withers and glanced at Edward.

"Tollkeeper!" he called, rending the silent night. After a moment he called again, still with no result.

"He must be dead asleep." The wind had risen, causing Charlotte to tug her cloak closer.

"Dead drunk's more like." Edward dismounted, strode to the tollhouse door, and knocked.

The door jerked open. A huge hand grasped his shoulder, dragging him inside.

"Edward!" Charlotte dropped the reins, peeled her aching leg from around the horn of the sidesaddle, and slid to the ground. She must get to Edward. As her boots hit the dirt, two men appeared from nowhere.

"Ha, got ya!" They grabbed her arms, their rough fingers digging painfully into her flesh.

Terror shot through her veins, stopping her breath in her throat. Still, she managed to pull back and forth, trying to break free. No use. Their big hands clamped down on her like a vise as they hustled her toward the toll booth.

"Edward! Help! Someone, help!" Charlotte shrieked as they dragged her toward the building. Dear Lord, they must be highwaymen. She had heard sickening stories about the dangerous criminals who roamed the roads, preying on unlucky travelers. Her stomach twisted.

At the threshold they loosened their grip to get her through the door. Charlotte swung around and raked her fingernails down one man's face.

He bellowed and pushed her away, into the house.

She wheeled toward the other man, bent on a similar attack, but stopped, shocked at the tableau before her.

The flickering light of the hearth revealed a large man holding Edward's head down on a crude plank table, a pistol pressed against his temple. The tollkeeper in his nightshirt and cap, eyes wide, face pale, stood in front of the fire, staring at the scene. To the left of the table stood her father.

All the strength ran out of Charlotte's legs and she began to sink toward the floor.

The man she had wounded grabbed her arm and hauled her up. "No, you don't. That's all, your lordship. Just the two of 'em."

Leaning on his silver-knobbed walking stick, her father fixed his dark eyes on her, his mouth a black line between thin lips.

Charlotte's heart thudded painfully in her chest. The light flickered, dimming to a dull gray as she began to slump again. Oblivion would certainly be preferable to what her father surely had in store for her.

Cold water hit her face and chest, forcing her back into consciousness.

"You will be awake to see this, Charlotte." Her father thrust a stoneware mug at the tollkeeper, who clutched it to his chest as if it were a shield. Then her father nodded to the man with the pistol.

"No! You cannot kill him." Charlotte wrenched her arms out of the man's grasp and lunged for the gun.

The side of the pistol slammed into her face, knocking her to the floor. He cocked the piece and returned it to Edward's head.

"Thrush, here, had the audacity to try to take what is *mine*." Her father's voice shook, his fury rising with each curt word.

Through her wavering vision, her father's face appeared impassive in the uncertain light, his voice now emotionless as he peered down at her. "If you assisted him in this, then his blood is on your hands much more so than mine."

"If you kill him, you will have to kill me as well." Narrowing her eyes at him, Charlotte carefully picked herself up off the floor, hatred of him so intense it must be oozing through her skin. "I will tell everyone exactly what you have done to Edward. As a peer you may be above the law, but you are not above the censure of the *ton*. I will make sure that they have every detail of his death and our elopement until the scandal-broth scalds you to death. If you want scandal, Father, I will choke you with it."

He chuckled, adjusting his grip on his walking stick. "Sometimes I wish you were my heir, Charlotte. You have a better mind than Caldwell, and much more of me in you." He sighed and rubbed the knob of his cane. "Pity you've begun to rave like a lunatic. I doubt you will like Bedlam, my dear. I would dislike having to put you there, but if you tell such grievous lies, what else am I to do?"

A wave of horror washed over her. Tales of the appalling conditions of the infamous hospital had sickened her. Her arms broke out in gooseflesh. Bitter bile crawled up the back of her throat. Tears trickling down her cheeks, she looked at Edward, who hadn't moved the whole time.

He mouthed silently, *I love you*.

Staring at him, she raised her voice until it rang to the rafters. "I love you, Edward."

"Sickening pap." Her father pursed his lips as though a bad taste filled his mouth. "I *should* kill you, too." He nodded to the man with the pistol. "Cates."

"Tollkeeper!"

The shout from outside froze everyone.

Dear God, a savior. Charlotte opened her mouth, only to have the dirty hand of her captor slam over it before she could shout.

"Attend to your business, tollkeeper." Her father's words were clipped as he stared down at the little man. "Leave me to mine and you will be rewarded."

Eyes wide, the tollkeeper nodded and headed for the door with shaky steps.

Charlotte elbowed her captor, wrenching her body this way and that, trying to break free. She bit down on the hand that muzzled her and stomped in an effort to mash his foot.

The howl the blackguard sent up was music to her ears. He jerked his hand away, swearing.

"Help! Oh God, help me. Someone!" She screamed so loudly something in her throat tore.

"Charlotte!" Her father slammed his cane down on the table an inch from Edward's face, making her jump back. "Andrews, for God's sake, stifle her."

Andrews grabbed her again, putting his arm around her neck. She almost gagged at the sour smell of his coat.

The door burst open and a tall man holding a large pistol strode in, the tollkeeper scuttling behind him.

Cates whipped his gun around, training it on the stranger.

The man, who seemed to tower over everyone in the room, obliged him by leveling his weapon on Andrews. Glancing from one figure to another, his gaze finally rested on Charlotte. "What the devil is going on here?"

His deep, commanding voice sent a thrill of hope through her.

"None of your affair, sir." Her father once again leaned on his cane, his mouth pinched. "You may pay your toll and be on your way. This is a private matter."

The stranger, bundled against the cold in a blue peacoat and black felt hat with the brim pulled down shading his eyes, shook his head. "I think not." He nodded toward Charlotte. "I heard the lady scream. I'll hear what she has to say."

Andrews tightened his hold and Charlotte's vision started to gray again. A loud thwack sounded near her ear and the arm smothering her loosened and fell. She coughed, then drew a deep, clean breath. Her father's henchman lay at her feet. The stranger now stood next to her, his gun pointing at Cates. Hope stole through her breast once more.

"Tell me what's going on, miss."

"I apprehended this horse thief," her father spoke up before she could say a word, "and was about to administer justice when you came along. As I said, it is a private affair."

"That's not true." Charlotte turned to their rescuer, her heart thundering. She must convince him to help them or Edward would die. "My betrothed and I were eloping. My father found out and waylaid us here. They are going to kill Edward." Her heart lurched at the sound of the words spoken aloud. She searched the man's face, praying with every fiber of her soul that he believed her. That whoever he was, he was a match for her father and his men. "Please, I beg of you, you must stop them."

"He was stealing my horses, taking my daughter as a hostage for ransom." Her father cut his eyes toward Cates.

Charlotte tensed. What would the wretched man try next?

"The lady seems rather enamored of her kidnapper, which I find odd if what you say is true." The stranger gestured to Edward. "What do you have to say, sir?"

Edward tried to rise, but Cates slammed the butt of the pistol into the back of his head. He fell forward onto the table.

"No!" Charlotte shrieked, her stomach twisting anew. She darted toward the still figure.

Her father grabbed her arm and jerked her behind the table next to him. His fingers dug into flesh, biting even through her clothing.

The stranger swung his pistol around, pointing it at her father's face. "Because you didn't want me to hear his reply, I'll assume it would have confirmed the lady's tale."

"And if it did, you have no authority to aid and abet their illegal flight to Scotland," her father countered. "My daughter has not reached her majority; therefore, I am fully within my rights to keep her from making such a mésalliance."

"Quite correct, sir. If she *is* your daughter, she does fall under your dominion. This man, however, does not. And you certainly have no authority to kill him."

"That was never my intention."

"Oh yes, it was." Charlotte tried to pull away from her father, but his strong grip on her upper arm pinned her next to him.

"I think I will take the lady's word over yours, all the same." The stranger smiled, and a chill ran down Charlotte's spine. "Get him on his feet." He gestured with the gun to Edward.

Cates glanced at her father, who nodded. The henchman grabbed Edward by the back of his coat and hauled him up.

Groaning and groggy but able to stand, Edward stared at her, the anguish in his eyes matching the ache that tore at her heart.

The stranger clasped him about the waist and they backed toward the door.

"Make sure you do not take any of my horses." Her father finally released his grip on her aching arm. Shaking it loose, she ran toward the door, shouting, "Take the chestnut mare. She's mine."

Cates blocked her way, but moments later the muffled sound of hoofbeats told her they were away, Edward safe at last. Her shoulders slumped and the tears began to flow once more, relief at his escape warring with the hollow ache of her heart. She would never see him again. If she could die right now, she would count herself blessed.

"Wake up Andrews and bring my carriage around." Her father barked out the order to Cates. Glaring at the tollkeeper, who was now cowering in the corner, he tossed a gold sovereign on the table. "For your trouble and your silence." At last he turned his attention to Charlotte, his lips twisted in a snarl. "You will fill an ocean with those tears before I'm through with you."

He grabbed her arm again and pushed her out the door into the chill air and pale moonlight that would be the rest of her life. Oh, yes. Death would have been a blessing.

"My lady, wake up." The insistent voice of her maid scarcely penetrated the fog of exhausted sleep Charlotte had fallen into early that morning. She grunted and turned over. If she never woke up she'd be perfectly happy.

"My lady." Rose shook her shoulder. "Your father wants you downstairs immediately."

Oh, God. Charlotte groaned and burrowed deeper under the covers. The reckoning she'd known was coming had arrived. Too heartsore to be afraid, she crawled out from beneath the covers. Best to get this over with, take her punishment as she always had at her father's hands, so she could come back here to mourn Edward's loss in private.

She peered at herself in the mirror and wished she had not. Her face was badly bruised where Cates had hit her. Rose would be hard pressed to cover the purple marks on her cheek even with cosmetics. And her arm throbbed from her father's brutal grip. Still, her heart ached more than her body. She wanted to be happy that Edward had escaped, but she couldn't ignore the empty pit in her heart.

An hour later, she entered her father's study, fighting not to wince as she straightened her shoulders and raised her chin. Unless she met the man with strength, he would trample her and never look back. She stood before the huge, worn mahogany desk, exactly as she had every time she'd displeased him in her eighteen years.

He continued writing, not even looking up to acknowledge her presence. Another of his ploys.

Remaining still, she stared at his hand as he made the small, neat letters. The trick was not to say a word. Allow him to make the first move.

At last he signed his name with a flourish, set the pen down, and capped the ink. Then he raised his head and looked at her. And smiled.

Charlotte's stomach sank. The smile meant triumph. It meant whatever the punishment he had set for her, he had gotten his way with it. She firmed her lips. She'd not give him the satisfaction of seeing her fear.

"Well, your little indiscretion of last night has cost us the Ramsay alliance." He leaned back, his hands clasped.

"It has?" She couldn't keep the surprise out of her voice. The settlements for her marriage to Lord Ramsay had already been signed. How had the betrothal been broken?

"Ramsay caught wind of your little escapade. I'm not sure how, but I'll find out which servant talked. They will never set foot in a decent household again." He tapped his forefingers together. "Nevertheless, he knows that my daughter tried to elope with her groom and now refuses to have you."

Well, good for Lord Ramsay. She had nothing against the man except that she didn't know him and certainly didn't love him.

"I could have forced the issue, but he has agreed to be discreet about the reason he now finds you objectionable. I have broken the betrothal on your behalf. Perhaps next year I will give him your sister Agnes." His intense stare made Charlotte's skin crawl. There would be worse news to come. "She's much more biddable than you ever were."

"Thank you, Father." Not that this situation pleased her much more than marrying Ramsay. Of course, now he'd have to send her down into the country to wait for him to choose the next-most-advantageous match for her. A plan with merit, for being out of his presence was a boon. Even had she found a man this Season at least palatable to her, her father would never allow her to marry him unless the alliance served his purposes.

"But do not despair, Charlotte. You shall have your wedding, and on schedule." His eyes twinkled and her stomach sank even further. "I have called in a favor from an old friend. He has agreed to marry you and take you off my hands."

"An old friend, Father?" Dread built slowly in her chest. This must be her punishment.

"Sir Archibald Cavendish. You remember him, I daresay. He's been my guest often enough at the hunting lodge in Kent."

Her breath stopped. No. That was not possible. Marriage with . . . "Sir Archibald? But . . . but he's your age." And balding and as big around as he was tall. The last time she'd seen him, two years ago at the lodge, he'd been so drunk he stank of whiskey and the strong clove scent he wore in his cologne made her sneeze. Now she'd be expected to marry the man? She had to clutch the back of the chair in front of her.

"Two years younger, but that's of no consequence." The jubilant tenor in his voice told her he was enjoying her horror. "Sir Archibald is just the man to curb that spirit of yours."

"I won't do it. You cannot make me marry that nasty old man." She had spoken with her cousin Jane when she'd been betrothed to Ramsay and been informed that English law required her to consent to her marriage. Well, she would never willingly agree to this alliance. Being a spinster or anything else was better than being that man's wife.

"Oh, I think you will, daughter." He leaned toward her,

menace etched in every line on his face. "Because it is Sir Archibald or the lunatics at Bedlam. Any woman who would disgrace herself by running off with a servant would easily be deemed mad by the authorities. I have sent inquiries to one of the physicians on the board, telling him of your irrational behavior and asking if they would admit you if you do not see reason."

"You would really do such a thing to me?" He would. She had no doubt.

"It is your choice, Charlotte. I will not have scandal in my house. Had you behaved according to your station and married Ramsay, we could have avoided these less-appealing options." He sat back again, cold, emotionless. Triumphant.

He had her trapped. She could not choose the asylum if she expected to live. Edward had not wanted that for her, even at the cost of his own life. She swallowed hard and prepared herself for the inevitable. It would have to be the odious Sir Archibald. Perhaps she could persuade the man to leave her in the country while he gallivanted around and thus spend as little time with him as possible. At least there was that hope.

With a heavy sigh, Charlotte nodded. "Then I accept Sir Archibald's suit. You can inform me of the wedding details when you have arranged them." She clenched her hands and spun on her heel, determined to leave the study without seeing her father's gloating face. Before her tears rained down again, as she knew they would, the ocean her father had predicted just beginning.

Chapter 2

London, June 18, 1816

Lady Charlotte Cavendish squeezed into the upstairs retiring room at Almack's, shaking in her new yellow slippers, half in excitement, half in terror. The parlor was already crowded with gaily dressed women eager to show their patriotism for the Waterloo veterans. She, on the other hand, attended for an entirely different reason— a reason that gave her joy for the first time in six long years.

Charlotte glanced around, unnerved by the crush of people. She was unused to such crowds after five years of marriage and a year of mourning. Surely she could find a bit of unclaimed wall where she could wait for her cousin, Jane, Lady John Tarkington, and contemplate the freedom she'd celebrate tonight. Not the normal return to society by a grieving widow. Then again, she had never grieved one day for the odious Sir Archibald. Considering she was still a virgin, she could hardly be called a normal widow at all.

She danced out of the way as two portly matrons hurtled past her.

"And then she said Lord Fairfax dragged her into the library . . ." The ladies moved off, heads still together, oblivious of the others around them.

Charlotte ran her hands over her skirts, checking for tears. She had never seen so many people here before. Had half of London turned up? Spying an open spot, she hurried toward it, tread on the hem of her gown, and stumbled against the cream-colored rear wall.

Drat. She turned her back to the wall and inspected the edging of the garment. The modiste had apparently cut it a little too long despite her exacting measurements. Why hadn't she noticed this at home? The lace wasn't torn, however. She sighed in relief, relaxing just a little. There was no reason to be nervous about rejoining society, yet she was on pins and needles. She must compose herself and wait right here for Jane so her clothing would not be further mussed.

She glanced down, smiling in satisfaction at her gown, which the seamstress had delivered yesterday. The fresh confection, cut daringly low in both front and back, in the most delectable shade of deep primrose yellow, boldly announced her eagerness to engage in life anew.

Time now to re-emerge, like a bright butterfly from a twelve-month cocoon, to stretch her wings. Charlotte fidgeted, shifting from one foot to the other, full of pent-up energy after years spent suffering through an empty marriage to a man she had never loved. *I'd have better spent the past twelve months grieving the loss of Edward. Or perhaps I should have mourned my stepson Hal. He set me free.*

Harold Cavendish, her husband's second son, had died at Waterloo. When the news had reached Sir Archibald, he'd suffered an attack of apoplexy and died. His elder son, Edgar, now Sir Edgar, held the title to the baronetcy. What a pity the fates of the sons had not been reversed. Charlotte had always gotten along well with Hal. Edgar was another matter entirely.

Near the entrance, the press of women seemed to thin a bit. She strained to see through the throng that still surrounded her. Drat. Had the dancing begun before her cousin arrived? She didn't want to miss a moment of tonight. Cocking her head, she strained to hear through the soft din of voices. Snatches of discordant notes drifted in from the ballroom as the orchestra tuned up.

Why hadn't Jane arrived? Charlotte eyed the doorway, willing her cousin to appear. As the first social function Charlotte had attended since her mourning ended, this fete represented her bid for freedom and she did not intend to miss a moment of the ball.

Thanks to her father's treachery, not since her ill-fated flight to Gretna Green had she experienced one moment of love or tenderness with a man. Her aging husband had made it quite clear on their wedding night that he would not demand his marital rights. He'd never given her a reason for his disinterest, although she had her suspicions. During the next five years, however, he'd been as good as his word, never so much as putting a foot over the threshold of her bedchamber. A circumstance for which she gave thanks to God nightly—Sir Archibald had been short, potbellied, with breath like an old chamber pot. Charlotte had often wondered who she despised more, her husband or her father.

What she wouldn't give to just once know the long-denied pleasure of a man's attentions. She imagined herself on the dance floor, held in the arms of a dashing gentleman who would sweep her around the room as if they trod on air. He would smile for her alone and perhaps hold her a bit more tightly than was proper. She would laugh and flirt with him, without a care in the world beyond who her next partner would be. Yes, she had dreamed of this night for years.

Her blood beat a quick rhythm in her veins. The air had grown quite stifling. Alarmed, Charlotte pulled out her fan and plied it vigorously. She simply could not faint here! Not before setting a foot on the dance floor.

Had she known Jane would be this tardy, she would have accompanied her to Lady Darlington's crush. Instead, Charlotte had preferred to have more time to dress, to perfect her first impression after so long an absence. If Jane didn't arrive soon, however, she might give in to desperation. Might even be tempted to go into the ballroom alone. A dreadful way to call attention to herself, but she'd been waiting all her life for this moment.

As if summoned by Charlotte's frantic need, her cousin rounded the corner into the retiring room. Panic receded. Charlotte breathed deeply and waved to her. Ever since they were children, Jane's presence had had a calming effect on her. Though truly sorry for the loss of her cousin's husband, she had been grateful when Jane had moved into the London town house with her and provided her with advice on widowhood.

"Oh, Jane!" Charlotte hugged her slight frame. "I thought you would never arrive."

"I told you to come with me, Charlotte. Then you wouldn't be in such a state." Jane straightened the topaz and gold necklace around Charlotte's neck. "You seem ready to fly to pieces."

"I am." Charlotte laughed, so giddy now the flickering candlelight spun. "I'm so tired of waiting."

"Well, you likely will still have your share of that once we enter." Jane nodded toward the ballroom. "We will probably have a devilish time attracting any attention at all from the gentlemen." She frowned and flipped open her fan. "That is a major concern, my dear. The Season is all but over."

Charlotte nodded. Now that they could accept any invitation they liked, the invitations had ceased to arrive.

"Our mourning ended at such an unfortunate time of year." Jane started toward the doorway. "What few events remain will not likely be well attended by gentlemen seeking to marry. The most eligible have either been brought up to scratch already or have managed to escape and think themselves safe for another year." She stopped and nodded to an acquaintance. "Despite the numbers drawn to the fete tonight, I fear we will find dancing partners scarce." Jane sounded miffed, but Charlotte smothered a smile at her words. She doubted her cousin would sit out a single set unless she chose to. Jane had always had a way with men.

"Then by all means, let us hurry to make our presence known." Charlotte bit her lip. Prickles of excitement coursed down her glove-encased arms. The moment she had waited for had arrived. Once again she would enter the giddy world of the *ton*. Shoulders straight, a pleasant smile carefully gracing her lips, Charlotte swept toward the glittering ballroom, ready for life to begin again.

"Demmed slim pickings this late in the Season, eh, Wrotham?"

Blandly surveying the crowded ballroom, Nash, twelfth Earl of Wrotham, had to agree with his friend, George Abernathy.

"Well, none of them showed great promise, even when out in full force in April. Too young and too silly if you ask me." A shame too, as Nash had determined he would do his duty and marry this year. He'd come into his title unexpectedly, only eighteen months before, and at thirty had no time to waste putting an heir in his nursery. Life was a chancy thing.

"You may be right at that." George surveyed the room, his usual look of boredom unchanged.

"I suppose we must wait and hope for a better crop during the Little Season." Nash sighed as several young ladies, dressed in all manner of frothy pastel gowns, congregated not ten feet from where he stood. He smiled pleasantly to acknowledge them, all of whom he'd stood up with before, but none of whom had drawn his interest for more than a dance or two. "I do hope at least one or two here tonight can dance tolerably. Such a shame Miss Benson is now betrothed."

Abernathy cocked his head and produced a quizzing glass, through which he seemed to study Nash. "You cherished hopes in that direction?"

"Not a bit." Nash chuckled. "The chit is as flighty as they come, but she moved like a sprite. I've not had a partner such as her in ten years." He shook his head. Not that he had indulged in dancing much at all in that time. "Fortunately, the ability to dance well is not my highest criteria for a wife."

"Now there we can agree." Abernathy settled himself to gazing about the room, likely looking for a suitable candidate for the opening reel. "Fortune is the primary consideration when seeking out a wife. Fortune and good breeding."

Nash shook his head. "A consideration perhaps, but not the highest one. I'm much more interested in a pleasant woman, a good companion. A lady who will not insist on dabbling about in my business affairs, although she must be an outstanding hostess." He looked expectantly at two young ladies entering; then he recognized them as Miss Olivia Sanderling and Lady Catherine Dole. Neither one old enough for his taste. "She should also enjoy living in the country and sharing quiet pursuits. I seek a woman I will *want* to sit across the breakfast table from, which means she can't be some miss right out of the schoolroom, fortune or not."

"Humpf." Abernathy swung around toward the ballroom entrance, where some sort of commotion had erupted.

Had the press of people entering become too great, creating a stoppage? The organizers should have foreseen that with this particular ball and fete. Everyone must want to attend this evening.

Nash peered at the little knot of people now filing through the doorway, his attention immediately drawn to a lady in yellow who chatted animatedly with another woman. The bright hue of her gown riveted his gaze on the elegant figure, an arresting, almost fierce expression on her face, as if determined to enjoy the evening no matter what.

"I say, Abernathy, do you know that lady there in yellow, just come into the room?" Nash had never seen her at any other *ton* event. Of course, this was his first full year on the Town and he certainly had not met everyone. One of the disadvantages of inheriting his title with no warning had been his lack of preparation for the duties expected of him. Including attending all these blasted functions and remembering names and faces.

I would have remembered her.

George once again raised his quizzer. "Well, well. Lady John Tarkington. She was widowed last year. I suppose this means her mourning is finished." He smiled and licked his lips. "Lady John is quite the figure of a woman, wouldn't you say?"

"Is she the one in yellow?" Nash couldn't take his eyes off her.

"In blue. With blond hair."

Nash shot his friend a sideways glance. "Bit older than your usual conquest, isn't she?"

George let the quizzing glass drop and straightened his

jacket. "Yes, but ever so much more fun. She led Tarkington a merry chase before and after their marriage, so I'm told. Always a breath away from scandal was Lady Jane Munro before she married. And now she's apparently back on the market." He started across the dance floor. "Come, let me present you so I can ask her for the first dance. Perhaps she will introduce you to her companion."

"But who is the lady in yellow?" Nash followed, frowning. He hated when things went on the fly. Fifteen years in the Royal Navy had taught him that lack of organization usually led to disaster.

Abernathy shook his head. "No idea. Didn't get a good look at her." He nodded toward the two women, talking and laughing together with several ladies they had joined. "But Lady John obviously does."

Nash trailed behind, weaving his way across the floor, where the first set was making up. If fortune shone on him, an introduction would be forthcoming in time to ask the lady in yellow for the honor of the first dance. If not, he'd ask for the second set and admire her during the first.

They arrived at the little knot of ladies and George's acquaintance turned toward them.

"Mr. Abernathy. How wonderful to see you again." The woman's eyes lit with pleasure and perhaps a touch of amusement. She turned her penetrating gaze on Nash, and he swallowed hard, unnerved by her bold assessment of him.

Managing a smile, he bowed as George made the introduction.

"My lady, may I present the Earl of Wrotham? Late of His Majesty's Navy. Wrotham, this is Lady John Tarkington, widow of the late Major-General Tarkington." Abernathy beamed at her. "I am so pleased this special light of the *ton* has reemerged."

"Delighted, my lord." The widow's low-pitched voice

managed to convey a touch of the suggestive in just those three words.

"Actually it's pronounced 'Rut-am,' my lady." He sent George a scathing look that was ignored. "Abernathy here has never said it correctly." He bowed to Lady John. "My pleasure, entirely."

Her eyes narrowed seductively, and an uncomfortable flare of heat touched his face. Well, George had intimated she'd had her share of scandal. So his friend had best beware this woman didn't sink her claws into him, although the man appeared unconcerned. Instead, he continued an avid conversation with her, leaving Nash at sixes and sevens and without an introduction to the intriguing younger woman.

From the corner of his eye he watched her, deep in conversation with two other ladies. She stood out among them, brilliant as a peacock among doves. Her laughter sent a little thrill down his spine. He clenched his fist. Would George never inquire about the blasted introduction?

"Wrotham."

Nash jerked his attention back to his friend.

"I told Lady John you wished an introduction to her friend." Abernathy picked up the quizzing glass once more and gestured toward the lady.

"My cousin actually, my lord." Lady John's broad smile dimpled her cheeks for the first time.

"I had hoped to ask her for the first dance, my lady."

"Splendid. Charlotte." Lady John stepped toward the entrancing figure in yellow, who turned at the sound of her name.

She smiled at her cousin, then glanced inquiringly at him. He held his breath.

The face he now saw close at hand confirmed his instincts. A vision of loveliness on the outside, with an energy that pulsed under her skin, making her the most animated person he had ever seen. Her eyes glinted green, sparkling in the candlelight like the sun reflected off the jeweled waters of the Mediterranean. The slight smile on her perfectly bowed lips made her appear both secretive and joyous, filled to the brim with anticipation of something long awaited.

With a rush of desire, Nash wanted to be the one to inspire that feeling in this lovely creature.

"May I introduce the Earl of Wrotham, my dear?" Lady John nodded and stepped back, her gaze darting between the two of them. "A friend of Mr. Abernathy's. My lord, this is Lady Charlotte Cavendish, my cousin."

Lady Cavendish stepped forward quickly, a smile curling her lips. "I am pleased to meet you, my lord." Her eyes widened, her gait faltered, then she pitched forward with a little cry, arms flailing.

Reflexes honed from years in the Navy, Nash stepped in neatly, catching her under her arms. She landed with a thump against his chest, sending a whiff of jasmine all around him and a thrill of lust straight to his loins. He paused, savoring the soft body pressed against him, the shining hair brushing his chin. With regret, he got himself under control and reluctantly set her on her feet.

Her neck and face had flushed, turning the color of the deep red roses that adorned the terraces at Wrotham Hall. She kept her eyes downcast and stepped back.

"The pleasure is certainly all mine, my lady." Not the most appropriate response, perhaps, but a heartfelt one surely.

Lady Cavendish gasped and raised her head, her green eyes flashing.

"Are you all right, Charlotte?" Lady John stepped forward, her lips puckered as if trying to hide a smile.

"Yes, I am fine, Jane. I stepped on the hem of my gown is all." She cut her eyes at Nash and her lips thinned to a line. "Thank you, my lord, for coming to my rescue."

Nash smiled. Even angry, the woman was a vision to behold. "Not a'tall, my lady. Glad to have been of service."

She seemed to collect herself and returned his smile, albeit tentatively.

There would be no better time to make his request. "My lady, I would be honored if you would dance the first set with me."

Her smile widened. "Thank you, my lord. I would enjoy that."

He'd enjoy having her in his arms again too.

"Lady Cavendish?" A blond young man in elegant evening dress had approached so stealthily behind her, neither he nor the lady had noticed. He touched her elbow and she whirled around.

"Oh, Mr. Garrett. You startled me." The pink had returned to her cheeks.

The buck immediately grasped her hand and had the audacity to kiss it. "My sincere apologies for that, my lady. It is nice to see you again."

"As it is to see you as well." Her voice had a high pitch, but a sweet tone, lilting and light. It suited her down to the ground. "Do you know Lord Wrotham?"

"I have not had the pleasure, I believe." Garrett nodded his head briefly, his eyes still on Lady Cavendish.

"Nor I, Mr. Garrett." Nash bowed, then straightened to his full six foot three, pleased to see he looked down on Garrett by a couple of inches.

"It has been several months since we met, I think, Mr. Garrett?" She clutched her fan, but smiled politely.

"March, I believe it was. And I am come to claim my dance as promised." His eyes glinted when her jaw dropped.

"Your dance, Mr. Garrett?" Her brows puckered and she tugged on her bottom lip with her teeth. "I don't recall we spoke about a dance." The lady shot Nash a fleeting look, but he was unsure if it was a plea for help or an apology.

"I remember it distinctly, my lady." Garrett claimed her gloved hand and squeezed it gently. "You said you would be glad when you could once again be out in society and that you couldn't wait to dance."

"Well, yes, I may indeed have expressed such a sentiment. But that did not mean—"

"To which I replied that I would be honored to partner you at the first opportunity. Then you smiled and nodded and thanked me." The blackguard raised his eyebrows, affecting an innocent air. "What else was I to assume except that you had given me permission to seek your first dance?"

She fidgeted, almost dancing now. Her eyes had the wild look of a horse ready to bolt.

Well, if she didn't want to dance with the man, he'd make sure she didn't have to. "I'm afraid her ladyship has just engaged herself to me for the first set, Garrett. Perhaps her second is still free." Nash took Lady Cavendish's hand from the man and turned them toward the floor, where the orchestra was tuning up.

"The thing is, my lord," Garrett stayed him with a touch on his wrist, "I have the prior claim."

Nash stared into the insolent blue eyes and forced himself not to call the man out. He'd really like to pummel him into the floor, but such tactics were for the battleship, not the ballroom. He shook off the man's hand. "The lady has not acknowledged that, sir. I think I will take her version of the events." Nash glanced at Lady Cavendish, whose face had paled. "Are you all right, my lady?"

She started, as though coming out of a dream. "Yes, I am fine. Something reminded me—"

"That I am supposed to be your partner. There, Wrotham, the lady herself has said it. Are you satisfied?" Garrett nimbly plucked her hand out of Nash's grip and before he could protest, whisked her out to the area where couples were making up the first set.

Stunned, it took Nash a second to register what the rogue had done. He started toward the dance floor, mayhem in his heart. He'd show the scoundrel how they took care of such slights in the Navy.

A hand on his shoulder made him swing around, his own hand coming up to fend off this new menace.

"Steady, Wrotham." George Abernathy held on to him and turned him away from the eyes that were beginning to take notice of him. "He's not worth starting a brawl that will get you banned from Almack's."

Nash exhaled sharply, hot blood still pounding through his veins. Another breath and he was closer to control. His friend was right. He didn't need to start a scandal that would help neither him nor Lady Cavendish. He glanced at Lady John, who had paled, a wan smile pasted on her lips.

"I am certain Lady Cavendish would be very agreeable to partnering you for the second set, my lord." She fluttered her fan and tried to meet his eyes.

"Perhaps I will ask for that dance when this one is concluded." Like hell he would. Nash snapped a bow to Lady John, took his leave of Abernathy, then turned on his heel and strode out of the ballroom.

Chapter 3

Drat. How could this have happened? With a sinking heart, Charlotte allowed Mr. Garrett to lead her onto the dance floor.

In less than fifteen minutes her triumphal return to society had dissolved into a complete disaster. Not only had she tripped and fallen into Lord Wrotham, but she had been unable to stop Mr. Garrett from stealing her away from him. To protest would have created another huge scene. She also resisted the urge to turn and took at Lord Wrotham, the partner she had actually chosen. What must he think of her? Well, she could at least give Mr. Garrett the rough side of her tongue.

"Mr. Garrett, you have taken unfair advantage of the situation." She dropped his hand and turned to face him. "I recall no conversation that would permit you to believe I had promised you the first dance at this or any other ball."

"My dear Lady Cavendish." He laughed, making his handsome face even more attractive. "I have built my reputation by taking unfair advantage of women. Did you think yourself immune?"

"I thought you a gentleman when we met at your aunt's home. Despite your reputation." A hum of voices had set off around the room the instant his lips touched her, singling her out. Lord knew what they would make of his stealing her out of the very hands of Lord Wrotham. The *ton* forever whispered about such things, especially when one of the parties enjoyed the reputation of a rakehell the likes of Garrett's.

He grinned and took her hand again. "I am a gentleman, my lady. However, being a gentleman attracts fewer women than being a rogue. Don't you long to be scandalous after a year of mourning?"

"Certainly not." The wretch was bad. How could he know she yearned to do something at least a little wild now that she was her own woman?

"You may say no, but a yes lurks in your eyes, my lady."

Charlotte gasped and dropped her gaze. Dratted man. Could he read her thoughts?

Jane had warned her about how wicked the man was. He existed barely within the pale—Mr. Garrett's reputation for affairs of the heart and ill-considered wagering of large sums at the worst gaming hells made him the bane of every matchmaking mama and the desire of each one of their daughters. His fine physique—broad at the shoulders, narrow at the waist, hard muscled all over—had caused many a maiden's desperate sigh.

Charlotte might have sighed right along with them, for he had made an impression on her in March. He had been gravely respectful of her loss and sweetly attentive— bringing her tea, listening raptly to her banal conversation ranging from the weather to her deceased husband. Yet, when he'd assisted her with her wrap, his fingers had brushed the skin at the back of her neck, lingering just a bit too long. Promising more. And more was what she so desperately wanted.

Jane's revelations, however, had acted like a cold bath to her budding longings for Alan Garrett. She'd had enough threat of scandal held over her head; she wouldn't likely heap more on herself. Now the rake was back and seemed to have set his sights on her. Well, she would nip that in the bud. One set and she could refuse him the rest of the evening. Hopefully, Lord Wrotham would ask her again.

"Lady Cavendish." Mr. Garrett leaned toward her. His blue eyes deepened and flickered with hunger.

"Yes, Mr. Garrett?" She stepped back, trying to keep a decent distance between them. Was the man trying to compromise her for some perverse reason?

"Are you afraid of me, my lady?" His laugh, utterly charming, gave him an innocent, boyish air. "I promise if you dance with me, I won't bite." He held out his hand.

A wave of heat rose to her face. "I will hold you to that promise, Mr. Garrett." Cautiously, she placed her hand in his.

He leaned toward her slightly and spoke sotto voce. "Very good. Perhaps we will also talk after our dance." He squeezed her hand and drew her closer. The scent of his spicy cologne—bergamot and something with a deep musk—tickled her nose.

Lord, she had to sneeze! Rubbing her nose to prevent the disaster, she stepped back and nodded. "Perhaps we will, Mr. Garrett." *Why did he have to wear so much scent?*

Mr. Garrett straightened and offered his arm. "The musicians are about to commence. Let us take our place in the set."

Charlotte slipped her arm through his, aware that they were causing a stir. She glanced around the room and noted several women darting inquisitive looks their way. Their countenances were anything but kind. The threat of incipient gossip about her made her shudder inside. She would never again dance with a rake.

They had almost reached their places on the dance floor when she caught sight of Jane talking to a young man Charlotte had seen several times at functions her late husband had taken her to. Her cousin stared at her and raised her chin, a summons Charlotte knew all too well.

"A moment, please, Mr. Garrett. I must see my cousin." She steered him around a group of young women and between two sets of young men who seemed to be gathering up the courage to ask them to dance.

Finally, they reached Jane and, as Charlotte feared, her frown and firm lips spoke of her displeasure. What on earth had happened now?

"Lady John, I am sure you remember Mr. Alan Garrett?" Charlotte smiled bravely, although Jane's glare did not waver. What had she done? Certainly Jane could see she had no choice but to dance with the wretch. "As you may remember, we all met at Lady Burrows's house? Mr. Garrett's aunt."

Squeals from instruments being tuned attested the orchestra would be ready shortly. Perhaps they would miss the dance. Of course, the perverse Mr. Garrett would likely try to claim the next one as a forfeit. She might not be able to get rid of him until supper.

"I remember you quite well, Mr. Garrett," Jane said with icy civility. "How lovely to meet you again."

Lord, judging from that tone, her cousin was in rare form tonight. Jane had the unfortunate habit of causing scenes in public places when trying to protect someone. The embarrassing incident during Charlotte's come-out always came to mind. Lord Reardon had ever after pointedly avoided speaking to her after experiencing Jane's scathing set-down in the middle of the hall. Just because he'd tried to claim a third dance.

"You are kind, Lady John. To be remembered by you is to gain immortality."

Jane chuckled.

The false tinkle told Charlotte her partner was in for it indeed.

"You have a silver tongue, Mr. Garrett. I trust you will not allow it to tarnish my cousin?"

"Lady Charlotte is in no danger from me, my lady." He patted Charlotte's hand. "Although the reverse may certainly prove true. She could well prove my downfall."

Charlotte cut her eyes toward Jane. What in the world did the man mean by that?

Jane gave her head a slight shake, then fingered her necklace of perfectly matched pearls. "Charlotte, allow me to present a dear friend of mine, Mr. George Abernathy. Mr. Abernathy was friends with Stephen once upon a time. He is also, quite suddenly, the heir to Lord Romney."

Jane's gaze took the man in from head to toe, slowly and sensually, all but undressing him as she spoke.

"Jane!" Charlotte whispered, scandalized at her cousin's behavior. She'd never have thought she would do such a thing in public.

"Mr. Abernathy, this is my cousin, Lady Cavendish, and Mr. Alan Garrett, with whom I think you are already acquainted?"

George smiled at her, a rather lopsided though charming sight. "My lady. I am so pleased to meet you at last." He then turned and inclined his head almost imperceptibly. "Garrett." The single word did not disguise the animosity in his tone.

"Abernathy. It has been too long." Mr. Garrett seemed amused at the other man's enmity. Charlotte glanced from one to the other, wondering what lay between them.

The music changed, signaling the dancing would commence soon. Mr. Garrett took her arm. "If you will excuse us, Lady John?"

They turned to go to the floor. By all means, let them get this dance over with.

"Charlotte."

Good Lord. They would never make this dance. "Yes?"

Jane glanced from Charlotte's face to Mr. Garrett's, settling on the latter with a determined stare. "Please return Lady Cavendish to me directly after the dance, Mr. Garrett. Lord Wrotham would like to have her for the second set, if I'm not mistaken." And with a sharp look at Charlotte, "You know he had particularly asked for that introduction, my dear."

Memory of the man's intense eyes, dark and fathomless, coupled with his blatantly sensual mouth caused Charlotte to swallow hard. She recalled vividly being pressed close against him, breathing a clean citrusy scent when her face lay against his jacket front. A riot of butterflies stirred in her stomach. And his voice. There had been something in his voice when he had argued with Mr. Garrett. Something familiar.

Charlotte surreptitiously scanned the area, but no tall, dark man of his description appeared. She hoped he would return at the end of the first dance and ask her for the second.

"It will be as you wish, Lady John; however, we must go now or miss the set." Mr. Garrett peered inquiringly at her. She nodded, and he finally led her onto the ballroom floor. All eyes seemed to fasten on them, though she tried to ignore them and smile.

He grasped her hand as they assumed their places in line. Heat baked her palm and she almost snatched her hand back. This would be the most agonizing set she had ever danced in her life.

"Shall we see if we can be scandalous enough to be banned from the ballroom?" Mr. Garrett spoke lightly, with a twinkle of amusement in his eyes as the music began.

Good Lord. Was the man mad? Did all rakes act like this? Well, she'd have to brazen it out until the end of the dance. Likely he was all bluster anyway.

"I am certain much more scandalous behavior has occurred within these halls than we could display in this one dance, Mr. Garrett."

He hissed as he tugged her into the correct position for a Scottish reel. "So you wish to play the game with me, Lady Cavendish?"

"And what game would that be, sir?"

"Bait the tiger, my lady. Shall I see just how much scandal it would take for the ball and fete committee to demand our removal?" He drew himself up, his spine even straighter than before, his eyes glittering and hard.

He wasn't bluffing. He would destroy both their reputations in the face of such a challenge and think it a great lark. Charlotte's pulse quickened. For the briefest of seconds she imagined herself looking him in the eye and saying, "Do your worst." Then sanity returned. Rash behavior on her part could jeopardize more than just her own reputation merely in the name of exercising her freedom. Besides, she'd already made enough of a spectacle of herself tonight.

"As I have just emerged from a different form of exclusion, perhaps it is best we not undertake that particular experiment." She grasped his hand and stole a glance at him as they marched down an aisle formed by the other dancers.

A knowing smile played about his lips. "As you wish, my lady. However, if you ever care to pursue that particular avenue, please let me know."

When hell freezes over, Mr. Garrett.

"Did you know I would be here tonight?" Had he made inquiries about her? Such attention from him would bode ill indeed.

They spun in a cogwheel, their eyes locked until the pattern of the dance reversed.

"I wasn't sure. But I hoped."

Those words, in his deliciously deep voice, sent chills trickling down her spine. They joined both hands and turned.

"Although you gave me to believe that your obligation to your deceased husband would be strictly observed, I trusted you would return to society as soon as you had fulfilled your duty."

He chuckled, and they moved into the grand chain.

"I am actually out of mourning a day early," she confessed when they finally met again, staring straight into his sinful blue eyes. "Scandalous, don't you think?" She couldn't help but smile at this, her first rebellion. "My husband did not receive word of his son's death until June 19, then was taken in a fit of apoplexy and so died the day after the battle."

"Then this is a grave breach of protocol, Lady Cavendish." He tried to look scandalized, but the playful twinkle in his eyes said otherwise.

"My marriage was arranged. While he lived, I did my duty to my husband. After his death, I mourned appropriately, as is expected of a devoted wife." She pursed her lips and shuddered. "Now, my life is my own." And, by God, she would at last live it as she pleased. "I thought it fitting that I rejoin polite society at this ball in particular. If that shocks everyone, so be it."

"I see you wish to become a rebel." Mr. Garrett laughed as Charlotte went into the center for her turn.

She tossed her head as she set and turned first with her partner, then with the other gentlemen in the circle. Much as she hated to admit it, she was enjoying her dance with this rogue. Did that make her wicked? When she finally regained her position next to Mr. Garrett, he resumed their conversation.

"A rather difficult role for a woman, although for a widow it may be more possible. I would certainly wish to be part of your rebellion, my lady. Given my many activities over the years, I am certainly not afraid of public censure. Are you willing to risk your reputation to seize the prize for which you lust?"

His voice deepened on the final word, sending a wave of fear through her.

She stopped in the middle of the last ladies' cogwheel, her gaze riveted on his face. Dear God, was he about to shock the *ton* with some public display? Her heart thudded. Had she baited this tiger unknowingly?

He pressed her onward, however, moving into the last grand chain and bowing to her with a flourish when the music stopped.

Relief swept through her and she valiantly curtsied, then took his arm as he led her from the floor. She actually leaned on him, for that last fright had turned her legs weak. Thank goodness that dance was over, although she must admit Mr. Garrett had proved a good dancer and a very exciting partner. She closed her eyes and breathed a sigh of relief. Jane would no doubt scold her anew for dancing with Mr. Garrett, but she thought she had managed to scotch any scandal brewing.

A shadow crossed her face and Charlotte opened her eyes to find they had entered a dim stairwell, with a flight of dusty stairs leading to the attics. Her mouth dried as though she'd eaten sand.

Before her eyes could adjust, he wrapped his arms around her, squeezing her against his granite-hard chest. When his hot mouth found hers, she gasped. Oh, drat. She should have known he would try something like this.

He darted his tongue through her open lips and she squealed, then quieted. The last thing she wanted was for someone to find them so engaged. His hands cradled her head as he explored every inch of her mouth with a gentle thoroughness she had not known for years. Had anyone ever kissed her thus? With an intensity designed to kindle flames in her soul? Perhaps Edward. But that had been so long ago, she'd forgotten how good it felt, except . . .

That blasted cologne of his. Pressed right up against him, Charlotte couldn't help but breathe in the overpowering scent of bergamot. *Lord, don't let me sneeze.*

That thought broke the spell. She pushed Mr. Garrett away from her.

He panted as if he had run a race. "Devil take it. Are you trying to get us thrown out, Charlotte?"

"Me?" Her voice rose and she stopped and lowered it. "You're the one trying to ruin my reputation. And do not call me Charlotte. I haven't given you permission."

"After that little interlude, I don't need permission." He grinned at her in the faulty light. "You can't deny you enjoyed it."

"I can and do deny it." She pressed her hand to her chest, where her heart still hammered. She hadn't enjoyed it. Not really. But it had been exciting. More exciting than anything in her life for the past six years. Pray God he couldn't see her face. It must be the color of ripe cherries.

"Methinks 'the lady doth protest too much.' May I call upon you tomorrow?" He grabbed her hand and placed his lips on the palm. The kiss burned even through the glove.

"I don't think that would be wise for either of us." She must hold on to what little sanity was left to her.

His eyes darkened and he ran his finger over her swollen lips. "Allow me to be the judge of what is wise, my dear. Come, I will escort you to Lady John before we are lost entirely." He took her hand, stuck his head around the doorframe, then pulled her quickly into the room.

Blinking in the suddenly bright lights, she stumbled after him as he made his way toward her cousin.

"Here you are, my dear. Safe and sound again." Mr. Garrett bowed, his eyebrows arched in innocence. "Lady John."

Charlotte finally focused on her surroundings enough to find Jane staring at her darkly, from beneath lowered brows. Oh dear. What on earth must she look like after such an encounter?

Dumbfounded, she stood before her cousins, quite at a loss for words or actions. Dazed by the overwhelming pulse that still throbbed through her, she could only glance from one to the other of them, praying one would be her savior.

"I will look forward anxiously to our next meeting, Charlotte." He kissed her fingers, the warmth of his lips like a banked fire. With a final flourished bow, he turned and strode into the crowd.

Stunned, Charlotte simply stood still, the chatter of the ballroom subsiding into one sound—the pounding of blood in her ears.

"Charlotte," her cousin said, grasping her arm until it hurt, "we must remove at once to the retiring room."

Distantly thankful that someone had taken charge of her, Charlotte followed docilely as Jane towed her back the way they had come. They descended on an empty corner and her cousin pushed her into a chair.

"Sit there. I must find a footman"

"Whatever for?"

"To send for some lemonade from the refreshment table. I'll go wet my handkerchief to repair your face and see if I can do something with your hair." Jane fired off the strategy as efficiently as any general, then picked up her skirts and hurried away.

Charlotte leaned back against the chair and sighed. She had managed to survive her first encounter with a rake with few people the wiser, thank God.

Jane reappeared, clutching a glass of lemonade.

"Tark would be proud of your martial skills, Jane." Charlotte grinned, although Jane seemed not to enjoy her compliment.

"You hold your tongue." She thrust the glass into Charlotte's hands. "Dear lord, he's mussed this whole section on the left side. Here." Jane dug into her own coiffure and produced two pins. "What on earth were you thinking, Charlotte? To be ravished at Almack's on your first night out!"

"I was just congratulating myself that it wasn't worse. At least no one knows what happened."

Jane looked daggers at her, then produced a wet cloth and pressed it to Charlotte's mouth. "Wha ah oo doing?"

"Your lips are swollen, dear. You have that delectable, very well-kissed look." Jane's eyes took on a distant aspect and her lips curved into a nostalgic smile. "Excellent after an evening in bed with your husband." The smile vanished, replaced by lips pressed into a thin line. "Disastrous in the public rooms, however. You'll be lucky if it's not being discussed over every breakfast table in the morning." She blotted Charlotte's swollen lips once more. "Now, the lemonade. The sugar will guard against shock and the astringency of the lemons may help the swelling."

Jane plucked the glass from Charlotte's hands and shoved it against her full lips. She drank deeply, savoring the cool, sweet liquid. She had no idea being seduced was such thirsty work.

"You must pull yourself back together and return to the ballroom in all haste. You will set the tongues to wagging even worse if you do not." She gave Charlotte a withering look. "As I feared, it is more difficult to secure a partner and hold his attention this evening. Yet you must attempt to do so in order to divert everyone from your unfortunate behavior." Jane pressed the sodden scrap of linen to Charlotte's temple. "I am particularly concerned that Elizabeth and Georgina did not attend tonight."

She shook her head and Charlotte sighed. Two of their friends, also widows, had not quite gotten over their husbands' deaths.

"Where is Fanny? I would have thought she would be here, certainly."

"She had a last-minute invitation to Lady Beaumont's masquerade. She said it suited her better to make a dramatic unveiling." Jane dropped into the chair next to Charlotte. "I doubt she will lack partners during the night."

Charlotte cut her eyes toward her cousin. Her arch tone spoke for itself. However, she did not doubt it either. Her other friends were another matter. "If we could have the men to ourselves somehow we might have a better chance of Elizabeth and Georgina making an impression on them." Charlotte took another sip of the lemonade as she turned her mind to the problem of her friends.

"Yes, these gentlemen who are left on the marriage mart have had the most beautiful girls fawning over them all Season. We need to get them alone." Jane paused and grinned. "Not alone *that* way, although I for one would not turn down such a tryst if offered."

"Jane!"

Her cousin had the grace to blush. "You have no right to say anything at the moment, Charlotte. In any case, we need to spend time with these gentlemen and make them see how our sterling qualities surpass those of the younger ladies. As we would at a house party."

"But who of our circle is able to host such a thing?" Charlotte slumped. Their situation seemed more doubtful given the reality of their situations. "Neither Elizabeth's nor Georgie's circumstances will allow it." Upon her husband's death, her best friend Elizabeth and her children had returned to her parents' home. Georgie had fared even worse. Currently, she was housed only by the grace and charity of her complaining sister-in-law, Mrs. Reynolds.

"I suppose I might be able to persuade Theale to allow me use of one of his estates," Jane said. "He was quite affected by Tark's death. He and his brother were very close. Of course I couldn't tell him why I need the use of it." She sighed and looked sad for the first time that day. "I do miss Tark, you know." She glanced around the almost empty room. "I will not marry again. He made some canny purchases in real estate. As a result, I'd be a fool to relinquish my jointure."

Charlotte tried to fix her cousin with a stern stare. The woman who had been her dearest friend and companion all her life had taught her well that all women were not conventional. Despite Jane's sweet face and soft, womanly body, her heart and soul thrived on breaking society's rules whenever she could. She had done so for most of her thirty years. "Then why do you wish to meet gentlemen again? Surely nothing can come of such attentions if you have so made up your mind?"

Jane patted her arm. "For the same reason you indulged in Mr. Garrett tonight." She smiled sadly. "Tark is dead, not I. And male companionship is so . . . stimulating, wouldn't you say?"

Charlotte clamped her hands over her burning cheeks.

"I am not adverse to a little dalliance, if given a quiet, secluded place to dally." Jane's face had taken on a faraway look.

Wishing for something a bit stronger, Charlotte sipped her lemonade and gathered her wits, trying to resolve the problem. A place for a successful house party was the very thing they needed. Such a secluded spot, however, could hardly be attempted here in London, under the scrutiny of their families. If they wanted true seclusion, they needed an estate in the country. None of them, however, had such a place to hand . . .

She sat straighter in her chair as Jane chatted on. An inkling of an idea presented itself as if a gift from the gods. She needed time to think about the organization of it, but yes, this notion just might do.

"Jane, are you free tomorrow morning?"

Her cousin glanced quizzically at her but nodded.

"Can you please send messages to the ladies of our circle and ask them to call upon us at ten o'clock? I believe I may have the answer to all our prayers." She stood and looked around the now-deserted retiring room, satisfaction welling up in her chest. "We shall have a formal meeting of the Widow's Club and plan our strategy to snare the gentlemen of our choice."

Chapter 4

Nash sat down to a breakfast of toast, kippers, and eggs, in a better mood than when he'd come home last night. He sipped black coffee, savoring the rich drink. It had been a luxury all the years he'd served in the Navy, so now it had become a morning staple.

He tucked away the note that had arrived earlier from Lord Grafton and smiled. The earl was coming to call upon him this morning. That had to mean he had finally decided to lend Nash his considerable support on the upcoming Yeoman Warder bill. One less matter he had to worry about as the parliamentary session ground on.

Next, he perused *The Times*, searching for news of the fleet, always his first interest. Then turned over to the marriages and obituaries. After several months as a member of Brook's and all the social outings this Season, he had some hope he knew the grooms; occasionally, he found he had danced with the brides before their betrothals. Nash sighed. He'd hoped to have his own engagement announced by now. How difficult should it be to pick a woman to marry?

He'd attended every soiree, ball, rout, crush, and musical evening he'd received invitations to this Season. Theatre parties, outings to Vauxhall, driving or riding in Hyde Park. Any potential way to meet young ladies of good family, he had tried. Was he truly so particular?

Nash savored the rest of his coffee and folded the paper. In all his perambulations, only three ladies had piqued his interest. Miss Bolton, a pretty brunette who danced well and smiled a great deal. A sweet girl, with whom he had been able to converse on a number of subjects. She had, however, developed a tendre for the heir to the Marquess of Ainwick.

Then there had been Lady Grace Knowlton, a daughter of the Earl of Braeton, who had held Nash's interest for quite three weeks. An elegant blonde who played the pianoforte beautifully, she'd been a touch reserved, but he believed they might suit. He'd been on the verge of offering for her when he'd opened the newspaper one morning to see her engagement to Lord Longford.

The last was Lady Cavendish from last night. He'd never been so attracted to a woman on such a brief acquaintance. The sum of his knowledge of her amounted to almost nothing: She was a widow, her given name Charlotte, she moved more gracefully on the dance floor than off it, and she had a propensity to carry on with unsavory men. He clenched his jaw at the memory of his last sight of her.

After he'd cooled his ire in the refreshment room with weak lemonade, he'd returned to the ballroom bent on asking the captivating Lady Cavendish for the next set. Instead, he'd spied her emerging from the stairwell, her hair mussed, her eyes glazed, in the company of that young buck. Had Nash been closer, he'd have planted the man a facer on principle alone. The woman, however, was none of his affair now. A lady that brazen in a public place could hardly be one he wanted for his countess.

Why then could he not stop thinking about her?

His reflections were interrupted by Hoskins's announcement, "Lord Grafton, my lord," followed by the sight of the man himself.

Nash leaped to his feet, his napkin flying off to the side. "My lord." He bowed. "I beg your pardon. Hoskins should have shown you—"

"He tried, Wrotham. Don't berate him for giving me my way." The tall, thin, gray-whiskered man smiled mirthlessly. "I told him to take me to you at once and he did so. Shows he's either a sensible man or a well-trained servant." Lord Grafton appropriated the chair on Nash's right, as imperious here as when in the House of Lords. An imposing man, whom age seemed not to have touched as far as dint of will or physical strength was concerned, the earl sat ramrod straight, staring at Nash with small, round, glittering brown eyes, his hands crossed gracefully over his silver-knobbed walking stick. Nash had seen that stick countless times in the Lords and had a healthy respect for it. Those who did not often found it had purposes that had nothing to do with walking. No, the Earl of Grafton was not a man to be gainsaid.

"I received your note this morning, my lord. I assume your visit had to do with the Yeoman Warder bill?" Nash tried not to sound too hopeful. The earl's face gave nothing away. He could just as easily be about to withdraw as to lend his support.

"It does, Wrotham, after a fashion." Grafton settled himself in the chair, straightening his shoulders, adjusting his hands on his stick. "I want you to marry my daughter."

Nash blinked several times, unable to speak. He stared at the older man, wondering if he was playing some elaborate jest. Grafton's face had not one laugh line on it.

"I beg your pardon, my lord," he said at last, grappling to maintain a stoic mien. He needed to stall for time to compose himself. "Would you prefer tea or coffee?" Had the man actually just asked him to be his son-in-law?

"Coffee, black."

Nash nodded to a footman. Not enough time to puzzle it out. Well, then, forward unto the breach. "You say you want me to marry your daughter, my lord? Yet this is the first time you have broached the subject to me. Is there some recent development that would precipitate such an offer?" God, his daughter was breeding and he wanted to marry her off to keep it quiet. Or, worse, thought him the cad who had ruined her. Gad, what a tangle.

"I see you are a man to come directly to the point. I was right about you." Grafton's smile sent a chill down Nash's spine. "Yes, there has been a development concerning my daughter that I will not countenance. She has taken up with the most unsavory of men, a rakehell who will see her reputation in shreds and laugh about it at White's afterward." The earl's face had turned a deep shade of red. "I will not have it, I tell you."

The footman appeared with the earl's cup of coffee and set it in front of the shaking man.

Grafton seized it and drank it half down at one gulp. "Therefore, Wrotham, you will oblige me by marrying this headstrong woman and put an end to her scandalous actions."

"I do understand your concerns, sir." Nash's breathing had slowed to an almost normal rate, his mind racing to find a way out of this highly distasteful proposal. "However, I don't believe that I have even met your daughter." What was the chit's name? The elder two were married, so the man must be speaking of the youngest one. He hadn't thought her out of the schoolroom yet. "I can hardly make a declaration to Lady Sophia—"

"Charlotte."

Nash jerked back in his chair. "I beg your pardon?"

"I am speaking of my eldest daughter, Lady Cavendish. She is a widow." The gleam in the earl's eye pierced Nash to the heart. "I believe you made her acquaintance last night at Almack's, for all the world to see."

The rag-mannered woman. With difficulty, Nash drew in a breath and slowly let it out.

"I did, my lord, render her some slight assistance last evening." Either their encounter had become the latest on-dit circulating this morning or the earl had excellent spies following Lady Cavendish.

"Then you know about her shameless liaison with that blackguard Garrett."

The memory of the lady, hair mussed, lips swollen, emerging from the stairwell with the young buck rose with startling clarity. His stomach clenched. Now he was more than sorry he hadn't planted Garrett a facer. Hadn't the lady's cousin warned her about the bounder?

Nash nodded. "I believe I had heard something to that effect." Best not say what he had seen or he'd never be able to refuse the earl. And refuse him he must. Despite his attraction to Lady Cavendish, if her actions were so scandalous as to drive her father to this desperate action, he was well shed of the woman. "But rumors run rampant in London, my lord. I suspect Lady Cavendish is merely the latest innocent victim of the *ton*'s need for gossip."

"She's not innocent, Wrotham." The earl leaned forward, gripping his cane head, eyes bulging. "There were *witnesses*. This morning they are calling her the 'Wicked Widow.'" He dragged the words out, making them as horrific as possible.

Damn. How could he escape now?

"Mark me, Wrotham, I'll have no disgrace attached to my name. I stopped her once before and, by God, I will do it again." He fixed Nash with a stare that would have caused apoplexy in a lesser man. "You will marry her, Wrotham, before she can do more damage. You owe me that at least."

"I beg your pardon, my lord?" That last sentence caught Nash off guard. "I'm sure I don't know what you mean by owing you."

"Come, now. I have not changed a great deal in six years."

Nash frowned. "I don't understand. We only met—"

"The tollhouse at Whetstone?"

His words recalled that chilling scene so vividly—the young man with a pistol to his head, the terrified woman, the icy voice from the shadows—Nash had to blink to bring Lord Grafton back into focus. "That was you? And the young lady . . ." Lord, he remembered her, so frightened yet defiant. Quite different from the woman he had met last night.

"My daughter. Disobedient and headstrong as always. Now to be your problem." He cocked his head. "I was surprised you didn't recognize me the first time we met in Parliament."

Still stunned, Nash shook his head and shrugged. "The firelight was behind you at the gatehouse. I couldn't see your face." Then he narrowed his eyes. "I never gave you my name that night. How the devil did you know who I was?"

"I had you followed, of course." Lord Grafton settled his hands on his cane, his lips pursed in displeasure. "My man lost you once you and Thrush reached London, although he managed to get your name from a tavern you stopped at in Highgate. I have sat on that knowledge until I required your services, as I do now."

Nash swore under his breath. "Surely there must be other, more illustrious alliances you could seek?" With his influence, Grafton could have his pick of victims.

"Had I more control over my daughter, I would do that very thing." The earl obviously did not mince words. "I did before. Now, however, she has a measure of financial independence and I cannot do as easily as I once did. Therefore, I decided to call in my favor from you."

He put up a hand to forestall Nash's protest. "You thwarted my plans once before; it is only fitting that you now pay the price. It should not be a totally odious one. While my daughter is willful, she is not without her charms."

"But—"

"You're respectable," the earl continued, undaunted by the interruption. "You have no vices I've been able to discover, you vote as you should in Lords, and you're almost of an age with Charlotte. She should like that." He laughed mirthlessly.

Nash cringed. Like a stallion the earl contemplated putting out to stud. Insufferable.

"And if I refuse, Lord Grafton?" Nash straightened in his chair. "I sympathize with your situation, however, my actions of six years ago hardly obligate me to marry your daughter. We met but briefly, both then and last evening. I cannot, in good conscience, marry a woman with whom I have scarcely spoken two dozen words." Even more especially because her own father had called her reputation into question.

"Ah, good conscience would have you decline the offer, you say?" The earl leaned back, rubbing the cane head with the palm of his hand.

Nash kept his gaze on that cane.

"What will your conscience have to say when your Warder's bill is voted down at my insistence?"

Every muscle in Nash's body tensed. He had worked hard in the past year to write this bill and worked even harder to gain it support in the House of Lords. Traditionally, every branch of service save the Royal Navy could apply to become a Yeoman Warder of the Tower of London. If his bill passed, the retired naval petty officers would have a chance at this honorable position as well, with good benefits the other branches of service had enjoyed for more than three hundred years. He had garnered a good bit of support for the legislation already. Grafton's considerable influence would make the victory all but sure. Now, however . . .

"I am sorry, my lord, but I fear I must decline your generous offer nevertheless." Where he would get the votes now he didn't know. But if not this year, there was next.

Grafton rose, bringing Nash to his feet as well, somewhat dazed at his easy victory. "I am sorry to hear that, Wrotham. I believe you would have been quite a force in Parliament from what I have seen in this last year."

"'Would have been,' my lord?" The sinking feeling of having a trap sprung about him nigh on suffocated him.

"Would have been, Lord Wrotham." The earl turned toward the doorway. "As I said before, a sensible man gives me my way. When I run into a stubborn man, one who thinks to turn me from my course, I fear I have not the Christian way of charity when dealing with him." He swung back toward Nash, his walking stick whipping around until it was aimed squarely at Nash's stomach. "You asked earlier for my support on your bill, and I would have been happy to grant it as a familial alliance. But know this, my lord: as no such alliance exists, not only will I remove my support from *this* bill, but from any other bill you may propose within my lifetime. *Any* bill you support, I will actively work to defeat. Members will avoid even being seen with you because I will make it known that such an association will incur my wrath and the immediate withdrawal of my support for *their* bills."

Nash stared at Grafton, icy anger flowing through his veins. How dare the earl blackmail him into marrying his licentious daughter? He opened his mouth to tell the old man it would be a cold day in Hades before he spoke vows with the wanton Lady Cavendish, when a niggling little voice whispered to him to close it instead. That voice had saved his bacon more than once. He'd better listen to it now.

"I do not take kindly to blackmail, my lord."

"Then look at it as my way of assisting you in your career in Parliament." Lord Grafton gave what Nash assumed passed for smile. "I give you my support, you give me yours. Quite simple actually. Once you come to know Charlotte, you may even develop a fondness for her. She has spirit, although she is one of the most stubborn women in England. As long as you keep her from becoming the talk of the *ton* and are betrothed to her by November first, when the bill comes up for a vote, you shall have my considerable weight behind you." The earl inclined his head and leaned toward Nash, resting his weight on his cane once more. "Do we have a deal, Wrotham?"

During Grafton's little speech, Nash had frantically counted each vote he had already gotten and tried to figure who else he could possibly persuade. Damn the rest of his career; if he could get this one bill passed he'd be satisfied. If he could convince Admiral Lord Hyland to come over, he might be able to swing a block of ex-military members. It would take the rest of the session to see it through, yet it might be possible. Let Grafton believe Nash was courting Lady Cavendish while instead he'd be doing courting of a different kind.

"I have no idea if Lady Cavendish will even receive me, my lord. But I will pay her a call at my earliest convenience." That had enough truth in it to appease his honor.

His butler appeared from nowhere. "From Wrotham Hall, my lord." Hoskins presented a sealed message precisely in the middle of a silver salver.

Nash plucked it from the tray and broke the seal. He perused the note and swore. What despicably bad timing.

"Not bad news?" Grafton raised an eyebrow.

"As I'm sure you know, my lord, estate agents never send anything else. I will need to postpone my call on Lady Cavendish." Nash sighed, the chance of garnering a sufficient number of votes to pass his bill without Grafton evaporating like smoke in the wind. The inevitability of becoming Grafton's son-in-law weighed like a millstone. "I'm for home this afternoon."

The earl cocked his head and frowned. "That serious?"

"Quite. There's been a gang of robbers terrorizing the neighboring county. Now they've moved into Kent. They wounded one of my tenants trying to defend his home. My presence is required."

"Robbers in Kent? I've an estate and a hunting lodge there." The earl's face darkened.

"I know. Lyttlefield Park abuts my property near the village of Wrotham." Nash had thought their proximity a boon earlier this summer.

"Then you won't mind keeping an eye out for my interests while you're there?" The older man peered at him, as if he were bestowing a great favor on Nash rather than asking one.

"Not a'tall, my lord. However," Nash snatched at a breath of hope, "I will be hard-pressed to court Lady Cavendish if she is in London and I am in Kent. This matter with the robbers may not be resolved easily."

Grafton waved a hand in dismissal. "I believe it will not be that difficult for you to find a way to court my daughter, Wrotham, if you put your mind to it. Keep her from public censure and put your engagement in *The Times* in short order and all else will fall into place. Good day."

"Good day, my lord."

Grafton strode out of the room. Nash stared after him, crumpling the note in his fist. The only place this could be deemed a good day was in hell.

* * *

"What is this Widow's Club Jane spoke of in her note this morning?" Mrs. Elizabeth Easton wrinkled her brow as she sat in the gold-figured Chippendale chair, a focal point of Charlotte's perfectly appointed drawing room, sipping tea as they waited for the rest of their friends to arrive.

"I've actually thought of our little set that way all along." Charlotte poured herself a cup of tea and added two lumps of sugar. "We are all widows, we met because our husbands died at Waterloo, or because of it, and we are now all on the hunt for male companionship once more. We have so much in common, it put me in mind of one of the gentlemen's clubs." As the clock struck eleven, she glanced at the door, but it remained closed. Her cousin was never punctual.

"Except we talk about fashion and children, and our husbands . . ." Elizabeth fought to contain a sob and bent her head to study her teacup. Her shoulders sagged.

Charlotte clasped her hand and squeezed it. "I know, my dear." Poor Elizabeth. She had been devastated by her husband's death. Almost worse, she had had to return to her parents' home. If Charlotte's plan for the widows worked, maybe she could help her friend.

One more squeeze of her hand and Charlotte let go. "Yes, we do talk of much different subjects than our male counterparts." She plopped in one more lump and stirred slowly. "Our conversations lately, however, have focused on our desire, or the necessity, of marrying again." She patted Elizabeth's arm, then sipped her tea. "Marriage is actually what we shall discuss this morning—a way I've come up with for us to find new prospects."

Elizabeth twisted her plain gold wedding band. She glanced up, met Charlotte's gaze, then folded her hands in her lap. "Do you plan to bring Mr. Garrett up to scratch, then?"

Charlotte sputtered back into her teacup. "Dear Lord, why do you ask that?"

Elizabeth broke into a rare smile and raised her cup. "I daresay you have not read the scandal sheets this morning."

Charlotte's cup rattled its way into the saucer. The dratted man. She'd be ruined. "What did it say, Elizabeth?" She held her breath.

"Only that Lady C had been seen behaving in a shameless manner with Mr. G at the Waterloo Ball and Fete." Elizabeth raised an eyebrow at her, a censure to be sure. "What on earth did you do, Charlotte? One scandal sheet is calling you the 'Wicked Widow.'"

Dear Lord. Not ruin, but close enough. Apparently, someone had noticed her emerge rumpled from the stairwell, so anyone who had seen her and Mr. Garrett dance together would assume the worst. Charlotte put her head in her hands. At the very least they would expect her to marry the man. Well, they could all go hang.

"Yes, I did meet him, and no, I do not have any desire to bring him to the altar. He is a rake who may be trying to ruin me. He certainly acted like it last night."

Elizabeth frowned. "So you were not a willing participant?"

"Hardly." Charlotte shook herself. "His attentions were most unwelcome. Well," she paused, and heat crept into her face, "mostly unwelcome."

"Mostly?" Her friend gave her an arch look.

"Please believe me, I didn't encourage him in the least. But when he kissed me . . ." Lord, she could feel his lips on hers with the mere thought of the word *kiss*. She shrugged. "I have had no warmth or passion in my life for so long, Elizabeth. It was a relief to know I could still feel something."

"I would never have doubted it, my dear. You have an amazing amount of love in you." She smiled and patted

Charlotte's hand. "Still, if you would not wed Mr. Garrett, there are others you might consider, I suppose."

"Actually there is not." Charlotte drew herself up. Her friend would not like her next statement at all. "I do not intend to marry again."

Elizabeth's face changed from confusion to shock. "Not wed again?" Her horrified voice rose two octaves. "But Charlotte, what do your parents say about such a thing?"

"They have no say over me now, thank God. Oh, they will be scandalized, no doubt, but I don't give a fig for what they want." She turned the cup to and fro in its saucer. "My mother practically abandoned me as a child, then did in earnest when I married Sir Archibald. Father's decree, I assume. No one in the family was allowed to contact me, although I did receive the odd letter at Christmas from Mama most years, so I do know some of what goes on. Mama was much taken up with my sister Agnes, Lady Ramsay, the good child, and her increasing brood this past year. And she'll be busy getting ready for Sophia's come-out next year as well, I daresay. She won't care that she does not need to plan another wedding for me."

Flustered, Elizabeth's face paled. "You never told me that, Charlotte. But even so, what about a family of your own? What about children?"

"I was married once and that was nightmare enough for me. I will not allow myself to be under the absolute power of a man ever again." She clenched her hands, the memory of Sir Archibald's cruelties never very far from her thoughts. "My husband commanded my every move, from town to country, country to town—whether he accompanied me or not. I could not stir from the house without his approval." Her jaw clenched. "After our wedding, he controlled all expenditures, including my clothing. He made me feel like a servant to whom he need not pay wages."

"Not every man is like that." Elizabeth set down her cup as well and grasped Charlotte's hands. "You need to find a good one who will love you and give you children."

Charlotte sniffed. "If I had a loving husband, of course I would want children. I would not, however, have wanted them with Sir Archibald, had it even been possible. They might have turned out like Edgar."

Edgar Cavendish had taken Charlotte in dislike upon their initial meeting six years before. Try though she might in the early days of her marriage, she had never been able to make Edgar thaw toward her. After he spread rumors about the nature of her elopement with Edward, the animosity had become mutual.

"Sir Archibald couldn't have more children?" Elizabeth's cheeks flushed.

"Not when he never visited his wife's bed, he couldn't." Charlotte kept her gaze firmly on her teacup.

"You had no marital relations with Sir Archibald at all?" Elizabeth's shocked whisper made Charlotte flinch.

"None whatsoever." Bitterness flooded her voice. She had not desired the physical attentions of her aging husband and had been glad when he made no move to claim his rights. He had made sure she suffered otherwise at his hands, however. To retaliate, she had filled her lonely bed with dreams of the husband she had been denied, the one with whom she could have shared a good and passionate life. It had not helped much. "The most loving thing he ever did for me was to die."

"Charlotte!" Elizabeth's face had drained of color.

Charlotte set her cup carefully on the saucer. "You may think me wicked for such thoughts, but I cannot help myself. Father dragged me from Edward's arms and threw me into Sir Archibald's." Resentment welled within her anew. "Can you imagine your disgust if you were forced to leave Dickon and made to marry . . . oh, I don't know,

Lord Bassingstoke?" Bassingstoke was a particular crony of Elizabeth's father, perhaps twenty years her senior.

Elizabeth shook her head, cringing. "That is not quite the same thing, Charlotte. Dickon came of gentle birth, a colonel in the army. Edward Thrush was a—"

"Servant; I know." Charlotte stared at her fiercely. She would never be ashamed of him. "My groom, and I loved him. He loved me. What he was didn't matter. We would have been happy."

"You would have been disinherited and forced to live God knows how once Edward was dismissed without a reference." Elizabeth met her eyes, a mixture of sympathy and censure in their blue depths. "It is hard to live on love alone. Georgie can tell you that."

Charlotte longed to rail at her friend, defend her love, but she had never been able to make anyone understand. Edward had been the only man who had ever cared for her. From the moment that summer when her father had assigned the new groom to accompany her whenever she rode out, she had felt at ease with Edward Thrush. He'd not shied away from talking to her, as her other grooms had. She'd been sent to the Glasbury estate as punishment for speaking back to her father and had been mad for company.

Edward had known so much about the land at Glasbury Park and had told her many fascinating things as they rode each day. He even made her laugh into the bargain. She'd loved that though a groom, he had wanted to better himself, in the hopes of owning his own small estate one day. Most of all, Edward had been kind to her. She had never had kindness from her father or brother, and precious little from her mother either, so it had mattered a great deal to her. Charlotte had not believed she was being defiant by eloping; she had simply wanted to be loved. There would never be another man as sweet and caring as Edward.

After that horrible night, she had never heard one word about him. The moment she learned of her widowhood, she had made inquiries, tried to find him. She now had the means for them to live comfortably for the rest of their lives. But the men she had employed had discovered no trace of him. Resigned to never know what had become of him, she prayed nightly he still lived. Now, at four and twenty, she had her freedom and the means to live life on her own terms. Precisely what she intended to do.

She shook herself, as if awakening from a dream. "I beg your pardon, Elizabeth. I was woolgathering. But I do believe I have found a way to solve our problem."

"What problem?"

"Well, Jane observed last night that eligible men were few and much in demand this time of year. What we need is a private place to entertain them, so we can have them to ourselves. But we couldn't think of a place to hold a house party." Charlotte arched her neck and raised her chin. "But I believe I have found just the place."

"Where?"

"Lyttlefield Park."

Elizabeth cocked her head sharply. "What is that?"

"An estate left to me at my husband's death as part of my dowry and to which I will remove before Edgar's arrival."

"Has Sir Edgar not yet returned from his grand tour? I must tell you, I thought it in exceedingly poor taste that he would go to the Continent immediately after his father's death." Elizabeth sipped her tea and lowered her voice. "It seemed so disrespectful."

Charlotte snorted. "Edgar's tour had been scheduled long before his brother's and Sir Archibald's deaths. As soon as his uncle told him the funds were at his disposal, Edgar refused to let anything stand in the way of his pleasure." She stared over her cold teacup at her friend and confided, "I am just as pleased that he has been absent these eleven months. I have almost six more weeks of respite until his return in early August."

"But what have you discovered about Lyttlefield Park?"

"Lyttlefield Park?" Jane's strident voice filled the small room as she strode in.

"Jane, at last." Charlotte rose to buss her cheeks.

"Good morning, Elizabeth." Jane stripped off her gloves and unfastened her spencer. "I didn't know you were here already."

Charlotte poured her a cup of tea.

"Two lumps and lots of milk, please."

Charlotte raised her eyebrows. "I would think after living with you for almost twelve months I would know that, my dear." She plopped the sugar into the cup and tipped the milk pitcher the required amount of time, then handed the cup to Jane. "Let's see how well I managed."

Jane smiled and sipped. "Delicious. So, Elizabeth, are you—"

"Lady Stephen Tarkington and Lady Georgina Kirk-patrick." Thorne, her late husband's staid butler, ushered them in.

"I sent the carriage around for them earlier, before I went out." Jane rose to greet their guests.

Lady Stephen, Fanny to her friends, had been married to a younger brother of Jane's husband. Lady Georgina, or Georgie, was the youngest of the widows in their little group, her circumstances the most dire. Thorne assisted them with their pelisses.

"More tea, Thorne."

"Yes, my lady." He withdrew, shutting the door with a loud click.

"Lady Marable was quite put out that you did not call with me, Charlotte. She said she had some questions for you about last night." Her cousin sent her a droll look before reclaiming her seat.

"Precisely the reason I did not accompany you." Charlotte nodded emphatically. She surveyed her circle with satisfaction. They had come, but would they all be willing to go through with the plan?

"I am so very pleased you came this morning, ladies." Charlotte embraced her friends. "I was just telling Elizabeth I propose we create a club—we have already, you know—called the Widow's Club." They all settled themselves and Charlotte poured tea. "It will consist of the five of us who seek to marry or," she shot a glance at her cousin, "take an interest in men once more."

"It's to be like the gentlemen's clubs," Elizabeth added.

Jane frowned. "Like White's or Brook's? How is that to help us find men? Unless perhaps you were thinking of a joint outing somewhere . . ."

"No indeed." Charlotte shuddered. "No, the club is simply similar in structure. We have always met to talk about fashion and children and—"

"Men." Fanny spoke up eagerly.

"Exactly." If anyone would get right to the point, it would be Fanny. "Except we will carry it a step further. Before the end of the Season, we will invite certain gentlemen of our acquaintance to a house party. Once there, we shall have the opportunity and the time to talk and flirt with them without constraint. Best of all, we will have these gentlemen all to ourselves." Charlotte raised her chin, her gaze darting from face to face.

"It is a wonderful plan, my dear." Jane beamed at her. "But the problem remains where to have this party? Gentlemen's clubs have particular buildings in which to meet. We are five women without property."

Charlotte smiled broadly. "That is not exactly true. Have you forgotten Lyttlefield Park?"

"Ah! Yes, you were speaking of it when I entered. I had forgotten you inherited it. Well done, my dear." Jane softly applauded.

Fanny leaned forward. "What on earth is Lyttlefield Park?"

"One of my father's unentailed estates that served as part of my marriage settlement. It is in Kent, just beyond Kingsdown."

The hum of soft voices threatened to drown her out as the other women broke into an animated exchange.

Charlotte had to clear her throat to get their attention. "I had been thinking to remove there permanently when we quit this town house, if you agree, Jane. However, we can open it early and make it ready to receive guests within a few weeks' time. This morning we shall make a list of the gentlemen with whom we wish to become better acquainted so I can issue the invitations. Lyttlefield Park will be the perfect place to relax and demonstrate our numerous charms."

The chattering that ensued resembled a gaggle of geese in a cornfield. Charlotte had to wait for the noise to subside again before asking, "Which eligible men shall we invite?"

Four sets of eyes stared at her expectantly.

Drat! Had they all read that silly scandal rag? Very well, she would turn the attention elsewhere. "Jane, you were talking to Mr. Abernathy for a good bit of the evening. Are you perhaps interested in him with an eye to matrimony?"

"I told you last night, Charlotte, I will never marry again. I am, however, very interested in Mr. Abernathy." Jane leaned back and licked her lips, a smile curling the ends of her mouth. "By all means, invite him."

Charlotte wanted to roll her eyes; still, she could hardly throw stones after her own performance last night and her resolve to remain unmarried. She held her tongue and moved on.

"Fanny? Your choice?"

"Well," Fanny couldn't repress a self-satisfied smile, "I renewed my acquaintance with the Earl of Lathbury last evening. We both attended Lady Beaumont's masquerade. I think we would suit, certainly for the weekend." She laughed, and her face became livelier than Charlotte had ever seen it. "Indeed I hope it lasts longer. He's a Corinthian, but I rather enjoy the horses and the hunting parties. I'm a woman who doesn't want to live in her husband's pocket." Her face lost all animation. "The less I knew about Stephen's comings and goings toward the end, the better off I was."

Fanny's lips pressed into a thin line, then she seemed to make herself relax and resumed her report on Lathbury. "We danced once, but he lingered, and after the unmasking we talked for a bit. Recalling old times." She paused, then blurted out, "He's very . . . big."

Charlotte's jaw dropped and the other ladies burst into giggles. Fanny's face had turned bright red. *Lord, how many of us have the same thing on our minds? And not necessarily marriage.*

To cover her embarrassment, Charlotte fetched paper and pen from her travel desk. "All right." She sat and began her list. "Mr. George Abernathy, the Earl of Lathbury." She paused and looked at Elizabeth and Georgina expectantly.

Georgina immediately looked guilty and hung her head.

"Has anyone taken your fancy, Georgina?" Charlotte asked gently. Her friend looked as if ready to bolt at the idea. "Someone you would like to know better?"

After several moments, Georgie nodded, and whispered, "Jane introduced me to Lord Fernley at Lady Gresham's when we called the other day. He seemed kind."

"Well, that's a start." Charlotte tried to sound encouraging, although Georgie obviously had not the slightest interest. "Shall I ask him down? You've spoken to him, so he won't seem a total stranger, and there will be others at the house party you likely know as well."

A curt nod of Georgie's head and Charlotte jotted down Fernley's name.

"Now, Elizabeth." Charlotte tried to infuse her voice with enthusiasm, but the stricken look on her friend's face made her feel like a torturer. "Have you someone you would like me to invite, dearest?"

Elizabeth shook her head. "I simply have not got my spirits up sufficiently to want to meet anyone else, Charlotte. I am sorry. I think it best if I not attend the house party this time."

"Nonsense. There must be someone you have met whom you would like to know better."

"Can I have you invite my brother?" Georgina asked excitedly.

Charlotte cocked her head. "Your brother? Why would you want to bring your—"

"For Elizabeth."

A rosy flush spread upward from Elizabeth's neck. "Georgie, you don't need to do that."

Georgina grasped Elizabeth's hands and smiled gleefully. "But don't you see, it will help me too. I'll know someone and feel more comfortable around all these strange men."

Elizabeth's blush began to recede. "Which brother, Georgie?"

"The eldest, Jemmy . . . um, Lord Brack." Georgie's charming one-sided grin brightened her face. "He is so much fun. You will like him, Elizabeth. Even if he is the heir, and six years older than I, he's always looked out for me. He didn't approve of Father disowning me or taking away Mr. Kirkpatrick's living for marrying me and his son, but in the end Jemmy could do nothing to dissuade him." She looked at Charlotte hopefully. "If you invite him, I will finally be able to see him. It has been three years since I last spoke with him, but you mustn't tell anyone I will be there or Father may forbid him to come."

Charlotte wrote the name with a flourish. "There, he is on the list. And if he is as wonderful as he sounds, Elizabeth will be well entertained." She laid the pen down and fanned the paper. "Ladies, I believe we have our first guest list."

A smile tugged at Jane's lips and she said in a teasing voice, "We appear to be one guest short. Who will you invite, Charlotte? You must choose as well."

Drat. After last night, they certainly must expect her to invite Alan Garrett despite her protests. Charlotte closed her eyes, and the darkly handsome figure of Lord Wrotham sprang to mind instead—black hair, intense blue eyes, and full, sensual lips. She remembered well the feel of his hard chest and the strong arms that had saved her and sighed softly.

"If you are squeamish about writing his name, I am not." Jane's words brought her back to the present to find her cousin had plucked the list out of her hands and was busily writing.

"Jane!" Charlotte dove for the paper, but her cousin held it out of reach. "Whose name are you writing?"

"Alan Garrett's of course." Jane laughed, fanning the paper before her face.

"What about Alan Garrett?"

A shiver of dread coursed through Charlotte at the sound of that loathsome male voice. Steeling herself, she turned toward the doorway.

Sir Edgar Cavendish stood stripping off his riding gloves, a snarl on his thin lips.

Chapter 5

"Edgar." The shock of seeing him took Charlotte's breath away. What was he doing here in June? Automatically, she rose. "I didn't expect you back until August."

"Really? Thought you'd be able to live off my charity for another couple of months, eh?"

The Continent had changed her stepson not one iota. Charlotte's arsenal of defenses against Edgar's bullying clicked back into place. After five years of taunts and disrespect, conveniently overlooked by his father, she had devised her own methods to cope with him. First, she'd get him away from her friends. No one save his relations should have to be subjected to Edgar's tirades.

"Come, let us remove to your father's office to discuss this privately." She moved toward him and he put a hand out to stop her.

"We might as well speak before your *friends*. I am sure they will be affected by your lack of means as well." He brushed past her to sit in the chair she had just vacated.

She narrowed her eyes at her loathsome prig of a stepson. "I have perfectly acceptable means, Edgar, as you very well know from the reading of your father's will. I have my jointure and I have the settlement from my dowry."

"Then I suggest you use them and find another abode." His gaze fell to the list Jane had dropped at his entrance. "What is this?"

Charlotte bit back a curse. Disaster loomed if she could not come up with a plausible reason for that list.

He picked it up, his eyes flicking down the list of names. They stopped at the last one. An evil smile curved his mouth. "Why have you written a list that contains Alan Garrett's name? He's one of the worst rakes in the *ton*."

Charlotte glanced at her friends and swallowed hard.

"We were making a list, Sir Edgar." Georgina spoke quietly, not looking at him. She resembled a child confessing to breaking china.

"Obviously." Edgar rolled his eyes. "But what kind of list?"

"Of ineligible men, Sir Edgar," Elizabeth answered with absolute conviction.

He shot a wary glance at Charlotte. "I was given to believe that women usually made lists of the eligible parties rather than the opposite."

"Yes, but you see, Sir Edgar," Jane leaned forward, arching her neck and thrusting out her chest toward him, "last evening Charlotte and I attended the anniversary ball at Almack's. On our first foray back into Society, we were accosted by so many undesirables, we compiled a list of the gentlemen we felt were simply not to be tolerated. Our friends are now back out in society as well and we wanted to warn them in case they should meet them."

He glanced down at the list again. "George Abernathy? He is undesirable because . . . ?"

"He is quite the rake, my lord." Jane smiled knowingly. "I have it on the best authority. He's not as blatant about it as some, but I've heard he's done some of the most outrageous things with women."

Edgar frowned and consulted the list. "The Earl of Lathbury?"

Fanny spoke up. "Drinks like a fish. Was in his cups last night so deep he couldn't remember my name. Kept calling me Sally."

"There's no drinking at Almack's."

"I attended a private function last evening, but the man had been drinking before he arrived at any rate. Pickled as a herring."

Edgar shook his head, looking at the faces surrounding him. "You were all accosted by bounders?"

Fanny nodded gravely. "There are so many rogues out there, Sir Edgar. At the end of the Season, all the decent gentlemen have already become betrothed."

Charlotte scarcely breathed. Pray God they could explain away that list to her stepson's satisfaction and mislead him from their true intentions.

"And I suppose you are going to say that this Lord Fernley is also a rake or a drunkard?" He stared at them one by one.

Georgina spoke up again. "I'm sure I don't know about that, but I do know he pulled me into the library at Lady Gresham's and tried to kiss me."

A collective gasp went up. Charlotte's vision wavered. That description came too close to her circumstances for comfort. But Georgina continued on, though her cheeks flamed. "I don't think that is very proper behavior toward someone you've only just met."

"I suppose not." Edgar's tone had turned speculative, and to her horror, Charlotte realized he was eyeing Georgie as though she were a horse he contemplated buying. Lord, she hoped that hadn't given him any ideas.

"I am also responsible for the next name on the list. Lord Brack is my brother."

Edgar continued to eye her askance. "And your brother is ineligible as well?"

Georgie shifted in her chair. "He is a cruel man, Sir Edgar." She hung her head. "I wanted to warn my friends about him. When I married a man he deemed beneath my station, he convinced my father to disown me. He has hounded me since my husband's death and tried to make me marry a man just to pay off his gambling debts."

Charlotte clamped her hand over her mouth to keep back the laughter. Georgie looked so miserable, her voice so pathetic, that if Charlotte hadn't known the truth, she'd have been completely convinced of Lord Brack's evil ways. Her friend had missed her calling as an actress.

"And of course the last name needs no explanation." Jane spoke up before Charlotte could do so. "Everyone knows Mr. Garrett's reputation."

Edgar lowered his head and squinted at each woman in turn. "And which one of you was accosted by that rogue."

"He didn't accost me, Edgar. But he did dance with me." Charlotte tried to diminish her encounter with Garrett. She had to admit the dance; a room full of people had seen them. But if her stepson knew the full story, she'd be ruined in society as soon as the man left the room.

"That alone could have ruined your reputation, Charlotte," Edgar admonished. "Not that it matters to me." He tossed the list back on the table. "You are on your own as far as I am concerned. I assume you have begun your packing?"

Charlotte raised her chin. "I have not. Your uncle gave me permission to continue on here at the town house in London until August because he thought it a more fitting place for me to live during my period of mourning." Her lips curled into a sneer. "I supposed he was grateful to have *someone* to mourn his brother."

Edgar squeezed the arm of the chair until his knuckles turned white. "I want you out of my house."

"I have permission—"

"Which I am revoking this instant. I want you," he looked around at the little circle of women, "and these *ladies*, out immediately."

Almost as one, her friends rose, their shocked faces riveted on her.

Charlotte took a deep breath and loosened her clenched fists. "Pray take your seats." She stalked over to tower over Edgar. "He has no right to send anyone from this house."

Edgar leaped to his feet and she thought for a moment he would actually strike her. "You lying—"

"He has not yet reached his majority, have you, Edgar?" Charlotte smiled sweetly as his black frown deepened. "You don't turn twenty-one until August second. On that day, you may do as you like with your property. But until then, because your uncle has given me leave to live here, I will do so. If you disagree with his decision, I suggest you take it up with him."

Edgar clenched his hands, a darkness flashing over his face that foretold a reckoning for her at a later date. "You will regret this insolence, my lady." With that veiled threat, he quit the room, slamming the door on the way out.

As if his exit had been a signal, Charlotte and her friends dropped back into their seats, chattering frantically.

"I am so sorry, Charlotte."

"How have you stood living with that horrible boy?"

"Has he always been cross as crabs?"

"What a dirty-dish." Jane settled herself into her chair. "Someone needs to plant him a facer."

Laughter burbled out of Charlotte at last. "I would truly love to see that."

Jane sobered. "What will we do now, my dear? We

only have a little over six weeks and that bounder will turn us out into the street."

"We will commence packing immediately and remove to Lyttlefield as soon as possible." Charlotte smoothed out her dress, thinking how much she would miss seeing her friends in Town.

"And the Widow's Club? Will you still be able to host the house party, do you think?" Fanny asked, her face stretched tight.

Charlotte looked about at her friends. This move would put a strain on her. A house party would only compound the stress. But these women had stood by her during the trials of the past year. They all deserved the chance to pursue their happiness. She would see the matter through, no matter what.

"If I set the servants to start today, I can begin the move perhaps by late next week. I intend to be completely free of this house before the middle of July. I'll see what needs to be done at Lyttlefield; hopefully nothing of major concern. In fact, why don't we celebrate our freedom with the house party the weekend after that?" Charlotte strode to the desk in the corner and produced a calendar. She ruffled through the pages until she found July. "Around the nineteenth of July, say?" she asked, looking expectantly at her friends, most of whom were nodding enthusiastically.

Jane, however, frowned and shook her head. "No, I'm sorry, my dear, that won't do for me. I'm to go to Scotland in July, don't you remember? The Munro clan Gathering?" She screwed her face into a comic moue. "I detest these things, but Papa is adamant about it each year."

Charlotte laughed, then sobered. "Then we must await your return, my dear. You will have something to look forward to while you are up in the Highlands. I had hoped to hold it sooner, but that cannot be helped now." She sighed as the thought of Lord Wrotham's strong arms assailed her. "Will the second weekend in August be enough time after your return?"

"Yes, that should suit admirably." Jane nodded, her tense face relaxing into pleasanter lines.

"I will send out the invitations next week so there should be plenty of time for the replies." Charlotte turned the pages of the calendar, counting the days.

"You never gave us the name of your gentleman, Charlotte," Elizabeth spoke up, a smile touching her lips. "I assume Mr. Garrett is not invited?"

"Indeed he is not, Elizabeth." Charlotte shuddered. "No, I believe I will invite Lord Wrotham, to make amends for not dancing with him last night." The perfect way, perhaps, to end up in his arms again.

"What will you do if one of the gentlemen can't attend?" Elizabeth sounded almost as if she hoped that would be the case.

"You will need to give me an alternate name to be invited." Charlotte nodded decisively. "Perhaps I should invite an additional gentleman, just in case." She smiled. "There can never be too many gentlemen, don't you think?"

"If we can each get the one we want to attend, we should consider ourselves most fortunate." Jane rose, which signaled the others. "We need to sit down and plan, Charlotte. I think Theale will loan us servants to help with the move." She gazed around the morning room and sighed. "This was always such a cozy room. I am sure I will miss it. I daresay you will too, my dear."

Charlotte glanced around, taking in the elegant Chippendale chairs, the Queen Anne escritoire, the white marble Robert Adams mantelpiece, and smiled. "Perhaps not as much as you might think."

Chapter 6

August 7, 1816

Pacing the confines of his study, Nash read Lord Grafton's letter once more, grinding his teeth as irritation built with every word.

"My daughter, Lady Cavendish, informs me that pursuant to the terms of her late husband's will, she will be removing from London to her estate (through dower rights) at Lyttlefield sometime in late July. This plan presents you with an opportune moment, Wrotham, to call on her once she and her cousin are settled in. Make sure she is in good health and spirits. And begin your courtship. Tempus fugit.

"I trust you are dealing with the robbers you spoke of to me in London, and that you will inform me when they are apprehended. I will not be able to travel into Kent until the autumn hunting season, at which time I would beg your attendance at Grafton Lodge near . . ."

He tossed it on his desk and picked up the small, elegant cream-colored card.

*"Lord Wrotham is invited to attend a house
party, August eighth through twelfth, at Lyttlefield
Park in Kent. Hostess ~ Charlotte, Lady
Cavendish."*

The invitation had arrived only two days ago, after languishing at his London town house, where it had been sent over a month ago. If he were to go through with this charade, the house party offered a perfect opportunity to woo his wicked widow.

Lady Cavendish. The woman rose before his eyes: her yellow gown showing off the swell of her bosom, her smooth white arms, and her long regal neck. The sweet, warm bundle she made pressed against his chest after her graceless fall. If only the memory could stop there. But then she was snatched from him, absconded with that insolent rakehell. Nash closed his eyes against that last sight of her, hair mussed, lips swollen but smiling, hand in hand with the blackguard. The image exploded, leaving his body tense, his mind cold.

Damnation. He would rather walk through a sea of crushed glass rather than pay a call on that wanton woman, much less attend her party, but he had given his word to the earl. The only thing that made any such visit even slightly palatable was the thought of his bill, now languishing in the House of Lords.

Nash sighed and laid the invitation on his desk. He consulted the calendar. Had the woman arrived in Kent? He pulled the bell, summoning the butler.

"Acres, have you heard anything about Lyttlefield Park being occupied?"

"Yes, my lord. Mrs. Lockhart met the new cook from the Park yesterday at the market."

"Ah." So the widow was in residence. "Did Mrs. Lockhart mention anything about our new neighbor?"

"No, my lord. Only that she had advised her cook not to buy chickens from Harnett's."

"Hmmm." Tomorrow was the eighth. "Thank you, Acres. That will be all."

The clock on the mantel struck three as the butler closed the door. Half the afternoon gone and he still had to ride out to see to that tenant issue near Pliny Woods. He'd leave the decision about Lady Cavendish's party until tomorrow. He'd put that meeting off until the Second Coming if he could.

Nash quit the study and headed to his suite. He'd change into riding clothes and, with luck, make it out to the Woods and back by dark. Thayer entered his dressing room, polished Wellingtons in one hand, brown tweed coat in the other. Nash nodded and gave himself over to the man's ministrations. It would be a long afternoon but eminently more pleasurable than one spent wooing Lady Cavendish.

Compelled to inspect each room one last time, Charlotte strode down the first-floor corridor, stopping at each doorway to assure herself everything stood in readiness for her guests.

It had been a hectic seven weeks of whirlwind activity, but she had managed to complete the move well before Edgar's birthday. She hoped he enjoyed himself however he had celebrated his majority and heartily wished never to see the wretch again.

She popped into the morning room to straighten a red rose in a vase of flowers. Perfect.

Nervous tingles shot down her arms and gave way to flutterings in her stomach. Only a few more hours and the gentlemen should be here. But would Lord Wrotham?

She'd had no reply from the earl, which boded ill for her plan to become better acquainted with him. Even in the midst of the move, this house party had always been in the forefront of her mind.

Their meeting at Almack's had occurred almost two months ago, yet she still vividly recalled the feel of his hard chest, his arms around her body.

If only Alan Garret had not intervened. Then the rogue had had the gall to call on her the next day, a mercifully brief interlude owing to an unexpected and unsatisfactory visit from her father. He had put in an appearance after years of absence from her life to upbraid her for her actions the night before. Charlotte had dismissed his concerns and him rather abruptly.

Of course his concerns were all for himself and his reputation—the Fownhope reputation rather—though why this was so she had never been able to fathom. She'd never heard of a man so proud of his name, nor so determined to rule his family with an iron fist to keep it spotless. When she'd eloped with her groom, she'd opened the possibility of public scandal to the family. His retaliation had been to silence her using Sir Archibald.

Sometimes, however, in the past six years, she hadn't known whom to pity more, herself or her mother. Mama had been married to the tyrant for almost thirty years. At his insistence, she had relinquished control of all the children to him while they were growing up. Rather like Patient Griselda from the *Canterbury Tales*. Charlotte had seen her mother rarely, though she'd been fond of her sisters growing up. That had ended with her attempted escape with Edward. Father hadn't wanted them contaminated by her *unhinged* behavior, so they had been forbidden to write her as well, even after Agnes had married and moved to Durham. Old chains still bound.

But Father couldn't control *her* life any more, thank goodness.

After his visit, she had focused her attention on supervising the packing and moving and therefore been unable to attend the few remaining social functions of the Season nor received any callers.

Including Edgar, who she chose to avoid whenever possible.

Fortunately, her stepson had elected to lodge with his uncle in St. James's rather than live under the same roof as her. Unfortunately, for a brief period, he had come every day to oversee her progress. She could not forbid him the house but made every effort to keep to her rooms or manage to be out whenever she thought he might show up. With the thankfulness of a pardoned prisoner, she had learned in mid-July he had repaired to Brighton. His absence lightened her burden considerably, and she had continued her move as planned but with brighter spirits.

Now the day had arrived; it remained only for the guests to appear. After assuring herself the morning room met her standards, she continued on to the drawing room, where Fisk would bring her company. She stepped through the doorway and stopped, her heart giving a little leap. A guest had already arrived.

He stood at the window, looking out at the front lawn, his broad back encased in an excellent blue superfine. From this vantage point Charlotte did not recognize him, although she had a passing acquaintance with most of the gentlemen invited. The man hadn't heard her enter, so she took the opportunity to study him, puzzling over who he could be.

Georgie had shown her a portrait of Lord Brack, who had blond hair; this gentleman was dark. Lathbury and George Abernathy had sent regrets. Lord Sinclair, who she knew, had accepted in Abernathy's place. Lord Fernley had asked to bring his cousin, Henry Marsh, whom she did not know, but at that point Charlotte, desperate to keep her numbers even, had agreed. This wasn't Fernley—who had a shock of red hair—but his cousin might have come separately. Gathering her courage and smiling her most gracious hostess smile, Charlotte said, "Good evening."

The man spun toward her, his expression wooden, his mouth pinched. "Good evening, Lady Cavendish." His voice, though stern, fell pleasantly on her ear.

A memory tugged at the edges of her mind. Something about his intense blue eyes . . . "Lord Wrotham." Charlotte's smile widened as she curtsied. He had come after all. Her heart gave an odd little beat.

He nodded and his mouth pinched tighter. "We have been formally introduced, albeit briefly." Something in his eyes flared. "I received a letter from your father, asking me to call on you."

"My father?" Strange news indeed. Other than that brief, curious visit in June, she had not seen him at all in six years. Her smile slipped. "Why would my father do that? I thought you had come in response to my invitation."

She scowled, at once wary. Any time her father tried to involve himself in her welfare, she ended up the worse for it. If the earl had come from her father, she'd have nothing else to do with him.

The transformation of her face from lovely to outraged took all of two seconds. Damn, if she had such animosity toward her father, he'd better find a way to explain the man's interest and do it quickly. "I beg your pardon, my lady. What I mean is, I received word from the earl that he wished me to see about your property. If you do not know, we have a band of robbers in the area. Neither your father nor I would wish to see you harmed." Well, that was true as far as it went.

Her eyes flashed green fire. "I see. Well, thank you, Lord

Wrotham. You may report to my father that I am perfectly safe here on my estate."

"I certainly hope so, my lady, for the threat is real." He stared sternly at her, waiting for her to break her gaze first.

She raised her chin and continued to glare at him.

Damnation. When the earl had said she was stubborn, he'd meant it. "Because I bear an action to discharge for the earl, does that mean I am not welcome at your house party?"

"That depends on how involved with the earl you are, my lord." Lady Cavendish stepped backward, her cool stare chilling his innards.

Not a good sign.

"I wish for no contact with my father whatsoever, my lord." Her eyes bore straight into him, as if searching out his secrets.

"I believe he said he would not be in the county until the hunting season, so you need have no fear that he'll come knocking on your door in the near future." Nash forced a pleasant smile and tone. Grafton hadn't mentioned her animosity toward him, curse the man. One more hurdle to overcome.

"How do you know him, if I may ask?" Her eyes narrowed, a calculating gleam flaring there.

"The Lords, for the most part. Although—" Nash paused. Redemption in her eyes lay close at hand if he dared take it. Well, faint heart never won fair lady. "I believe we met originally six years ago."

She cocked her head, her brow still puckered in a frown.

"At the tollbooth in Whetstone."

It took a moment for the words to sink in. Her head straightened and her brows rose to an impossible height on her forehead as her eyes widened alarmingly, the green dots swimming in a sea of white. Blood drained from her face, leaving it as white as uncooked pastry and she staggered toward him. She grasped his arm, fingers digging into him with a death grip.

"You?" The word came out a croaked whisper.

"Yes, my lady." Damn, he didn't want her to faint. "Here, you must sit." He slid his arm around her shoulders and sat her gently on the chaise. "I wondered if you had recognized me before, but I suppose not." The warmth of her against him felt amazingly familiar and disconcertingly pleasant.

She shook her head, but her gaze searched his face. "It was dark and you had a hat pulled over your eyes."

"I was a naval officer at the time. A mere lieutenant does not want his commander informed of his more unsavory activities. A discreet shadow over the face works wonders." Nash removed his arm, suddenly aware of the impropriety. The loss of contact left him unaccountably sad, although she still clutched his arm.

"Your voice." She sat straighter and leaned toward him. "It sounded familiar at the ball, but I didn't quite recall . . ." Her hand clamped down on him. "Oh, God. What happened to him? What happened to Edward? Please, for pity's sake, you must tell me." Then she burst into tears.

Nash fumbled for his handkerchief and thrust it into her hand, then returned his arm to her shoulders. Dash it all, he hadn't meant to upset her so. "Hush, my lady. It's all right. He is fine; at least he was when last I heard from him."

Her sobs intensified. "Thank . . . you," she hitched out at last. "I lived in . . . fear this last six years that my father had followed you and managed to kill him anyway."

Her body shook with weeping and he tightened his hold.

"I promise you, I believe he is well and happy." He settled her more comfortably against his chest, her warmth seeping through his jacket. Touching his heart. "I would have kept him with me, as servant to my captain, although he was a bit old for it. I thought it best he stay away from London and your father. Unfortunately, Thrush proved an appallingly bad sailor."

Her crying had ceased and she gazed up at him, drinking in every word.

"To this day, I cannot describe the shades of green he turned when we made a short run into the Channel."

She smiled at that and charmed him all over again. "Then where did he go?"

"I sent him to Devonport, near Stoke in Devon. My mother's family is there and he became head groom at her brother's stable."

A light shone in her eyes, although she tensed as if expecting a blow. "Did he marry?"

"Yes. With three sons now, I believe."

She raised her chin and swallowed, then leaned away. "I am glad he found the happiness he deserved." Her face took on a fierceness found in mother animals defending their young. "He was the best man I ever met. Kind, gentle, loving. What did it matter that he was a groom?"

"Nothing at all, my lady." Nash could imagine the insults she had endured regarding her affection for a stable servant. Her defense of the man, even now, spoke volumes to him. Had he misjudged her at the ball and fete? "I knew him but briefly, but I saw in him all you claim. I am very happy to have been of service to him. To you both."

She bit her lip and nodded, her gaze now on the floor. "I cannot thank you enough, Lord Wrotham, for your kindness that night. Many would simply have paid the toll and been on their way."

"But they are the ones with no taste for adventure, I'll wager." That particular adventure continued still, with surprises all along the way.

The clock on the mantel chimed three and Nash reluctantly rose. "I should be going, my lady. I have discharged my duty to your father, although if I can render you any service regarding these plaguey robbers, please send to me at once. At times they seem more a nuisance than a danger, although I do not like that they have lingered here in Kent so long."

She turned those sea-green eyes on him and he caught his breath.

"Will you not stay for the house party, Lord Wrotham? There is ample room here at Lyttlefield Park and I would consider it an honor to have you as my special guest." She grasped his hands and heat danced along the tops of his forearms. "I can never repay you for the kindness you did for Edward. But please allow me to offer some entertainment to you this weekend. I am sure you would like a rest before returning to London."

Nash couldn't repress a chuckle. "Not quite so far, I'm afraid. Your invitation followed me from Town to Wrotham Hall, scarcely a mile down the road from your estate."

"Oh, dear, yes, of course." She released his hands and her cheeks pinkened prettily. "The village is Wrotham. Why did I not realize it was you?"

"I am sure you had many other things on your mind, my lady, than my name." He missed the warmth of her hands. "And I was situated in London when we met in June." Nash recalled that evening and some of his lightness dimmed. "I understand you are widowed?" There must be a story there. Why marry if she had been in love with another man?

"Yes. My husband died just after Waterloo."

"My condolences."

"Thank you." She nodded curtly, although her countenance did not seem grieved.

"Was Almack's your first venture into society after your mourning?"

"Yes." Her hands tightened in her lap. "My cousin and

I thought it fitting to emerge from mourning at the ball to commemorate the anniversary of that dreadful battle." She sent him a fleeting smile, then dropped her gaze back to her lap.

"I was sorry not to have had the benefit of your company longer that night, Lady Cavendish. I had hoped to partner you for one of the dances." Nash waited, keen for her response.

"Oh, Lord Wrotham." She clasped his hand once more, and Nash was hard put to stand still. "I am truly sorry for that inexcusable breach. I assure you I had given Mr. Garrett no cause to believe I had promised him that dance." She hung on to his hand as though it were a lifeline. "I would never have accepted you if I had. Please, I hope you can find it in your heart to forgive me, especially as we are to be neighbors."

He raised her hand and kissed it, the soft, rose-scented skin intoxicating. "Consider it forgiven and forgotten, my lady. I will therefore live in hope of another opportunity to claim you for a dance."

She nodded, another brilliant smile lighting her face. "I will look forward to it, my lord."

As would he.

"Look forward to what, my dear?" Lady John Tarkington's voice startled them both. Nash jumped back and Lady Cavendish rose to greet her cousin.

"Jane! May I present the Earl of Wrotham?" Her eyes sparkled, darting her gaze from him to her cousin.

Overly excited for a mere introduction. Had his confession made such an impression on her?

"I have just discovered his lordship is our neighbor."

"Indeed? His lordship and I met at Almack's in June, my dear. How do you do, my lord? I am so glad you have turned up after all. Dear Charlotte was quite in a dither that she had not heard from you. It is excellent news that we have you close to hand if we ever require assistance."

"Jane!" Lady Cavendish gasped and blushed for a third time. The lovely color in her cheeks was even more becoming, although he feared she might overheat at any moment.

"I was just telling Lady Cavendish I hoped for another chance to dance with her."

"Splendid, Wrotham. You shall get your chance at the party this weekend."

"Indeed I had hoped so."

"So you will attend, Lord Wrotham?" Lady Cavendish's face glowed with happiness.

How could he deny that face? "It will be my pleasure, my lady. Although I beg to be allowed to reside at home, for tonight at least. I have several matters that must be seen to first thing tomorrow."

"It will be as you wish, my lord." Lady Cavendish took his arm, steering him toward the entrance hall. "I enjoy keeping country hours, therefore dinner is at six."

"Lady Stephen will be in directly," Lady John called after them. "She insisted on repairing herself before her entrance." She peered around. "Is she the first to arrive other than Wrotham?"

"Yes." Lady Cavendish leaned toward him, conspiratorially. "We are celebrating our move to the country, you see."

"So let the celebration begin. Oh!" Another young woman, a trifle older than Lady Cavendish, had flounced into the room and stopped dead, obviously not expecting his presence.

Nash bowed. "Indeed, my lady, a joyous sentiment that all can agree with."

Lady Cavendish dropped his arm and reverted to the role of staid hostess. "Lady Stephen Tarkington, may I present the Earl of Wrotham? The earl is my neighbor, Lady Stephen. Lord Wrotham, Lady Stephen is my cousin's sister-in-law."

The lady curtsied as he bowed and remained standing. There was no telling how many more women might come bounding into the room.

"If I am to return in good time, I fear I must say au revoir for the moment." Odd, but he suddenly felt reluctant to leave. Lady Cavendish had surely beguiled him this afternoon. Perhaps he *had* misjudged her at Almack's. Who was to say Garrett hadn't dragged her off against her will?

"Until then, my lord. We will look forward to it." Her generous smile sent a warm thrill through him.

"As will I, my lady." Nash bowed again and left, relieved, excited, and puzzled at the turn of events. Such an intriguing woman. Dinner tonight should prove enlightening indeed.

Chapter 7

"Oh, my dear Lord." Charlotte sighed and plopped onto the sofa beside her cousin, completely spent.

"So Lord Wrotham has accepted your invitation, Charlotte." Jane sipped her tea, eyebrows raised. "Well, well. I believe he has a certain admiration for you, dear. He seems to have forgiven your rudeness at Almack's."

"I was not rude, Jane. Mr. Garrett was. Should I have made a scene instead? And Wrotham said he came only because Father asked him to."

"Indeed." Jane leaned closer to her. "And why, pray tell, would he do that?"

"I don't know. Lord Wrotham said he'd received a letter from Father asking him to call on me." Charlotte shook her head. Such behavior by her odious parent was baffling. "Father has not taken a smidgeon's interest in me for six years. Then, the day after Almack's, he appeared and invited himself to dinner. He spent two hours admonishing me about my behavior the night before and threatening to take a hand in my affairs if I became embroiled in a scandal."

It had not been an idle threat. Given the opportunity

and enough of an excuse, her father would find a way to take over her life again, she had no doubt. "Now he's asking strangers to look after my welfare. Trying to rule my life again." She would not brook his interference. Not this time.

"For once I am grateful not to have parents to interfere with my life." Fanny smoothed her hands over her light blue mull gown. "It's bad enough to have Theale forever questioning me."

"Fanny, you should be thankful he's not as high a stickler as some would be about his sisters-in-law." Jane turned back to Charlotte, idly swirling the tea in her cup. "At least Wrotham seems to have forgiven you." She chuckled to herself and sipped. "Most important because we are now neighbors and may be much in company." A mischievous smile played over her face. "He's a very eligible *parti*, you know."

"I know, Jane. You have not ceased to remind me of that since the invitations went out." Charlotte laughed. "He is almost good enough to make me throw away my resolve never to marry again."

"Really, Charlotte." Jane sniffed and jammed her cup down in the saucer with a vicious clink. "You should pitch that resolution into the middle of the lake. Lord Wrotham would be the perfect match for you."

"Perhaps." Charlotte remembered his deep blue eyes, the warmth that tingled through her whenever she touched him, and sighed. "I have already made my choice, Jane. I will not have men control me as they have in the past. Not even one who—" She bit back the words about Lord Wrotham's startling revelation regarding his involvement with Edward. She would treasure that secret for herself alone a while longer.

"'Not even one who . . . ?" Jane leaned forward, all ears.

"Not even one who seems perfect on the surface."

Charlotte sipped her tea and leaned back, trying not to smile. Lord Wrotham might not be a man to marry, but he would certainly be one with whom she'd enjoy having a discreet affair. A thrill of excitement shot through her, making the hairs on the back of her neck stand up. A vision arose of them together, tangled in the sheets, his strong arms around her, his heat pressed against her . . .

"Charlotte. Whatever is wrong?"

As if a shower of cold rainwater had doused her, Charlotte shivered as Jane's face swam into view. "Wrong? Why would anything be wrong?" Drat. Had she said something whilst thinking of her and Lord Wrotham?

"Your face is splotched, as if you've got a fever. Are you well?"

Fever indeed.

"I am fine, little mother hen." Charlotte felt her cheeks, which did seem quite warm. "I suppose the tea was a trifle too hot for me."

"Tea. Yes, of course, that must be it." Jane lifted her cup, scrutinizing Charlotte all the while.

"Charlotte," Fanny broke in from her perch on the Queen Anne armchair opposite the sofa, her brows puckered. "Isn't this the same furniture as in your town house? Sir Archibald's town house? I know this is the chair you always sat in . . . and the sofa is the same." She glanced around the room, her frown deepening. "It's all the same." Her gaze fell on the fireplace and she gasped. "Even the Adams mantel. You must be mad. It had to have cost a fortune to gather all the pieces."

Charlotte laughed and patted Fanny's hand. "No, it cost me only the transportation from London to Lyttlefield. These are the same pieces that were in the town house."

"Dear God." Fanny leaned forward, her face pale. "You stole them, Charlotte? What possessed you? Your rotter of a stepson will have you clapped in irons!"

Charlotte laughed and caressed the sofa's beautiful floral upholstery. "Edgar may have some choice words to say to me, but he can do nothing. I was completely within my rights to take them. They are mine." She surveyed her sweet revenge, fruit of a scheme begun before her marriage.

"You are looking at a master chess player, Fanny." Jane nodded toward Charlotte. "She planned her strategy six years ago in her marriage settlement."

"I had Father insist that anything—clothes, furniture, cattle—that I brought to the marriage would revert to me upon Sir Archibald's death. Then I took a small inheritance from my grandmother and furnished everything in the London town house with the exception of Sir Archibald's private office, library, and the master chamber. All the furniture, linens, bedclothes, my trousseau. Everything. Including my horse and carriage. When Edgar takes possession of the house, he'll have one cracked leather chair, a desk, a library table, two straight-back chairs, and a rickety old bed." A thrill of satisfaction washed through her every time she thought of the look on her stepson's face when he realized he barely had a place to lay his head.

"Oh my dear." Fanny's peals of laughter warmed the room. "You are a genius, Charlotte. I will take care to stay on your good side."

Fisk entered and announced, "Mrs. Wickley," and gave way to a petite brunette, hardly old enough to be out of the schoolroom.

Charlotte rose, utterly at a loss. This person wasn't on her guest list. Had Father sent her as well? She stepped toward the girl, who looked frightened as a mouse in a cat's parlor.

To her surprise, Jane rose and swept toward the trembling young woman. "Maria! How delightful you could come. Charlotte, may I present Maria Wickley,

the daughter-in-law of my cousin? Her husband was trag-
ically another victim of Waterloo. A most sad story."

She stared, aghast. This child a *widow*?

"Maria," Jane continued, "this is Lady Cavendish, our
hostess for the weekend. I promise she will take good
care of you."

Maria bobbed a curtsy and said in a small, high voice,
"Thank you, my lady. You and Lady John are too kind to
me." She looked around with jerky movements of her
head, as though frightened of something.

Jane embraced her friend and ushered her over to the
sofa, leaving Charlotte gaping in the middle of the room.
She shot an inquiring glance at Fanny, who shrugged and
muttered, "What else would you expect from Jane?"

More than a little perturbed at this unexpected addition
to the weekend, Charlotte nevertheless returned to the
sofa, hoping to discover who her additional guest was
and how she had come to be here.

"My dear, how well you are looking," Jane crooned,
patting the child's hand. "The journey from Oxfordshire
seems to have done you a world of good. I hope this
weekend will be a pleasant diversion from your grief."

"Thank you, Lady John." The girl tore at the handkerchief in her lap. "You have been ever so kind." She risked
a glance toward Charlotte. Liquid brown eyes in a sweet,
heart-shaped face would be lovely without their stricken
appearance.

"And I must thank you properly, Lady Cavendish, for
your invitation. I am sure such good company will help
cheer me. I have been so sad this past year, since William
died." Maria twisted and tugged at the handkerchief so
tightly, Charlotte feared she would tear it asunder. "My
husband, my lady. Ensign William Wickley, of the 52nd
Light Infantry. His commanding officer, Sir John Col-
borne, wrote to me that William fell during an advance

that routed the French. His sacrifice helped turn the battle, he said." She bit her lips and sighed. "But I do still miss him, you see."

"William's father is my cousin, Charlotte." Jane took up the tale. "I visited him on my way back from Scotland and met Maria, who lives with his family now. Her family resides nearby and there had always been the understanding of a marriage between them." She smiled. "To which the young couple agreed completely. But young Mr. Wickley felt it his patriotic duty to fight when Boney threatened once more. Their parents consented to their marriage being moved up several years so they could wed before he went off to war."

"Several years? Then you were not out when you married?" She had been right about the girl still being in the schoolroom.

"Oh no, my lady." Maria sighed. "I was only sixteen when we wed. I will soon be eighteen, although I will not of course have a come-out."

Stunned, Charlotte could not help asking, "Were you married long, Mrs. Wickley?"

"A very short time, my lady. We wed in May, once the call for troops had gone out. He was gone within the week. I never saw him again." One tear cascaded down her cheek and she dabbed it with the abused handkerchief.

"Such a tragic story, my dear." Jane squeezed her hand. "Lord Byron should take you for his next subject."

"My condolences, Mrs. Wickley." Charlotte's heart went out to the poor girl. "You are very welcome here at Lyttlefield. I hope we will be able to cheer you a little." Another challenge for the hostess, but she believed she could cope. Except she now had an odd number of women that would throw her dinner placements askew.

Charlotte frowned. Such disorganization set her teeth on edge. Even with the inclusion of Lord Wrotham, they would be odd. She would need to relinquish her partner, it seemed, for the good of the party, although perhaps she might be able to secure him for one dance at least.

"Lord Sinclair, Lord Fernley, and Lord Brack."

Fisk's announcement sent a flurry of activity through the party. Charlotte rose to greet the gentlemen and make introductions. Jane moved to take Lord Sinclair's arm. She had suggested him when George Abernathy had sent his regrets. She had just finished introducing Maria when Fisk returned to announce Elizabeth and Georgie.

"Jemmy, Jemmy!" With a squeal, Georgie launched herself at her brother. "How wonderful to see you again."

They embraced, then Lord Brack stood back, laughing. "Georgina, you have not changed at all, my dear. Still the hoyden at heart." He bussed her cheek. "I have missed you too."

"And we shall have the whole of the weekend to catch up, my dear. But wait." She beckoned Elizabeth, and Charlotte nudged her over. "You must meet my dearest friend."

While Georgie performed that introduction, Charlotte surveyed the room. Fanny had engaged Lord Fernley in a conversation about his cattle, Jane, with Maria in tow, already flirted with Sinclair, and Georgie's brother was explaining the workings of his curricle to Georgie and Elizabeth. She lacked only Lord Fernley's cousin and the return of Lord Wrotham. Where the devil was Mr. Marsh?

She rang for Fisk and ordered more tea. The clock on the marble mantel struck four. Dinner at six left ample time for them to dress and mingle beforehand. She could, perhaps, relax a trifle.

As she sank gratefully onto the sofa, she could not help but be pleased with her efforts thus far. The busy room hummed with guests who seemed excited to be there. The two unexpected visitors had been handled to her satisfaction. Henry Marsh's absence remained the sole thing marring the perfection of the house party. She sighed, determined not to fret.

Tea arrived and her guests seated themselves, still chatting avidly. Smiling, Charlotte poured, although she glanced at the clock more frequently than she should. It was now going on five. Soon the company would need to retire to dress for dinner. Well, if Mr. Marsh did not come, she would have to carry on as best she could with very odd numbers for dinner.

"Lord Fernley, I expected your cousin to arrive with you," Charlotte said, setting her teacup in its saucer with a firm clink. "Do you suppose he has been detained in Town?"

Fernley had just taken a sip of his tea. He held up a finger, making a show of swallowing. His face had turned almost the same shocking red as his hair.

"Forgive me, my lady, I should have explained the moment I arrived, but I had just been renewing my acquaintance with this ravishing young creature." He nodded toward Georgina, who turned scarlet and clutched her cup like a weapon. "So all other thoughts flew right out of my head. My cousin sends his regards and his regrets. A sudden turn in his business—he is a barrister, you see—and he was called to the bar for a most infamous case, you must have heard of it . . ."

Lord Fernley droned on as Charlotte sat, sick at heart. Only four gentlemen to six ladies. And she knew none of her neighbors well enough to call on for reinforcements. As hostess, she must be the one to give up her claim on the gentlemen. She'd be lucky to have two words with Lord Wrotham the entire time. The weekend that had held such promise now loomed like a gloomy cloud over her happiness.

"I do wish you had sent a note, Lord Fernley," she said

as he finally paused for breath. "I might have been able to invite another gentleman to round out the party."

"My lady, do not fret yourself. I have managed to save the day." Fernley beamed at her, revealing the frightening sight of large crooked teeth in a wide grin. "I persuaded a dear friend of mine to attend when he had already sent his regrets."

Charlotte's heart skipped a beat. That would leave her lacking only one gentleman. Perhaps the party wouldn't be as gloomy for her after all. "Excellent, my lord. May I expect Lord Lathbury or Mr. Abernathy?

"Mr. Alan Garrett." Fiske's rumbling voice cut through the guests' low chatter.

Charlotte jumped, her head jerking toward the tall man in the doorway. Attired in buff and blue, his curly hair in ringlets around his brow, he smiled brilliantly at her, his eyes sparkling in triumph.

"Mr. Garrett." She rose on unsteady feet to greet him, her heart beating a tattoo in her chest. The mere thought of his hand on hers sent dread coursing through her and the room wavered.

"I have missed you, fair one," he murmured in his deep, velvet voice as he brushed a kiss over her knuckles.

Her eyes closed and the sharp tang of his cologne assailed her senses. Not so strong this time, thank goodness. Still, she couldn't wait for him to raise his head so she could withdraw her hand and step back.

"Has all of your little party assembled?" He glanced around the room, nodding to Lord Fernley.

"Yes, you are the last, but for Lord Wrotham, who will return for dinner." Dear God. Wrotham would think she had invited Mr. Garrett. She would attach herself to Wrotham at dinner—he would be seated beside her—and inform him that this last-minute substitution was not of her making. "Do you know everyone here, Mr. Garrett?"

He scanned the drawing room until his gaze fell on Maria. "All but the young one there. Is she a daughter of Lady John?"

"A distant relation only." Charlotte took his arm. "Pray, let me introduce you." She led him toward the unsuspecting Maria. Mr. Garrett might focus his attentions on the young widow instead of her, but she doubted it. From the corner of her eye she caught the rake's quick smile as he squeezed her arm. Yes, she doubted it very much indeed.

Dinner proved rather a victory for Charlotte. Lord Wrotham arrived in good time and established himself as an excellent addition to their party. He was previously acquainted with Lord Brack and Lord Sinclair, having attended a hunting party last autumn with the latter and a dinner party hosted by the former's elder sister.

As a result, the dinner conversation touched on literature, politics, sports, and the Season past. Amazed to find Lord Wrotham, seated at her left, had a lively interest in poetry, Charlotte listened, rapt, while he talked of Byron's *The Corsair*. Lord Sinclair, on her right, proclaimed himself a regular at Jackson's and gave her a blow-by-blow account of his latest round, so stirring the women near him applauded when the final blow fell.

By the time she and the other ladies retired to the drawing room for tea, Charlotte genuinely looked forward to dancing with several partners at the evening's entertainment. She had enjoyed herself more tonight than she had in years, despite her worry over Mr. Garrett's presence. He had talked devotedly to Maria Wickley at dinner and so far had been a model guest. The evening, however, was young.

Once the gentlemen joined them, natural groupings

seemed to arrange themselves. Georgie, Lord Brack, and Elizabeth appeared inseparable. Good for Elizabeth, although Georgina needed to push herself to converse with the others as well. Jane gathered Sinclair, Wrotham, Fanny, and Maria together, talking about gaming. And Garrett and Fernley were deep in a discussion about curricles.

"We can have dancing now, if you like," Charlotte announced and sat down at the rosewood pianoforte to play "Miss Gayton's Hornpipe." Couples formed the set quickly, the pairings ending much as she expected, except Wrotham partnered Georgie and Garrett claimed Maria.

The energetic country dance that ensued put everyone in a playful mood. She followed it with the "Duke of Devonshire" and "Grimstock" before giving way to Elizabeth. Charlotte hurried to the refreshment table, seizing a glass of lemonade. While she drank, she looked around and discovered, to her dismay, Mr. Garrett the only unpartnered male. Drat the luck. With as good a grace as she could muster, she accepted him for the next dance, a set called "The Mercury," a particular favorite of hers.

"You have been a lovely hostess, my dear." Mr. Garrett met her in the middle and they sashayed down the line.

"Thank you, sir. The company seems to mix together well." They circled round each other, closer than the dance called for. Waves of heat from his body assailed her.

"We should mix together well, Charlotte."

His low words and the use of her first name sparked tension in her, putting her on alert.

"Shall I come to your room this evening?"

Charlotte's foot came down on top of his and she stumbled. Her face must have turned bright red for heat seemed to burst from her cheeks. How dare the wretch propose such a thing in the middle of the drawing room?

Of course that was his design. She could not upbraid him here without causing a scandal. Oh, yes, he was a rake through and through.

His strong arm steadied her and she shot him a scathing look. He grinned and winked at her, a most lecherous glint in his eyes. Well, she would put an end to those notions forthwith.

"You go too far, Mr. Garrett. I have neither given you permission to use my first name nor done anything to suggest I would be agreeable to such advances."

"But my dear Charlotte, you most certainly have." He grasped her hands and whirled her around. "That amorous interlude at Almack's was all agreement, if I remember correctly."

"You remember incorrectly, sir. I was not a willing partner in that bit of debauchery."

"I recall you exactly, Charlotte. In my arms, pressed against me, my lips thrilling to the taste of you. I have wanted another taste for months." He had pulled her close so those last words brushed her ear, sending a shiver down her spine. "And I usually get what I want."

They broke apart and the dance continued, although she moved mechanically through the rest of the steps. When at last he led her from the dance floor, she trembled in earnest and excused herself as quickly as she could.

She fled to the refreshment table once more, thankful for a moment's respite to gather what remained of her wits. But oh, dear. Lord Wrotham appeared immediately to take possession of her, and the look on his face did not bode well for her. Naturally, he'd seen her little tête-à-tête with Mr. Garrett. The whole company had seen it unless they'd been struck blind. How could Lord Fernley have invited that rogue? She would have a few choice words for him shortly.

Lord Wrotham's big, rough hand took hers, but instead

of leading her back to the floor, he made his way to Elizabeth, speaking a word in her ear.

She laughed and nodded, then rearranged her sheets of music.

He pulled Charlotte onto the floor to stand in front of him. "I hope you will not be too scandalized by my request, my lady." His eyes said he hoped she was, and a thrill ran from her head to her toes.

"I doubt you can shock me, my lord." She raised her chin and stared straight into his coal-black eyes.

"We shall see." He grasped her hands, the power in his a tangible thing. His touch spread delicious warmth throughout her body. They bowed and Elizabeth began a waltz.

Not exactly scandalous, yet a bold choice. The first figure moved easily, with little intimate contact. Then, in the second figure, his arms were supposed to embrace hers. Instead they reached all the way around her back until they touched. He pulled her closer to him, his lips pressed against her ear, and whispered, "And now, my lady? A waltz can be a scandalous dance if your partner is of a mind to make it so." He pressed her tighter, almost indecently.

Yet she did not struggle. Could not. His big body against her—the hard strength of him leaving nothing for her to imagine—persuaded her that to fight him was futile. She would never be free. Never wanted to be.

They twirled in time to the music, yet the room faded until his face alone remained illuminated by the candlelight. "You never answered me, my lady."

Had there been a question? She couldn't remember.

He gazed into her face and leaned forward.

She stared, fascinated, as his lips drew near—

A discordant jangle stopped the music. She froze, then looked at Elizabeth, who hastily picked up the scattered sheets of music. "My pardon, ladies and gentlemen." Her color high, she rose from the instrument and Georgina took her place and began a quick-paced mazurka.

Wrotham led Charlotte off the dance floor, and before she could protest, out the French windows to stand on the veranda.

She shook herself, trying to cool down in the slight chill of the evening breeze. Coming back to reality.

"Thank you for the dance, my lord."

So much more than a dance. And a dangerous one at that, for in the few minutes of that waltz, everything else had ceased to exist: guests, music, ballroom. The man before her had been her whole world and she had reveled in it. Such a thing had never happened before.

Even now, the phantom touch of Wrotham's arms embraced her, heating her to a fever pitch. An overwhelming desire arose to feel his lips on hers. Just once.

She looked up at him but couldn't read his face in the faint light of the stars. Still, she understood his desires. His body had proclaimed them eagerly enough when they had danced. She'd been eager too, and now . . .

He stepped toward her, his eyes black and alive with passion. For her. She leaned forward—

Raucous laughter wafted through the French windows, wrenching her back to the present. Her guests required her attention. This was not the time. But soon . . .

Putting a hand out, she stumbled back and murmured in a shaky voice, "I must see to my other guests, my lord, if you will excuse me."

She turned without a backward glance and fled to the house, completely unsure whether she required its safety or not.

Chapter 8

By two o'clock, the house had quieted down, although Charlotte wasn't quite sure how settled all the inhabitants were. She went from room to room on the ground floor, looking for anything not as it should be. Caution—at least in some things—had always been her motto. She listened as the sounds of the retiring guests diminished into murmured good nights and closing doors.

Elizabeth and Georgie, she would wager, were already snug in their own beds, alone. Elizabeth had seemed more animated and in better spirits than usual. She had talked and even laughed with several gentlemen this evening but showed no great partiality toward any one. Charlotte had not expected her to. Her devotion to Colonel Easton had been akin to that found in the fashionable romantic novels available from the Minerva Press, so her personal period of mourning might extend until circumstances forced her to marry. And knowing Elizabeth, she would certainly wait for marriage before indulging in bedroom pleasures once more.

Georgina had finally been persuaded to dance a second time with Lord Fernley, although she had eventually cried off from dancing altogether, pleading fatigue. She had instead accompanied the others, seeming very accomplished and comfortable on the pianoforte. It might take several meetings of the club before Georgina became accustomed to dancing—and men—again.

Charlotte paused before the library door, the muffled sound of voices straining through the polished oak door catching her attention. Some of her guests still stirred? She reached for the latch, then paused, hand on the handle.

What if this was a tryst? Both Jane and Fanny were eager to resume the pleasures of the bed, although why they would wish to do so in a library she could not fathom. Leaning her head against the panel, she pressed her ear to the smooth wood, listening for voices. The denizens of the library chose that moment to fall silent. Drat! She pressed more intently, aware that if the door opened she would fall into whoever stood there.

The murmuring resumed, in a register so low it could only be a man's. Was there a woman in there also? Did she really want to know? Easing away from the door, Charlotte changed directions and headed for the stairs, her heart beating quicker at the thought of the assignations that might be going on all around her. She could have had one of her own if she'd accepted Mr. Garrett. She shivered at the prospect and sped up the stairs.

Jane had warned her about him in March and the man's reputed escapades would make any decent woman blush. Last spring alone, rumors had circulated regarding his pursuit of three different women. Two widows and a viscount's wife, so the story went. She certainly didn't want to be his next conquest. If only there was some way to make him leave the house party, but it would be rude to ask him to go if he'd done nothing except suggest an assignation. She would simply have to be on her guard. Surely he would not try to force her in a houseful of people. A sudden foreboding made her look over her shoulder, but the dark staircase remained empty. When she made the landing, however, she picked up her skirts and raced to her suite.

Quiet reigned in the blue- and cream-colored room she had claimed as her own. A fire crackled in the grate, her gown and wrapper laid out on the tall bed to warm, a decanter and glasses twinkled on a side table.

"There you are, my lady. I wondered why you hadn't come up yet." The door to her dressing room opened and Rose emerged, a pair of emerald-green suede shoes in her hands. "You have a full day tomorrow. You'll be needing your rest. Let me put these down and I'll help you get ready for bed."

She gave another brush to the shoes and set them back in the dressing room. "Now, stand still, my lady." Deftly, Rose unbuttoned, unlaced, and untied Charlotte's clothes until she stood gloriously naked and free.

A sudden vision of standing thus before the Earl of Wrotham sprang to mind, his dark eyes full of approval, his rough hands caressing her body. She shivered and glanced down to see her breasts peaked into hard, pink points.

"Are you cold, my lady?"

Her maid's voice dragged her back to the present. "A sudden draft. I'll take a short wash only." Perhaps the water would cool her down.

Moments later, she emerged from behind the screen and the fine lawn and lace nightdress slithered over her head. She pulled her wrapper around her shoulders and sat, forcing herself to relax as Rose brushed out her hair. The soothing routine now rubbed her nerves like a cheese grater. The more Rose slid the brush through her hair, the more sensually aware she became of the touch of the bristles on her super-sensitive scalp. She could imagine Wrotham's hands in her hair, raking his fingers through the length of her thick locks, cupping her head, drawing her closer until he engulfed her body with his.

A sharp rap on the door sent Charlotte staggering up with a squawk on her lips. She stood swaying, every nerve tingling as she tried to calm her racing heart.

"Who's there?" Rose opened the door.

"Fisk," the butler replied, standing straight, completely unruffled. "I am sorry to disturb you, my lady, but one of the guests is leaving and insists on speaking with you before he goes."

Charlotte clutched her wrapper tighter. "Which guest?"

"Mr. Alan Garrett."

Good Lord, an answer to a prayer. Or a ploy by a very clever rake? Well, she could be clever too.

"Tell him I will meet him directly. Is he in his room?"

"The drawing room, my lady."

"Thank you, Fisk." Charlotte dismissed the servant and turned to Rose. "I'll wear the dress I just took off but without the stays. Too much trouble for the ten minutes I will be with Mr. Garrett. I'll use my nightgown in place of the chemise." The quicker she could get this over with, the better off she would be.

Rose nodded, disappeared into the dressing room, and reemerged with the pale blue silk gown. In moments she had dropped it into place and was fastening the back.

"It's a bit loose without the stays, my lady."

Charlotte could see that. The small puffed sleeves sagged onto her shoulders, revealing the top of her undergarment. Bother it. "Hand me the paisley shawl. I can cover up with that."

Draping herself as best she could, Charlotte stepped into her slippers, grabbed the candle from Rose, and hurried out the door.

Shadows played up and down the staircase as she descended, distracting her as she fought to manage her skirt, her shawl, and the candle all at once. If she took a tumble she'd either break her neck, set the house on fire, or both.

At last she reached the drawing room but found it dark. No sign of the man. Frowning, Charlotte peered into the blackness of the hallway. "Mr. Garrett?"

Silence. What was the rake playing at now? Perhaps she had been correct in thinking this summons was a ploy to get her alone. He might even have thought she'd come to him in her nightgown. More fool him.

She darted out into the hall, bent on returning to her room. Mr. Garrett could go hang. About to mount the stairs, she paused, a light beneath the library door catching her attention. Had the dratted man changed rooms? Even if not, Fisk should have extinguished the sconces long ere this. She whirled around and strode to the door, reaching for the handle, then stopped. There had been voices in the library earlier. Had those guests gone? Would she humiliate herself by walking in on a passionate scene?

She took a deep breath, pressed her ear against the oak panel, and listened.

Nothing. Drat it. Her shoulders slumped. She would have to take a chance. With a fervor born of desperation, she grasped the handle, shoved it down, and threw open the door.

Nash knocked back the last of the brandy in his glass and set it down on the sideboard. He should have left hours ago, but the company at Lyttlefield Park had been stimulating in a variety of ways. Lady Cavendish had been his dinner companion and they had enjoyed a surprisingly spirited conversation. About Lord Byron's flight from England, of all things, and had discovered a common interest in his poetry. She had turned out to be a remarkably agreeable dinner partner and more of his distrust of her had eased.

The gentlemen of the party were also a pleasant lot; he'd been acquainted with two of them already. He'd recognized Garrett, curse him, from their encounter at Almack's. The earl had been right; Lady Cavendish played a dangerous game, flirting with scandal in the form of this rakehell. She'd declared to him at dinner, sotto voce, that she had not invited the scoundrel. Something about Lord Fernley and a misunderstanding.

Nash shook his head. Good thing she'd invited him to this party. He could keep an eye on her and Garrett while he wooed the lovely lady right out from under the rake's nose.

Should he indulge in another brandy? Strange he felt no compulsion to shove off home. Of course, he and Brack had fallen into a great discussion about Egypt, which they both had happened to visit. That had led them, eventually, out of the drawing room and in search of the answer to a question about the Great Library in Alexandria. Having settled the point, they had quite abandoned the ladies and fallen to talk of their cattle and the coming hunting season. The clock striking two had roused them from conversation and, after a final snifter, Brack had gone off to bed.

Nash had lingered, however, sipping his brandy in the soothing darkness. The house had settled into a peaceful quiet. Restful, in fact. He was loath to disturb it by opening the door and seeking a servant to fetch his carriage. Too bad he hadn't taken Lady Cavendish up on her offer of accommodation here. Now, dash it all, he couldn't just bed down on the sofa. With a sigh, he turned from the sideboard and started toward the door. He was reaching for the handle when the door burst open.

He staggered backward as a pale vision strode toward him. Gorgeously disarrayed, hair flying around her like a battle maiden of old, Lady Cavendish presented a formidable sight to behold. His mouth dropped open as the full effect of her dishabille struck him like a kick from an ornery horse.

Her pale gown hung close to her body, outlining delicious curves, delineating shapely legs. Her shawl had slipped from her shoulders, exposing her chemise and a lot of very tempting skin. His gaze strayed lower, to the neckline of her low-cut gown, gaping away, showing off her voluptuous breasts. And her feet . . . were bare. Despite the shadowy light, his gaze riveted to the small white toes and his groin ached with wanting.

"Oh, dear." Her face paled to the hue of the moonlight streaming in the window. Recognition of him stopped her in midstride. She trod on her shawl, wavered for a long moment, then pitched forward, the candle flying from her hand.

Here we go again.

Nash grabbed her, his arms going around her as they had that evening at Almack's. Once more each contour of her body pressed against him intimately, every inch of them seeming to touch. Her head landed on his shoulder and the sweet, exotic scent of tuberoses filled his head. Erotic beyond belief. His already aroused member stiffened as if by magic.

Dear Lord, she had to feel his prodding presence. Yet she offered no resistance whatsoever. He expected her to recoil, to scream, to slap his face at the very least. Instead, she simply lay against him, panting. He relaxed his hold on her slightly, expecting her to ease away from him. To his astonishment, she nestled against him, as if at home there.

What the devil did she mean by this behavior? Had she known he was still in the house and been seeking him out? Their earlier encounter suggested her more enthusiastic about him than he had believed, despite her abrupt departure from the veranda. But women had played hard to get with him before—at least for a short while. Dressed in her current attire, she might very well be in search of a rendezvous. He'd still heard no protest about being in his arms.

Nash shifted her onto one arm. With his other hand, he brought her head up, her pale visage now inches from his. She searched his face, no fear in hers, only a question. He answered it the only way he could.

Lowering his head to hers, he took the lips offered to him, sweet and smooth and soft. Her body trembled, but she didn't struggle. He pressed harder, demanding surrender as a fire quickened in his veins. Slipping first one, then the other hand behind her head, he angled her mouth to his best advantage. A slight turn of her head and their lips melded.

Emboldened, he opened his mouth and ran his tongue back and forth across the seam of hers. A low whimper emerged. When it turned into a guttural moan, he pressed more insistently against those soft lips. They opened like the petals of a rose in the morning sun, and he slipped between them, the silken gateway to paradise.

Nash repressed a groan of need. At this moment he'd like nothing better than to lay her down on the thick carpet and sink his all into her. Too soon, too impetuous. Best move with caution lest he frighten his prize.

Instead, he contented himself with a slow, thorough exploration of her mouth. He reveled in the sensuous feel of her—silky and smooth. The taste of her almost drove him wild, like a sweet liqueur of which he could not get enough.

When she slid her arms up and around his neck, pulling him to her, he thought he would explode with desire. Every inch of him tingled with the need to touch her skin, enfold himself around her, possess her completely in every way. No other woman had ever moved him this deeply. Scary as hell, yet satisfying beyond belief.

Still, he must move with caution. Despite her sweet responses, he couldn't assume she wished to pursue an even deeper intimacy tonight. Best give her the opportunity to make her intentions known.

Nash began to ease away from her when he became aware they were not alone.

Damnation! At the worst . . . well, almost worst possible moment. Instinctively, he spun them around so she stood behind him, her identity shielded slightly at least. Too bad she was not a young miss. The earl could have them leg-shackled before the ink dried on the special license. Still, it would be enjoyable to spend some time wooing Lady Cavendish.

Nash swung back around, frowning at the intruder, who should have been abed by now anyway.

"My pardon, my lord. My lady. But if you desired more privacy I would have suggested you close the door." The dark figure's voice held a wry tone—respect tinged with knowing laughter.

Before Nash could upbraid the man for his impertinence, the lady poked her head around his side. A sharp, indrawn breath.

"Mr. Garrett?"

Chapter 9

If she could have sunk through the floor and deep into the ground, Charlotte would have praised God as a merciful deity. Of all the people to discover her in such a compromising position, it had to be this rake. Now he would think her a light woman and she'd never be rid of him. He'd just bide his time and wait his turn. She had no choice save to stand beside Lord Wrotham, guilty as sin.

"My lady. Were you perhaps looking for me?" Mr. Garrett made no other utterance, God curse him. The wretch's implication could not have been clearer.

Wrotham jerked his head around and stared at her.

"Yes, Mr. Garrett, I had come down to meet you." God, that sounded badly. "You sent for me . . . I mean, you sent Fisk to tell me to meet you." Worse and worse. "You said you were leaving?" Charlotte raised her head and wrinkled her nose. "Do you smell something burning?"

Both men stared at her; then Wrotham, scowling like a gargoyle, stomped behind a chair and ground something into the carpet.

"I suppose you two weren't the only heat in the room," Garrett said, grinning at Charlotte.

She itched to smash something into that leering face. "I tripped, Mr. Garrett, and fortunately, Lord Wrotham caught me." Heat crept into her cheeks as she thought of how they must have looked to him.

"Again? He's always there when you need him, isn't he? I suspect you needed a great deal of comfort after such a tumble." He seemed to enjoy mocking her. His gaze flicked over her appearance.

Automatically, she pulled her gown up over her shoulders. She curled her toes on the scratchy carpet, at once aware she'd stepped out of her slippers somewhere along the way. Likely when she'd tripped and fallen into Wrotham's arms.

"I see no reason for insolence, sir." The deathly calm of Wrotham's voice drew her attention back to him. "This is really none of your affair whatsoever." His glare would have made a sensible man shut his mouth and be on his way. She'd not want to see it turned on her. A warm wave of gratitude washed over her at his gallant defense.

"You are correct, my lord. It certainly is not." He eyed Charlotte once more. "You are, however, correct also, Lady Cavendish. I must take my leave. I received word almost an hour ago that my uncle, Lord Kersey, is gravely ill and not expected to live past a day or two. I regret that I must immediately journey to his estate in the north of Essex."

"Oh, dear. I am very sorry for your uncle, Mr. Garrett." She hoped her condolences hid her relief at his departure.

"I as well, Garrett." Wrotham spoke up, startling her anew. She had forgotten he stood next to her.

"Is there anything you require for your journey, Mr. Garrett?" Charlotte forced herself back into her role of hostess, despite the bizarre circumstances.

"No, thank you, my lady." At least he sounded a bit more civil now. "I've ordered my carriage and it should be coming around front shortly. My valet is seeing to the packing. I had only to speak to you." He stared at her, and a softening in his eyes made her heart leap with dread. "Therefore, I take my leave of you, Lady Cavendish. Will you be returning to London in the autumn?"

Taken aback by this sudden change in attitude, she stuttered, "I . . . I had not thought about it yet. But perhaps Lady John and I will visit during the Little Season. However, I will likely be here most of the time. I had thought to have another party here at the end of harvest." Why couldn't the man just leave?

"Good. When you are in town I would ask to call upon you. I may be in need of solace if the worst happens with my uncle." He shifted awkwardly and tapped his hand against his leg.

"I pray all is better than feared."

"I as well, my lady. Wrotham." Garrett bowed and left.

Charlotte watched him go, sighing in relief, alone once again with Wrotham.

The gravity of their situation reared its head once more. Not so much that they had been found out, but that she had behaved so wantonly with this man she hardly knew. What had possessed her to kiss the earl like that?

Standing apart from him like this, she felt nothing of the burning passion that had seized her when he had caught her in his arms. No fire ripping through her veins as when his mouth sealed itself to hers. If she touched him again, would it reappear?

Charlotte turned toward Wrotham to find the earl watching her, as coolly detached as he had been hot with desire. She opened her mouth, not knowing what words might emerge.

He saved her the trouble. "You *were* expecting Garrett just now when you ran into me, weren't you?"

Her sharp gasp sounded loud as cannon fire to her ears.

In the silence that followed, he sauntered to the sideboard and poured a good three fingers of brandy into his glass and downed it in one gulp. "Did you simply mistake me for him, or did the man matter at all to you?"

"How dare you!" Outrage at his insinuation shoved all her guilt over her actions into a far corner. Just whom did he think he was to judge her?

"I dare to speak the truth, my lady. You seemed genuinely desirous enough just now to fool me into believing your passion was aimed at me. Either you thought me your lover or you wanted me to be. I merely wish to know which is true." Wrotham's gaze glittered in the guttering candlelight, unreadable as blank stone.

"I came to meet him, as I said. But he is not my lover."

His eyebrow rose. "Surprising."

She gasped, and anger made her bold. "Why? Because I'm the 'Wicked Widow'?"

He chuckled and shook his head. "No. Because I have tasted a depth of passion such as yours only once or twice. If he is unwilling to take you to his bed, he is a fool."

The last he spoke with such vehemence she jerked her face up to his.

His eyes gleamed with dark desire.

Her stomach plunged to her toes.

Wrotham stalked toward her, and she fled backward until she pressed against the wall of the library, the chair rail digging into her back.

He towered over her, the expanse of his chest filling her field of vision with the black superfine of his jacket and the starched white of his cravat. He grasped her head and lifted it until his dark eyes bored into hers.

"No one has ever called me a fool." Then his mouth seized hers again and she melted once more, damn him!

The heat of his lips burned like the red-hot embers of a well-banked fire. She struggled to pull in enough air, as if he had sucked it all from the room. When his tongue thrust into her mouth she welcomed it, cherished it as it ravaged whatever it touched. An ache she had only felt once before began to pulse between her thighs, one that magnified as his tongue plundered where it would. Her knees buckled and she would have slid down the wall except he grasped her arms, steadying her. Time ceased to be as he caressed her shoulders, her arms, her breasts.

The throbbing below intensified when his thumbs circled her nipples, making them peak and strain against the thin fabric of her gown. She moaned low in her throat, a sound full of longing, full of need. Lord, would he never stop? Never let him stop. Heat flushed her entire body until she burned like a furnace. He lifted his head.

"Marry me, Lady Cavendish."

"What?" She couldn't have heard that correctly.

"Marry me and let us continue this evening's activities to their inevitable and glorious conclusion." His voice, ragged with need, rumbled from his chest. He seized her lips again, pressing his big body against her until she could feel his shaft, hard, hot, insistent.

Desire for what he offered welled up and her resolve slipped. It would be glorious to give in to these feelings that made her doubt her sanity. But once married, she would have no recourse against him, as she'd had none over Sir Archibald.

He slid his hands behind her derriere, pushing her against his hips and grinding them together until she broke the kiss, gasping at the need he inspired in her.

"Why bring marriage into it, my lord?" she whispered, pulling his ear to her mouth. With one slow stroke, she licked the outer rim and thrilled when he shuddered in her arms. "Surely we can reach that 'glorious conclusion' without benefit of clergy?"

Then he was gone.

Charlotte blinked, coming back to her senses as if being pulled out of a well.

Wrotham stood before her, breathing heavily, hovering as though he might pounce on her again. "I need a wife, Lady Cavendish."

"I am sorry for that, my lord, but I don't need a husband." She licked her lips and hoped she looked seductive. "Can we not find a way to compromise?"

He wavered. Charlotte would have sworn he started toward her and the throbbing between her legs became agony. Then he leaned back and crossed his arms. "No. I'm afraid where you are concerned, Lady Cavendish, I cannot."

Damn him! She raised her chin. "Then I fear we are at an impossible impasse."

"It would seem so, my lady. And I for one am truly sorry." He shrugged and sighed, then headed for the door. At the last moment he turned, his black eyes burning into her. "If you are ever in need, I am close at hand." With that outrageous statement, he disappeared through the doorway.

Charlotte slid down the wall until she bumped into the floor, her strength spent. That annoying ache still hounded her body, though it had eased once his hands no longer claimed her. She leaned her head on her knees and tried to slow her heart from its frantic pace.

What a beginning to her house party. Garrett gone to Essex, over fifty miles away. Wrotham fled home, scarcely a mile from her. Rakes, both of them, and good riddance. Something in the recesses of her practical mind, however, whispered that she had not seen the last of either one. And something else, with a naughty gleam in its eyes, rejoiced.

Chapter 10

Charlotte passed a wretched night, tossing and beating her pillow, pretending she had the Earl of Wrotham under her fist. How dare he insult her, propose to her, then flee with that disgraceful suggestion that she contact him if needed. The fact that he had excited her as no other man ever had just made the whole episode worse.

At some point she dozed off and woke late into the morning, still weary but determined to be the perfect hostess. Her hopes for a dalliance with Wrotham might have crumbled, but she, nevertheless, had to carry on for her guests as if nothing was amiss. The house party had, however, lost some of its luster.

With her maid's assistance, she managed to present a decent appearance. The freshness of her rose sprigged muslin—her favorite of the new post-mourning day gowns—helped boost her spirits. Her face told another story when she gazed in the mirror. She sighed.

"Rose, bring the Pear's Bloom of Roses." A little on her cheeks would hide the pallor brought on by the strains of the night. She usually disdained the use of cosmetics, but better a touch of the rouge than be thought pale from pining for someone.

Charlotte arrived in the cheery breakfast room, around haft past eleven o'clock, to find her cousin alone, sipping tea and spreading marmalade on toast. Not the best companion this morning. Jane could always wheedle information out of Charlotte no matter how hard she tried to withhold it. She braced herself for a battery of questions.

"Good morning, Jane." Charlotte kissed the cheek that looked younger than her own and slid into the chair at the head of the table. "I see I have missed breakfast."

"Good morning, my dear." Jane eyed her face, then raised an eyebrow. "Yes, they've just put the things away, although I'm sure there's still plenty in the kitchen." She peered closer at Charlotte. "You're certainly out of looks today. Did you not sleep well?"

Charlotte signaled a footman to bring her a plate. "I may have tossed and turned a bit," she admitted. That much at least was true. "Worrying about the guests and today's activities. Are you aware Alan Garrett left in the middle of the night?" Best get that piece of information out in the open. Her cousin either already knew or would find out shortly. "He was called to his uncle's death bed."

"Yes, I heard that while dressing this morning. Nichols had it from Fisk. Shame about his uncle, but I daresay it's for the best in the long run." Jane sipped her tea with an air of nonchalance.

"How so?" Charlotte took a piece of toast and began to butter it, listening carefully for her cousin's point.

"I suspect his elevation to the title and the attendant responsibilities will steady the man. Make him less of a rakehell." Jane cut her eyes at Charlotte, then back to her teacup.

"Lord, I will pray for that from this day forward. Perhaps then he will stop his unwanted attentions to me."

Charlotte finished with the butter and began to slather marmalade on the bread. She didn't like to coat the jam so thickly, but she needed something to do with her hands. "Unfortunately, I've noticed that such behavior is a rare occurrence. They inherit their titles, more funds become available to them than they have ever seen before, and they go off on a spree of drinking, gambling, and whoring—"

"Charlotte!"

"Well, that's what happens, isn't it?" Charlotte turned a sour eye on her companion. "I have been married, Jane. I've seen Edgar at close range for years. Men gamble away all their inheritance before they know what's what or take up with mistresses or some other type of bird of paradise."

Of course, some men might take up with a discreet widow instead. Much better for a man's purse in the long run, if she had her own money and would be content to simply share his bed. The Earl of Wrotham's face came to mind, as darkly handsome as ever. No, she would not think of the wretched man this morning.

The footman laid her plate before her and she studied the eggs and kidneys with loathing. She'd be violently ill if she took a mouthful of that. Determinedly, she crunched into the sticky toast.

"Lord Wrotham seems to have weathered that storm successfully. He is very pointedly looking for a wife."

The toast stuck halfway down Charlotte's throat. Grasping her teacup, she sipped a mouthful, trying to make the gluey mass go down. She coughed, praying she would not finish the morning by casting up her accounts. A bit more struggle and the food continued on its way. Charlotte gulped her tea, then set the cup down with a vigorous clink. She wiped her tearing eyes with her napkin. "Why bring up Lord Wrotham? And how do you know he's looking for a wife?" Her cousin certainly knew how to get a reaction from her.

"Most titled gentlemen his age are." Jane sipped tea tranquilly, a slight smile on her lips. "He's only been in *ton* circles for a year or two. Inherited his title from an uncle when he and his son were killed in a carriage accident. I'm sure you heard about that? The son was Lord Berkley."

Charlotte vaguely recalled a tall, blond young man of that name from her come-out Season, so she nodded. She carefully turned the teacup around and around its saucer.

"And I know for a fact Wrotham was very taken with you at Almack's. If only Mr. Garrett had not been so insistent."

"May I remind you, I am not in the market for a husband, my dear?" Charlotte would swear her cousin rolled her eyes.

"Nonsense, Charlotte."

"Nonsense? You yourself told me you would not marry again. Why should I?"

"Because you need to experience a real marriage." Jane squeezed Charlotte's hands. "You were married to an old brute who used you badly. You should marry a young man who will thoroughly woo you, bed you, and give you children. That's what a woman needs." She released Charlotte. "And if Lord Wrotham is not the perfect man to do it, I will eat my best bonnet." Jane pursed her lips. "Perhaps my second-best bonnet. I do adore the cream straw with the blue trim. I would hate to have to eat that one."

Charlotte burst out in giggles. "Jane, you are a wonder. Only you could annoy me to the point of distraction and then make me love you for it." She had often marveled at the captivating way her cousin had always gotten her way with everyone, from the servants to her late husband.

"Now tell me," Jane gave her an arch look, "just between us. If Lord Wrotham proposed, would you really say no?"

Charlotte went still, seeing the image of Wrotham's dark eyes boring into her when he demanded that she marry him. Memory of the incredible heat their bodies had created pressed against each other sent a rush of warmth through her again.

"Charlotte?" Jane's voice sounded a long way away. "Charlotte."

With a gasp, she came to herself to find Jane peering at her, her brows puckered.

"Are you all right?" Jane grasped her hand and rubbed it. "You went quite pale and then your cheeks flushed. Have you taken a chill?"

"I did."

"You've got a chill? My dear, you must go back to bed." Jane had risen and was urging her to stand.

"No, I refused him. Wrotham. Last night." Charlotte fanned her hot cheeks. Lord, if this happened each time she thought about the earl, she'd have to start wearing lighter clothing.

"He actually proposed? Last night?" Jane's mouth had dropped open.

At last she had surprised her unflappable cousin.

"Yes. It's quite the story. First, he accused me of being Alan Garrett's lover, then he kissed me, then he asked me to marry him. Somehow I don't think this is the behavior of a perfect gentleman."

"Perhaps not," Jane said, sipping her tea, her eyes still wide. "But you have to admit it is extremely dashing. Was he very disappointed when you turned him down?"

"Not half so much as when I suggested we have an affair instead."

Jane dropped her cup. It rattled into the saucer without spilling a drop.

"Charlotte! You didn't!"

"I did indeed. And I would have done it, but he simply refused to entertain the notion." Charlotte adjusted her napkin. "He must wish to marry rather badly. I thought men generally jumped at the chance for a dalliance."

"Generally they do." Jane picked up her cup and shook her head. "One does wonder why he would insist on marriage on such short acquaintance. Perhaps he's in love with you."

Charlotte snorted. "Love at first sight, Jane? In Minerva novels only, I assure you. No, I'm not quite sure why only marriage will do for him where I am concerned, but should he persist, I will find out."

"I will be very interested in what you discover. So, my dear," the brisk Jane returned, "how do you propose to even your numbers now that Mr. Garrett has gone?'

The abrupt change of subject jarred Charlotte so thoroughly she knocked her hand against the teacup. It rattled alarmingly, almost turning over. "Drat. I had forgotten Mr. Garrett's departure would make the party most uneven."

"Yes, you are now down two gentlemen, Charlotte, for dinner and your outings, which will make for an awkward time of it for one of your guests. As hostess, you can stand to be unpartnered, but at least one of the ladies will likely be made to feel left out." Jane poured more tea and dropped in two small lumps of sugar, all the while staring at Charlotte with an air of expectation. As if Jane hadn't realized her invitation to Maria Wickley had caused the problem in the first place.

"I hadn't thought about it yet," she confessed, suddenly aware that she should have been thinking about the situation almost immediately. It wasn't as though she'd never hosted a party before. Just never one where she had been completely distracted by the men in her life.

"Lord Wrotham is returning, is he not? He seemed to

get on well with everyone last evening. And if he is absent, I simply don't know what you shall do with only three men."

Charlotte's heart sped up at the mention of his name again. This would never do.

"Lord Wrotham hinted he had more important things to do than socialize with his new neighbors. That is why he did not stay last night. He said he had business to attend to this morning." Charlotte comforted herself with the thought she'd spoken some snippet of truth, although he'd said nothing about being otherwise engaged this evening.

Jane flashed her a knowing look. "Indeed. It sounds as though he enjoyed himself immensely. I'll wager he returns tonight. He dances divinely, but of course you know that. You seemed to take great pleasure in the set you shared." A satisfied smile spread across her face. "In fact, you appeared quite enthralled when you looked at him. Are you sure you turned him down?"

Face now flaming, Charlotte stared down at her cold plate. "Yes. And if you doubt me, you may ask him yourself when he arrives tonight. If he arrives." Best turn the tables before Jane could ask any more questions. "But then, what about you and Lord Sinclair? How have you been getting on?"

Jane's narrowed eyes spoke volumes. "Robert and I have been friends for years, while I was married to Tark." Her voice firmed and her gray eyes flashed. "And that is all we were." She softened once more. "Now I believe he has developed a tendre for me. And I have encouraged him in it. This weekend, therefore, I think we will become better acquainted."

Her voice softened as she returned to their previous topic. "So tell me, what do you plan to wear on the lovely outing you have planned for this afternoon?"

* * *

The village of Wrotham lay picturesquely nestled at the foot of the North Downs of Kent, only a mile from Lyttlefield Park. Why, therefore, had Charlotte only visited it once in the whole of the four weeks in which she'd been resident? Oh, she could give herself excuses aplenty. There had been so much to do and oversee at the Park that unless she deemed the need urgent, she'd vetoed any excursions in order to make sure the house and grounds were all in readiness for her guests. That meant, however, that planning an outing to the village had been done with almost no knowledge of the points that might be of interest to the company.

Charlotte managed to smile pleasantly at Georgie as she and Elizabeth chatted about the sights of the village as the carriage rumbled forward toward Wrotham. Then she went back to brooding, praying her ignorance of the village would not earn her the label of poor hostess. She had attended only one house party before her marriage and none thereafter, so she had little personal knowledge to guide her.

Her original hope had been that her guests would be so exhausted from their nighttime frolics that they would be content with a turn around her park and gardens. But Jane had assured her this was an error on her part. The ensuing discussion this morning had led to the hastily planned visit to Wrotham.

On her one trip into the village, Charlotte and Jane had visited a couple of shops looking for a cobbler to mend Charlotte's riding boots, had peeked into St. George's Church and been accosted by the rector, who welcomed them to the community, and had lunched in a private parlor at The Bull Inn and Posting House. Not a grand tour, but a start at least. Perhaps Mr. Micklefield, the pub owner, could suggest some other sights for their tour. Otherwise they would be returning to Lyttlefield in short order.

* * *

Nash downed his second pint, set his glass on the dark-stained plank table, and called for a third. "And another for you as well, Mr. Smith?"

The burly man in stained linens grinned and nodded quickly. "Aye, if you don't mind, my lord. Smithing's a hottish business come August, even with our weather these days."

Nash nodded to Micklefield, who came at a run with more of the inn's best ale. "I cannot imagine." He shook his head and raised his glass. "You seem to take it in stride, however."

Smith shrugged. "It's in me blood, so to speak. You can't deny what's in yer blood." Alfred Smith could trace his lineage all the way back to the tenth century in Wrotham, every generation producing at least one smith to carry on the family name and tradition.

It boggled Nash's mind to think of so many hundreds of years of Smiths all in the same village. His family couldn't be traced back half so far. And they certainly hadn't remained in the same place nor taken the same occupation, though he had carried on in his father's footsteps until the death of his uncle and cousin had thrown him into the business of estate management.

Nash grunted acknowledgment and sipped his ale. He'd come to like his role at Wrotham Hall more than he'd expected to. Although he'd never before planned for planting or harvesting or animal husbandry, he too had taken it all in his stride, read books and asked questions of the estate manager, and had gotten along fairly well last year. Surprisingly, he actually enjoyed the cyclical life, bound to the land. Perhaps this love of the land flowed in his blood, begun somewhere back along the line of St. Claires.

"So you've begun the preparations for the harvest home already, Mr. Smith? Last year's celebration impressed me quite a lot. I'm looking forward to an even better one this year." Nash leaned back in his chair, the memory of happy villagers clear in his mind. "Have you chosen your lord of the harvest yet?"

"Aye, we have. Michael Thorne's the lord this year." Smith's smile split his face from ear to ear.

Nash winced inwardly. The lord of the harvest negotiated wages for the harvesters and Thorne had a reputation for being a sharp bargainer.

"You'll be partin' with a bit o' brass this year, my lord, if I don't miss my guess."

"If Thorne lives up to his reputation, I've no doubt of it." Nash chuckled ruefully.

The door to The Bull opened behind him, a loud chatter of many voices invading the otherwise quiet pub. Nash twisted around to see what the commotion was all about and froze as Lady John Tarkington, Lady Stephen, and Lady Cavendish, followed by the rest of the party from Lyttlefield, entered with the bright enthusiasm only ladies on a party excursion possessed.

Nash groaned. He'd not expected to meet the lady quite so soon after their tête-à-tête in her library last night. Especially while he was so hard pressed to know his mind about the woman. Just as he'd concluded he'd been mistaken about her, her obvious penchant for assignations had confirmed his fears.

Of course, if she had accepted his proposal in the heat of the moment, he wouldn't have cared who she'd been seeking originally. Sheer folly, unless he could persuade her to marry him quickly and save her from her own baser nature. Or channel them only toward him. He closed his eyes as his blood rose at the thought of her warm, soft body pressed against him. At least he now knew she would warm his bed spectacularly. This unexpected and intense desire for her, however, might prove inconvenient while convincing her to marry him.

She turned toward the bar, and something in her grace-ful movement recalled the image of her lightly clad body and bare feet. Why he'd acted so rashly became perfectly clear. Thoughts of her lusting after another man had roused a jealous streak hitherto undiscovered. He'd wanted her for himself, plain and simple. And now most likely im-possible if she truly meant her words last night. He turned back to Mr. Smith, who seemed to enjoy the parade of Quality.

"Have Thorne come see me on Monday, Mr. Smith. I doubt this harvest will be as good as last year's with the cold weather we've had. We may need to postpone it for a bit, so I need to prepare Thorne and the harvesters for that possibility."

"Aye, my lord. I'll speak with Michael directly." The smith rose, tipped his cap, and moved to the door just as Lord Brack and Georgie brought up the rear of the party.

Brack's gaze swept the room, coming to light on Nash. "Ho, Wrotham!" He guided Georgie over to his table. "Didn't expect to see you here after our late night."

Nash rose immediately. "Lady Georgina. Brack." He bowed and smiled. "How nice to see you once more."

The young woman seemed less frightened of him than she had last night, when she could barely string two words together to greet him. "Lord Wrotham. It is a plea-sure, to be sure." She blushed, though Nash had no idea why. Perhaps a deep shyness afflicted her.

Micklefield hurried toward them. "My lord, my lady. Your party has settled in one of the private parlors. Would you care to join them?"

"Excellent," Brack said, shepherding Georgie toward the doorway the innkeeper indicated. "Join us, Wrotham. We'd be delighted if you would."

Every grain of sense Nash possessed screamed at him to decline. Coming face-to-face with Lady Cavendish would likely be disastrous on many fronts. A quick but respectful refusal and he could be on his way back out to the fields.

"Thank you, Brack. Much obliged." Like a moth driven to seek the flame, he could not stay away from the woman. Hopefully, he would merely be singed and not immolated outright by her wrath.

He fell in line just behind Lady Georgina. If he walked in with another woman he could pretend interest in her was his major objective. Perhaps his lady would then think she had a rival. Women often did not perceive a man as desirable until another woman found him so.

That might be the key to his campaign to get Lady Cavendish to accept his suit. He meant to turn her head from thoughts of Alan Garrett and fix her attentions on him. And what better way to achieve that than a little harmless flirtation with another woman? He prayed Georgina could play the role. Now if only he could do his part justice, perhaps he'd win himself a wife.

Chapter 11

When Nash strolled into the largest private parlor The Bull boasted, only a step behind Lady Georgina, he sensed someone immediately to his right, almost behind the door. Out of the corner of his eye, he glimpsed Lady Cavendish, looking like a vision this afternoon. Her straw bonnet with a jaunty feather on the side allowed only one shiny chestnut curl to escape, a ringlet that hung to the left side of her face. Her green- and white-striped gown, with a tight-fitting Spencer in matching green, accentuated her breasts.

Nash gave an inward groan. Why did the woman insist on torturing him like this? Thank God she wore no more provocative clothing or he'd be undone in the middle of The Bull. He fought the impulse, but in the end he gave in and glanced down at her feet. They were, of course, encased in sturdy half boots. Had he expected her barefoot in public?

He must get hold of himself.

With a deep breath, he slowed and turned toward his hostess. "Lady Cavendish. Such a wonderful surprise to see you all here. I trust you passed a pleasant morning?"

Her face paled, then flushed. "Lord Wrotham. I . . . I did, thank you." The hectic color in her cheeks approached the hue of a ripe strawberry. Obviously she remembered their early morning meeting as well as he did. Nevertheless, she curtsied, her lips pursed. "Will you join us, my lord? We were about to take some refreshment before exploring the village."

"I would be delighted, my lady. How fortunate for me to have come upon your party."

"Indeed. Fortunate." The lady fidgeted with her reticule. "Will you take a seat—?"

"Thank you." He turned toward Brack and his sister. "May I wait upon you, Lady Georgina?" When she nodded, he moved to the nearest end of the table and assisted her with her seat. One irresistible glance back told him his lady had not expected that maneuver.

She stood staring at him, her brows dipped in a puzzled frown. After a moment she seemed to shake herself and took a seat halfway along the table beside Lady John.

So far, so good.

"You have a splendid day for your outing, Lady Georgina." Nash nodded encouragingly, bringing a blush to the young widow's cheeks and a small smile to her lips. She seemed too young to have had a husband, although he'd learned the tragic circumstances of her marriage from her brother over brandy last night. The lady deserved better from her father, and under other circumstances Nash might seriously have considered courting her. She seemed sweet and companionable. Excellent qualities in a wife.

But the Earl of Grafton's grip tightened on him the closer they drew to November. And truth to tell, after last night's amorous entanglement, he had set his heart on conquering Lady Cavendish. Her scandalous proposition had startled him. Not the offer most ladies would make, but he shouldn't underestimate his "wicked widow." The game was on between them, though she didn't know it. How long before he could persuade her to accept him? His body prayed for sooner rather than later.

"It is indeed lovely, my lord." Lady Georgina's merry voice broke into his thoughts. "I am quite looking forward to seeing the sights of your village. I had heard of The Bull before. It has quite a history, does it not?" She gazed around, avidly taking in the rustic half-timbered, half-whitewashed walls hung with gleaming coats of arms and ancient weaponry.

"Indeed it does, my lady." Nash spoke in a clear voice designed to carry down the table. Lady Cavendish glanced their way and he relaxed in his seat. "In the Middle Ages Wrotham acted as a stop on the Pilgrims' Way."

"The Pilgrims' Way?" Georgina's glass-green eyes sparkled. "I've heard of *The Pilgrim's Progress*, my lord. Are they similar?"

He chuckled. "Not exactly, my lady." Nash searched her face but couldn't tell if she spoke truthfully or if the young minx had decided to flirt with him. "They both had to do with a religious journey, however. The Pilgrims' Way was the route that stretched over a hundred miles from Winchester to Canterbury that many pilgrims took when traveling to the cathedral. A perilous journey, with many a soul lost on its way there."

"As dangerous as that?" the lady whispered and inclined her head closer.

Definitely flirting. He might well enjoy this.

"Yes, I'm afraid so." Nash leaned toward her, peering intently into her eyes, which sparkled with mischief. What had brought about this change in her? What the devil was she up to? Could he believe she had developed a tendre for him overnight? He pulled himself back into the conversation. "Although I daresay Wrotham provided a safe haven for them if they made it this far."

"I am convinced your ancestors would have made sure

of it, my lord." Her smile broadened and she laid her hand on his arm. "If they were anything like you."

Lord, what on earth had he started? Perhaps something a bit more gruesome would cool the chit's interest a trifle.

"Did you know Wrotham has also been the haunt of kings? In fact, the story goes that King Henry VIII was in residence here when he received word that Anne Boleyn had been executed for treason." He intoned solemnly. "The next day he betrothed himself to Jane Seymour."

"Oh, my!" Lady Georgina jerked upright, her eyes growing big and round. She clutched his arm. "How horrible."

"King Henry wasted no time, apparently. He wanted an heir and one disappointed him at their peril." Nash chuckled at Georgina's shudder and patted her hand. "Fortunately, today men are not quite so driven, although it is their ultimate duty to their family to secure its succession."

"Hah!" Lady Cavendish tossed a glance at him, then continued her quiet conversation with Lady John.

Had his statement drawn her disdain or something else entirely? Did she not want children? Dangerous woman indeed.

"I had no idea the village's history was so colorful." Georgina withdrew her hand and sat back in her chair, her face a trifle paler.

Nash shot a glance once more toward Lady Cavendish, whose ears had now turned a bright shade of pink. He'd wager she'd been listening. Good. He hoped she had also noted their earlier flirtation.

"Still, Wrotham Village is quite charming, Lady Georgina." He smiled and settled in his seat. "What sights are you planning to visit today?"

Her fresh face lit up again. "I think after here we are to walk to St. George's Church, which is ever so old."

"Thirteenth century, I believe. There is a magnificent view of the village from the clock tower."

Georgina leaned toward her hostess. "Charlotte! May we actually go up in the clock tower? Lord Wrotham says there is a lovely view of the village from there." Her wheedling tone was not lost on Nash, although he assumed Lady Cavendish had already planned that particular excursion. That view alone often drew people to the village.

The lady in question, however, turned toward them and raised her eyebrows. "Is it indeed, Lord Wrotham? Then I suppose we should avail ourselves of that prospect."

"Have you not climbed the clock tower, Lady Cavendish?" Given her current tone, Nash doubted it.

"No, my lord. I must confess I have only visited the village once before today." One end of her pursed mouth turned up in a charming smile, making Nash stifle a gasp. The lady could be unpredictably enchanting.

"Therefore, may I be so bold," Charlotte leaned toward him, deepening the décolletage of her gown, "as to impose upon you to act as guide to us? You obviously have more experience in the area than I."

The winsome look of a maiden in distress became her very well.

Nash licked his lips. Damn. How must that look with his eyes fastened on her cleavage?

"And you will, of course, be in attendance at Lyttlefield tonight?" Lady John interrupted the conversation as she poked her head over the table, beaming seductively at Nash.

Another delightfully bold woman.

"You are part of the party, you know."

"I will be delighted to attend, Lady John."

"Thank you, my lord. We are devilishly short of men now that Mr. Garrett has been called away." Lady John turned liquid blue eyes on him, half-closing them like a cat satisfied with the cream it has stolen.

He would have agreed to anything the woman asked. As she had intended. Lady John knew how to get her way, that was for certain. Had she also deliberately dropped the information that Garrett had gone? Lady Cavendish had not disclosed their encounter, then. Did that bode ill or well?

"How wonderful that we may count on you." Lady John gestured to the party members. "I believe we are to have dancing again and cards. Men are useful in so many delightful ways."

"Indeed we are, my lady." A fascinating woman. But too audacious for him by half. He turned to Lady Cavendish, vividly reminded of several ways he longed to be useful to her.

"But we must not trespass too much on Lord Wrotham's time, cousin." Lady Cavendish smiled at him, setting off a small riot in his chest. "I have just beseeched him to show us the village. How can we expect him to donate so much of his valuable time when he may have other pressing engagements?"

"But I will be honored to escort your guests around the town. And as I am not engaged this evening, *nothing* would give me more pleasure than to attend your gathering." Nash couldn't resist one more taunt. "Or almost nothing. Pleasure can be had in so many ways, don't you agree?"

Lady Cavendish's eyes widened, then narrowed. Her cheeks reddened as if by magic. "Yes, my lord, I do. I will remember that. Thank you."

If looks could kill he'd be in the Wrotham kirkyard this minute. He chuckled, then glanced around the room, bent on putting his words into deeds immediately. The first thing to strike him as odd was the lack of beverages on the table. "Have you ordered some of The Bull's famous ale for your guests, Lady Cavendish? It's quite the local specialty."

After a fleeting look of annoyance, the lady shook her head and shrugged. "I had no idea of such a thing." For a moment her face shadowed with embarrassment. "I suppose I should have made better arrangements for the party."

How had she learned so little of the place in the time she's been here? Well, he would fill the breach.

"Not a'tall. But you are all in for a treat. And ladies, although I know it is highly unusual for you to drink ale, you really must indulge just this once." He rose and went in search of the innkeeper. In moments, they were all sampling the light, nutty ale for which The Bull had gained quite a reputation.

Nash sipped his fourth pint, glad he had insisted the ladies try the beverage before moving on to the tea, which he had also ordered. Several of them seemed quite taken with the ale. Lady John and, surprisingly, little Georgina were making headway with their half-pints. Lady Cavendish too seemed to enjoy it. The others were less enthusiastic.

Mrs. Easton took one sip, sputtered, and pushed hers toward Lord Brack.

He laughed and said, "Much obliged," before downing his own and pulling her glass toward him. He fixed his eyes on the lovely blond woman as he sipped. A conquest in the making?

Nash returned his attention to Lady Georgina, still sipping her ale. "I see you like the Wrotham ale. 'Tis said those ladies who esteem it find a true husband." Against his will, his gaze strayed to Lady Cavendish to find her staring back at him.

"Indeed, my lord?" Georgie shook with mirth. "I suppose if they both liked the ale sufficiently, the wife wouldn't care if the husband was true or not."

"I take your point, my lady." Nash grinned, pleased at the way she had put herself forward today. Dash it, she was a winning little thing. Not at all like the prickly Lady Cavendish.

Well, not always prickly of course. She had been soft enough last night. He shook his head and finished his ale. Enough of that. He needed to keep his wits about him. Perhaps some fresh air would be agreeable.

With a small inclination of his head to Lady Georgina, he rose and turned to his hostess. Had she been staring at him the whole time? Her dusky green eyes, tip-tilted up at him, said she had indeed noted his conversation with Georgie.

Splendid.

"If you will have the party meet in front of the inn, we can start toward the church."

Lady Cavendish nodded and rose to stand beside him. A weariness in her face spoke of their late night, the strain of which lay at his door. Had she tossed and turned as he had, consumed with unfulfilled passion? He shook the thought from his mind.

"There are several places of interest in the village in addition to St. George's. I will be honored to act as guide for the afternoon. I'm certain I can keep the party sufficiently entertained."

The look of appreciation she sent him spoke volumes. "You are very kind, my lord." Her soft voice sounded warmer than before. "If you will not be too inconvenienced? I am sure you did not come here with the expectation of leading our party."

"I am delighted to be able to show off our village to your friends."

"Our village?"

He cocked his head. "Both our properties adjoin Wrotham Village. It is as much yours as mine."

She shook her head. "I am only just come into the neighborhood, my lord. It is your home, not mine."

He grinned. "Not as much as you might think, Lady Cavendish. But if you will excuse me?"

Nash made his way toward the convenience at the back of the inn and in five minutes time stood in front of The Bull, talking to Brack as the rest of the party assembled around him.

The little knot of women off to his right on the grass beneath a shady oak had their heads together like the witches from *Macbeth*. Perhaps deciding which gentleman they would like to escort them, for when Lady Cavendish emerged from the inn they broke apart en masse. Each one then engaged one of the men who stood in a staggered line in the dusty road.

Lady John claimed Sinclair with a determined arm through his. Lady Stephen slipped her hand through the crook of Sinclair's other arm. Mrs. Wickley sidled up beside Lord Fernley and began to speak animatedly to him.

Nash wasn't greatly surprised when Lady Georgina attached herself to his right arm.

"Shall we be off now, Lord Wrotham? I am so excited to see the church tower."

Before he could answer her, to his amazement, Mrs. Easton appeared on his left.

"We truly have a lovely day to see the village, don't you think, Lord Wrotham?" she asked, her voice musical and low-pitched. "The weather has been so unseasonably cool."

Nash swallowed to moisten a suddenly dry throat. Two ladies at his side? Well, with Garrett gone, the party lacked more than one man.

He shot an innocent look toward Lady Cavendish.

She had stopped next to Lord Brack to stare back at him. Her shoulders squared as though pierced with a ramrod and after one wintry flash from those devastating eyes, she fell into conversation with her escort, as though she had taken no notice of Nash's companions.

With difficulty, he repressed a grin and turned to Mrs. Easton. "I quite agree, ma'am. A beautiful day for a walk with two lovely ladies." His voice carried just far enough on the windless air.

His lady twitched her shoulders, then continued to nod at a comment from Brack.

Nash glanced at first one, then the other woman beside him, sighed, and started down the road toward St. George's. This could prove to be an exceedingly interesting afternoon.

Chapter 12

Strolling down the dirt-packed lane to St. George's, arm in arm with Lord Brack, Charlotte couldn't help but think she should be a happy woman. Her disastrous outing had turned golden: The weather couldn't be better—blue sky, a gentle breeze, the sun beaming down pleasantly warm for such a cool August. The company seemed to be enjoying themselves, though they changed partners with alarming frequency. The idyllic setting, with leaves rustling in accompaniment to the birdsong overhead, had put her party in good spirits. And best of all, a guide had appeared who knew everything about Wrotham Village. All in all, a splendid day to her credit as hostess.

Then what had her so on edge? Her heart kept up a fluttery beat and the pit of her stomach ached from that blasted ale. No wonder ladies weren't supposed to drink the vile stuff. She might have known Lord Wrotham would suggest a beverage that upset her digestion. Disagreeable man. Too cheerful by far for what he had been up to last night. The memory of lying still against his chest surfaced and her breath came in gasps.

"Whoa, Lady Cavendish!" Lord Brack's words checked her headlong flight toward the rugged gray building. He turned a quizzical gaze to her. "We're not racing to the church, are we?"

"Of course not, my lord. Please, do forgive me." Charlotte immediately slowed down to a normal pace. They were now at the head of the group; when she and Brack had set off, they had been dead last. "I confess I was thinking about everything I need to do for tonight's entertainment and got quite run away with the details."

The pleasant, ruddy-cheeked young man chuckled. "You almost ran away with me."

Charlotte had to restrain the urge to fan herself. The gentle breeze no longer cooled her sufficiently. "I do beg pardon. Georgina would never forgive me for stealing away her brother."

"I believe today you could kidnap me here in broad daylight and she'd not even notice." He glanced back at Georgie, still on Wrotham's arm. "I am so glad to see her coming out of her shell a bit."

"Yes, we were very concerned that she would not enjoy herself this weekend." Charlotte winced at a high-pitched peal of laughter that wafted from behind them. "I am so pleased to find this not the case."

Lord Brack snorted a laugh, then apologized. "I'd say she's finally on a fair way to recovering from Kirkpatrick's death. A blessing I must lay at your feet, Lady Cavendish."

"Oh, but I—"

He put a hand up to stop her protest. "Having friends she could grieve with, who were experiencing the same loss as she, proved a godsend, not only for Georgie, but for all you ladies, I suspect. She is so miserable in town with the Kirkpatricks. Your calls and at homes during her mourning were the highlight of her week. She wrote to me, you see, even though Father forbade it. She was so lonely until she met Eliza . . . Mrs. Easton. And through her, your little circle."

He glanced back at Georgie again. "I must say I am particularly grateful to Wrotham for his attentions to her. And thankful he'll be at this evening's party as well. Father might well approve of an offer from someone as steady and well-established. It would be a good match for everyone all around."

"Not everyone." Charlotte gasped, appalled that the words had slipped out. Brack peered at her oddly.

"You disagree, Lady Cavendish? Are you acquainted with Lord Wrotham?"

Charlotte took a deep breath to compose herself. She wanted to say neither too much nor too little. "I fear I do not know him well. I know few particulars of his life other than what I gleaned last evening. He seems fond of dancing." Of course she could not broach their encounter in the library to Brack. Or his rescue of Edward.

Her companion looked thoughtful. "I will make inquiries when I return to London. If Georgie has a genuine interest in the earl, I must make sure everything is as it seems. He appears an amiable gentleman, but one must be certain."

"Very wise, my lord." Charlotte relaxed a trifle and continued her sedate stroll, although her stomach still lurched uncomfortably. It must have been the drink that upset her. She firmly squelched any thoughts to the contrary. The encounter with the earl last night, as wonderfully arousing as it might have been, would not do. He desired a wife. Even Jane had said so. And Charlotte's resolve held firm: marriage was not for her.

Brack opened the thick oak door of the church and Charlotte passed into the cool, dim interior. She turned to walk down the central aisle of the nave toward the brighter light near the pulpit. Once there, the windows in the northeast transept drew her attention. Beautiful stained glass illustrating scenes from the life of Christ in jeweled tones calmed her flustered nerves. The window depicting the adoration of the Virgin called to her especially. The brilliant Della Robbia blue robe, ruby red throne, emerald hangings all glowed, the sunshine appearing to light it from within. Unearthly beauty that sent an aura of peace through her.

"This window dates from the fifteenth century. A generous donation by the then-major landowner, Thomas Wrotham."

Like a dash of cold water, the deep baritone voice sent a shiver down Charlotte's back. She turned to Lord Wrotham, her momentary peace fled. He stood smiling at her, Georgina and Elizabeth on either side of him.

"An ancestor of yours, my lord?" She tried to keep her emotions at bay, but the sight of him with her two friends sent a frisson of hurt through her, irrational though it might be. She had no designs on the earl. So why did his attentions to other ladies bother her?

"Alas, no." When he chuckled, the blue of his eyes deepened. "Our title only dates back to the sixteen hundreds and the family name is St. Claire. The Wrothams were here from the beginning. Richard de Wrotham gave his name to the village and parish in 964." The impudent man had the audacity to wink at her. "It is rumored he is here still."

"Whatever do you mean, Lord Wrotham?" Georgina cocked her head prettily to the side.

He widened his eyes innocently. "Come with me and find out, Lady Georgina. If you dare."

Elizabeth glanced from Wrotham's mischievous face to Georgina's eager one and put a hand on her friend's arm. "I think I heard your brother call to you just now, Georgie."

"You did? I didn't hear—"

"I'm certain I did. You were likely distracted by Lord

Wrotham's explanation. Come. He's there in the narthex."
With a long-suffering glance at Charlotte, she shepherded
Georgie back down the center aisle.

Wrotham turned to her with a wicked smile. "Do *you*
dare, my lady?"

He was teasing her unmercifully, reminding her about
their encounter. Well, she'd be hanged if she'd let him get
the better of her. "Of course I do, my lord. 'Lay on, Mac-
Duff.'"

"'And damned be him that first cries, 'Hold! enough!''"
He finished the quote with a wry twist to his mouth and
started down the near aisle, Charlotte following close behind. About halfway down, he stopped. Making a sweeping gesture up and down, he proclaimed, "This is the
north aisle. Thomas Wrotham is buried somewhere along
here, according to the rector. No one knows precisely
where." Close to her ear, in a deep voice that shook her to
her core, he whispered, "Perhaps beneath our very feet."

Gooseflesh pimpled her arms and neck. Charlotte
couldn't help a slight squeal as she danced backward,
imagining a phantom rose before her eyes. She had never
enjoyed ghost tales and avoided contact with any ghostly
places at all costs. She sidled toward Wrotham and the
protection his solid frame provided. His arm went around
her and her shudders stopped.

"Not to worry, my lady," he said, his voice normal
once more, with a touch of amusement. "Spirits seem to
rest well here in Wrotham. In the time I've been here,
I've heard of no local hauntings." He steered her toward a
side door, then turned to address the company, scattered
throughout the church.

"If anyone would like to see the clock tower, please
follow me. The stone staircase that spirals upward is narrow and steep, with only a rope to hold on to. But if you
care to ascend, there is a fine prospect from the top."

Wrotham paused, eying her. "Are you game, Lady

Cavendish? The climb is nigh vertical and the way extremely close." He grasped her hand and held it.

Charlotte looked at Georgina and Elizabeth, who had moved away from Lord Brack to stand with Jane. Georgie sent a glance to the earl, as if weighing her choices. In the end, she turned back to Jane and began to talk in a low voice.

"Of course I am, my lord. As you said earlier, it is my village too. I should be familiar with all its sights and eccentricities, should I not?" She could not resist adding, "Next time I may not be so fortunate as to find you available to guide me."

"But I told you, my lady, if you are ever in need I am close at hand." His voice became a liquid whisper in her ear. "And I mean what I say."

Charlotte froze. The church melted away until she stood half clothed with this man in the library. A deep desire to throw herself into his arms welled up inside her.

Madness. She squeezed her eyes shut and gripped the strings of her reticule. A breath. She must take a breath. The man was merely flirting with her, as he had been with the other ladies in the party all afternoon. Nothing more than that. After her adamant declaration this morning, he could not still be considering her as a prospective wife.

She dragged air into her lungs, determined to hide her disturbing feelings from him. With great effort, she managed to gesture easily toward the clock tower door. "Please, lead the way, my lord. I am eager to see what delights await us at the top."

A blatant lie. Next to ghosts, heights had always given her the whim-whams. She'd loathed high places, even as a child. Her mother had never had to worry about Charlotte becoming a hoyden—she refused to climb trees or ladders or walk on rooftops, as her younger sisters had done. But she could not give Wrotham the satisfaction of seeing her decline. Pray God she did not fall from the parapet.

"Well done, Lady Cavendish. But I insist you go first. In case you lose your footing, I will be behind you to assist." Wrotham opened the door and they allowed Jane and Sinclair and the rest of the gentlemen, except Fernley, to precede them up the staircase. That gallant had elected to remain as protector of the rest of the ladies.

Charlotte took the moment of confusion to gather her courage. *Just put one foot before the other.*

Lord Brack shoved his wiry frame through the narrow doorway and disappeared.

Her breath sped up. Panic chased its own spiral path through her body. Pride be damned. She could not do this.

Wrotham's steady hand clamped her shoulder, warm and comforting. "Your turn, my lady." He gently urged her through the opening. "Watch that first step. The rest are quite even."

She lifted the skirts of her gown, a fleeting prayer sent on high that it would not be ruined. The first step was very high, and Charlotte grasped the scratchy rope on her right, where a railing should have been, to keep her balance. Some light filtered down from above, but they remained in an uneven darkness. She must feel her way upward. Slipping her right hand along the rope, she resolutely stepped up.

Immediately, Wrotham's presence close behind her reassured her. The heat of his warm breath caressed her nape. The clean scent of his citrusy cologne calmed her nerves. Still, she could not help thinking if she fell they likely would both tumble to their deaths. Serve him right for suggesting this excursion.

She took a deep breath and raised her foot to another step. This was torture. No view was worth this dangerous a feat.

Another step, another inch higher. She might as well crawl up the blasted staircase. What if she missed a step? What if the rope broke free? At that terrifying thought, she jumped and wobbled on the well-worn stone.

A hand came out of nowhere to steady her.

"Do not fret, Charlotte." His whisper soothed her. "I have you safe."

The conviction in his confident words staved off her rising panic. But wait; he had called her Charlotte. The wretch had taken the liberty deliberately, knowing she could not upbraid him due to her distress. Of course he had saved her from taking a nasty tumble. So perhaps she could overlook the slip this once. His even breath touched her neck, his warmth so comforting. Yes, she would let it go. This time.

Another step. Did she see more light now? She tried to hurry the last few steps, grateful to have the ordeal over. Her shoulder banged into the narrow passageway, unbalancing her. With a yelp of fright, she dropped her skirts and grabbed for the rope with both hands. Her ankle twisted and she screamed as she fell backward.

Her back thumped against Wrotham's chest and she expected them both to hurtle down the cold stairs and dash their brains out on the stones below. A moment of sheer terror passed before she realized she still stood upon the stairs. Wrotham might as well have been made of the same stone as the staircase. A solid pillar, he withstood her fall without so much as a grunt of surprise. His arms snaked around her waist, and a sense of security welled up in place of the earlier fright. Whatever else, she knew Lord Wrotham would not let her come to grief.

"Steady, my dear. I have you." His arms squeezed tight, and a stab of yearning shot through her, rendering her immobile. "Wait a moment and get your bearings."

Not with his arms around her. She shook the disturbing thought from her head and nodded. A moment later, she was able to lean forward, breaking his grip.

"Thank you, my lord. I am sorry." Charlotte sighed. "I seem to be forever falling into you." She drew a deep breath to steady herself.

A warm chuckle sounded loud in her ear. "My pleasure, my dear. Take your time and be careful."

His deep voice reverberated in the enclosed space, filling it with his essence. Even though she had moved a little way away from him, his presence at her back was still palpable. Still, she must focus on getting off this dratted staircase. Carefully, she lifted her skirts once more and grasped the rope. One step at a time.

Four more slow, torturous steps and her head emerged into the sunlight. Lord Brack offered his hand and she nodded her thanks as her feet finally made contact with the smooth, wide expanse of the roof's flooring.

"The view is simply splendid to the north, my lady," Brack said, taking her arm and leading her to the waist-high parapet.

Charlotte gazed around, drinking in the incredible sights. Wrotham had been correct—the prospect was magnificent. She peered over the edge and regretted it immediately. The sheer drop down the clock tower to the grassy lawn below made her head spin. Abruptly, she pulled her head up and turned to stare at Wrotham, who had joined them.

"An impressive view, would you not say, my lady?"

"Indeed, Lord Wrotham. If one does not look down."

Laughter rumbled from his chest and he smoothly took her hand from Brack and wound it through the crook of his elbow. "Much obliged, Brack."

"Not a'tall." The amiable young man grinned at him and shot a speculative look at her. "I was just about to point out that odd round building there on the left," Brack continued. "I wonder what it is?"

"That is the artesian well and pump house that supplies water for the village. We can visit it later if you like." Wrotham then pointed to a large white manor house beyond the pump house. "And that is the rectory, just beyond it. You will hear the rector, Mr. George Moore, in church tomorrow. I think you will enjoy his service."

"Did you enjoy growing up here in Wrotham, my lord? You seem very proud of it." Charlotte smiled to think of him as a small boy, running wild in the village.

His brow wrinkled as he shook his head. "I have lived in Wrotham for less than two years, Lady Cavendish. I passed my childhood in a small house outside London."

She stared at him, thoroughly confused. "You weren't raised on your father's estate?"

"My father was a naval officer. His elder brother held the title and would have passed it on to his son had they not both perished in an accident almost two years ago. Until then, I too served in His Majesty's Navy." His gaze rested on her face, as if searching for some reaction to this news. "I am surprised you hadn't heard this."

She shook her head, shock making her stare at him in amazement. "I believe Jane mentioned it to me this morning, but I didn't quite understand. You seem to know everything about the village, the people. How have you done this in such a short period of time?" Shortened still further by months spent in London during the Season.

"When I became earl, I vowed I'd do the best I could for the people who depended on me for their living. The most efficient way to do that was to learn estate management—pull myself up by my bootstraps, as it were. Running an estate isn't too different from running a ship. You need knowledge and organization. After fifteen years on board, organization came naturally to me. So I concentrated on studying everything about Wrotham Hall and the surrounding environs." His grin flashed like quicksilver. "I'm a fast learner, Lady Cavendish."

"I commend you on it, my lord. I only hope I can prove as adept as you at settling down in this pleasant county. I do wish to become more supportive of the community."

Lord Wrotham turned an innocent gaze on her. "And the community will welcome you with open arms. But now you mention it, I don't recall seeing you in church, my lady. I am certain I would have noted you."

Heat sprang into her cheeks. She had been sadly remiss in her church attendance and she turned slightly away from him. "You are correct, my lord. I have been so intent on putting Lyttlefield Park to rights, I have sadly neglected my duties as a parishioner of St. George's."

"And now that your renovations are complete, may I look forward to seeing you at services in the morning?" The deep blue of his eyes intensified and he seemed to hang on her next words. What on earth did he want with her? Had she not been plain enough in the library this morning?

A devilish imp seized her and she laughed, bringing a puzzled frown to Wrotham's face. "You may indeed, my lord. As soon as you devise a way to get me down from here."

Chapter 13

"Lord Wrotham, my lady."

Nash frowned briefly, then recalled himself. So unfortunate that Fisk's die-away voice managed to make his name sound dour. He set his face into more pleasant lines and sauntered into the well-appointed drawing room at Lyttlefield Park several hours after their tour of the village. He moved directly to his hostess, who looked ravishing in a pink silk gown, the very first stare of fashion. Had she worn it to impress someone, perhaps?

"Good evening, my lady." He bowed, then lifted her hand for a chaste kiss.

"Good evening, my lord. You are well after your exertions this afternoon?" The minx grinned at him unabashed, alluding no doubt to the hour-long trek down the stairs of the clock tower. She had insisted on taking the staircase one step at a time, her arm plastered around his waist in a death grip.

His ribs ached this very moment from it.

"Indeed I am in fine fettle, my lady. I trust you have suffered no ill effects from your little adventure in the tower?" She seemed in excellent health, cheeks a pretty pink, eyes sparkling. Dare he hope some of her cheerfulness this evening meant a change of heart toward him? Had he indeed made inroads in her opinion of him?

"None at all. In fact, I seem to have gained a grand energy from that brush with danger." Her eyes laughed at him; the danger had nothing to do with the clock tower and still lurked between them.

"I am pleased to hear it. Would you care to take a turn about the room?" He glanced around, immediately noting everyone's position in the room. A strategy that had served him well more than once before. "I would like to hear your impressions of the village, now that you have had time to reflect and are once again on solid ground."

She nodded her agreement, and Nash offered his arm, hope rising in his heart. One hesitant look from her, then she placed her arm through his and they began to stroll around the drawing room.

"Did you think I would bite, Lady Cavendish?" He loved to tease her. She rose so excellently to the bait.

"Not at all, my lord. Though you have teeth, I'll warrant it." She looked straight ahead as they approached the French windows that led out onto the veranda.

"The better to eat you with," he murmured.

"Highly unlikely," she returned, not missing a step. Her mettle truly set her apart from the other women of his acquaintance. He chuckled and tucked her arm more securely in his.

"So other than your unfortunate fear of heights, did you enjoy your first real visit to Wrotham Village?"

"I did." She gave him a slight smile. "I am looking forward to the services in the morning. It is a beautiful church."

"Even more so when it is decked out with all the trimmings at Christmas or with dozens of flowers for a wedding."

She cut her eyes toward him and sniffed. "I am sure it

is lovely at all times, my lord." Her voice, so recently warm with the memory of the afternoon, now echoed with the coolness of an autumn night. "Perhaps you would like to make up a table for cards with some of the other guests? We were about to sit down when you arrived." She gestured toward Lord Brack, flanked as usual by his sister and Mrs. Easton.

What had put her off him this time? The woman was changeable as the March wind. He sighed but nodded. "I would indeed, Lady Cavendish. The company here is so pleasant."

She managed half a smile before striding off. A moment later, she joined Lady John, Sinclair, and Fernley, laughing at some jest the latter gentleman made upon her arrival.

Nash clenched his jaw, then forced himself to relax. The woman had no intention of changing her mind about marriage. Still, he had some time. He'd simply have to continue to charm her and wear her down.

Putting on a more amiable countenance, he strode over to Brack, paying his respects to the two ladies as well. The suggestion of a game of whist brought smiles of agreement to the ladies and Brack good-naturedly consented as well, although Nash suspected he'd have preferred something a bit more challenging. They settled to play, Elizabeth partnering Brack and Georgina across from him.

"We will trounce them soundly, will we not, Lord Wrotham?" Georgie giggled as she shuffled the cards and placed them at Elizabeth's elbow. "I know all of Jemmy's best tricks."

Nash couldn't help but smile. She seemed to have shed her shyness and found a new confidence literally overnight. As he shuffled the cards and began the deal, he flicked glances at her fresh face. Bran-faced of course—that went with her red hair—but they were a charming dusting over the bridge of her nose. Her cheeks were pink with excitement, her green-eyed gaze darting from him to her brother. The green taffeta gown, checked in light and dark green, was fashionable, if a little worn. It suited her youth, even as the low-cut bodice revealed her womanly attributes.

An engaging little thing. He finished the deal and picked up his cards. As he arranged his hand, the thought that Lady Georgina would be a very suitable candidate for his countess did more than cross his mind. They seemed to get on well together, her youth suggested she might be more compliant than an older woman, and her family connections were impeccable. There would have been many advantages to paying Lady Georgina his addresses had he not been under the earl's edict.

Laughter from the other table, where Charlotte sat partnered with Fernley, jolted him out of his speculations. Damn the woman. He shot a glance at her, irked at the way she leaned over the table for an intimate word with her partner. And cursed himself for a fool. Why did he constantly follow her movements? He might just as well ask why the sun shone in the morning. As he turned back to the play at his table, he heaved a mental sigh.

Another long night ahead of him.

Charlotte laughed and shamelessly leaned over the cards toward Lord Fernley, aware as always of Lord Wrotham's attention on her. Well, this time she wanted his focus trained on her. She planned to show him for the last time that she had no intention of accepting his offer. To that end, she deliberately flirted with Fernley. If she could make the earl believe she had designs on another, perhaps he would cease dropping his hints about marriage.

He already suspected her of carrying on an affair with

Mr. Garrett. So much the better. Surely if he thought her a scandalous wanton, giving her favors to a number of men, he wouldn't want to marry her. He might, however, consider her as a possible dalliance. The best of both worlds, as far as she was concerned. After their encounter in the library, she had dreamed more than once of a tryst with Lord Wrotham. His kisses had urged her to be shameless with him and she was more than willing to comply. Judging by his manner with her last night, he undoubtedly knew how to pleasure a woman. Their *glorious conclusion* would be glorious indeed. If only he would stop thinking of marriage.

Charlotte looked again at Lord Fernley, his florid face and thinning hair a stark contrast to Wrotham's lean, tan features and full, curly head. Yet appearances were not everything. Fernley might be a good man. She knew little of him past what Jane had told her, but he had acquitted himself well with the party, save for bringing Mr. Garrett with him. Georgina, for whom he had been ostensibly chosen, had given him almost no notice, being much more taken with Wrotham.

A sly glance over at their table told her that infatuation had not diminished. Georgie was giggling at her partner, eyes bright, trilling laughter filling the room. And Wrotham, to her consternation, was smiling back. Laughing at whatever comment her friend had made.

Her heart twisted, but she ruthlessly renewed her attention on Lord Fernley. Perhaps it was best for Lord Wrotham to turn his attentions toward someone else. A lady, like Georgina, who would want to marry him. Although a tryst with him would have been wonderfully exciting, it could have been fraught with problems as well.

Had she persuaded Wrotham to take her to bed, once he found out her virginal state, his sense of honor might have made him demand that they marry. And she refused to relinquish her independence, even for the best of lovers. Never again would she be helpless in the face of a man's cruel control of her life. Her father and Sir Archibald had taught her to cherish freedom above all else. One more wistful, last glance at the earl and she turned back to her partner, redoubling her efforts to flirt with him.

Fernley flashed her a knowing smile.

Drat. She mustn't overplay her hand. He needed to feel one of a cadre of her possible lovers, not the one she had chosen. That twinkle in the man's eye, however, could mean she was too late.

When the final trick had been taken, Charlotte and her partner winning soundly, Fernley rose. "I believe a mouthful of fresh air would be pleasant about now, don't you agree, my lady? Let our opponents regroup if they desire a rematch." His swagger, so true to form for the man, grated on the nerves, even on short acquaintance. Still, she should accompany him, if only to engage him in a private conversation designed to curtail his hopes.

She nodded and rose. "That sounds like a splendid idea, my lord." She took his arm, aware once more that his clothing approached the extreme in fashion. His starched collar, so tall and stiff, threatened to put his eye out if he turned suddenly. His evening coat was in good taste, although cut extremely tight. And she had shuddered earlier that evening when he had appeared in a pair of black, skintight inexpressibles that left little to the imagination. Discerning, elegant attire, such as Lord Wrotham's, was more to her liking than Fernley's excessively bold dress.

The veranda proved cooler than the house, pleasant with the scent of the roses that wafted up from the flower garden that edged the perimeter of the manor. Fireflies fluttered and a gentle breeze cooled her face, already hot at the thought of the subject she needed to broach with

Fernley. Usually her favorite haunt in the early evening, the terrace had now taken on a battleground aura. Charlotte steered Fernley toward the nearest balustrade, seeking the courage to begin the conversation regarding her interest—or rather noninterest in him.

Fernley's abrupt seizure of both her hands told her she was indeed too late to put him off. "I wanted to say how flattered I am by your attentions this evening, my dear Lady Cavendish." His eyes widened, shamelessly ogling her in the flickering light of the veranda lanterns. "I think I understand your desires and can assure you they are mine as well." He lifted her hands and placed a hot, fervent kiss on each one.

Oh, Lord, he had indeed taken her flirting for an invitation. Charlotte stared in horror as he turned her palm up and pressed his odious mouth to the center.

"Lord Fernley!" She squirmed with revulsion and clenched her hand, trying to withdraw it.

He grasped it firmly instead and pulled her into his arms.

"Please call me Hugh, Charlotte," he whispered in her ear, then ran his tongue around the outer rim, a sickening parody of her more pleasant encounter with Wrotham. His breath rasped in her ear and she shuddered.

"Lord Fernley, you forget yourself." She tried to push away from him, but her hands were pinned between their bodies and she had no leverage.

"Not for a second in your presence, my dear." His mouth traveled down her neck, the greasy feel of it making her cringe. The image of a snail dragging its slimy body across her flesh didn't help matters at all.

Damn him. If she screamed she'd bring ruin down upon herself. Despite the naughty intent of the weekend, her plan had always been discretion. With a sickening twist of her stomach, the memory of the conversation with her father in June arose. He had warned her that the very hint of disgrace would be disastrous for her. His dire threat to remove her to a lunatic asylum if she became once more embroiled in a scandal was not an idle one. And even in their closed circle here, there would be talk. Especially from Fernley if she rebuffed him. Abruptly, all the fight went out of her.

"My lord, it is not seemly to act this way in such a public place." If she could put him off until later perhaps she could find a way to avoid an actual assignation.

"There's no one looking on, my dear." He ran his hand into her hair, and she cursed him anew. She would look exactly as she had when she'd come from that tryst with Garrett at Almack's—an advertisement for a wanton wench. Except she clearly would take no pleasure in this encounter.

She struggled back from him, bent on further chastise-ment, when he pulled her head to him and plastered his lips onto hers. Unfortunately, her mouth had been opened to speak.

He trust his tongue into her mouth, almost down her throat, making her want to gag. He tasted of the wine from dinner, thank God. Anything more noisome and she might have cast up her accounts all over him.

Still, she thrashed against him, fighting to break free of his grimy grip.

One huge push against his chest seemed to make no difference; then, as if by magic, she was freed of his loath-some tongue. Her eyes popped open in time to see Lord Wrotham, his furious face twisted in a scowl, grasp Fern-ley by the scruff of the neck and the waist of his inex-pressibles, and heft her unwanted suitor into the air.

Fernley's heels kicked as a muted squeal escaped his lips.

With a look of utter disgust at her, Wrotham pitched the unfortunate lord over the balustrade to land squarely in the midst of a rosebush. The muted groans of the unfortunate peer made Charlotte grin as she watched him gingerly roll out of the thorny brambles.

Wrotham jerked her around to face him, wiping the smile from her face, his handsome features now distorted by a rage aimed squarely at her.

"I told you if you needed me to call me. I meant it." Eyes dark, brows knit in a sharp V, jaw clenched, the earl had never looked more desirable. A dangerous animal, with the power to break her, bend her to his will, devour her body and soul. She could think of no more pleasant way to die.

Her breathing quickened until the sound of her panting shut out all else.

He closed the distance between them so slowly she could swear she could see the ripple of each muscle as he approached. She could fend him off if she so desired, but his eyes held her mesmerized. She would gladly drown in those blue depths. When he cradled her head, the silky touch of his fingertips on her scalp almost drove her mad. How could such an innocent touch arouse such a passion within her? Her belly ached as it had in the library, with a painful longing she must deny. Could not deny.

When he urged her lips toward his, her legs weakened, and it took all her willpower to simply remain standing. His incredible softness was the perfect antidote to Fernley's rough assault. He molded their lips together, compelling hers to open. Her willingness to do so frightened her, yet she could no more deny him than she could stop breathing. Warmth stole through her, loosening muscle and bone, until she leaned fully against his hard, magnificently aroused body. Completely uncaring who came by or what they saw.

After what seemed a lifetime, he leaned her away from him. She let his lips go reluctantly, sad that the blissful interlude had to end. As always, once she had lost contact with his body, her senses returned to normal.

Fernley.

She stepped back from Wrotham, shook her head, groggy as if coming out of a deep sleep, and glanced over the railing. The young man in question sat nursing several deep scratches that had bled onto his ensemble. In the poor light she could not tell which circumstance pained him the most, the scratches on his person or the ruination of his suit. Had he seen her and Wrotham? Did it matter? The earl's actions would certainly make him think twice before spreading scandalous gossip.

She stared at Wrotham, his face as enigmatic as she had ever seen it. What was he thinking, blast him? He obviously desired her as much as she did him. Could they resolve their differences enough to allow them to act on them?

The French windows opened with a lurch. Jane, Fanny, Sinclair, and the others crowded out onto the terrace. How would the earl explain?

"Ladies and gentlemen, thank you for rushing to our aid." A hum of questions sprang up at Wrotham's words and he moved toward the nearest stairs leading to the garden. He glanced at her, and the wretch had the audacity to wink. "Lord Fernley, I am afraid, has succumbed to a slight misadventure."

A general murmur of surprise rippled through the assembled crowd.

"On a bet of some sort, I suppose, or perhaps a request to show some skill at balancing, Fernley attempted to walk along the balustrade. A misstep occurred and the poor man tumbled into Lady Cavendish's rosebushes. Can one of you gentlemen give me a hand righting him?" With that, he picked his way through the grass to stand above the fallen nobleman. He extended a hand, but his eyes glinted with an emotion that was not sympathetic.

"Let me assist you, my lord. You have a nasty scratch across your cheek."

By this time, Sinclair, scarcely containing his mirth, had reached Wrotham's side. "Are you otherwise injured?"

They grasped Fernley under the armpits and hoisted him to his feet. "If you feel unable to continue downstairs this evening, I am sure Lady Cavendish will be most forgiving. The last thing any of us wants is for someone to be *hurt*." Wrotham seemed concerned, yet he squeezed the man's arm unmercifully.

"I believe it may be prudent if I retire, my lord." Fernley's voice certainly sounded pained. "If Lady Cavendish will forgive me, I will remove to my room." He glanced at Wrotham and winced. "Indeed, my arm is beginning to ache."

Wrotham suddenly released the viscount. "It may be that, if it is no better by morning, you must needs seek medical attention in London. The local apothecary is still firmly of the bleeding-with-leeches school of medicine. It is the one area where I believe I need to lend a firmer hand concerning change."

He clapped Fernley on the back. "Allow me to follow your progress, my lord, once you return to the city. I cannot tell you how much I will hang upon word of your recovery." Wrotham nodded to a servant, who assisted Fernley into the house. "Now," he said, gazing about the stunned company, "shall we continue at cards or is dancing in order again?"

Charlotte stared at him, as startled as anyone at how Wrotham had smoothly taken charge of the evening. Could she ever hope he would bend to her will? Despite the desire that raged through them both, she wouldn't wager a brass farthing on it.

Chapter 14

Charlotte came down early to breakfast Sunday morning, yet found Elizabeth there before her, sipping tea and looking thoughtful. A smile curled Charlotte's lips at the pleasant prospect of a chance for private conversation. She and her friend had scarcely had time to speak this weekend, much less have a comfortable coze. Now, unless the other ladies appeared in the next half hour or so, she'd have time to learn Elizabeth's impression of the gentlemen she'd met.

"I might have known you would be here before me, Elizabeth," Charlotte said, greeting her with a kiss on the cheek, then signaled for the footman to bring her plate. "Have you always been an early riser?"

Elizabeth smiled and put down her cup. "Not until Colin and Kate were born. We didn't have a nursemaid at first, so I tended them night and day." She chuckled. "And early morning. Once they were older, that was the best time to play with them, before the routine of the day called me away." Her smile faded. "Dickon used to say we made the prettiest picture, down on the nursery floor playing with blocks and toy animals. I wish," her mouth trembled, "I wish they'd had more time with him. They were only five when he . . ." She glanced at Charlotte with pain-stricken eyes. "I wish I'd had more time with him."

Charlotte grasped her hand. "I can't imagine how difficult it's been for you, my dear. And for the children. But you will help them remember their father always." This was not the path she'd hope this conversation would take. How to change to talk of the future instead of the past?

"Are you finding yourself more at home with your parents these days?" Charlotte settled to her plate, waiting to hear the latest in her friend's struggle. Lord and Lady Wentworth adored their grandchildren and had welcomed their grieving daughter back to their estate in Dorset. They had, however, also assumed the right to give unwarranted advice on child-rearing to Elizabeth. A kindly gesture that had driven her friend to distraction when she had first taken up residence there.

"It's still a struggle." Elizabeth frowned. "They mean well, they truly do. But Mama is so used to getting her way about everything, I feel badly when I have to tell her I must raise the children as I see fit. As Dickon and I agreed."

"Of course, that will be more easily accomplished when you are in your own home again." Charlotte rushed on past the reference. "I couldn't help but notice you seemed to enjoy Lord Brack's company this weekend. The short time I have spoken to him, I have found him a very amiable gentleman. And he's so kind to Georgina. Do you like him, Elizabeth?"

Her friend smiled briefly and shook her head. "I know what you are about, Charlotte. And the short answer to your question is yes, I do like Lord Brack and find him to be, as you said, both amiable and kind. I cannot, however, know on such short acquaintance if we would suit for more than friendship."

"Have you told him about the children?" That might be a bone of contention Charlotte had not planned on. Some men did not like to raise children not their own.

Elizabeth picked up her tea and set it down again. "Georgie took care of that revelation the first night. Lord Brack knows all about Dickon and the children. And I must say, he seemed very sympathetic. He knows how hard a time Georgie's had." She sent Charlotte an intense look. "And that's something I wanted to talk to you about."

"About what?"

"Georgina."

Charlotte poured tea and reached for the sugar. "Georgie? Has something happened?" Bizarre images of Georgina being accosted by Fernley surfaced. She shook them away. The man would not dare do such a thing after last night. But perhaps earlier in the weekend?

"Well, not happened exactly, but Charlotte, it's her circumstances. Lord Brack, in thanking me for taking Georgie under my wing, also confided how desperate her situation is."

"He may have mentioned something of it to me as well, though it did not sound as dire as all that." Charlotte's conscience smote her. She had not taken in all of Brack's conversation about his sister because she'd been too busy thinking about Wrotham. "He did say she was miserable, but I thought he referred mostly to her missing her husband."

"There is of course that burden." Elizabeth sighed. "However, he told me that the tension at home is very bad indeed. Mr. Kirkpatrick's daughter, a Mrs. Reynolds, blames Georgie completely for her father's dismissal of the vicar." Elizabeth wiped her tearing eyes with her napkin. She seemed to weep at any provocation since her husband's death.

"Well, that is hardly fair," Charlotte said, settling to

her breakfast. "Mr. Kirkpatrick married them. He must have known the risk in going against the wishes of the marquess." Georgina had been guilty of nothing but falling in love.

"Oh, Charlotte, Mrs. Kirkpatrick had to actually beg her daughter to take poor Georgie in when Isaac died. She agreed, grudgingly, but the daughter has treated Georgie horribly, more as a servant than a guest in her home. Every day she makes sure Georgie knows she's there only out of Christian charity." Elizabeth sniffed. "If that's what you want to call it. The Kirkpatricks can't say much to her, though, because they have nowhere else to go. The vicar is still without a parish."

"I am so sorry, Elizabeth. I truly had no idea. Georgie never said a word." Charlotte's conscience smote her. Why had she not realized her friend was suffering so? Georgina had apparently tried to hide her circumstances and succeeded very well in doing so.

Elizabeth ducked her head. "I had several of my old dresses made over for Georgina to wear this weekend. She has had no clothing allowance for over a year. One reason she wore full mourning for so long is that those were the best clothes she had."

Lord, Georgina had certainly never let on the situation was so dire. How appalling she had not known this. No wonder Georgie had been trying to catch Lord Wrotham's eye. Marriage to any decent gentleman would be preferable to such an existence. And Wrotham had the makings of an excellent husband . . .

Charlotte stopped as anguish flooded her heart. The idea of Georgie marrying Wrotham was both wonderful and terrible. It would be a brilliant match for Georgina, one that, as her brother had pointed out, might reconcile her with her family. She and the earl had rubbed along well all weekend. Had she not known of Wrotham's desire for her, she'd have been convinced his affections lay with the younger woman. Who was to say that they might not if given time?

"So, Charlotte," Elizabeth's voice jerked her back to the breakfast table, "I thought perhaps you could invite Georgie to stay with you here at Lyttlefield Park."

Charlotte froze, her mind racing. If Georgie lived here, she would be in close proximity to the earl and could continue to pursue his courtship. In which case, if Charlotte truly wanted to help her friend, she should relinquish her budding tendre for Lord Wrotham.

That thought sent a pang to her heart. Even though the man was a new acquaintance, his charm and physical attractions had captured her interest. And he had rescued Edward. How could she not feel warmly toward him for that act of bravery?

She sighed, then glanced at Elizabeth. It might all be a tempest in a teapot. She had no idea whether Wrotham would choose to woo Georgina or not. However, if he showed any interest in her, she would steel herself to bow out gracefully. Although she'd enjoyed his attentions, it wasn't as if she'd set her cap for him.

"Georgie would be good company for you and Jane," Elizabeth continued, so eagerly Charlotte's conscience smote her again for even hesitating.

"Of course I'll ask her. That is the perfect solution, isn't it?" A lead weight tried to settle in her stomach, but she disregarded it. Georgina would be infinitely happier here than in London and she would love her company. "I only wish I had thought of it first."

Elizabeth's shoulders dropped, as if a heavy burden had fallen from them. She sipped her tea and smiled broadly. Charlotte hadn't seen her this content in months. If she could bring about the happiness of two of her friends, she would count herself fortunate, no matter the cost to herself.

Gay chatter down the hall turned her attention to the

doorway. "Perhaps I can broach it to her this evening. Let me figure out how to put it so that she does not feel she will be an imposition on me."

"Excellent." Elizabeth relaxed back into her chair as Jane and the rest of the ladies swept into the breakfast room.

"What smells so delectable this morning, my dear?" Jane sailed over to the sideboard and began removing the covers. "Oh, I adore kippers." She grabbed a plate and began to pile her plate with herring fried to crispy perfection. "Maria, child, you must try some. They look quite scrumptious."

As the ladies filled their plates, Charlotte sipped her tea, biding her time until she could speak with Georgina alone. Now if she could only get the image of the Earl of Wrotham out of her mind . . .

During the church service, Charlotte pondered her predicament once more. She tried to focus on Mr. Moore, but when he took his sermon from the story of the Canaanite woman, her mind drifted back to Georgie's plight. Her friend was very proud. Would she agree to whatever aid Charlotte could offer?

She continued distracted on the ride home and throughout luncheon.

Surreptitiously, at the table, she studied Georgina and found her friend sparkling and vivacious in her conversation with her brother and Elizabeth. She had even spoken pleasantly to Lord Fernley, on his best behavior today. He hadn't even dared look at Charlotte.

Yet now Charlotte looked for strain in Georgie's face, she found the signs. When Georgina listened to the other guests, her attention sometimes seemed to wander. A wistful look came over her face when Elizabeth talked about her home and family. Once she smoothed down her dress, a lovely white and blue sprigged frock, although Charlotte recognized it as one of Elizabeth's garments from two years ago. Yes, she must extend the invitation immediately.

"Do you hunt here in Kent, Lady Cavendish?"

Charlotte started, then smiled politely at Lord Sinclair. "I have never done so, my lord, although my father has a hunting lodge in the eastern part of the county."

"Jane has told me you are an excellent horsewoman. I would have thought you had ridden to the hounds at least once. Do you not enjoy the chase?" The tall, handsome man with a distinguished touch of gray in his hair, grinned at her, then back at Jane. His own gaze had a predatory gleam when it rested on the woman by his side.

"Sadly, my lord, neither my father nor my late husband approved of ladies joining in a hunt, although I do know those who relish the pursuit. Perhaps this year, as I am no longer constrained, I will join in the chase." A freedom she might be forced to forgo should she marry, only to find her husband also disapproved of such activities for ladies.

She glanced away from Sinclair, who had already turned his attention back to Jane. As she stared at her plate, her situation clarified itself in her mind and new resolve made her straighten in her chair. Independence had been given to her, a great gift she would make the most of. To marry and relinquish it, even to the perfect man, would leave her wondering for the rest of her life. If that meant forgoing a husband and a family, then that was simply the price she would have to pay.

The afternoon wore on interminably. After luncheon her guests were free to walk about the grounds or chat at will. Charlotte had planned that in order to give any newly formed couples some time alone together. The only couple conspicuously absent were Jane and Lord Sinclair. Charlotte assumed they had retired to one or the other's room for a private conversation. Georgie and her brother had gone out to walk in the gardens. Maria and Fanny were playing cards and Elizabeth had opened a book beside the fire.

Hearing a step on the stair, Charlotte left gazing out at the sunlit roses and turned, expecting to see Jane. Instead, Lord Fernley entered and stopped when he saw her. He glanced around the room; then some of the stiffness went out of his shoulders.

"Good afternoon, Lady Cavendish."

"Good afternoon, Lord Fernley. We were sorry you could not attend church with us this morning. And we missed you at luncheon as well. Your arm is no better?"

Fernley flinched and turned pale. He rubbed the offended appendage and shook his head. "I am afraid not, my lady. I think it best that I return to London, as Lord Wrotham suggested." He peered around the room again, and Charlotte had to bite back a laugh.

"We are certainly sorry to lose your company, my lord. I wish you a speedy recovery." Charlotte dipped a curtsy as Elizabeth and the others gathered around. "Lord Fernley is taking his leave, ladies."

They murmured their farewells, Fernley bowed, narrowly escaping putting out an eye with his high-pointed collar, and left.

"Did Lord Fernley seem a trifle nervous to you, Charlotte?" Fanny had returned to the card table. Her grin as she shuffled the cards belied the need for her question.

"He did seem to be looking for someone," Elizabeth said, a smile touching her own lips.

"Lord Wrotham apparently made quite an impression on him last evening," Charlotte ventured. He'd certainly made an impression on her. She rubbed her arms and went back to the window. She had no idea if he would turn up today or this evening. He'd not been at church this morning, even though he'd made such a point of wanting to see her there. Perhaps he'd grown tired of the party. Charlotte sighed. The cheerful afternoon sunlight masked the perpetual chill in the outdoor air. If they were lucky, however, there would be some warmer days ahead.

Dinner that evening did not improve. A pall had been cast over the whole party and Charlotte was at a loss how to lift it. She feared herself at fault and redoubled her efforts to engage her guests, yet she sensed the whole party overcome with melancholy. Were they unhappy with her hospitality? She thought not. Everyone had complimented her throughout the weekend on how well her first entertainment in her new home had gone.

She doubted Fernley's departure had upset the company, but he had left her number of men sadly depleted. Perhaps that accounted for everyone's lack of spirits. Or the fact that they would leave on the morrow, all except her and Jane. That thought left her melancholy as well. Still, she tried to rally the conversation when the ladies gathered for tea in the drawing room.

"We shall be sorely in need of company after tomorrow, won't we, Jane? The party has been so lively, we will be quite at sixes and sevens for at least a week. Perhaps we should think about going up to town as well?" Charlotte hoped to plan a long visit to London shortly. Living so close to Lord Wrotham might prove detrimental to her in several ways.

"Oh, my dear, I am to be in such a whirl for the next month!" Jane beamed at Maria. "Sinclair has invited Maria and me to his estate in Suffolk. We are going to teach Maria how to ride. The poor thing never learned properly. Then, when hunting season arrives, he plans to have a ladies' hunt." Jane laughed, her eyes gleaming. She glanced around the room. "And you all are invited. Sinclair plans to make accommodations for all of this party, as well as a few new faces."

"Do you know when you will return?" Jane's news had thrown Charlotte into a dither. "I had hoped we could go up to Town before the harvest season begins in earnest. Of course, that may be delayed until late in September with this horrible cold, wet weather we've been having. Apparently, the farmers are hoping for a final spell of good weather to help ripen the crops."

"I believe I shall have returned by then, my dear. And you know we are always welcome at Theale's town house." Jane smiled and turned to Maria, at her side as she had been all weekend.

"Thank you, but whatever am I going to do for company while you are gone?" Charlotte straightened her shoulders. The perfect opportunity to kill two birds with one stone had just presented itself.

Jane snapped her attention back to her cousin. "I can ask Sinclair to include you in the party of course." Her gaze flicked over Charlotte's face. "We would not dream of abandoning you."

"I'm sure you would not, my dear." Charlotte turned to Georgina beside her, who had just picked up her cup of tea. "However, I have actually hit upon an idea that will give you a bit more freedom to pursue your own entertainments without worrying about me being left alone." She put her hand on Georgie's arm. "I have come up with a scheme, my dear, that will be to both our benefit if you agree."

Georgina stopped with the teacup almost at her mouth.

Her brows furrowed and she carefully set the cup back into its saucer. "What do you mean, Charlotte?"

"After all the company I have had this weekend, I fear I am not inclined to the solitude of the country. Elizabeth, Fanny, and now Jane even are leaving. If you have no fixed engagements, I wondered if you would care to remain here with me? We will be great company for each other and when Jane returns, we can all go up to London."

She'd already decided that if Georgie agreed, she'd have her fitted out completely for that hunting party and the Christmas season when they went to Town. Shopping would make the trip even more enjoyable.

Georgina sat in stunned silence, her hands working in her lap. "Charlotte, that is too generous an offer." Her bright eyes said she longed to take it, yet something, perhaps pride, held her back. "I would need to write to Mrs. Kirkpatrick, to make sure I am not needed at home." A hint of blush on her cheeks told Charlotte she knew how little she was needed—or wanted—in her sister-in-law's house.

Thinking only of the greater good for her friend, Charlotte made the final argument, one Georgie could not refuse. "You would also be in close proximity to Lord Wrotham, Georgina." Charlotte spoke his name without a qualm, although her stomach clenched painfully. "If some affection has begun to grow between you, surely you would be better able to pursue it here than in London?"

Georgie blushed but nodded. "I am not sure if there is anything to speak of yet." She peered keenly at Charlotte and said, "I thought some affection had begun to develop between the two of you, Charlotte. Was that not true?"

Charlotte waited, steeled herself, and shrugged. "There may have been some interest early in the weekend, but that has passed. By all means, if you have a tendre for him, we must help foster it. And that is easier accomplished here." Charlotte smiled at the reluctant widow, in whose face she saw a glimmer of hope. Perhaps this scheme would be the best thing for all concerned. Now she could put this weekend behind her and focus on helping Georgina bring Lord Wrotham up to scratch. The sinking feeling in her stomach said she was making a mistake, but if so, at least it would be her own to make.

Chapter 15

September 16, 1816
Dearest Charlotte,
Thank you so much for your kind letter of con-
dolence. It quite touched my heart. My uncle died
peacefully and I talked with him and sat at his bed-
side until the end. He was most adamant in his
hope that I would carry on the title in an accept-
able manner and do my duty in every way possible.
My reputation was much on his mind, which I can
certainly understand. But I reassured him that I
would not bring shame to Kersey, but do my utmost
to carry on as he would have me do. I hope he be-
lieved me.

As a result, the responsibilities of the earldom
weigh more heavily upon me than I anticipated. I
am spending my early mourning period here, at
Kersey Hall, locked away with the account books,
trying to make sense of bills of sale and prospec-
tive acreage yields on five different estates. Most of
my friends would simply not believe the lengths to
which I am going for the properties. My head

aches with the figures and I long for some feminine companionship.

By happy circumstance, I find I will be in London next week and would ask to call upon you and your cousin at your earliest convenience. Lady John informed me of your intent to meet her there for the beginning of the Little Season. She, Sinclair, and Mrs. Wickley have been much in company with me at Sinclair's estate, where they have resided for the past month, is not far from Kersey.

As we have some unfinished business to attend to, I look forward to being in your excellent company once more.

I remain, as always, yours to command,
Alan, Lord Kersey

When Charlotte had read this missive for the tenth time, the once-crisp cream-colored stationery, edged in black and crested with the embossed image of a lion couchant, had become creased and bedraggled. She still did not know quite what to make of his words.

She had been surprised to receive a letter at all. Astonished, in fact, as she'd given Mr. Garrett—rather, Lord Kersey now—no encouragement whatsoever, unless one could call a perfunctory letter of condolence encouraging. So she had read the missive with some trepidation the first time and sighed in relief to find it rather straightforward. A new sense of responsibility seemed to have been instilled in the earl, as Jane had predicted. A dutiful letter sent to acknowledge hers.

Until that final sentence.

As we have some unfinished business to attend to, I look forward to being in your excellent company once more.

To what unfinished business did the man refer? There could only be one. That outrageous question he had asked while they danced in August. *Shall I come to your room this evening?* Why would he still want to pursue a dalliance with her after all this time? His other words echoed eerily in her mind as well. *I usually get what I want.*

Surprisingly, the more Charlotte thought about the possibility of an affair with Lord Kersey, the more appealing it became to her. She did long for the excitement of male companionship, especially since Jane and Sinclair's liaison had put the matter right before her face, so to speak. Warm arms and hot kisses, like those in the stairwell at Almack's, would be much more welcome now she knew very well what she was missing. She had even gone so far as to daydream—scandalous images of her entwined in bed with Lord Kersey had played tantalizingly in her mind ever since she had received his letter. The daydream, however, had the unfortunate habit of changing to one of her entangled with Lord Wrotham instead. Oh, Lord, but she had tried more than once to rid herself of the thought of the man.

She had done her best to put Georgina forward as a replacement candidate, although so far her strategy had met with little success. An invitation for both her and Georgie to dine at a neighboring estate had seemed promising when Lord Wrotham turned up as part of the party. He had, fortunately, not been seated with her, and when the gentlemen joined the ladies after dinner, she had latched onto an elderly relative of the hostess, asking all manner of questions about the neighborhood and the harvest, ignoring everyone else.

Georgie had taken the opportunity to engage Wrotham in conversation instead. Several times, Charlotte had caught them laughing out of the corner of her eye. On the carriage ride back to Lyttlefield, she had pounced on her companion, demanding to know everything about the evening and her conversation with Wrotham.

According to a very enthusiastic Georgina, they had touched on her move to Lyttlefield, those awful robbers who still remained uncaught, books they'd read, her brother . . . and Charlotte.

"What did he want to know about me, Georgie?" Charlotte fought against the agonizing leap her heart took at that statement. Drat the man.

They climbed the stairs to the first floor and headed to Georgie's room.

"Just the usual polite questions. He asked after your health. If you'd been riding out, and whether or not you had an escort." Georgie chatted gaily as Charlotte helped her off with her stays. They had found they enjoyed assisting with each other's toilettes since Georgie had come to stay at Lyttlefield.

"The gall of the man." Charlotte jerked the laces.

"I'm sure he's just concerned for your welfare. Ouch! I want them off, Charlotte. You're tightening them."

"I'm so sorry. Here." She unthreaded the laces, and the stays loosened. "That should be better." She took the stays and shift and handed Georgie a nightgown.

Slowly, she folded the garments, lost in thought. Lord Wrotham still asked after her. The notion filled her with both longing and resolve. She laid the clothing on the dresser for the maid to attend to the next day. She'd hired a local woman, Martha Grant, to see to Georgie.

"Did Lord Wrotham ask anything else?"

Georgina began brushing her hair, avoiding Charlotte's eyes. "He did ask if you'd been up to London yet."

Hmmm. He was still interested in her. Interested, perhaps, in who she would see in London. Part of Charlotte thrilled to the idea that he was still attracted to her. Yet her mind insisted nothing could come of an *affaire de coeur* between them. The best thing to do was put him out of her mind and try to move on. If she set her cap for another man and let Wrotham know about it, hopefully he would take the hint, put her out of his mind, and pay his attentions to Georgie instead.

That dinner party and the ensuing conversation had been two weeks ago. As soon as Lord Kersey's letter had arrived, she'd begun to plan for a rendezvous.

He would call on her at the Marquess of Theale's London home, where she would be staying with Jane. They obviously could have no assignation there. Perhaps his town house would be more discreet. Or they could go to an inn outside Town. Outside of a country house, she had no idea where people usually went to conduct illicit affairs. The problem with being innocent was a lack of knowledge about so many very important things.

Since she'd emerged in June, she'd lived from one exciting event to another: the Almack ball, the move to Kent, her house party, Lord Wrotham's proposal. The culmination would be this chance for the physical intimacy she'd been denied with Edward so many years ago.

Charlotte folded the letter and put it in her escritoire once more, thoughtful. If the new earl had indeed turned over a new leaf, as Jane suggested, then he might also be in search of a wife rather than a mistress. Who would have thought it so difficult to find a man who wanted a night of passion without it being followed by an offer of marriage? She'd believed men were in dire dread of being leg-shackled. That they considered widows safe women with whom to indulge their passionate natures. She had obviously not found those particular gentlemen. Except for Fernley, who disgusted her. Was there no middle ground when it came to taking a lover?

Charlotte stood, wandered over to the window, and gazed down the driveway, playing with the small locket at her throat. Only two miles to Wrotham Hall. It might as well be a thousand.

Worse, she had to admit she missed Lord Wrotham's

company. She had come to admire him for so many more reasons than just his physical attributes. His intelligence attracted her more than she would have suspected. Conversations with him had never been dull and often she had to focus, as much as in a game of chess, to stay abreast of his wit. His interest in his land and its people too had struck a deep chord with her. With the harvest finally approaching, she hoped she could work half so well with the tenants as he. The only area where he had not succeeded was with the capture of the robbers, who still plagued the countryside. Still, given time and his determined nature, she had faith that Wrotham would triumph there as well. Truly a man to be admired.

Unfortunately, no matter how much she esteemed Wrotham, she still refused to agree to marry him. The horrors of her first marriage made her value her hard-won freedom too much to consider relinquishing it.

So Alan—she'd best learn to use his first name now— remained her best choice if she simply wanted a dalliance. He had agreed to call on her and that was a start. She must set Rose to begin packing for her departure. If only she could as easily set herself to the task of seducing her rake.

Almost a week later, on her first night in London, Charlotte made ready for bed in the comfortable chamber allotted her at the Marquess of Theale's town house. She and Jane had had a long, comfortable coze to catch each other up and her cousin had just risen to retire when she grasped Charlotte's hand and asked, "Why do you not wish to marry, Charlotte?"

Charlotte sank onto the bed, amazed at the question, which came from nowhere. They had just been talking about Lady Havercourt's invitation to dine tomorrow evening, certainly nothing to do with marriage. Once the question sank in, Charlotte's shoulders slumped. Why did she have to keep answering that question?

"You have had a declaration from one of the most eligible men in England." Jane gave her arm a shake. "Why did you not accept him?"

"Other than the fact that I have no wish to marry?" The hair on the nape of Charlotte's neck rose.

Jane shrugged. "I do not believe that. I think you are afraid to risk being hurt again. Mind, you have every right to be wary. Between your father and Sir Archibald, you have had a miserable life. However, as bad as it has been, it will be that much more wonderful if you find the right man. I can assure you, Wrotham's interest in you is genuine. I'd wager my fortune on it. You should have seen his face that night at Almack's. He looked ready to throttle Lord Kersey for stealing you away."

"I have been married." Charlotte sniffed and stared into Jane's narrowed eyes. "It is not an experience I wish to repeat."

"You were married to a man much older than you who may not have been kind, but—"

"He was definitely not kind, Jane." Charlotte twisted her handkerchief. Perhaps, at last, she needed to explain how horrible her life had been to her cousin, to make her understand why she feared losing her independence so much. It was a tale she had told no one.

"Sir Archibald made the five years of our marriage a living hell for me, Jane. I don't know if he was under orders from Father or if he simply hated me from the moment we wed. From the beginning, he would insult me at dinner, whether we had guests or not. He would tell me I had no intelligence, no grace, no manners. That I was ugly. That I never did anything right."

She took a deep breath, trying to keep the tears at bay. She refused to cry over his insults any more. "He kept me buried at a cottage in Itchingfield most of the year, a small property with only one servant. I had little allowance for clothing and I had to be frugal just to eat and stay warm." She fisted her hands, then slowly unclenched them. "All the while he kicked up his heels here in London. He and Edgar. I was brought to Town only when it suited him, when he needed a hostess for some political dinner or party. I'm not sure which I despised more, the lonely months in the country or the loathsome weeks in his company."

As she spoke, Jane's face had paled. She swallowed several times and clutched her throat. "My dear! I had no idea . . ." She grabbed Charlotte into her arms, tears trickling down her cheeks, falling onto Charlotte's back. "Why did you not tell me?"

"I told no one." Charlotte sniffed and blinked back tears. "No one knew, unless Sir Archibald told someone, which is unlikely."

Jane sat back. "Was he . . . did he ever physically harm you?"

"No, he never struck me." She kept her eyes on her lap. "He never touched me at all."

"What?" Her cousin's eyes rounded. "You mean he never once came to your bedchamber?"

Charlotte shook her head. She still thanked God every night for that. "I don't think he was capable. To my knowledge, he never dallied with anyone else either."

Jane sniffed. "He may have been very discreet. If you were so often in the country, you may not have known of it."

"Humph." Charlotte snorted. "Do you think Edgar wouldn't have known? The slightest thing he could have said to hurt me, he would have shouted it gleefully—in the most public place possible."

Jane shook her head and sat up, staring into her face as if searching for something. "All the more reason, my dear, to think before throwing away this new chance for happiness. Charlotte, you have the opportunity to make a good marriage now. A marriage with a man near your age, who you yourself have said you are drawn to. Why not accept Wrotham? You cannot seriously believe he will behave as Sir Archibald did?"

Charlotte had to bite her tongue to keep from laughing. "No, Jane. I truly do not believe Lord Wrotham would be anything but a good husband. But why should I tempt fate and leap into another marriage when I need not? He may not have Sir Archibald's faults, but he will certainly have some of his own. As it is now, I can do as I please, run my estate as I see fit, and find male companionship as I like." She gave her cousin an arch look. "Considering your declaration never to marry again, I would think you understood my reasons."

Jane nodded but grasped her hands. "I do, my dear, but my situation is much different from yours. I had a satisfying marriage, children, and financial reasons not to marry again."

"As have I."

"But you do not have children, Charlotte. If you do not marry, you will end up alone. Or worse, you will not be careful and be forced into marriage with a man who seemed delightful in the dark but less so in the light."

Charlotte blotted away her tears. Why could she not have it all as she wished with no fuss? "I do want a husband and children, but not so badly as I want to make my own decisions. And mistakes. For the first time in my life, I have that ability. If I cannot have the man I loved, at least I will have a choice in what I do."

Jane's kind blue eyes looked sad, but she nodded. "I believe I do understand, my dear. Now, what may I do to help you?"

* * *

"You look positively ravishing, Charlotte! But then, that is the idea, is it not?" Jane remarked as Charlotte entered the drawing room of the Theale town house.

She smiled and flushed, nervous that at last she would see the Earl of Kersey. Ostensibly she awaited with her cousin for the fashionable callers now in town to make an appearance, but they both knew one particular caller was the reason for her grand appearance.

Her white sprigged muslin, so sheer it left little of her shape to the imagination, dipped down low over her breasts, inviting male attention. Unsuitable for afternoon? Definitely. She cared not a fig. When the earl arrived, she wanted to be sure his gaze would be only on her.

"Exactly the point, Jane." Charlotte paced about the room, glancing out the window as she passed by. One o'clock in the afternoon. Alan had written yesterday, asking permission to call today. If only he would arrive, this panicky feeling might subside and she could once again be the gracious, flirtatious woman he had kissed in June.

"Do sit down, Charlotte." Jane sipped her tea and frowned. "You look ready to fly to pieces. Not the effect one wants to project when one is angling for a lover."

Giving her cousin a speaking glance, Charlotte dropped into a Queen Anne chair.

"Take this tea, my dear. It will fortify you."

"Only if it has a large dollop of brandy in it." Charlotte grinned and sipped the hot, sweet beverage. Her hands shook, and she forced them to steady. He would appear eventually. Pray God, no one else did.

As the long-case clock struck the half hour, Fisk appeared. "The Earl of Kersey, my lady."

Charlotte sat straighter, which pushed her bosom straight out, jutting like the prow of a ship. She licked her lips, then bit them slightly to deepen the color. Her cheeks were already blooming, thanks to the Attar of

Roses she had applied. Setting the teacup on the table before she spilled it, she turned toward the doorway and smiled broadly.

Lord Kersey swept into the room and she caught her breath, for the change in him was immediately evident. The handsome blond looks were still there, curly hair still charmingly riotous, blue eyes alert and sensual. His clothing, as fashionable as ever—deep brown coat, cream silk embroidered waistcoat, and fawn-colored trousers—save the addition of a mourning armband. He looked to be the same man who had earned her the reputation of wicked at Almack's.

Yet his demeanor had changed. He moved with the presence of his station rather than the relaxed devil-may-care attitude that had proclaimed him unconcerned with anything save the next wager or woman to be won. Before, his eyes would have sought her out hungrily. Now he strode toward her cousin, avoiding Charlotte's avid gaze entirely.

He spoke to Jane and bent low over her hand, his countenance poised and respectful. Her cousin had been correct. The rake was gone. In his place a man of purpose stood, one who might also insist on a more permanent arrangement between them.

Plague take him.

At last, he turned to her, and his eyes warmed.

That warmth at least was encouraging. With luck, it might be all right after all.

"My dear Lady Cavendish. I am so pleased to see you once more." He lifted her hand and his lips grazed her knuckles.

Delightful shivers shot up her arm. That certainly boded well.

"I truly regret the necessity of having to quit your house party so early in August. Indeed nothing would have persuaded me to leave your excellent company except the sad news of my uncle's impending death." His gaze searched her face, a mocking lift to his eyebrow. "I do hope you have forgiven me?"

"Of course, my lord. Such an event must take precedence over any other engagement. I am sorry for your loss."

He continued to hold her hand, and Charlotte's heart pounded in her chest, almost visible, she'd wager, due to her extreme décolletage.

"You are kind, my lady." He squeezed her hand and she returned the gesture. Looking deeply into his eyes, now darker and wider than just moments before, a fleeting thought arose that he might sweep her into his town house this very evening.

"Will you be seated, Lord Kersey, and have tea with us?" Jane asked, interrupting their heated gaze. "You must give us the particulars about your uncle's funeral and all the fascinating things one must do to take over an earldom."

"I beg your pardon, Lady John, but I am, as usual these days, pressed for time." He continued to stare into Charlotte's eyes. "I had hoped to have the pleasure of Lady Cavendish's company in my curricle for a turn around the park, if she is willing?"

Charlotte clutched the arms of the chair. She hadn't expected a drive alone with him, although it should not draw attention if she rode with him in an open carriage. If she was going to do this, they would need to be discreet above all else. He must understand that. She allowed him to assist her as she rose.

"I would enjoy becoming reacquainted very much, my lord. And a ride in the fresh air is always welcome." A quick glance at her cousin showed her nod of approval, though she also noted Jane's silent sigh. "Let me prepare for the outing and I will meet you in the hall shortly."

He nodded and released her hand, giving it another squeeze as he did so.

Charlotte kept a sedate pace until she exited the room, then picked up her skirts and ran for her chamber. She had no idea what this ride would lead to, but considering the man's reputation, she needed to be ready for anything.

Chapter 16

"Did I tell you how lovely you look, Lady Cavendish?" Lord Kersey asked as he handed her into his curricle. The sleek vehicle, drawn by a team of smart matched bays, looked new.

"I believe you said we were beyond Lady Cavendish and Lord Kersey since Almack's." Charlotte arched a brow at him as he climbed in and took the ribbons.

He glanced at her sharply, then started the horses. "I did say that, but as you never seemed comfortable with that level of intimacy, and because we have not had a private moment in three months, I thought to err on the side of caution." He looked at her with a wry smile. "You do look lovely, Charlotte."

His words and warm tone sent a thrill coursing through her. "Thank you, Alan. You too are looking extremely well."

"I thought of you often while I worked at Kersey." He frowned. "Although usually I thought of the tableau I stumbled upon of you and Wrotham." His voice grew cool. "Are you now betrothed?"

Charlotte's heart gave a lurch and gripped her reticule.

"No, we are not. He offered, but I refused him. What you saw was an accident." She placed a hand on his arm, giving it a gentle squeeze. "It happened as I explained that night. I did not find you in the drawing room, and when I saw a light under the library door I rushed in, expecting to find you there, and came upon Wrotham instead." She struggled to control her voice, the vivid memory slicing through her resolve, bringing with it a warm tingle in her breasts. "I tripped and landed in his arms. Before I knew what had happened, we were kissing."

"Very thoroughly, from my perspective."

Charlotte's cheeks heated, but something new in his voice made her curious. "Were you jealous?"

"Of course." He frowned as he expertly turned the horses into Hyde Park. "I could only think that it should be me standing there with you in my arms. I had gone to see to the carriage and came back to find you otherwise engaged."

Face now aflame, she paused, ostensibly searching the park for other acquaintances, although in truth she badly needed a moment to recover. The remembrance of that night was swift and sharp. She could feel Wrotham's arms around her again, could smell a phantom splash of his citrusy cologne. The intensity of the memory shook her, made what she had come here to do seem almost a betrayal. A silly notion, as nothing had come of their embrace.

Thank goodness the hour was early. Only one or two people walking and one carriage in the distance. No one would see them together. If she were to shake off the shade of the Earl of Wrotham it was time to be bold.

"Have you forgotten that I never answered your question during our dance in August, Alan?"

"What question?" He looked completely blank.

Well, it had been a long month and he'd had other things on his mind.

"You asked if you should come to my bedroom later. I have an answer, if you'd like to hear it." Lord have mercy, had she really said that? Her heart beat oddly, blood pounding in her ears.

His eyes widened and his hands tightened on the ribbons. "My, my. You *are* the Wicked Widow, aren't you? I am all ears."

Charlotte smiled, confidence returning. "If one has a reputation, one should live up to it, wouldn't you say?"

"Indeed. That has always been my motto." He kept glancing toward her, as though she were some new creature he'd never encountered before. His admiration made her quite giddy. Was this what being wicked felt like?

She prayed, however, he would keep his eyes less on her and more on the path. The last thing she wanted today was an accident in the curricle.

"Perhaps it should become mine as well. You can teach me all you know about being scandalous." Was she actually saying these things to him? She *had* become the Wicked Widow. "Because my answer is yes. Come to my bed, Alan."

He grinned at her, deftly turning the horses toward a lesser-driven path. In moments, they were in a more secluded part of the park than Charlotte had ever seen. But of course a rake would know all the best places for seduction. He pulled the horses to a halt and turned to her.

Grasping her hands, he peered into her face. "I scarcely think you need lessons in being scandalous at all, my lady. So why do you want me in your bed?"

His blunt question stunned her. Her head whirled until she finally blurted out, "Because I want to have passion in my life for once. My husband had no idea of the meaning of the word."

"Hmm. I thought it might be something like that. Or laying to rest a tendre for Wrotham." He squeezed her hand, an excited gleam in his eyes.

Shock rippled through her and her stomach clenched. For a moment, she thought she might cast up her accounts, at which point her embarrassment would be so acute she would pray for death.

"Wh . . . why would you think such a thing? I just told you I had refused him." She pulled her hands out of his grip. Her palms had gone clammy and she rubbed them against the folds of her spencer, trying not to shake. This ride had been a mistake. The whole plan to be seduced by Lord Kersey had been a huge mistake.

"I know what I saw that night in the library, Charlotte. Passion, or the simulation of it, has been my forte for years. That little scene had the ring of truth to it."

"No." The denial came as quickly as she could spit out the word. "He . . . I . . . was taken unawares."

"That is quite often the best way to elicit true passion."

She shook her head violently, although in her heart she suspected he was right. "No. There is nothing between the earl and me."

"Methinks 'the lady doth protest too much.'" His voice remained calm, but he watched her with the tension of a cat at a mouse hole.

"And if I did have a tendre for him . . ." Even that much of a confession sent her heart racing. She tried to calm it and continued, although her patience with him was nearing an end. "Would that prevent you from acting on my request? Why should it matter to you? You're a rakehell of the first water with a scandalous reputation. All I'm asking is for you to act like it."

He threw back his head and laughed.

Charlotte wanted to crawl under the carriage just to get away from the amused wretch. She settled for straining away from him until she clung to the far edge of the seat. At the first bump, she'd likely go flying out. Then, at least, her worries would be over.

His chuckles subsided and he leaned back in the leather

seat. "Regrettably, my circumstances have changed, Charlotte. When I inherited the title, I promised a dying man I would renounce my wild ways and take up the responsibilities of the earldom." He shook his head. "I can scarce believe it when I say it. I have never cared before what people thought of me, which is why they think so little of me now."

He stared out at the lane, a determination tightening his jaw. "So despite having made the declaration to become a better man, I find I do not wish to relinquish my status as a rake so easily. Which makes your offer quite tempting, my dear. Unfortunately, as I am trying to repair my reputation, taking you as my lover during my mourning period would scarcely qualify as reparation."

Charlotte blew out an exasperated breath. "If we were discreet no one would have to know."

"True. Not all my exploits became public property." His eyes pierced her, and she squirmed in her seat. "There is, however, another solution." He paused and grinned. "You could marry me."

Charlotte closed her eyes and silently cursed all men. Her hand itched to slap his handsome, self-assured face. Why did marriage seem the only answer for every man she found attractive?

"I do not wish to marry again."

"From your earlier statement, it hardly seems as if you were married the first time." He leaned in toward her, his lips less than an inch away.

"I hardly was." She need only lean forward and their lips would touch. "So now I want the freedom to make my own decisions about what I do, where I go, who I have in my bed. A husband would not allow that."

"Well, naturally not the last one." He laughed and his eyes went dark. "Not even I, dear Charlotte, would want my wife in another man's bed." He pressed his lips to hers.

Madness seized her. She grasped his head and pressed back, with an urgency designed to obliterate the image that came to her—Wrotham's mouth on hers. Could the man not leave her alone?

Alan slid his tongue inside her mouth. She waited for the frenzy of desire to claim her again; however, after a few moments of him vigorously thrusting in and out, all she felt was a vague sense of disgust. It seemed too stilted, too practiced. Not at all like the intense, soul-stirring experience Lord Wrotham had given her.

She quickly broke off the kiss and peered around. Lord, if anyone had seen that wanton display she'd have little choice in the matter of marriage. There were some lines even a widow could not cross. Discretion remained the best virtue, especially as her interest in the man was fast waning.

"Will you marry me, Charlotte?" He kissed her temple and pressed her head against his shoulder.

She jerked back. "That is the exact thing Lord Wrotham asked me."

Alan disentangled them and looked at her with raised eyebrows. "Indeed."

"He proposed to me just after you saw us in the library." A proposal she now found much more appealing by far.

The earl sat up straighter and collected his ribbons, though he did not start the horses.

Charlotte noted his tension and smiled to herself. "Lord Wrotham has proved a persistent suitor, with very persuasive methods." She stared into his eyes. "Remarkably similar to yours just now."

"Yet he has not persuaded you."

"To marry him, no." She glanced around. "We should perhaps return to the more-frequented areas of the park. Remember, you now have a reputation to protect."

"I believe I will remain untarnished if we let the horses

rest a few moments longer." He looped the ribbons around the whipsocket and adjusted his position so that he faced her fully. "If he has not persuaded you to marry him, then has he persuaded you to some other action?" He drew off his driving gloves and began to tap them lightly on his thigh.

Repressing the urge to laugh, Charlotte merely shook her head. "That would have been my desire precisely. Lord Wrotham, however, is a stickler where it comes to women, even widows. He will have a wedding before a wedding night. Nothing else will do."

"He did seem that type." Kersey's disgruntled tone caught her attention.

"Arguments for a marriage between Wrotham and me are sound and well thought out, I must say." Her gaze lingered on Alan's face. A fine straight nose above the wide mouth, his lips full, though somewhat strained at the moment. The strong chin completed his chiseled look. Attractive an hour ago, but now . . . "Our properties adjoin, I am of sufficient station for his rank, and, as I said, he can be very persuasive when it comes to the physical aspect of marriage."

"But you said—"

She sighed. "He draws the line at the extreme of physical intimacy, although he has no compunction about kissing and caressing me, a bit more . . . energetically than we just did."

"Huh."

"An *arousing* experience, to say the least." Wrotham had aroused her instantly in the library and on the veranda, and on the staircase in the church, if truth be known. "I fear that if he attempts to persuade me one more time, I am liable to be so carried away by his ardor, I will acquiesce and accept him." God, it was true. Having tasted the likes of Kersey and Fernley, she needed no other inducement to choose Wrotham.

Alan stared at her, a tic jumping near his left eye. "Even though you do not wish to marry? Can you not find another man who will warm your bed without requiring matrimony as the price?"

She stared directly into his eyes. "That seems to be rather hard to do these days."

He growled and snared her hand, holding it still against the warmth of his leg. "You will consider him as husband but not me? For the first time I need a wife, Charlotte, not a mistress."

She winced at the word, though it was only the truth. "Indeed nothing seems to exist in-between. There is no way to enjoy one another fully without the need for more."

"What if you find you want more?"

The question took her completely by surprise. She hadn't contemplated the possibility of wanting more of him. Wanting marriage. She'd thought no further than the initial passionate conquest. Could she propose the same thing to Lord Wrotham? The notion tantalized her. Now that Alan was hell-bent on marriage as well, she'd need to find another man with whom to tryst, or choose between the two she'd already approached. And between the two, Wrotham held many more charms than Kersey.

If Wrotham had not already begun to woo Georgina. The thought acted like a dash of cold water in her face.

"Then the morning after I would accept your proposal and be happy." The words came automatically, as Charlotte fought to bring her focus back to the man beside her.

But the wind had shifted.

Faced with the choice between Wrotham, Kersey, or the other few men she'd met at the end of the Season, there was no choice really. If truth be told, she'd known before she came to London who she desired and hadn't wanted to admit it. Hadn't wanted to acknowledge that she might want to give up her freedom for another man.

She could fool herself no longer. She had no more long-ing for Lord Kersey than she had had for Lord Fernley. A shiver went through her. She would consult Georgina as soon as she arrived home. If Lord Wrotham were still free, she would see if she could persuade him anew. If not . . .

Alan unwound the ribbons and clucked to the bays. They stepped out, prancing into a trot as they raced back to find a few more vehicles had joined them. Charlotte nodded to several acquaintances, though they did not stop until the horses drew up in front of Theale's town house. A groom came up to hold them and Alan handed her down the steps.

"How long are you in London?" he asked, holding her waist lightly.

"Almost no time." She hastened to make that clear. She wanted no more calls from the Earl of Kersey. "Less than a week, I'm afraid. They have had to push back the harvest because the crops are so poor from the cold and wet. But I am determined to be there for my first ingath-ering as mistress of Lyttlefield." The thought filled her with a sense of purpose and contentment. *Her fields.*

"I am likewise engaged with the business of the earl-dom for the next several weeks. I will be visiting all my properties, using London as a base." He paused, as if thinking, calculating. "Will you be in London or Kent by the middle of October?"

"In Kent assuredly, for the harvest and celebration af-terward. I don't plan to return to London until the middle of the Season."

"That is right, you mentioned in the library that your second house party would be held at about that time. I hope I am invited this time." His lascivious grin set her teeth on edge.

Lord, she'd forgotten that bit of madness, born on the spur of a very dangerous moment. "Yes, so good of you to remember." She forced herself to continue. "It would be lovely if you could attend." She'd almost rather have a repeat of the Fernley performance.

"I will look forward to it with the utmost anticipation. By the end of the party I hope we will be able to reach an understanding." He licked his lips. "I will be counting the days until I see you again. Think of me, will you?"

He kissed her hand, lingering over it so long she had to repress the urge to squirm. With a bow, he climbed up and took the ribbons. A quick shake set the team to their paces. As soon as the curricle turned the corner, she wiped her hand on her skirt and strode into the house.

Tomorrow she'd return to Kent and seek out the Earl of Wrotham. One way or the other, she would make the man declare himself. A wave of dizziness made her grab the newel post as she remembered the last time he had done so. After all that kissing, her legs had been so weak the library wall couldn't hold her up. Oh, to be kissed that way again. Very well, this time they would come to an accord, even if it meant relinquishing her hard-earned freedom.

Chapter 17

Nash knocked on the door of Lyttlefield Park, still pondering his invitation to tea with Lady Georgina. Except for church services, he'd not seen her since the evening they'd spent at the Stokes dinner party, talking about banalities while he plucked up the nerve to ask if Charlotte had been to London.

He'd been busy with matters having to do with the estate. The harvest was in full swing at last, although it would be a dismal one this year. The poor stand of wheat barely needed gathering, but it had to be done. According to Alfred Smith, this year would hold the distinction of latest harvest on record.

Neither had he solved the problem of the robbers, whose attacks had become less frequent but more daring. Throughout all these calls on his time, he still thought daily about Lady Cavendish.

Fisk answered the door and showed him into the drawing room, just as on the first day he had met Charlotte here. He'd thought of her as Charlotte ever since her slip on the steps of the tower had given him the excuse to call her by her first name. He hoped soon he would be allowed the privilege in truth instead of in secret.

The woman who awaited him there today, however, could not have been more different from his lady. Lady Georgina Kirkpatrick stood perhaps five feet tall, no bigger than a child really. Her tiny figure and effervescent attitude toward life enhanced this youthful aura. The bright auburn hair and green eyes—so like Charlotte's, his mind insisted—and the sprinkle of bran across her nose completed the fresh face. Dressed in a lovely pink-and-white-striped day gown that accented her luscious figure, Lady Georgina appeared a marvelous mixture of youth and maturity.

"Lord Wrotham. How kind of you to come. Let me ring for tea." Georgina pulled the bell and Fisk entered the room as though he'd been standing guard.

"Yes, my lady?"

"Bring the tea, Fisk, please." Composed as any London hostess, Georgina smiled at Nash and indicated a seat on the sofa. "Won't you sit down, my lord?"

Nash returned her smile and sat. "Thank you, my lady." Nash paused, then plowed ahead. "How have you been, Lady Georgina? It has been too long since we met."

Georgina laughed. "We saw one another at church on Sunday, my lord. Scarcely three days ago."

He shook his head and glanced away. "I meant more than just a nod at church. We haven't spoken since the Stokes dinner party in August."

"A lack I am seeking to remedy today." The butler entered with the tea tray. After he deposited it on the table, Georgina poured.

"Milk or sugar?"

"Sugar only, please."

She smiled, added the required items, and handed Nash a cup. "You have been well also, I trust?"

"In excellent health, thank you." Time to leap past this

banal conversation and get to the reason he'd accepted the invitation. "I noticed Lady Cavendish did not attend church this Sunday past. I hope that does not indicate she is unwell." Perhaps the reply to that innocent question would answer his more burning one.

"No, Charlotte was in fine fettle when she left on Saturday. She's gone to London to meet Jane and enjoy some of the Little Season." She looked brightly at him, unaware of the dagger she'd thrust into his heart.

He dropped his gaze to stare dully at the teacup cradled in her hands. Damn. He'd known it was inevitable she'd go to London. The possibility she was meeting Kersey there turned his stomach. If so, there was nothing he could do about it, despite the letters he would surely receive from Lord Grafton or his own fears for Charlotte's reputation. He could not leave with the harvest nigh upon them and the robber gang still unchecked.

If only he'd been able to woo her properly before she left, he might have managed a better proposal than that slipshod affair in the library. The problem had been persuading her to talk to him. If he called at Lyttlefield, she was out or indisposed. At the Stokes party she had acted afraid to speak to him, practically barricading herself with old Lady Penelope in the corner of the drawing room after dinner.

"Lady John, that is." Georgina broke in on his thoughts. She pouted her lips and frowned comically. "I do wish we could all be just Jane and Charlotte and Georgina."

"You may call me Nash, my lady." The words came automatically to his lips, his mind still churning at the information of Charlotte's departure. Had she gone to Lord Kersey's bed rather than marry him? The earl's vengeance seemed mild in comparison to the devastation of having lost his chance with his daughter.

"And you must call me Georgina, or Georgie, as the others do." She beamed at Nash. "I feel ever so much more at ease when I can address someone by a name rather than a title. More tea, Nash?" Her eyes twinkled when she said it.

He nodded, distracted for a moment by her charm and lively demeanor. She should enjoy all the entertainments in London during the next Season. He'd be surprised if she wasn't quite the rage in the spring. A question tugged at his mind. "Why did you not accompany Charlotte, Georgina? Did you not wish to enjoy the Little Season as well?"

She poured more tea into his cup and moved the sugar dish closer to him, all the time avoiding his eyes. "I actually enjoy it here more. There is peace and quiet and a chance to rest without . . . feeling guilty." Georgie finally lifted her gaze to his. "The truth is, I pretended to be ill the morning we were to leave. I pled a megrim, which I have suffered from on occasion."

"So you wished to remain in the country? I'm sure Charlotte would have understood that." Nash dropped two lumps of sugar into his cup and stirred. He raised the tea to his lips, savoring the fragrant aroma of the blend before putting the cup to his lips.

"I wished to meet with you, Nash, without Charlotte's knowledge."

Nash had to fight to keep from spewing tea all over his hostess. His mouth on fire, he took a deep breath and swallowed. The burn traced a path into his belly, where it seemed willing to stay.

When he could speak, he asked, "You wished to talk to me?" What on earth might Georgina need to say that she didn't want Charlotte to know about? Was this invitation some sort of ploy to compromise him into marriage? He'd noticed Georgie's partiality at the house party, and she'd seemed very attentive toward him the other times they'd met as well. They might indeed suit. If not for Charlotte . . .

"Yes, and I'm going to be rather forward, Nash. Are you in love with Charlotte?" Georgina tilted her head expectantly.

His breath stopped. So fortunate he had not drunk more tea. This woman, in her own way, was as unconventional as her friend. Not his experience with ladies at all. Did all widows behave this way? He put the cup back in its saucer and rose. Pacing to the window, he stalled for time to figure out the reason behind such an outrageous question and how to answer it.

After discarding several scurrilous replies, he decided to simply tell the truth and shame the devil.

"Yes, Georgina, I am in love with her." To say it so baldly made it sound like a confession. "I haven't always wanted that, but then, love does not always come from the head." He tried to keep some of the bitterness from his voice. A losing battle at best. "She refused me, did you know that?" A glance at her showed a slow nod. "And she would not let me even talk to her before she left. I suspect I know what that means."

Georgina sipped her tea and shot him a peculiar look through narrowed eyes. "I wonder if you do indeed, Nash. But continue."

He sighed and seized a cut-glass tumbler from the sideboard. Something stronger than tea was necessary for this conversation. A quick survey of the sideboard revealed no spirits. Damn. He set the glass down again. "You said she is in London. I suspect I know who she plans to see while there."

"I would be surprised if you did not."

With a mumbled curse, Nash threw himself back down into the chair. "Then I suppose it does not matter at all whether I love her or not. She has made her choice. I cannot take a complete wanton to wife." It was on the tip of his tongue to add, "No matter what her father wants."

"I'm sure Charlotte is not as shameless as you believe." Georgie sipped her tea, looking thoughtful. "Until just before her trip to London she was completely disinterested in Lord Kersey."

"I suppose she received the name the 'Wicked Widow' for completely innocent reasons?"

"Actually, she did."

His mouth must have fallen open in astonishment because Georgina laughed and pushed it closed.

"Lord Kersey took advantage of Charlotte's inexperience at a public entertainment. That is how he managed to take her away from you in the first place. She'd only attended one or two balls before her wedding and none afterward. He led her astray and she followed. Fortunately, nothing came of it, save that silly nickname." She met his eyes steadily. "I believe she has a deep regard for you too, Nash."

Their heated encounter in the library surfaced effortlessly. That kiss had all but undone him. A minute more and passion would have overtaken them, for she had protested not a jot. Passion, therefore, didn't seem to be the problem.

"It is not her regard for me that creates the difficulty, Georgina. Her desire to be a free woman trumps anything she may feel for me." The agonizing truth became clear to him. Charlotte did not fear he would be unkind or an unskilled lover or a bad provider. His attributes mattered not at all. "The institution of marriage itself is her enemy. One to which, I fear, she will not surrender." He smiled kindly at Georgina, a melancholy stealing over him. "So, you see, I am left with a dilemma. I need to marry and produce an heir to inherit my title. As Charlotte refuses, I must take another woman to wife." He stared into green eyes that widened as he took her hand. "Have you thought about that, Georgina?"

Her hand trembled in his and he rubbed his thumb over the white knuckles.

"Yes, I have." She dropped her gaze to her lap, silent for so long Nash began to shift in his seat. Had she gone into shock? He chaffed her hands, trying to bring warmth back into the cold little fingers.

A profound sadness settled over his heart, but he disregarded it. If Charlotte would not be his countess, did it truly matter who would? He liked Georgina. She would make a good companion, an excellent wife. Just not the one he wanted.

Finally, he slipped two fingers under her chin and tipped her head back until he could see her beautiful face, so pale the bran that dusted her nose and cheeks stood out like dark stars.

He gathered his courage, looked deep into her eyes, and asked, "Then will you marry me, Georgina?"

Chapter 18

"Have some more of the gooseberry tart, Georgie." Charlotte offered her the last bite then sat back, watching as her friend shook her head and sighed contentedly. Charlotte had returned home late last night and could scarcely contain her curiosity about Georgina and Lord Wrotham.

"I could not hold one more berry." Georgina smiled and sipped her tea. "You should have it, Charlotte. You've barely eaten anything. I should not have asked so many questions, but you've had such adventures in London I am quite jealous. However, as you've described them in such detail, I almost feel as if I had been there with you."

Charlotte toyed with her teacup, pushing the handle to and fro. "I do wish you had been, my dear. I would have relished your company. But we will have a visit there together after the harvest, with lots of shopping. We must start in good time to outfit you for the Season."

"Now, Charlotte—"

"We have been over this, Georgie. I am determined you will eclipse every woman in the *ton* next spring." She gripped the cup's handle. "Unless, of course, you have decided to marry before then."

Her friend made no response other than to smile and sip her tea. The girl had said nothing about Lord Wrotham since Charlotte's return, and her silence on the subject was driving Charlotte to distraction. Had something transpired while she had been in Town? Her pulse beat hard and fast, wondering what she would do if Wrotham had indeed declared himself.

"Now you must tell me what you have been doing since I left. Did . . . did you have any callers?" Charlotte tried to appear nonchalant and failed miserably.

"Yes, I did have several, who helped me pass the time quite well. Lady Fitzroy called the day after you left. She was all in a dither about . . ." Georgie continued, laughing animatedly about the local baronet's wife and her feud with her neighbor, Mrs. Lawson-Smythe.

Charlotte made herself pay attention, although she couldn't help but wonder who else Georgie had seen this past week. If Lord Wrotham had come, would she even tell her? But her friend couldn't know about her interest in Wrotham. Could she?

"And then, of course, I asked Lord Wrotham to tea on Tuesday."

Charlotte stared at her, stunned beyond belief. "You did?" A sinking sensation began in her stomach and radiated out toward her limbs, down to her fingers and toes.

"Yes. He is such a kind man, with such charming manners. I do wish now I had danced with him at the house party, although I suspect I shall have another chance shortly." Georgina sat back, a satisfied smile on her face.

"You do?" A sense of foreboding gripped Charlotte with icy fingers.

"Why, yes. Don't you plan to have dancing at your upcoming party?" The girl cocked her head, as if puzzled, but a twinkle of mischief showed clearly in her eyes.

"Of course I do. Georgie . . ." Oh, drat it. At this point, her nerves stretched tighter than a violin string, she didn't care about propriety. "Did Lord Wrotham . . . ask you something?"

"Oh, yes. I meant to tell you." Georgie leaned toward her.

Charlotte steeled herself for the blow.

"He asked me about you."

Charlotte stared at her, relief cascading through her. "He did?"

"Yes, just before he asked me to marry him."

"What?" Her blood froze in her veins. She stared into her friend's smiling face and simply wanted to die.

"It wasn't the grand romantic gesture Isaac made, going down on one knee and bringing me flowers, but it was a proposal." Georgie's face lit up at the fond memory.

"So I am to wish you happy, Georgie?" Numb all over, Charlotte wasn't quite sure what to say. She didn't want to accept what she'd just heard, but she had no choice. Lord Wrotham had taken her at her word and found another woman to be his wife.

"Oh, no, I didn't accept him, Charlotte." Georgie shook her head, her red ringlets bobbing beside her face. "I simply couldn't do that."

Warmth flooded Charlotte's cold body, as though the sun had come out radiantly after days of snow and ice. She gasped and covered her face, fighting tears. After a few breaths to steady herself, Charlotte recovered enough to ask, "Why not, Georgie?"

"Because, my dear, I don't love him." She grasped Charlotte's hands. "I am not unaware of the honor it would be to become the Countess of Wrotham. And I confess I did consider it during the house party."

Charlotte nodded. "I suspected as much. You seemed to get on well with Lord Wrotham."

"Jemmy broached it to me. He made me see how good a match it would be. He even hinted that it might reconcile me with Father." She smiled wistfully. "Lord Wrotham is a very amiable gentleman. He looked out for me at The Bull, helped me be part of the conversation."

"You were flirting shamelessly with him, Georgie."

Her trilling little laugh filled the room. "I did, didn't I?" She sounded quite proud of it. "Quite astonishingly, he made me want to have fun again. Something I never thought I'd do after Isaac died." Her face sobered and a fierce light shone in her eyes. "But I had true love in my first marriage. I'll not settle for less the second time." She patted her lips, laid her napkin down, and rose. "I must write to Jemmy. He will be disappointed, I fear, but he will understand when I explain it to him."

"How did Lord Wrotham take your refusal?" Charlotte folded her napkin, carefully keeping her eyes down.

"He seemed a bit confused," she said, frowning at the memory. "As if he didn't think he'd heard me correctly. Then I told him I understood the great honor he bestowed upon me by asking me, but I thought it would be a mistake."

Charlotte's head came up. Georgie had mettle she'd never dreamed of.

"He didn't protest at all." She smiled straight at Charlotte. "I believe he knew I was right."

After Georgie left, Charlotte stayed at the table, her head spinning with her friend's story. She needed to confront the earl immediately. He had meant it when he said he wanted a wife. If she didn't act fast, she might find he had already asked yet another woman, although she could think of no reason for such haste on his part. Still, if she wanted to secure Lord Wrotham, she had best do it now.

Did she want to secure him? The outrageous thumping

of her heart when she had thought him betrothed to Georgie told her she had already made her choice. Her interest in him, which had begun that night at Almack's, had grown stealthily over the ensuing weeks and months. His admission to saving Edward, if nothing else, would make her esteem him above all other men. His manner toward her during the house party had persuaded her that he might have similar feelings for her. Of course, their encounter in the library left no doubt whatsoever of his attraction and his intentions. A pity he would consider nothing other than marriage, but if the man was bound and determined to have her as his wife, she would renounce her independence. And perhaps be happy at last.

Contentment flowed through her like a river of joy. She would go now. An urgency swept through her, a desire to see him again, to touch and hold him before she lost him. The sensible thing would be to send a footman to Wrotham Hall, requesting him to call on her. Her stomach twisted at the thought of waiting even an hour. No, she must do something. Go to him, pursue him. Her last act of freedom.

A scandalous proposition for her to visit a bachelor household unaccompanied, but a necessity in this case. She wanted him to herself, without a companion in tow. If she went on horseback rather than in the carriage, she could go to him and return with no one the wiser.

Both Rose and Georgina would try to dissuade her from this rash action, so she must employ stealth. Her next problems, therefore, would be how to change into her riding habit and escape the house and stables undetected. She would address those obstacles first. Planning her capitulation to Lord Wrotham could wait until she was underway.

* * *

Contrary to her expectations, donning her black wool riding habit undetected had been simple. She had summoned Rose, who had assisted Charlotte with her gown, and told the maid she would be riding alone in the park.

"You aren't taking anyone with you, my lady?" Rose pretended to be removing a piece of lint from the tailored jacket when she cut her eyes slyly toward Charlotte.

"A little solitude after all the constant company in London will be a welcome respite." Charlotte placed her most fetching bonnet on her head and adjusted it to her satisfaction.

"As you say, my lady," Rose sniffed. "You've put on fine feathers to impress the grooms, it seems." Her eyes widened as she clamped her hand over her mouth. "Oh, my lady. Not . . . not again?"

Charlotte cocked her head, truly befuddled. Then it dawned on her. Rose had been her maid since her comeout. She had been with her all through the miserable debacle of her secret affair with Edward.

With a laugh, Charlotte squeezed the maid's hand. "No, I promise, I am not in love with James or Clarence. But who knows who may see me going to or from the stable? One should always be dressed impeccably, no matter what."

Rose's shoulders slumped, her worried frown lifting. "Well, you'll certainly turn the head of whoever sees you, my lady."

Charlotte smiled at the compliment. She prayed the woman spoke true.

Rose headed into the dressing room to put away the discarded day dress and Charlotte slipped out into the hall. No one stirred, but she wasn't sure where Georgie might be. The secrecy might seem silly, but she didn't want anyone to know what she was up to until she returned, a betrothed woman. She hurried to the end of the corridor and down the servants' staircase to the kitchen. At the bottom of the stairs, she paused to listen to Mrs. Hatchette giving orders to the scullery maid about the dishes.

Holding her breath, Charlotte eased across the archway unseen and quietly opened the door to the garden. She ducked around the side of the house and, once out of sight of any of the kitchen staff who might look out the back door, stood gauging the next part of her adventure—the stable.

Chapter 19

From the kitchen garden, Charlotte fled stealthily toward the stables. Now how to saddle up without anyone being the wiser? If she took her groom, even if she swore him to secrecy, he still might talk. Such tittle-tattle in the servants' hall was as good as an on-dit in the *Times*. But drat it, she had no idea how to saddle a horse.

Why hadn't she gotten Edward to show her how to do it? Of course, she'd thought he'd always be there to do it for her. And then, they had had more important things to do, like eloping. She paused, prepared for the ache to settle in her heart as it always had when thinking of him.

Over the years since that horrible night, she'd thought of Edward almost constantly. First, in grief over his loss, then as an escape from life with Sir Archibald. She would lay in bed at night and remember the first time she and Edward had kissed. They had ridden out, even though the sky had threatened rain. As they approached the far side of the estate, it had begun to pour. He had called, "I told you so" and led their horses to a thick copse of trees. She'd slid off Bella straight into his arms and then raised her face to his. The touch of his lips had been both expected and completely surprising. He had held her to his strong chest as the rain drenched them and she had been overwhelmed by a sense of safety and happiness she'd never experienced before in her life.

After that day, she'd plotted incessantly how they could be together. Edward had been reluctant at first, but she'd coaxed him to help her plan their escape. She'd known it would be a shocking mésalliance—she would be shunned by everyone in the *ton*—but she hadn't cared. All she had cared about had been Edward's arms around her, his kiss on her lips, and a life with love and happiness and children.

That dream had been snuffed out in Whetstone. And for six years, whenever she had thought of him, her heart had ached for what might have been.

This time, however, only excitement and anticipation at the thought of seeing Lord Wrotham pulsed within her. Another sign, perhaps, that her present course was the true one. That Nash had been the one to save Edward still left her in awe. Did that circumstance have anything to do with her current affection for the Earl of Wrotham? She had certainly thought more of him and less of Edward since his revelation. Perhaps it was time to put aside her dreams of Edward and embrace Nash wholeheartedly. The two men resembled one another physically only in their height and dark coloring. But in their manner, in their caring natures and regard for her, they seemed almost as one. If she could make a life with Nash, she might finally find the love and happiness she had been denied for so long.

Charlotte crept into the stable, beguiled anew by the warm, comforting smell of horses, hay, and manure. Now to devise a way to have the groom saddle her horse without asking any questions.

The answer came with such startling clarity and simplicity that it took her breath.

She squared her shoulders and strode into the middle of the stable. "Clarence! James!" At her bold call, the grooms came scampering out of several stalls, one tucking the tail of his work shirt into his pants.

"Yes, my lady?"

"Please saddle Ajax for me immediately." She glanced from James, perhaps fifteen years old, to Clarence, who might be a pair of years older, both local lads who had been on the property when she took possession. She'd had little interaction with them herself, usually sending word to have her horse readied for a ride.

They exchanged a glance before looking back at her.

"Will there be others in the party, my lady?" Clarence asked, looking behind her.

"No. I'll ride alone today." Charlotte raised her chin and tried to affect a nonchalant air. In truth, her stomach twisted itself in knots.

"Very well, my lady. Clarence, I'll ready her ladyship's horse. You get yours saddled so you can accompany her." James turned toward the stall where her horse whinnied.

"That won't be necessary, Clarence. I am going for a short ride in the park today. I won't need a groom with me."

It had occurred to Charlotte, out of the blue, that she was mistress here. She need not answer to father, husband, or stable boy. If she wanted to ride without a groom, then by God she would. Who could stop her?

"Ride alone, my lady?" James stared, uncomprehending. "But you always ride with one of us to protect you."

"I'll not be gone long, and I doubt I'll need protection in my own park." Why would the lads argue with her?

"There's robbers about, my lady," Clarence said, his face grave. "It's not safe no more."

"Well, I doubt they will accost me in the little time I wish to be out. Please saddle my horse now." She firmed her tone to a command. If it took that to get her way in this, so be it.

"Yes, my lady." The boys spoke in unison and jumped into action. In less time than it had taken to persuade them, Charlotte found herself up on Ajax and headed out the stable door with the admonition to be careful ringing in her ears.

A thrill of power rushed through her. She had gainsaid someone and gotten her way for the first time since her marriage. Even if they were only stable boys in her employ, she hoped it boded well for her coming meeting.

She headed the gelding toward the park, just in case the grooms were watching. When she topped a rise near a stand of trees, she turned left and struck out for the road that led to the drive at Lyttlefield. According to Lord Wrotham, Wrotham Hall lay two miles farther down the road. A quick ride on a cantering horse, he had declared. She decided to test his word and touched her heel to Ajax.

In what seemed truly no time, Charlotte turned between the huge carved marble pedestals, lions rampant as though daring her to enter and beard her lion in his den. She ignored the fanciful thought and continued to canter down the drive, until the grand edifice of Wrotham Hall came into view.

Nothing the earl had said about his home had prepared her for the vast mansion that rose before her. She slowed Ajax to a trot, eventually stopping completely to gawk at the amazing structure. A yellow-white Palladian house sprawled amid manicured lawns, woodland rising in the distance behind it. Three stories high and perfectly proportioned in width, with four flattened columns, two on either side of the front door, the house appeared to be a model of Georgian architecture. The symmetry and grandeur quite took her breath away. To be mistress of such a house, to put her own stamp on this magnificent estate, would be such an exciting challenge. Much more so than her efforts at Lyttlefield, which she had enjoyed immensely.

Finally recalled to her purpose, Charlotte urged her mount forward. By the time she had arrived at the front portico, a groom had appeared to hold her reins and assist her to the ground. She thanked him, marched up to the imposing oak and ironwork door. Focusing only on her purpose, she summoned all her courage and raised her hand to the knocker.

Nash stared at the list of names, fighting not to crush it in his fury. He needed the information it contained, although he'd read its contents often enough he'd almost committed it to memory. Six of his tenant families had been attacked in the last week by this gang of what purported to be ex-soldiers. Unable to secure work after the war, they had taken matters into their own hands by robbing and pillaging in hopes of stealing enough for their families to survive.

Nash shook his head. Soldiers. He could scarcely credit it.

He'd received the report late last night and this morning, he'd ridden out to the latest victim, James Wright, a wheelwright by trade. What he had found had not been pretty. He closed his eyes and swore under his breath.

There was a knock at the door, and Acres opened it to announce, "Lady Cavendish is here, my lord. She's in the small reception room."

Nash's head jerked up. *Charlotte?* He tossed the list onto his cluttered desk and all but ran from the room. He strode swiftly into the green chamber and stopped. She stood in the middle of the room, severe in a black riding habit, but with a ravishing hat sitting jauntily on her head, its ostrich feather trailing over her shoulder. Like an invitation to likewise run his fingers down her back.

"My lady, what a lovely surprise." Nash rushed toward her and raised her hand to his mouth. He let his lips linger as he studied her face. What could have brought her here without a companion?

"I am so pleased to see you, my lord. I recently returned from London and wanted to call on you." She stared back at him, eyes bright, smile wide. Then she squeezed the hand he still kissed. Not as if to say, "Let go." Rather as though . . . good Lord, was the woman flirting with him?

Taken aback by this possibility, Nash released her hand and bowed. "I am delighted to see you again as well, my lady. When I heard you had removed to London, I feared we would be deprived of the pleasure of your company for quite some time to come. I am pleased to see that those fears were unfounded."

Her brilliant smile went straight to his heart.

"Please, my lord. I believe we are beyond the formalities. Will you not call me Charlotte?"

A rush of hot blood shot from his head straight to his groin. His breathing came sharper and a metallic taste flooded his mouth.

"I would be delighted to do so . . . Charlotte." The name sounded like liquid gold.

Her eyes crinkled, as though she enjoyed it as well.

"Then you must call me Nash."

"Nash." She tried it out, elongating the single syllable, savoring it.

His heart raced like a runaway carriage.

"You have been well, Nash?" Her eyes sparkled and she hummed with the same energy as that night at Almack's.

"I have been very well, thank you." The memory of his errand this morning, unfortunately, sobered him from the giddy aura her presence had created.

"Is something wrong?" Even her frown was charming.

"I rode out earlier to see one of my tenants who had been burned out last night."

"What?" The flirtatious woman fled like a lantern snuffed; in her stead was an outraged landowner. The lines on her face deepened. "Who?"

"James Wright, the village wheelwright, is the latest victim of the gang that's been terrorizing Kent for the last two months." He motioned her to a leather wing-backed chair and sat in its companion beside her.

"James's family has lived on Wrotham property for over six generations. The family works together to farm the land while James plies his trade. Now their house is in ruins, the contents ransacked, James's tools stolen." The sight had sickened him. "Even worse, James and his wife looked on helplessly while the gang of masked men looted and burned their home in broad daylight."

"Was anyone hurt?" Charlotte asked.

Nash shook his head. "They were lucky. Neither they nor any of their six children were harmed. I spent the morning arranging lodging for them until their house can be rebuilt. I'll see about replacing James's tools also, though I'll have to send to Maidstone or perhaps Rochester for them."

Charlotte looked at him, a softness in her face. "You're a good landlord, Nash. You care greatly about the people here."

"They depend on me." As simple as that. "I can't fail them. That's why I'm working so hard to find this gang and see justice done. They seem not to be local men. No one has identified them. And their violence seems to be escalating. There's no telling who they will attack next." He gazed into her eyes. He'd thought them green, but today they were gray-green flecked with brown.

"That is appalling. I had no idea they had gotten so out of hand." She looked indignant rather than frightened, which concerned him not a little.

"In fact, when you leave, I'll send one of my grooms with you. Only one person to protect you is not enough any longer." Nash patted her hand. "I want to keep you safe, Charlotte."

Her gaze suddenly plummeted to her lap, where her hands now twisted in her skirt. What did that mean? Nash lifted her chin.

"Charlotte? What's wrong?"

She sighed and her hands stilled. "I suppose you'll find out anyway."

He gripped her hands. "Find out what? Were you attacked on the way over?"

"No, but . . . I rode here alone."

"Alone?" His blood froze. "Don't you know how dangerous that is?"

"No, I didn't. The grooms mentioned a gang of robbers, but I didn't think they would attack in the daytime." Her voice rose, petulant.

"Obviously they will attack whenever they please." He couldn't believe she had been so stupid. "You were lucky you were not robbed or worse."

"Well, I wasn't, so there is no harm done." Charlotte pulled her hand from his grip and stood. The light had gone out of her eyes.

Nash rose as well, scowling. "There might very well have been. I know you have been told you should always ride with a man present. Every girl is given that instruction from the schoolroom."

She rounded on him, her formerly gray eyes now a furious green. "I am not a girl, I'm a woman. A woman free to make her own decisions. If I want to ride to London without an escort, I can do it. No one can tell me what to do and not do."

"Well, perhaps someone should!"

Charlotte's face went white and she drew back her hand to slap his face. He caught her wrist and pulled her against his chest, imprisoning her. He expected another attack, but none came. Surprisingly, as in the library, she relaxed against him. Nash gently drew his arms around her waist. The woman was such an enigma. Never could he predict what she would do next.

She lifted her face, slid her arms around his neck, and pulled him toward her.

Nash groaned as her soft lips met his. She turned her head, sealing their mouths perfectly, then opened herself to him. He needed no further invitation, by God, and thrust his tongue into her mouth.

Raging heat blasted through him, filling him with a lust he could scarcely contain. His shaft swelled until it strained against the fall of his breeches. He hoped she could feel it prodding against her, seeking that for which it was meant. He didn't care what she had come for; she had found this instead.

The incredible taste of her overwhelmed him. Wine and sweetness, like a single drop from a honeysuckle, mixed together created a delicious treat for him to explore. He slowed his frantic pace, licking, tickling, savoring every inch of her.

When she pressed her tongue into his mouth, he thought he would burst. She took her time, advancing an inch, retreating a bit, exploring as he had done but languorously, as if she had all the time in the world.

He didn't. If he didn't make a move to get her into his bedroom quickly, their first lovemaking would be on the hard floor of this receiving room. Not an auspicious beginning to their marriage.

Her hands moved to the waistband of his breeches.

To hell with the floor. He scooped her up in his arms, their lips becoming disengaged. "Come with me?" Nash had to ask. Had to make sure she wanted this . . . with him.

Charlotte nodded against his chest. "It's why I'm here."

The world spun. She was his at last. He crushed her to

him and ran for the stairs, taking them two at a time. On
the first floor he turned toward his suite of rooms, which
took up the whole north corner of the house. He slammed
the door to his sitting room open, then kicked it closed.

He stood in the middle of the room, spun in a circle.
What must he do first? His breath puffed like a steam en-
gine. His heart pounded frantically. He still clutched her
to him, yet she made no protest. Slowly, he released her
and she slid down his whole length, clutching his neck
until her toes touched the floor.

Charlotte looked into his face. "Oh, Nash." Desire
flickered once more in her green eyes.

God, if this was a dream he'd rather die than awaken.

He ran his hands through her hair—her hat had been
abandoned downstairs—scattering pins as he drew it down
around her shoulders. The glossy chestnut curls slipped
through his fingers like strands of silk. What a joy it would
be to see them fanned across his pillow.

The image swelled his erection even more, though he
wouldn't have believed that possible. They needed to
hurry or he might be rougher with her than he intended.
"This way, love." With his arm at her waist, Nash urged
her toward his bed chamber. She strode across the threshold, his at last.

She approached the bed, somewhat hesitantly, though
that seemed natural under the circumstances. At last she
turned and beckoned him. When he stood in front of her,
scarcely daring to breathe, she leaned forward and raised
up on her toes to whisper in his ear, "I am yours, Nash."

"Oh, Charlotte." He ran a finger down the length of
her arm. Her shudder fed his heat and he pulled her close.

"I am yours," she repeated, raising her hand to cup his
face, "if you want me."

Chapter 20

"**M**y God, Charlotte." He seized her again and crushed her against his chest. "I have wanted you since the moment I saw you across the dance floor at Almack's."

"You did?" Her words were muffled, and she turned her head. "I tried to find you after Mr. Garrett—or rather Lord Kersey—brought me back to Jane, but she said you had gone."

"I left early." He didn't want to think of her with that rakehell. Not now of all times.

"Why? I wanted to dance with you. You had to have known that."

He released her and stepped back. Best get this out in the open if they were to marry. "Because I saw you emerge from the stairwell, your hair mussed, your lips swollen."

She gasped, turning her back on him. "Oh, no."

"Yes. The sight convinced me you were involved with Kersey. Next morning, when I heard you being called the 'Wicked Widow,' I dismissed you out of hand. I will not marry a woman tainted by scandal." God, but he hated to ask this, but he had to know from her own lips. "Did you have an affair with Lord Kersey?"

She rounded on him, her eyes glowing with anger. "No. I never sought his attentions. It may have seemed that way to you, but I will swear to you that he has done nothing compared to what you just did."

At that his stern demeanor melted. He grabbed her and pressed his lips to hers again.

"Good," he said when he could speak at last. He pushed several strands of hair away from her face. So beautiful and strong. And vulnerable. How could he not want the responsibility of keeping her safe from everyone, including herself?

"Then will you marry me, Charlotte?" He feathered kisses along her hairline, down over her forehead. "I want us to have passion for each other that lasts until neither one of us knows the meaning of the word." He kissed the tip of her nose. "And I want it to begin now. I must marry and produce an heir for the earldom. And I cannot do that, and have a passionate life with you, unless you marry me."

He continued to trail kisses down to her mouth, brushed it with a kiss. He would have continued to her cheeks, but she suddenly pressed his lips again, holding him there.

Nash slid his arm around her, pulling her closer to him. She molded her body to his, aligning her hips to his and inflaming his desire once more. He caressed her back, sensitive even through her clothes, for she sighed at his touch, then moaned louder when he squeezed her bottom. God, she responded to his every touch so sweetly.

Nash ground his hips against hers, letting her feel his member, once again hot and hard and ready for her. She groaned, wrapped her arm around his buttocks, and tried to pull him toward the bed. After a moment's resistance, Nash allowed it, walking her backward until she fell onto the mattress with him on top of her. Good. Right where he wanted her.

He found her ear and rimmed the outside shell with his tongue, wetting it. Then blew gently, delighted when she shuddered beneath him. He traveled the short distance to her tantalizing lobe where a jet teardrop hung. Pushing the ornament aside, he nipped and sucked until she panted in his ear. She kneaded his back, tearing at his coat as she writhed beneath him. When he dragged his tongue down her neck, frantic, incoherent cries burst from her.

Slowly, Nash began a series of shallow thrusts, rubbing himself against her in an attempt to stimulate the spot he knew sent many women into climax. At the same time, he continued licking and sucking her neck, searching out the sweet spot that drove women mad with desire.

"Nash. Oh, Nash." Charlotte's moans deepened. "Nash, please." She began to pull at his clothing and thrust her hips against his already throbbing cock.

Oh, but this would be sweet. He sat up, shedding his coat, then unbuttoning his fall. On their wedding night he'd make sure to go slower, but now—

Christ. She hadn't accepted him. Repressing his own groans of need, Nash stopped and rolled off her. He lay on his back, trying to will his erection to calm before it was too late.

Charlotte sat up, eyes wild and dark with desire. "Nash! What are you doing? Why did you stop?" Her words were breathy, strained. She grabbed his hand and tried to pull him back toward her.

He rolled onto his side and stared into the face he longed to see beneath him once more. "I cannot until you give me your answer, Charlotte. I will not make love to you unless we are wed. Or at least betrothed."

"Ah, you wretch!" She flung herself back on the bed. "Yes, yes. There, I have said it." She lay still, panting. "Why did you do that to me? I want you!"

"Oh, God, thank you." Nash grabbed her hand. "Do you think I do not want you as well?" He pushed it down to his groin, held it against his rock-hard staff. "Ever since you arrived, I have wanted to do nothing so much as sink this into you and revel in the passion we could share." He released her hand and pounced on her.

She laughed and twined her arms around his neck.

"But I would not dishonor you if there was no contract of marriage between us. I gave your father my word to protect you, not debauch you."

"My father? What are you talking about?" She stilled, as if turned to stone.

Damn his tongue.

She pushed at his chest. "Let me up."

He rolled off her and she bolted up, her brow furrowed, her jaw working as she ground her teeth.

Christ. He was in the suds now. Nothing for it but to tell her the truth and hope for the best. She had agreed to marry him at least. "Your father heard about your antics with Lord Kersey at Almack's. He asked me to make sure you did nothing to bring shame to your family."

"And just how were you supposed to do that, my lord?" The deadly stare of her vivid green eyes pierced him like a lance.

Nash swallowed hard. "By marrying you." Why did it sound worse when spoken aloud?

Her face drained of color and her hands clenched at her sides. "So that is what your 'attraction' to me has been about?" She gestured toward his groin.

"No, that part has been painfully real."

She ignored him, swinging her legs over the side of the bed. "My father wants to run my life again and you agreed to be his minion?" She sprang off the bed and stomped toward the door.

Nash clambered after her and seized her wrist before she could open the door.

"No." He jerked her around to face him. "I told you the truth. My attraction to you began before your father spoke a word to me. At Almack's." He gripped her hands. "When you fell into my arms I never wanted to let go."

She stared at him and her eyes narrowed. "That's not all there is to it, I'll wager. My father must have dangled something before your eyes to gain your cooperation. That has always been his way."

Nash glanced away, hesitating. Damn the earl.

Her frown deepened and she jerked her hands away. "Was it money? Did he sell me to you as he did to Sir Archibald?"

He shook his head. "No. I'd not do that, Charlotte." He sighed. "He offered his political support for a bill I've drafted to go before Parliament."

Her jaw dropped. "Political support for a bill!" She shook her head and laughed, a raw sound that hurt his heart. "My value has decreased most grievously in six years. He gave Sir Archibald ten thousand pounds to marry me." Tears started from her eyes.

"Charlotte." Nash tried to put an arm around her shoulders, but she elbowed him in the ribs.

"He has only ever sought to control me. To make me bend to his will and my own happiness be damned. Never again." She shook her head, tears flying. "You can tell my father for me that he dictates nothing in my life. I will marry or not as I choose." She drew herself up and stared at his face.

He'd seen kinder eyes behind a pistol aimed at him.

"As far as your suit is concerned, Lord Wrotham, it will be a chilly summer in hell before I marry you." She turned on her heel and ran from the room.

Charlotte urged Ajax to even greater speed, pushing the gray horse into a gallop. Perhaps her face would have cooled sufficiently by the time she reached Lyttlefield Park. Even if it did, no speed would erase the memory of this afternoon. She wanted to weep each time she thought about it. Every moment, in fact, since she'd stormed out of Lord Wrotham's house, cursing the moment she had first set eyes on him.

To think she had been duped by the earl's treachery. And she had thought herself in love with the man. Her whole body flinched at the thought. Of course, now she understood why Wrotham had insisted on marriage all along. Her father thought to get his way no matter who he had to use to do it. Well, not this time.

Charlotte pulled Ajax back to a canter. She could not run him into the stable as if all the demons of hell chased her. In truth, only one did. She glanced back over her shoulder at the two burly grooms who were just catching up to her after her headlong flight. They had been ordered by Lord Wrotham to see her to within sight of the Lyttle-field stable. For discretion's sake, it was the one concession Nash would make regarding his decision to have her seen home.

High-handed wretch. She might have known he'd been working in tandem with her father, *for her own good*. She'd show them what was best for her. She had the freedom to live her life the way she wanted it. Make her own decisions and her own mistakes. Neither one of them could take that from her now.

The scene that had followed her declaration had been anything but pleasant. Nash's stony silence as she attempted to repair her appearance—one pin she hastily shoved into her hair certainly stuck straight into her head—continued as he followed her from the bedroom to the receiving room.

Had she thought it would not have given rise to too many questions at home, she would have abandoned her hat. However, she did not think herself up to much of an inquisition, so she diligently scoured the small room, finally spotting her ostrich plume curling out from under a corner table. She had pulled it onto her head, secured it with a lone pin and, with one defiant look at Nash, had stalked from the room and demanded her horse. His curt order for the two grooms to accompany her had done nothing to temper her anger, although given the recent savage events in the county, she saw the value in their presence.

Charlotte finally rounded the stand of oaks that shielded her manor house. Hers and no one else's. She stopped and waited for the grooms to catch her up.

"As you can see, you have discharged your duty." She pointed to the house and then dragged her manners forth. "Please thank Lord Wrotham for my escort."

Without waiting for an acknowledgment, she touched Ajax and he shot away toward the stable. She hoped the men had the good sense to leave before they were spotted by her servants. The last thing she wanted to explain was how a ride in her park had produced an escort of Wrotham's making. Bitterness had exhausted her powers of invention for the foreseeable future.

Chapter 21

October 1816

The full sun of the brilliant early October sky beat down on Charlotte as she pulled Ajax down from a trot to a walk. Glorious heat soaked into her black riding habit, warming her in the chilly autumn air. Nature blazed in all about her in a splendor Charlotte had never seen before. Much better to be out in the fresh air than brooding indoors.

She had been reluctantly planning her next house party when Mr. Courtland, her estate manager, had suggested she ride out with him to oversee the harvesting in the fields.

"You said you wanted to learn about the land, my lady. There's no better time to do so than ingathering." The round-faced young man, newly married, had laughed. "Unless it's planting time in the spring. You'll want to watch the cycle of the seasons on the property, how the ground is prepared and sown in the spring, how the crops are managed during the growing season, and how we bring the harvest in. You're starting at the end of the process, but next year you'll see it from the beginning."

Charlotte had been delighted at the prospect. It gave her purpose, a sense of becoming tied to the land and the people. It also kept her from fretting about the Earl of Wrotham's treachery. She had written a scathing letter to her father, demanding that he cease to meddle in her affairs and proclaiming her intention to remain unmarried, no matter the circumstances. She had received no reply, which had been expected. Neither, however, had she heard anything from Wrotham. After his passionate appeal to her, she'd thought he would attempt a visit or at the least write, imploring her to marry him and save his political career.

Not that she would do it, of course. Still his silence perplexed her, hence her relief at Mr. Courtland's suggestion of working closely with her land.

They had been riding out almost daily for the past week, inspecting the different groups of harvesters. This morning Courtland had called for her at nine and they were on their way to her furthest fields by half past the hour. The morning had melted away as they inspected the fragrant fields, met the harvesters, and received early yield reports on the hops, a major crop in Kent. By noon they had finished with one entire sector of the estate and had turned toward home and a good lunch.

Charlotte slowed Ajax as they approached a stand of trees. The path that meandered through the little wood wasn't wide enough to allow them to ride abreast, so they had ridden through single file on the way out this morning.

"I'll take the lead this time," Charlotte called, touching her heel to her horse. The stand of oaks was small but dense. Little sunlight filtered through the tree cover and the chill air intensified as she headed under the canopy.

Shivering even in her woolen clothes, Charlotte glanced up, wondering that the leaves were still so thick. The cold weather should have brought most of them down by now.

"Why haven't the leaves turned more, do you think?" Charlotte called over her shoulder.

"Likely the cold year has confused their cycle. They're used to the temperature changing from warm to cold. This year it's been so chilly all summer they don't know it's time to change." His tone said he didn't find this amusing at all.

"Just as the crops have taken so long to mature." Charlotte gave Ajax his head in the dim light, allowing him to pick his way along the path strewn with twigs and small branches. She peered ahead to where it brightened at the end of the stand. A dark shadow lay across the path about halfway to the light.

"That's odd. There's a small tree down up here. It wasn't there this morning." She turned to him, eyebrows raised.

He shrugged and shook his head. "I don't know, my lady. Might be a deadfall. Or it's not so big that something couldn't have rooted it up. We do have wild pigs here about."

A likely explanation. She nodded and urged her mount toward it. "Too big to step over, I think. Let's try to go around to the right." Charlotte pulled her reins to the side, heading off the path when the forest exploded with howling men. They came at her from all sides, trying to grab the reins, her skirt, her legs.

The robber gang.

"Courtland!" she screamed, holding on for dear life as Ajax reared up in fear, his hooves flashing out at the nearest attacker. The man gave way, though others still tried to seize her. She slashed her riding crop across the face of the nearest man. He cursed and grabbed it out of her hand, almost unseating her. Slipping her foot from the stirrup, she took aim and kicked the nearest body, the pointed toe of her half boot connecting with the man's head. He yelped and fell back.

"Ride, my lady! Ride!" Courtland yelled.

She heard a shot. God knew who had fired it. She hammered her heel into Ajax's side. The horse shot forward, trampling one of the robbers before crashing through the trees in a mad flight.

Anchored only by her right leg in the sidesaddle pommel, Charlotte grasped the reins in one hand as she clutched the horse's mane in the other and prayed she could stay on. The gelding fled straight through the trees, branches scratching her face as they whipped past her head. Sounds of the attack faded and still the panicked animal ran. Charlotte tried to pull back on the reins, but in her hunched state it did little good. She feared without her foot in the stirrup she'd fall if she loosened his mane.

At last they burst out of the trees onto the short grassland of the park. Ajax continued his headlong flight, though after some minutes of steady pulling on the reins he slowed sufficiently for Charlotte to regain the stirrup. She breathed easier and looked quickly about, trying to get her bearings. She had to get help to send back to her manager. God knew what those blackguards had done to him.

The land looked totally unfamiliar. Was she still even on her own estate? She set her heel into the horse's flank and he took off at a canter. Charlotte decided to make for the ridge on a rise to her left. Perhaps from its height she could locate help.

They crested the hill and Charlotte gave a sigh of relief. A field in the process of harvesting lay spread out before her.

Men. Thank God.

They tore down the hill pell mell, Charlotte peering into the fields, searching for someone who seemed to be in charge.

"Help! Help! My manager and I were attacked by robbers." She reined Ajax in and they slid to a stop, almost running down several of the harvesters. She glanced around, but none of the men looked familiar.

"Here, now, what's the to-do?" One tall worker ran up, followed by the others.

"I've been attacked. They were waiting for us in a little stand of woods on my estate. I'm Lady Cavendish of Lyttlefield Park. Please, you must come. My manager, Mr. Courtland, is still there. They may have killed him!" The truth of Courtland's dire circumstances hit her like a punch to the stomach and she burst into tears.

"My lord." The biggest worker, a giant of a man, turned toward a man who'd come running out of the wheatfield.

"Nash!" Charlotte screamed and vaulted off the horse.

"Charlotte? Charlotte, what's the matter?" He came flying toward her and caught her up in his arms.

"Robbers. In the stand of trees at the edge of my property. They've got my manager, Will Courtland. You have to come." Charlotte gripped his jacket, panting as though she'd been running instead of the horse.

"Thorne, Ashford, Stockley, get horses and follow me." He pried Charlotte's hands from his coat and ran to his horse, standing tethered at the corner of the field.

Dazed, Charlotte watched as he leaped into the saddle. "Hurry, lads." He pulled the horse around.

She stared after him, panic receding as determination set in. Did he think he would go without her?

"You there." She pointed to a young man who looked at her with eyes big as saucers. "Give me a leg up." She ran to her mount and glanced back at the boy, still standing stock-still. "Now!"

He reluctantly approached and gingerly made a stirrup for her to step into, then tossed her up and backed away just as Nash rode up beside her.

"What do you think you're doing?"

"I'm going with you." She glared defiantly at him, waiting for his denial.

He opened his mouth, then shut it abruptly. With an exasperated snort, he growled, "Come on." His horse shot away.

He hadn't argued at all. She sat still on the prancing horse, shaking her head and watching his straight back as he rode away. It took her a moment to realize she needed to follow. She urged Ajax after him, back the way they had come, trailing Nash on his big chestnut stallion. By the time they hit the crest, the other men had caught up and they rode hard toward the stand of oaks that now sounded eerily quiet.

As they neared the entrance to the trees, Nash pulled a pistol.

Charlotte gasped. She'd not expected him to have a weapon.

He held up a hand and they slowed. Nash entered first, Charlotte right behind him. There was no sign of her attackers. The tree still lay across the path, behind it in the dim light a crumpled figure.

"Mr. Courtland." Charlotte pulled her horse to a halt and slithered down. She hurried around the end of the tree to the body of her estate manager.

But Nash had gotten there first. He crouched beside the man and felt his neck for a pulse.

Charlotte's heart leaped into her throat.

Then he lifted the man's head, and a groan issued from him.

"Thank God he's still alive." Her shoulders sagged and she wanted to sink to the ground.

"He's not out of the woods yet." Nash winced at his words when Charlotte laughed nervously. "He's been beaten rather badly." Courtland's face had turned black and blue, one eye almost swollen shut. Nash pointed to a dark red stain spreading from the manager's shoulder.

"And he's been shot." He began to tear at his own neck cloth.

Nash's men had spread out in the woods. The big man now approached them. "No sign of them, my lord. They must have taken his horse. P'rhaps that's what they were after."

"Thank you, Thorne. They might have thought two horses worth the risk in broad daylight. It's an isolated spot." He glared at Charlotte as he finished untying his cravat. "A single man and a woman would seem like easy prey." He unwound the cloth and pressed it against Courtland's shoulder to staunch the blood. The man moaned and his eyes fluttered open.

"Lady Cavendish?" he whispered fiercely, his gaze riveted to Nash's face.

"Safe, Courtland. You are to be commended for making good her escape." Nash's voice soothed as he gently moved the man into a sitting position. "Do you think you can ride?"

The man nodded, then slumped against Nash.

"No. Right, then. Stockley, take Ashford and ride back to the field. Unload the wagon and drive it back here." He turned to the big man who towered over them. "Thorne, go to Wrotham Village and fetch Mr. Putnam, the apothecary. Take him to Wrotham Hall. We'll meet you there. Take my horse; he's faster."

"Yes, my lord." The big man swung up on the chestnut stallion and raced off. The other men had also gone, leaving her alone with Nash and the unconscious Courtland.

Awkward silence ensued. This was the first time she'd seen Nash since their encounter in his bedchamber weeks ago. She bent her head as her face heated at the memory, yet she yearned to throw herself into his arms and let him hold her, keep her fears at bay after this horrific experience. Fortunately, he still cradled Courtland's body instead. Perhaps her manager needed the comfort more than she at the moment.

After a painfully long time, during which she tried to come up with something to say, she settled for, "Thank you, Nash. I cannot tell you how thankful I was to see you running out of the field toward me." She gazed into his eyes, held by the deep blue pools that made her weak.

"I'm only glad I was there, Charlotte. Glad that Courtland here got you out of danger. Good man." Nash pressed the cloth harder into the man's shoulder. He stirred but did not wake.

"Yes, he is. Will he be all right, do you think?" She crinkled her brow, worry about her manager and his new wife surfacing.

"Hard to tell. The beating will mend. And it would be best if the ball passed all the way through his shoulder. We can pray it won't fester." Nash shifted the man to lean against his shoulder and Charlotte saw an expanse of chest left uncovered by the lack of cravat and an open shirt.

She swallowed, her mouth suddenly dry. That small patch of pale exposed skin set the blood in her veins on fire.

"What were you and Courtland doing out by yourselves today?" His stern voice dashed cold water on her budding ardor.

"I assume the same as you, Nash." She tried to give the words a nonchalance. "We had gone out to the far acreage. Mr. Courtland's been teaching me about the estate and the harvesting. We were heading back to the house when the gang stopped us."

"I thought I told you before, Charlotte, not to venture out without an escort. That means more than one man."

She sighed. She might have known he'd bring that up. "I had my manager with me. I thought that would be sufficient. Would you have thought the gang would attack us in the middle of the day?" And before he could answer she added, "There were perhaps six or seven of them. Do you honestly think two more grooms would have dissuaded them?"

He grimaced, as if caught with a bad taste in his mouth. Finally, grudgingly, he admitted, "If there were that many, and the grooms weren't armed, then likely the gang would have struck in any case. They'd have believed taking four horses worth the risk." He swore under his breath. "I beg your pardon, Charlotte," he said, gazing at her with hungry eyes. "I simply want to keep you safe."

"I know," she said softly. "And I want to thank you for allowing me to come back here with you without an argument." She still couldn't believe she had gotten her way about that.

Nash gave her a wry smile. "You said you wanted to make your own decisions. As a fellow landowner, I have to respect that." He grinned mischievously. "And because I was going to accompany you, I decided you'd be safer with me at any rate."

The smile disappeared, leaving his face drawn. "I've been trying to apprehend this group of blackguards for months. It's time I finished with them. I will not rest until they are caught and punished to the fullest extent of the law." The lines in his face deepened as his eyes came to rest on the still form in his arms.

Charlotte sat silently on the ground beside them. How wonderful Nash was in his present mood, protective yet respectful of her position. A woman would be lucky to have such a man.

She shook off that seductive thought. The last thing she needed in her life was a husband. The respect she'd already begun to command from her workers would be undermined or completely absorbed by any man she married. Soon she hoped they would treat her as any other property owner. Such esteem brought with it a heady feeling. She prayed the workers' regard would continue to grow. As Mr. Courtland's injuries would impede his actual running of the estate, she steeled herself to assume the duties as best she could until he was sufficiently recovered. God grant it be soon.

"If you would like, Charlotte, my estate manager and I can help with your harvest as well as our own." Nash broke in on her reverie, as though picking up her thoughts. "You can even ride out with me when I go to see to it." His smile was genuine. "The more you learn this year, the easier it will be next. Believe me, I know."

Stunned by his generous offer, Charlotte stared at him, unable to speak. Instead, he took her hand and kissed it. "It's a gesture of friendship, my dear. One neighbor to another." He squeezed her hand and let it go.

Charlotte's heart beat like a drum. His touch still had the power to set her body on fire, even if only his lips on her hand. Her mind leaped to thoughts of his mouth kissing her elsewhere, melting her into a puddle of desire.

A shout from without the stand of trees pulled her back to the present. Nash struggled to his feet, supporting Courtland, then hefting him in his arms as the wagon pulled into view. Charlotte grabbed her horse's reins and followed him. Once more the heightened awareness of Nash's power over her called to her like a siren song, to make a different decision about her path to happiness.

Chapter 22

"My dear, I do not see why you didn't simply die when the gang jumped out at your horse." Georgina had said the same thing at least five times since Nash had accompanied Charlotte home and the story of the ambush had come out. Even now, with dinner almost over, her companion seemed particularly upset by the incident. "You are lucky to be alive, Charlotte." Georgie shivered. "Had you not escaped there's no telling what might have happened."

"I fully credit Mr. Courtland and an excellent horse with my escape, Georgie. Had it not been for them, yes, I believe the outcome of that encounter would have been much different." Charlotte sipped her wine and tried not to think about the leering look on the face of the man she'd kicked. Death might not have been the worst thing that would have happened to her. A little shiver shook her.

"And Nash proved a gallant rescuer as well. At least of Mr. Courtland." Georgie gave her a sideways glance. "Did Nash scold you at all?"

Charlotte shook her head, still puzzled by that turn of events. "No. He actually admitted that the attack in broad daylight was unforeseeable and that a larger escort likely would not have discouraged it. Perhaps he is no longer so concerned about me."

Georgie snorted. "That was evident when he escorted you into the drawing room, shouting for Fisk to have the fires stoked, for the housekeeper to bring blankets, and then poured brandy down your throat to guard against the cold and shock." She grinned at Charlotte. "Yes, he seemed quite unconcerned."

"Humpf." Charlotte finished the last bite of Cook's excellent trifle and put down her fork. "He didn't even put up a fuss when I insisted upon going back with him to help Mr. Courtland."

"And did you want him to argue with you? Waste valuable time?" Georgie stared her, frowning. "He probably knew he couldn't stop you anyway. Perhaps he's accepted that you are capable of making your own decisions."

"Perhaps." Charlotte couldn't decide how that sat with her. A fine line existed between having her wishes respected and having her welfare in mind. She straightened her dress and put her shoulders back. It shouldn't concern her, really, whether Nash wanted to protect her or not. Nothing could come of their friendship, but as long as he respected her as a landowner, they'd get along fine.

"Shall we have our tea in the drawing room?" The after-dinner ritual seemed a godsend to Charlotte, who was ready to change the subject.

Georgina nodded and they removed there, chatting about the newest blend of tea Charlotte had brought from London. She'd bought a dozen or so samples so she could include Georgie in deciding which one she favored best. They had been trying a new one every few days since her return.

"I quite enjoyed the last one, Charlotte. Very light and delicate. Is it the Assam?"

Charlotte shook her head. "That was the day before. Remember, it had malty hints to it? And I said—"

"That it tasted a bit like Wrotham ale." Georgie giggled. "Yes. So what was the one yesterday? I found it very refreshing."

"Darjeeling. From India." Charlotte sighed. The name Wrotham seemed to be everywhere today.

" Well, then, if you do not choose it to be your particular blend, perhaps I will be able to eventually." Georgina sat in her favorite chair before the fire as Charlotte rang and ordered tea.

"The one we're having today is very different from the others I purchased. A smoky blend called lapsang souchang. More of a masculine tea, I think, but I particularly liked the fragrance of it in the shop. If you do not care for it, we can order some of yesterday's for you."

Charlotte sank onto the Queen Anne chair and surveyed the cozy room. "I loved seeing Jane again, but I do love being home as well." Her gaze fell on the Adams mantelpiece and her brow wrinkled. "It suddenly occurs to me that I still have not heard anything from Edgar. I would have wagered he'd be down here demanding his furniture back before now."

"Oh, I had a letter from Jemmy last week in which he mentioned Sir Edgar. Let me run get it." Georgina rose and hurried from the room. Charlotte relaxed against the back of the chair and stared idly into the fireplace. Perhaps Georgie's letter held an explanation for Edgar's absence. God knew she didn't want to see her stepson, but neither did she want to be surprised by his unexpected arrival.

Charlotte closed her eyes, the warmth of the flames relaxing her at last. Well, she'd had quite a day, hadn't she? She'd rest her eyes until Georgie returned.

A warm touch on her cheek. Her eyes fluttered open and widened to find Lord Wrotham bending over her.

"Nash?" She struggled to sit up. She must have fallen asleep and slid down in the chair. How embarrassing. "Why weren't you announced?"

His eyes twinkled. "When Fisk opened the doors and you sat here so charmingly in repose, I asked him not to wake you." He sat opposite her on the sofa. "Your tea arrived, and though I thought I'd let you sleep for a bit, I couldn't resist your rosy cheek."

"Hmm." Charlotte fought the urge to yawn. "You seem to have little resistance indeed."

"To you, Charlotte? None whatsoever." He grinned at her, so bold and unrepentant she had to chuckle.

"You would say such lack of restraint in a woman foretold a wanton life."

"So it is extremely fortunate that I am a man and can withstand such slanders upon my person," he replied with a droll twist of his mouth.

He would have her laughing outright in a moment.

"Goodness, Nash." Charlotte glanced around. "Have you seen Georgie? She went to get a letter." She poured the fragrant tea, hoping it hadn't cooled too much. "How long have you been here?"

"Only a few minutes. And no, I've not seen Georgina. I stopped in—"

"Here it is, Charlotte. Oh!" Georgie burst into the room and skidded to a stop. "Nash." Her eyes widened. "H . . . how nice to see you again." She looked from Charlotte to Nash and back again and sat abruptly.

Nash stood and bowed. "Georgina. The pleasure is all mine." He smiled, and Charlotte could have sworn he winked at Georgie. *Was* something going on between the two of them? Georgie had said she'd refused his proposal, but their behavior suggested something was afoot. Her heart stuttered and she ruthlessly ignored it. She had closed that avenue. Determinedly, she poured a cup of tea and handed it to Georgina.

"I had stopped in, ladies, to make sure you have had no ill effects from your ordeal, Charlotte." He peered at her, looking her up and down as he would a horse he thought to buy. "And to give you the latest news on your estate manager."

At the mention of Courtland, all other thoughts fled. "Oh, please, Nash. Tell me how he is."

"Better than expected, thank goodness." Nash settled back onto the sofa. "Mr. Putnam has dressed his wounds. The worst of it, of course, is the gunshot. The hole goes all the way through his shoulder—a blessing, actually—although cleaning it pained Mr. Courtland sorely." Nash shook his head. "It will be touch and go for several days. Fortunately, I managed to keep Putnam from bleeding him. He'd actually brought the leeches with him."

Charlotte grimaced and Georgie shuddered.

"I was hard pressed to keep him from what he considered his duty. If we can keep the leeches at bay, your manager resting, and make sure he takes his medicine, I'd say he has a good chance."

"Thank God." Charlotte closed her eyes as relief swept through her. She hadn't known until that moment how worried she'd been about the man. He was one of her people, and he'd put himself in danger to save her. "If there's anything he needs, or anything I can do, Nash, please let me know."

He nodded. "Of course I will." He sipped his tea and his eyes widened. "Delightful, Charlotte. A new blend from London? It's very bold. I like it."

She nodded and smiled. "Yes, I quite like it too. I'm thinking of using it exclusively. Well, except for Georgie. She prefers a milder taste. Oh," she turned to Georgina, "did you find the letter you were looking for?"

"Yes. I'm sorry it took me so long. I had not placed it where I always put my correspondence." She laughed and glanced at Nash. "Without fail I put all my brother's letters in a particular box. But the letter I told Charlotte about wasn't there. So I had to search the box, and when I still couldn't find it, I rummaged around until I remembered I'd kept it out to show Charlotte." Georgie held up the letter, cream paper with rows of scratchy writing. She hesitated, glancing from Charlotte to Nash.

Charlotte nodded, then said to Nash, "Earlier I'd been wondering why I hadn't received word from my stepson. We parted on . . . difficult terms and I'd expected to hear from him by now."

"Your stepson?"

"Sir Edgar Cavendish."

"Ah." Nash settled back. "I believe I've had news of the young man from my friend, George Abernathy."

Charlotte sat up, instantly alert. "What have you heard, if I may ask?"

Nash shrugged. "Only that he has gambled excessively since returning from the Continent. And he does not always pay his debts promptly."

Frowning, Charlotte said, "That makes even less sense, then. If he's in need of money, why hasn't he contacted me?"

Nash cocked his head. "You have some obligation to him still?"

"No," she shook her head, "though he must think I do." She sighed. "It's a rather long story, the gist of which is that I took what I owned from his father's house in London, though I doubt he knew the extent of what legally belonged to me." Charlotte grinned at Nash. "Suffice it to say, there is little left for him to use to raise money for his debts. I just don't understand why I haven't heard from him. He took possession of the house in early August."

"I think I have the answer to that, Charlotte." Georgina waved her letter in the air. "Jemmy writes that after leaving us in August, he traveled to Brighton with friends. There he met Sir Edgar, who apparently had come to the seashore to celebrate his majority. He's been in residence there ever since, gambling, drinking, and carousing." Geogie gave Charlotte a speaking look. "My brother says Sir Edgar has managed somehow to scrape an acquaintance with the Prince Regent and so is fixed at Brighton indefinitely."

"He must not have gone back to the London house, then." Charlotte tried to suppress a giggle. "Oh my, but he is in for such a surprise." What she wouldn't give to see his face when . . . She lost the battle and laughed aloud.

Georgie joined in, leaving Nash looking bewildered.

"I can just imagine his look when he finally goes home." Charlotte went off into more peals of laughter. "Pardon me, Nash," she said finally. "I don't know what came over me." She dabbed at her streaming eyes.

Nash smiled and shook his head, then looked at her thoughtfully.

The change in his demeanor sobered Charlotte immediately and set her on alert. Why did his eyes have that particular gleam in them? What was he up to?

"I hope you won't think this impertinent, Charlotte," he began, feeling around in his coat pocket. A moment later, he drew out a small, framed oval of ivory and handed it to her.

Eyes wide, Charlotte took the delicate disc gently in her hand, the smooth bone still warm from his pocket. On the pale surface lay an exquisite pen and ink drawing of a church. The intricate details—tiles on the roof, a clock in the clock tower, stained glass in the windows—brought the image to life, making her think . . . "It's St. George's, isn't it?" She glanced up at Nash, whose face lit up with a soft smile.

"Yes. I know you've taken a great liking to our little village and thought you might enjoy this. I had it commissioned last year after I moved here."

"It is beautiful." Charlotte gazed at the lovely work, recalling the outing to the church with Nash. A happy memory. She shook her head to stop from going deeper into those recollections. Too dangerous.

With a sigh, she handed the miniature back to Nash. "Thank you for showing it to me. Perhaps you will share the artist with me? Then I could have one commissioned."

His hand closed over hers, arresting it. "This is a gift for you, Charlotte. I'd like for you to have it."

Her mouth dropped open, shock and protest rendering her speechless. Such a present, while completely appropriate, seemed suddenly too intimate coming from him. Her gaze flew to his face to find his eyes flickering over her, as if searching for something.

"It . . . it . . . I . . . can't . . ." She had never been this incoherent in her life, but the look in his eyes, the warmth of his hand on hers, took her wits away.

"I insist, Charlotte." His hand squeezed hers. "I want you to have it."

"May I see it, Charlotte?" Georgie's voice broke the spell and brought her somewhat back to herself.

"Of course."

Nash released her hand and she gave the miniature to Georgie, then returned to her seat, disturbed at her reaction to the gift. It was merely a drawing. Yet it seemed so much more.

"It is lovely. This artist is exceptional, Nash. I wonder that you can bear to part with it." She shot an approving look at Nash, who raised his brow, then grinned at her.

"One must do as the heart dictates, Georgina. I found myself thinking that after that ordeal today, such a gift would raise Charlotte's sprits." He turned to gaze at her. "I feel responsible because I haven't been able to apprehend these brigands yet."

"That's not your fault, Nash." Charlotte would not

have him take all the blame. Their neighboring landowners had been unsuccessful as well. "They've eluded everyone."

"Well," Georgie broke in, "I still think this is a lovely present. Where shall you put it, Charlotte? You need to display it so those at the house party can see it." She handed the piece back to her friend.

Charlotte's face heated. She hadn't sent out all her invitations, but she hadn't intended to send one to Nash. It would be more than awkward for her to be in the same company with him at a party and remembering the previous one. Georgie, however, had now taken that decision out of her hands.

"You are quite right, Georgie. They will enjoy seeing it, especially those who attended the outing last time." She turned to Nash, who had resumed his seat also. "You'll be receiving an invitation shortly, Nash. I do hope you'll be able to attend again. The party will start on the tenth."

"You are too kind, Charlotte. Of course I will attend. Do I know any of your guests?" Nash leaned back on the sofa, seemingly relaxed. The lines around his mouth firmed, however.

"Yes, I believe so. My cousin Jane, Lady Stephen, and Mrs. Easton. Only Mrs. Wickley has sent her regrets. And several of the gentlemen are the same as well." Charlotte grinned at him. "Except for Lord Fernley. He will not be receiving an invitation this time."

"Indeed." Nash's brows went up in mock surprise. "A wise deletion from your guest list in my opinion." He hesitated, and Charlotte knew the next question he would ask. She steeled herself for it. "Will Lord Kersey be in attendance?"

"I have issued the invitation, yes," Charlotte said evenly. "I have received no word from him as yet."

Nash nodded, but made no further comment. Indeed what could he say?

Hating the awkward silence, Charlotte desperately cast about for another topic.

"Your party comes at a fortuitous time," Nash said, coming to her rescue. "They must attend the Harvest Home that Friday."

"Harvest Home?" Georgie's brow wrinkled. "What is that?"

"It is the festival to celebrate the end of the harvest. Traditionally, it's held on September twenty-third, but this year the cold weather has delayed the harvest several weeks. So we've settled on the eleventh of October, quite the latest Harvest Home ever held. But it means your guests will have a different sort of outing to attend this time." He smiled, though it didn't reach his eyes. "I would be honored to personally escort you both, Charlotte and Georgina. I will be the envy of the village—and the party too, if I don't miss my guess." Nash leaned forward, as if hanging on Charlotte's answer.

"I would be delighted to go with you," Georgie spoke up before Charlotte could open her mouth.

"And I as well," Charlotte added. "It would create a good appearance in the village to have the major landowners attend together, don't you think?" She relaxed and laughed. "I think this will be fun, although I'm sure I don't know what one does at a Harvest Home." She looked inquiringly at Nash.

"I'm surprised Courtland didn't tell you about it." He arose, that mischievous twinkle in his eyes once more. "Perhaps he didn't have a chance. Still, I think it will be much more entertaining if you don't know what happens." A fire lit behind his eyes, warming her pulse. "So we will all have something to look forward to."

"What will you look forward to?" Georgie's question

sounded far away as Charlotte stared into Nash's eyes, enthralled.

"Your response to the festival." A smile crept slowly over his face. "There are some interesting customs attached to it. I found them quite . . . stimulating last year."

Georgie gasped and turned pink.

"Ladies." He bowed to them with a mischievous smile and left.

Charlotte sank back against the chair, suddenly weary. Lord Wrotham had the ability to sap her strength in the most unexpected and provoking ways. Now, in addition to the demanding preparations for her weekend party, she would be fretting about this festival as well.

Drat the man. Would he forever turn her world upside down? Charlotte had the distinct impression that the answer to that question was yes.

Chapter 23

Just after breakfast two days later, Charlotte shivered in the cold, misty air as she headed toward Wrotham Hall. It was only the beginning of October. What on earth would it be like by Christmas? She'd be surprised if they didn't have to move the date of the festival yet again. This nasty weather must be delaying the harvest even further.

She scrutinized the road, all too aware of the target she made for the gang. The robbers might be desperate enough that the cold would not deter them. She would take no more chances, however. Glancing left and right, she made sure her armed escort—James, her groom, and Jeffers, her coachman—still flanked her, easily keeping pace. Their faces, set in determined lines, turned back and forth as they also scanned the land along the road for trouble.

Her journey today had been prompted by Nash's silence on Will Courtland's progress. She'd heard nothing in two days, which might not bode well for her estate manager. Would Nash keep it from her if his health had begun to decline? She couldn't be sure, even though he'd agreed to keep her informed. So she'd decided to go see for herself. She might have sent a note, but it would be better to go in person in case she could do something to add to her manager's comfort. And, deny it though she would, she wanted to see Nash as well.

Why the devil did her father have to spoil everything again? She tried to stay strong, to remain steadfast in her determination not to bend to her father's will in this. If he wanted her married to Nash, he'd wait an eternity. It irritated Charlotte to no end, however, that despite his involvement with her father's schemes, Nash occupied her thoughts much more often than he should.

Acres showed Charlotte into the rather masculine reception room with pictures of naval battle scenes gracing the walls, where she'd waited before. She always forgot Nash had served in the Navy, although he'd never had command of a ship. He seemed so at home on his estate, it amazed her he had not been born to the life. She was peering at a rather gruesome painting of the Battle of Trafalgar when Nash walked in.

"Charlotte. I am delighted and surprised to see you out on such a chilly day." He grasped her hand and kissed it, lingering just a second too long. Her pulse leaped and she withdrew her hand before he made her forget her purpose.

"It's nice to see you too, Nash. I was admiring your paintings. This one is a bit shocking, however." She stared again at the mayhem depicted on board the *Victory*. "It must have seemed like Dante's *Inferno*."

"Trust me, it did." His smile had gone, replaced by a hardness she had rarely seen in him.

"You were there?" She glanced back at the painting, at the fallen men, and shuddered. He had been so close to death . . .

"Not on Nelson's ship, but on the *Minotaur*. Not the first battle I'd ever been in either, but one of the hottest." He in turn stared at the painting, a distant look in his eyes.

"But isn't Minotaur the name of your horse?" Such an odd name for an animal.

He grinned at her, his mood lightening. "Yes, I confess to that. *Minotaur* was my first ship and I did well by her. First in the Egypt campaign in 1801, when I was still wet behind the ears. Then *Trafalgar* in 1805. After that, the Naval Office reassigned me to the *Temeraire*, and we saw a bit of action off the coasts of Spain and France." He motioned her to the sofa and they sat.

"Sad to say, the *Temeraire* came back to Britain for repairs in 1813 and instead of re-fitting her for war, they turned her into a prison ship. I was about to take another assignment, as captain of my own ship, when news of my uncle's and cousin's deaths reached me and I had to resign." Nash shook his head and sighed.

"So why didn't you name your horse *Temeraire*?"

Nash chuckled. "As I said, *Minotaur* was my first ship." That devilish twinkle came into his eyes. "And I thought the name sounded a good deal more dashing and less French than *Temeraire*, even though it means bold." His gaze softened as it took her in. "But I doubt you have braved the cold just to ask me about my war service. Shall I order tea to warm you up, Charlotte?" His voice dropped to a low purr.

How did he manage to make tea sound sinful? As if he'd rather warm her up in other ways instead? Despite the cold, her cheeks heated.

"Tea would be lovely, thank you." Charlotte smiled pleasantly, determined to carry on, despite his flirting. Was he flirting? Or had she misconstrued his words because she wanted to? She closed her eyes to keep her thoughts from spinning out of control. Her purpose was to ask about her estate manager and she needed to focus on that.

"I hadn't heard from you about Mr. Courtland's condition. You promised to keep me informed of his progress.

After two days I feared the worst." Charlotte tried to put a touch of reproach into her voice, but her genuine concern for the man overrode it.

"I'm sorry, Charlotte. I did not realize you meant to be so closely informed about your manager." His eyes glowed with warmth. "Would you like to see him for yourself? I'll tell Acres to hold the tea until we return." He pulled the bell and gave the order, then took her hand and assisted her to rise. "This way, my dear."

Nash led her up a grand staircase, all gleaming oak, to the next floor. "I have hired a nurse specifically to tend to Mr. Courtland. That way he gets thorough care and my servants' routine isn't interrupted, although," he leaned toward her, "he's become something of a hero belowstairs." Nash chuckled. "I don't think any of the maids would have complained of extra work had they been assigned to his care."

His eyes sparkled with merriment. "I believed it prudent, in that circumstance, to insist that his wife attend him as well in his suite." He grew grave again. "I also thought it best that Mrs. Courtland not remain alone in their house. Her husband thwarted the gang's plan. I did not want them to retaliate against his family while he was unable to defend it."

Another thoughtful, prudent move. The man certainly thought of everything he could to keep people safe.

Nash stopped before the door to what looked to be a guest chamber, his face etched in long lines of tension. "I didn't want to alarm you unduly, but I have also taken the precaution of sending patrols around both our properties. I don't know if it will act as a deterrent, but my hope is to keep the robbers off balance long enough for me to catch them."

"Do you have a plan yet, Nash?" Charlotte's heart beat faster at the memory of the men who had accosted her.

The sooner they could be apprehended, the sooner she would sleep soundly in her bed.

"Why don't you see Mr. Courtland first? Then we can retire to my study to have our tea and I'll explain the plan." He opened the door and Charlotte entered, immediately aware of the elegant if somewhat outdated style of the chamber. The furnishings were solid pieces that could be kept, though the hangings and wall coverings were sorely in need of changing. With a few simple alterations this could be a stunning room.

A stirring in the bed brought her attention to the figure lying there and the young woman sitting beside him.

Courtland lay motionless with his head resting against a multitude of white pillows, the blue satin coverlet pulled up to his neck. Dark circles rimmed his eyes, in stark contrast to his pale face.

It might have been her lying thus if not for the grace of God and William Courtland. Charlotte shuddered to think of what might have befallen her had this man not been at her side.

The woman who sat at his head occupied herself with a small embroidery hoop. Every couple of stitches she glanced over at her charge, then resumed her work. So intent was she that Charlotte and Nash had approached the bed before she became aware of them. When she realized they were in the room she arose, put her hoop down, and came toward them.

"Lady Cavendish, have you made the acquaintance of Mrs. Courtland?" Nash spoke softly and glanced at the figure on the bed.

"No, I am afraid I have not had the pleasure." Charlotte inclined her head toward the petite blonde. She had a soft prettiness about her that Charlotte found charming.

"My lady, it is an honor. Mr. Courtland has spoken of you often, with great admiration." Her hushed voice had a high sweet tone.

"How is he this morning, Mrs. Courtland?" Nash again looked at the sick man, who now stirred beneath the covers.

"Another uncomfortable night. And his fever is back, my lord." The woman pressed her hands together, her worry almost palpable.

Nash went to the bed and felt the patient's forehead and cheek. "Did you give him another dose of Putnam's elixir?"

"Yes, my lord. Early this morning. We've finished the last of the vial."

Nash sighed. "Do not be distressed. Putnam said the fever and discomfort would last for about three or four more days. But I will send for him and ask him to bring more of the medicine." He put his hand on Mrs. Courtland's shoulder and squeezed gently. "I believe he will recover."

"I pray so, Lord Wrotham." She turned to look at her husband, concern etched in the lines around her eyes.

"Mrs. Courtland." Charlotte took both of the woman's hands. "If there is anything at all I may do to see to your comfort or that of your husband, you must send for me at once. He saved my life. If I can do him a like service, I would be most grateful."

"You are kindness itself, my lady. Will . . . Mr. Courtland will be so pleased when I tell him of your visit." A fleeting smile gave way to a grimly clenched jaw that betrayed her distress.

The figure on the bed began to moan and thrash about. Mrs. Courtland released Charlotte's hands and flew to her husband's side. She grabbed a cup from the bedside table and deftly held it to his lips. "Here, Will. Drink this down."

He sipped it avidly, then shook his head.

"No, my dear. All of it, if you please." She succeeded in getting him to drink the whole cup, then eased his head back onto the pillows.

"I'll send Putnam up as soon as he arrives," Nash said and Mrs. Courtland nodded absently, her attention fully taken up by her husband.

Nash motioned to Charlotte and they left the room as quietly as they had entered. "I do believe he will recover," he said as he steered her toward the staircase. "With such a pretty and devoted wife to live for, I suspect he will fight valiantly."

Startled, Charlotte stopped and gave him a quizzical look. "Do you think such things make a difference?"

"I know if it were me, it would make all the difference in the world." His eyes flickered briefly with desire; then he took her arm and once again led her toward the stairs.

Flustered by that look, Charlotte cast about for another topic—any other topic—to distract him. "I want to thank you again, Nash, for taking such good care of him."

Nash shrugged. "It was the least I could do for the man. I'd have put him in the countess's apartment, though it's in sad need of renovation. I need a countess to take it in hand."

Charlotte halted at the top of the staircase. Her heartbeat stuttered. She glanced at Nash, who looked back with hopeful eyes. She burst into laughter. "Then you need to find a wife. You have offered for someone?"

"I have." He motioned for her to precede him down the steps, but Charlotte stopped, stunned.

Dread stole into her heart. "Do I know the bride-to-be?" Perhaps he spoke of his proposal to Georgina.

"Yes, you do." He smiled. "Intimately."

"Who—"

Nash held up a hand. "I offered, and she very eagerly accepted me." He touched her hair, smoothing a stray tendril into place. "Then treacherously reneged."

Her heart gave a great thump and she grabbed the banister. "I'm sure she had an excellent reason for jilting you." She started down the staircase, determination in each step. He'd not win her over with kind words and a touch. Even if that touch set her aflame.

"According to her, I had betrayed her trust." Nash trailed her down the stairs. "But she gave me little chance to explain or apologize."

Charlotte reached the bottom step, at a loss to know what to do. Her first thought was to flee home rather than continue this conversation, but he'd offered to talk about the robbers. Drat. She needed to know what plans he had made.

"This way," he said, and led her around the stairs and down a hall to a door on the left.

They entered the study and Charlotte stopped just over the threshold, amazement dismissing their disconcerting banter.

Chaos reigned here.

The room seemed a depository for every book, paper, or ledger in the whole of Kent, none of them in any discernible order. Stacks of books created myriad pathways throughout the room. Piles of papers lay strewn over every flat surface. Maps peeped out from between books on the shelves.

Stunned at this completely new side to Lord Wrotham, Charlotte edged carefully into the disarray. "How on earth do you ever find anything in here?"

He chuckled and nonchalantly strode to the bell and rang it. "I have a method to my madness." He grinned and tapped his head. "It's all locked safe in here. I can put my hand on anything you've a mind to ask for. Unless Acres has been in."

The butler must have seen them come downstairs, for he appeared with a tea tray in hand. Nash nodded for him to come in. "For the first two months, I couldn't find a thing because each night Acres would enter and *tidy* the room. After that we came to an accord. I would hold dominion over the study. Acres would be in charge of everything else in the house."

Nash swept away a pile of papers and Charlotte gingerly sat on what turned out to be a rather delightful Chippendale sofa in the Chinese style. With a long-suffering look, Acres set the oval tray down precariously on a stack of papers and left.

"Would you mind pouring, Charlotte? Then you can come over here and I'll acquaint you with the map and see what you find."

She grasped the teapot, and the whole tray wobbled. Teacups swayed alarmingly in their saucers. A glance at Nash showed him absorbed in the papers on his desk, not the hot beverage that would soon be in her lap. Charlotte grabbed a cup for Nash and rose. She set it on a bare spot at the edge of the desk and poured a generous cup for him. The fragrance was familiar, but she and Georgie had sampled so many teas since her return from London she couldn't be sure which one it might be.

"Do you take milk and sugar?"

"Sugar only."

Charlotte handed him the sugar bowl and he dropped in three large lumps. The man must have a sweet tooth.

She then carefully poured her own cup, added a modest two small lumps and milk, and tasted it. "Your tea reminds me of the blend I just brought from London."

"Yes," he said absentmindedly, his eyes still on the map. He looked up. "I quite prefer yours, however. It has a delicious smoky flavor."

Charlotte smiled, unaccountably pleased that he liked her blend. "The base is lapsang souchang, with hints of Assam and Ceylon. From Jacksons of Piccadilly."

His eyes never left hers. "I shall have to get some when I am next in London. If you do not mind, that is."

Flustered, Charlotte shook her head. "No, of course not."

He flashed a smile that quickened her pulse before bending his head to the map again.

She sipped her tea, hoping it would soothe her, then took it behind the desk to stand beside him.

The map spread out over various other papers showing the county of Kent. Their properties were outlined in dark lines. From this bird's-eye view, Wrotham Hall resembled a large rectangle to the north of Wrotham Village. Lyttlefield Park looked more like a wedge with a blunt instead of pointed top to the south of the village. There were clusters of red and blue dots and swaths of green.

Charlotte sipped as she studied the map. "What are the red dots?"

"They represent our tenant cottages." He pointed here and there on the map.

"And the blue ones?"

"The attacks by the gang so far."

The frequency of those marks appalled Charlotte. Eight blue dots, all but one sitting beside a red one. A lone blue dot sat next to a small patch of green. She placed her finger next to that site. "This was the attack on Mr. Courtland and me?" A shiver ran down her back and she clutched the warm cup.

Nash nodded, still absorbed in the map.

Determined to show him her mettle, she shook off her fear and concentrated on the dots. "What have you found out so far?"

His lips stretched thin and hard. "Precious little, and I've been working on the problem since late June. The gang must be receiving help from a local resident, for I have eliminated every other possibility. I've taken men and traced them through my woodlands and yours. We found traces of camps in both woods, but each time they had moved on."

"Do you know how many are in the gang?"

"How many did you see when you were attacked?"

Charlotte closed her eyes, trying to remember. Her impression at the time had been of a swarm of bees, but she supposed that had been prompted by her fear. "I would say no more than eight. If the entire gang attacked us."

Nash nodded and smiled grimly. "Good. That number tallies with what we found in the woods. Not too big for us to handle, I think." His smile broadened. "With a little help from some friends."

Charlotte cocked her head. "You are up to something, Nash." He seemed suddenly very pleased with himself.

"Indeed I am." He swallowed the last of his tea and set the cup down on the edge of the map. "I suspect another attack will occur during the Harvest Home festival. All the tenant families will be in attendance. You and I will be there. It's a day-long festivity that takes place out in the fields, away from the houses. How tempting a prize would that be to such a bold gang."

Charlotte stared at him, appalled at the logic of his words. Even her house at Lyttlefield or the very manor house in which she stood could be attacked and destroyed. Her face must have drained of color, for he ran his thumb and finger down her jaw as if to warm it.

"Do not be afraid, Charlotte. I will hire men when I go to London next week—some strong workmen, some Bow Street Runners—to stand guard during the Harvest Home. They will be discreetly placed and will be instructed to take the gang should they appear."

Charlotte sighed, a smidgeon of relief countering the fear that had seized her. "I do hope that works, Nash." She worried her lips as another thought occurred. "Drat! The house party will be here. Will they be quite safe, do you think?"

Nash dropped his hand and nodded, his face blank. "I don't believe the gang would be so foolish as to attack a house with four or five grown men inside, plus your servants. They only chose you because you were isolated, with just one man." He shrugged. "And your party will also be at the festival, so there should be little danger to them."

He picked up his cup, found it empty, and set it down again. "The company is fixed, then? Your guests have responded?"

"Yes, I believe I received the final response just yesterday." Charlotte grasped her cup and sipped, though she grimaced to find the tea grown cold.

Nash assumed a relaxed stance that did not fool Charlotte. Her own stomach had clenched, knowing what he would ask and dreading it.

"And everyone you invited has accepted? You were unsure when last we met whether Lord Kersey would be in attendance."

Charlotte let out a breath, glad to get the question over with. "Yes. I received the earl's note yesterday, informing me that he is indeed looking forward to attending once again. Especially as his time was cut so short at the last party." Her voice wavered. "He still regrets having to leave when he did."

Nash's face resembled the carved stone statues of warriors she'd seen at the museum in London. He pursed his lips, as though he longed to say something. Charlotte cringed, expecting some scathing comment.

But he paused, seeming to gather himself, and simply said, "Indeed. Then I am pleased everything is as you wish, Charlotte."

"Humpf. I would not say it is exactly as I wished." She hesitated, in two minds about confessing to him, then plunged on. "Lord Kersey rather trapped me into inviting him, much as he did with that first dance at the ball in June."

Nash gave her a piercing look and said, "Then let us hope it is the last time he is able to do so." He opened the desk drawer and removed a small oval, the exact size and shape of the one that now hung on the wall to the side of the fireplace in the drawing room at Lyttlefield Park. This one depicted The Bull Inn in pen and ink. He handed it to her.

"I thought you might like this one as a companion to the drawing of St. George's."

"Oh, Nash." Tears sprang to her eyes. Drat the man. Just when she'd settled her mind against him, he had to go and do something like this. "I can't accept it."

He smiled, warming her as the tea could not. "Of course you can. A friendly gift is always appropriate. Besides, they should be together." He put the miniature into her hand and closed her fingers around it. "Let me insist upon this if I cannot insist upon anything else."

Knowing she had been beaten, Charlotte nodded and clutched the ivory disc. She settled it in the left pocket of her riding habit and patted it securely. "Thank you, Nash." She tried to avoid looking into his eyes, afraid of what she might find there. Instead, she moved from behind the desk.

"I must go. Georgie will be wondering what has become of me, although with an armed escort, I daresay I'm as protected as she is at home." Charlotte found her gloves in her other pocket and struggled to pull them on.

"Allow me." Nash took the black leather glove and held it open for her hand. Swallowing the sudden lump in her throat, Charlotte slid her fingers smoothly into the glove. This was torture. She stole a glance at him. He seemed absorbed in the task.

"Thank you, N—"

"The other one, please." He held his hand out, and she hesitated before dropping the other glove into it. "You say your escort is armed? Two men or one?"

"Two." Charlotte stared defiantly into his eyes, only to find them shining with approval.

"An excellent move." Nash pulled the other glove down

over her hand, smoothing the fingers one by one. When he'd finished, Charlotte could barely breathe. She longed for escape from him and the fire he'd started in her belly.

He grasped her hand, raised it for a kiss that seared her through the leather, and said, "I hope all your decisions are as wise." Then he ushered her into the corridor, calling for Acres.

Charlotte couldn't take her gaze from him as he gave orders for her men to be fetched and the horses brought round. It had finally happened. She had declared her independence and won the grudging acceptance of this wonderful, stubborn man. She should be elated. Why, then, did she suspect she'd made the wrong choice?

Chapter 24

Almost as if the clock had turned back to August, Charlotte stood in the drawing room once more welcoming her guests to Lyttlefield Park. The only difference seemed to be the chill of the room. Mid-October had settled its cold grip on the countryside. She shivered and drew her shawl closer around her shoulders.

Fanny had been the first to arrive, this time with Lord Lathbury dancing attendance. They had been quite an item in town this whole time, according to Jane. Charlotte wondered about that. Fanny looked tired, her face pinched. When Lathbury sidled up next to her, she stepped away, chatting with someone else. Ignoring him. A lover's spat, perhaps? Charlotte hoped it would not escalate into a quarrel this weekend.

Jane, as she might have expected, seemed determined to be true to her word. She'd been closely attended by several different men in London since leaving Lord Sinclair's estate in September. During Charlotte's short stay with her, she'd seen Jane entertain two different gentlemen. And now she'd invited the young man Charlotte had met at Almack's in June, George Abernathy, for the weekend. Charlotte had no misgivings about the man himself, although she wondered at Jane's seemingly frivolous acquisition and discarding of these men. Did she change her suitors frequently to keep from forming an attachment or simply because she could?

Charlotte gave a perfunctory smile and made small talk with her guests, all the while awaiting Lord Kersey's arrival with real apprehension.

The last time she'd met the man had been in mid-September—what seemed an eon ago. So much had happened since then—the revelation of her father's and Nash's perfidy, the escalation of the robber gang's attacks, the assault on her and Courtland, and Nash's unexpectedly loverlike attendance on her. The latter circumstance gave her the most pause.

Nash had been so kind and attentive of late, Charlotte had become hard pressed to summon reasons why she should not give in and simply agree to marry him. Her father's involvement, of course, galled her, and she'd love to refuse all thoughts of marriage with Nash solely to set up her father's bristles. She couldn't quite convince herself to do that, however. Nash had managed to become rather dear to her.

Just then, Lord Brack and another handsome young man, with deep brown hair and stormy-gray eyes that danced with merriment, appeared in the doorway.

"Lord Brack and Lord St. Just." Fisk turned and gave way to the two striking gentlemen.

Brack smiled immediately and strode over to Charlotte near the window. "My lady, I am delighted to see you again." He bowed and his smile broadened. "I am also very pleased to present Lord St. Just. He was at Eton with me and we made a tour of Italy together. Lord St. Just, Lady Cavendish. Our most amiable hostess."

The young man with the unusual eyes laughed and bowed. "I am delighted to meet you, my lady. And very grateful for your kind invitation." He glanced at his companion, then back to her, mischief lighting up his face. "I am to meet the fairest of the fair here, according to Brack. And I see he has told the truth for once." St. Just took her hand and pressed a not-so-brief kiss onto it.

Charlotte bit back a laugh and reclaimed her hand. St. Just would make the weekend quite lively, she had no doubt. "You are most welcome here, my lord. I was only too happy to include you in our party." She fluttered her eyelashes at him boldly. "Even more so now that we have met. I do hope you will enjoy yourself and the company."

St. Just's eyes widened and she chuckled to herself. She'd never have done such a thing, even before her marriage. Independence had given her a new perspective, a new confidence in herself. She had no more interest in this young man than she had had in Fernley, although this one promised to be more fun to flirt with because he knew a game when he saw one. Definitely a welcome addition to the weekend's festivities. The man was a charmer, through and through.

"Is Mrs. Easton here this weekend, my lady?" Brack could not disguise the eagerness in his voice.

Charlotte smiled and gestured toward the sofa. "She is indeed, my lord. Will you introduce your friend or shall I?"

"That will be my pleasure." His gaze darted toward Elizabeth and his eyes sparkled. "Come on, Rob. You must meet this most enchanting creature . . ." Brack bowed and turned to shepherd his friend over to the sofa.

She chuckled softly. Brack certainly seemed smitten. Pray God Elizabeth returned his feelings in some measure. It would be such a brilliant match for her.

As Brack and St. Just moved off, another arrival took their place.

"Lord Kersey," Fisk intoned.

Charlotte's heart stuttered, then beat so quickly blood rushed to her face. She glanced up to find the earl, elegantly attired in black, towering over her. My, had he always been so tall? Almost menacing. Why did she not remember that? Nash stood at a comfortable six feet. Had she gotten used to that height? She shook her head and smiled as she extended her hand to him.

"How lovely to see you again, my dear Charlotte," he said, bending over her hand and pressing warm lips to her flesh.

"Y . . . yes, it is wonderful to have you here again, my lord." She quietly removed her hand from his. It would not do to be rude to a guest, even one she hadn't wanted to invite.

The look in his eyes helped not at all. They had fastened on her the moment Brack had moved away, devouring her with the hungry expression of a wolf eyeing a rabbit. Did he think to make her his prey tonight? The thought set her to trembling. His presence had never sent such trepidation through her before, but something in his manner now bespoke purpose.

"Am I the last to arrive?" He scanned the full room until his gaze rested again on her.

"Why, yes, I believe you are, although Lord Wrotham will be joining us for dinner." Charlotte hurried on now that his predatory gaze had softened. "You are, however, in good time. Dinner is at six, as usual."

Alan glanced to the clock on the mantelpiece. "Ah. It is but four o'clock. We have time at hand."

The innocuous words sent a shiver through Charlotte. Time at hand for what?

"Might I claim you for a short tour of the house?" His eyes deepened to darkest blue.

Oh, no. Her stomach twisted. She could not be alone with this man.

"I fear I was unable to properly appreciate your beautiful appointments the last time I was here." A flicker of amusement lit his face. "Would you care to show me what I missed?"

Charlotte doubted the house held any charms for this rakehell. "I would be happy to accommodate you. Let me see if Lord St. Just would like to accompany us. He has never—"

"I believe he is otherwise engaged with Lady Georgina." He indicated the group before the fireplace. Georgie was indeed chatting animatedly with St. Just, whose attention seemed fixed on her with a decided intensity. It would be a shame to interrupt such a promising match.

Charlotte turned back to Alan, who grinned wickedly.

"I would love to steal you away all to myself for just a few minutes. I'm sure your guests won't mind."

But she would. Her gaze strayed to the grouping of miniatures on the wall beside the fireplace, three in total now. The third one Nash had delivered earlier this week on his way to London, a beautiful view from the clock tower. Although she hadn't decided what to do about her feelings for him, she knew she felt nothing for the man before her. Still, she was his hostess, like it or not. She would spare a few moments to show him the house, and perhaps find a way to indicate her lack of interest.

"I'm sure they will not," Charlotte said, taking his arm and allowing him to lead her from the room. They headed toward the back of the house, stopping to peep into the formal receiving room, the study, her office. Arriving at the library, Charlotte simply waved her hand toward the open door. That was one memory she wanted to avoid.

"I've sadly neglected the library since I removed here this summer. I'd like to start several collections, one containing works of poetry through the ages, but particularly of the current age. I'd also like to acquire volumes regarding architecture and the decorative arts, a personal interest of mine." She hurried on, talking as she walked, trying to evade any mention of the last time they had stood together in the library.

His hand closed on her wrist, he gave a tug, and Charlotte gasped to find herself pulled onto the burgundy carpet inside the library. Alan released her, closed the doors, and twisted the key that stood in the lock.

"I prefer that we not be interrupted." He turned to her, that hungry wolf look back in his eyes.

Startled, Charlotte backed up a step. Her heartbeat raced as he came toward her. "Alan, I don't think . . ."

"No, don't think at all." He reached for her, captured her arms and pulled her to him.

Before she could protest further, he sunk his mouth onto hers. She stiffened as he slid his hands down the shoulders of her amber brocade gown to cup her breasts. Dear Lord, this couldn't be happening. When his thumbs rasped across her nipples, she shuddered and arched away from him, trying to pull out of his embrace. His caresses made her skin crawl.

He pressed her to him and thrust his tongue between her lips, then ground his hips against her—

The door handle rattled.

Charlotte froze.

Alan moved his lips next to her ear. "Stay still. It's locked."

She nodded, willing whoever stood on the other side of the door to go away. To be caught in this compromising position with him would surely spell disaster for her. Even worse, what if it was Nash? Fear streaked through her like a shot. He was invited to dinner but had no reason to be here yet. If he came crashing through that door, she would die on the spot.

The door rattled once more, then footsteps sounded on the polished corridor floor, fading into the distance.

Charlotte broke away from Alan and dropped onto the sofa, gripping the arm so she wouldn't shake to pieces.

"This is obviously the last room you should ever come to if you intend to dally, Charlotte."

The wretch would try to make a joke of it. She looked up to find him grinning.

"I believe you may be right." She tried to laugh, but the sound stuck in her throat like the cawing of a crow.

"Your bedroom should be safest tonight, my dear," he leaned down and whispered. "Make some excuse early in the evening. The sooner the better. I'll follow you as soon as I may."

"What?"

His lips grazed hers and he strode to the door. The key rattled softly as he unlocked it and disappeared down the corridor.

Charlotte sat stunned, unable to completely comprehend what had just happened—except to understand her tryst with Alan was finally at hand, whether she wanted it or not.

Chapter 25

What on earth had given him the idea she still wanted him in her bed? Charlotte stared at the thick burgundy carpet, a feeling of dread closing in on her as she tried to reason it out. When they'd met in London she'd been ready to pursue an affair, had even been the one to bring it up. He'd been the reluctant one, seeking marriage instead. But then he'd asked her what would happen if she wanted more than just one night and she'd said she would accept his proposal and be happy. Dear God. So now he wanted to take her at her word and give her the one night. Only when she'd spoken those words, she'd been thinking of Nash.

Charlotte dropped her head into her hands. She needed to find Alan now and plainly disabuse him of her interest in a tryst now or at any other time. Perhaps she should marry Nash just to keep from being accosted by other men.

With a weary sigh, Charlotte rose, intending to return to the drawing room. Her guests should dress for dinner shortly and she would have time to cancel her assignation. She steadied herself with a deep breath and a hand to her stomach. The evening had already assumed an air of unreality.

As she entered the hallway, hysterical sobbing in the foyer caught her attention.

Lord, what crisis now?

Charlotte hurried toward the entry where, to her astonishment, she found Maria Wickley crying brokenheartedly. Fisk stood before her, his unflappable cool shattered as he stared at the weeping young woman, for once at a loss for what to do.

"Maria!" Charlotte called softly to the girl, who turned to her with stricken eyes.

"Oh, Charlotte!" She ran into Charlotte's arms, burrowing against her like a small animal going to ground. "What am I to do?"

"Hush, my dear. The company is gathered in the drawing room. You don't want them to see you like this." Charlotte wrapped her arms around her and nodded to Fisk. "Light a fire in the small receiving room and fetch Lady John, please." The butler nodded, squared his shoulders, and sped off. Slowly, she walked Maria toward the formal chamber, giving Fisk plenty of time to light the fire and leave before they arrived.

"I am so surprised to see you, my dear. Your note said you were otherwise engaged this weekend, so I did not expect you, although I am pleased you could attend the party. Did your plans change?" Charlotte peeped into the room. All clear. She led Maria to the chair nearest the fire and gently sat her down.

The distraught widow clung to her, tears still flooding down her cheeks.

She disengaged her arms from Maria and sat next to her. What on earth was all this to-do about?

Maria wiped at her streaming eyes with the back of her hand, her face pinched and miserable.

Charlotte rifled her pockets and produced a handkerchief. The girl snatched it up, covered her streaming eyes, and bowed her head. "I just want to die, Charlotte. Just die."

"My dear, you must tell me what has distressed you so." Charlotte patted her hand but could not fathom the reason for the girl's distraught behavior. Had something happened to her family? Had a suitor jilted her? Where was Jane? Surely she would know what to do.

"I am sorry to appear so suddenly after declining your kind invitation, but I didn't know where else to go." Maria wiped her eyes and raised her head to stare desolately at Charlotte.

"Well, of course you should have come here." Charlotte patted Maria's hands again, peering at the doorway. Drat. Still no Jane. "We are your friends, Maria. If there is something we can do to help you—"

"No one can help me!" Sobs shook her slight frame as she bent forward, her head on her knees.

God in heaven, what could be the matter? What had happened that Maria would think there could be no remedy for it? Well, one thing might help the poor girl. Charlotte rose and paced to the sideboard. She removed the stopper from the cut-crystal decanter and poured a good shot of brandy into a tumbler. On second thought, best pour one for herself as well. This afternoon's events had shaken her. She needed reinforcements before she pried Maria's problem out of her.

"Here you go, my dear." She pulled the young widow into a sitting position and thrust the glass into her hand. "You need to catch your breath. Drink this and then when Jane comes we will puzzle this out together."

Charlotte took a sip of the amber liquid, relishing the burn that traced a path down her throat into her stomach. She'd never drunk spirits much, only wine at dinner and a sherry now and then. The popular ratafia she had never cared for. Another good swallow and her muscles began to relax. This brandy seemed to fortify her. No wonder men preferred it. She could deal with Maria and Alan much better now.

Maria held her glass in both hands, as if a child with a cup of milk. She had not tasted it yet.

"Here, dear, drink this up. It will make things ever so much better." Charlotte urged the cup to the girl's lips. Maria wrinkled her nose and took the smallest of sips. Her grimace told Charlotte she would get no more of the spirits down her. Indeed, Maria pushed the glass into Charlotte's hand and shook her head.

"Ugh. That tastes nasty, Charlotte. Please don't make me drink it." Maria settled herself in her seat, a measure of calm seeming to steal over her.

"All right. But I daresay Jane will say the same thing."

"What will I say, Charlotte?" Her cousin sailed into the room, going directly to the distressed young woman. "Maria. What a pleasant surprise." Jane bussed her cheek. "Charlotte said you were unable to attend this weekend." She took in the red eyes and woebegone face. "But whatever is the matter, my dear?"

The poor child arose and threw herself into Jane's arms, the weeping recommencing with renewed vigor. Charlotte took another swallow of brandy, then carried the glasses back to the sideboard. The sobbing behind her quieted. Thank goodness Jane had a calming effect on Maria. Charlotte's patience with the girl had begun to thin.

"Jane, what am I to do?" The pair sat on the sofa, Maria twisting the handkerchief to and fro.

"First, you must tell me what the matter is." Jane stroked the pale, woebegone face. "Then I will be able to advise you accordingly." She looked expectantly at her friend.

Maria cast a wretched glance from Jane to Charlotte, her eyes so stricken that instantly Charlotte understood this problem to be grave beyond her experience.

"I had hoped, up until yesterday, I had nothing to fear. That I was simply making a storm in a teacup. But I have counted and recounted and I have—" She came to a dead stop, bowed her head, and whispered, "I have missed my courses."

Charlotte and Jane exchanged a puzzled look. This was the dire circumstance that had brought Maria hurtling into the country?

"My dear, that is not an unusual occurrence," Jane said, wrapping her arm around Maria's shoulder. "Some women do miss their time occasionally, with no ill effects. It is only when you have been having marital relations that this event becomes more momentous."

Maria's silence sent a shiver of unease through Charlotte. Surely this could not be so. Had Maria had a dalliance with someone? Charlotte would never have believed it of the shy little widow. There must be some other explanation.

"Have you had any distress recently, Maria?" Charlotte asked, praying for some domestic argument with the girl's parents. "Any grave illness? That will sometimes upset your monthly courses." Dread filled Charlotte even as she spoke. A sickness of any sort would be a godsend at this moment.

"No, I have been extremely well. Except . . ." Maria studied her handkerchief as if her life depended on it. "Except in the mornings sometimes. I have been ill just after rising from my bed."

Oh dear God. Charlotte could feel the blood drain from her face.

"And the last time you had your courses was . . . ?"

"In August."

"So you have missed them twice?"

Maria lowered her head and nodded.

"And you have taken a man to your bed during this time?" Jane, though pale also, straightened her back and seemed determined to face this crisis head on.

Again the young widow nodded.

"When did this happen?" Jane's voice remained calm, matter-of-fact.

The girl glanced fearfully at her hostess and said, "At the first house party here, in August."

The light in the receiving room wavered before Charlotte's eyes.

"And was that the only time?" Jane continued her questioning while Charlotte tried not to consider the possibilities of who Maria had taken to her bed. Any of the men she had invited could have been the culprit.

With a hitching sob, Maria shook her head. "No. The first time was here and then later, in London, we met . . . often."

Charlotte squeezed her eyes shut and clasped her hand over her chest, trying to keep her hammering heart from escaping. What had she expected to happen? Her parties had been designed to throw men and women together for the purpose of seduction. Still, a widow had to have known the risks involved. But who would think of those risks while being seduced? Charlotte had not. If not for the grace of God, she might this moment be with child as well.

Abruptly, she arose and headed for the brandy decanter. Perhaps the fiery spirits would burn away some of her guilt. She poured half a tumbler full and took a huge swallow. It brought tears to her eyes, but she took a deep breath and the slow burn reached through her stomach toward her legs and arms.

"Charlotte."

Jane's voice finally penetrated her brandy-fogged mind. She glanced at her glass to find it empty. Had she truly

had so much? She shook her head, trying to brush away
the cobwebs. Jane might need her yet.

"Yes?"

"You should take Maria to her room and see that she is
comfortably settled. She must be extremely tired after her
journey. Especially in her condition." Jane rose, taking
Maria by the arm.

Charlotte nodded. A bad idea, that. She held a hand out
to steady herself as she walked with them to the door. If
only the dratted wall would stop running into her.

At the threshold she stopped Jane to whisper, "Did she
tell you who . . . ?"

Jane shook her head. "She wants to confront him with
the news first. She says you invited him here this weekend."

"Dear Lord."

"I will have a talk with her after dinner and see if I can
get her to confide in me. Then I could lend my support if
the man refuses to come up to scratch." Jane peered at
Charlotte with narrowed eyes. "Perhaps you should lie
down before dinner, dearest. If I'm not mistaken, you are
more than a bit foxed. It has been an eventful day and will
likely be an even more eventful evening. You will need
your wits about you."

Charlotte closed her eyes and the room started to tilt.
She opened them immediately and said, "I think that an
excellent plan." Glancing at the none-too-steady corridor,
she grasped the doorframe and asked, "Will you help me
get Maria settled? Perhaps I need more rest than I thought."

Jane stared at her, then raised her gaze to the ceiling. "Of
course, my dear. The hostess must be at her best for all her
guests. I'll inform Fisk to send her luggage to the . . . ?"

Charlotte paused, the layout of the bedrooms and their
occupants spinning through her head. They had been or-
derly in her mind only an hour or so ago. "The green
room is unoccupied. Or is it the pink room?"

Jane's eyebrows were dangerously close to her nose. *Whatever have I done now?*

"I will ask Fisk." Now her mouth was pursed as well. "I will take Maria to her room, then announce to your guests that you have had to retire early due to an indisposition." Jane leaned close. "It will not do for you to appear foxed before your guests, Charlotte. I suggest you go directly to your room, crawl into your bed, and stay there. Tomorrow you will feel exceedingly worse, but with luck you will be able to appear for luncheon."

"But Jane, this is all my fault." Tears threatened as Charlotte searched in vain for her handkerchief. Drat. She'd given it to Maria.

"There are at least two others who share a somewhat larger part of the blame, my dear." Jane patted Charlotte on the arm and escorted her across the threshold. Maria stood waiting, wringing her hands in the corridor. "You cannot be held accountable for their actions. Now, off to your bed. I will make your excuses."

Charlotte nodded and trailed behind the two women as they climbed the stairs. If only she could lie down and sleep, perhaps when she woke up the world would have righted itself.

She grabbed for the banister as the steps suddenly listed to the left. Would anything ever be right again?

Chapter 26

When Charlotte reached her suite of rooms, she paused in an attempt to let her head clear. She'd had to walk very carefully from the staircase to the door because the floor kept tilting at an alarming angle. No wonder men drank to forget their sorrows. They had to concentrate too hard on doing everything else to think about them. She leaned against the door, pushed down the latch, and slid into her sitting room.

The blazing fireplace created an inviting cocoon of warmth. Charlotte staggered to the nearest chair and slumped into it. Apparently she had not drunk enough yet. She still remembered her house party had perhaps led to the ruin of a young woman. She glanced at the small table that held a decanter and two glasses. It had remained untouched in her suite because she had placed it there, hoping to offer it eventually to a male companion.

Charlotte sighed and leaned her head against the back of the chair. She'd had no thought her idea to host a weekend party would result in such an unfortunate turn of events. True, she had assumed most of her guests would eventually find their way into bed together. And of course widows should know all the dangers of such liaisons. But the possible consequences hadn't crossed her mind. Until now. How stupid of her. First, an unfulfilled wife and now a bad hostess.

She stared at the amber liquid in the decanter that seemed to glow in the firelight. Perhaps a small amount more would be enough to push those thoughts out of her head. Trying to summon the energy to move, she lay back, allowing the question she had been avoiding to come to the forefront of her mind.

Who had fathered Maria's baby?

The guest list from her first weekend party danced tantalizingly clearly in her otherwise foggy brain. Brack, Fernley, Sinclair, Kersey, and Nash. She closed her eyes and concentrated on each man and his actions as she remembered them. Any one of them could be the culprit.

Lord Brack had seemed devoted to Elizabeth. They had spent a good deal of time together over the course of the five days. In her judgement, he had appeared not at all interested in Maria. Hadn't Georgie also informed her that her brother had gone from Kent to Brighton in August, not to London? Very well, then, one less candidate on the list.

Fernley was a top contender, even though he had seemed ill-suited to the company. Still, as an eligible parti, his enticements might have tempted Maria to succumb to his dubious charms. He possessed a title and enough wealth to be persuasive. If she had invited the little weasel, she could bring him up to scratch in no time. The image of Nash pitching the unfortunate Fernley into the rosebushes popped into her head and she laughed.

From the midst of her befuddled brain, Jane's earlier words surfaced: "She says you invited him here this weekend."

Maria had asked who would be attending before she had declined her invitation. Charlotte had written her and enclosed the guest list. So the girl knew Fernley would not be here. He could not be Maria's seducer. A relief in one way—Charlotte would not have the poor girl saddled with Lord Fernley for life. A distressing circumstance in another way as now there remained only three gentlemen who might have fathered the child. Sinclair, Kersey, and Nash. Unwelcome possibilities all.

Charlotte rolled her head back and forth against the chair until the room began to spin. With an effort she sat up and focused on the decanter. She would need another libation if she decided to continue her line of reasoning. The outcome seemed bleak at best. She tottered up onto her feet, lurched to the table, and managed to pour a glass of brandy, only half full by the time she'd finished sloshing the liquid around and sat back down. Just as well. The spirits needed to slow her thoughts, not render her insensible. Thank goodness carpets could be cleaned.

The fire of the liquid exploded in her stomach, seeming to radiate outward at an alarming rate.

"Is it getting hot in here?" she said to the empty room. Rose had not come to assist her into her nightgown yet and her clothing had begun to suffocate her. She must ring for her maid.

Drink in hand, Charlotte made her way into her bedroom. The fire here did not burn so intensely, rendering the air a touch cooler. She rang for Rose, then flopped onto the blue brocade coverlet, holding the tumbler out from her in an effort to avoid spilling any more. She closed her eyes and her body sank almost out of existence.

"My lady!"

Rose's indignant and loud voice jolted Charlotte back into herself. She sat up abruptly, spilling brandy onto her gown.

"Drat." Charlotte handed the drink to Rose and tried to wipe at the stain with her hand.

"My lady, what are you doing?" Rose set the glass on the nightstand, then peered at her mistress. Mouth set in stern lines and a frown deepening her eyebrows, the woman tsk-tsked until she had stripped Charlotte completely.

Charlotte lay back once more, luxuriating in the soft coverlet cool against her naked skin. Nash should see her like this. She doubted he'd be able to resist her then, wedding vows or not.

Rose pulled her into a sitting position, drew a plain white nightgown over her head, and sighed. "I'm sure I don't know why you've gotten yourself in this state, my lady. You've never been one to hold with strong drink." Rose maneuvered Charlotte under the covers.

"Well, I'm holding it now." Charlotte reached for the glass on the table and slid dangerously close to falling out of bed.

"Not well, you're not. What has gotten into you?" Rose removed the tumbler to the mantel.

"It's not what's gotten into me, Rose, it's what's gotten into . . ." From somewhere deep inside, caution about gossip with servants surfaced. "Never mind. My head aches." She put her hand to her head where a nagging little pain had begun.

"You'll feel worse tomorrow, if I may say so, my lady."

Charlotte shook her head and winced. "I believe you may be right, Rose. So let me be until morning. You may come in and pick up the pieces then. But for the love of God, do not disturb me tonight."

Rose sniffed, picked up Charlotte's clothing, and carried it to her dressing room. After an inordinate amount of time, she reemerged. "Everything is put to rights, my lady. I'll see to you in the morning. Sleep if you can."

The maid returned to the bed and slid a chamber pot under it within easy reach. "In case you come on sick during the night." With a final puzzled shake of her head, she left Charlotte alone with the quiet of the cozy room.

Blessed silence reigned. So quiet in fact, Charlotte caught herself nodding off.

That would never do. It was much too early to go to sleep. She struggled to sit up in the bed. She needed something to occupy her. Another drink would taste fine about now. But the glass sat all the way over on the mantel. She could make it there, of course, or to the table with the decanter, although both seemed very far away. Drat Rose!

There must be something else to keep her occupied. What had she been thinking about earlier? Nash? No; well, maybe. Alan? Yes. She'd been puzzling over the identity of Maria's lover. Three possible men left: Sinclair, Alan, and Nash. None of them a name to relish. Charlotte hated to think that Sinclair had been toying with Maria while wooing her cousin. He had invited both of them to his estate after the last party, so he had been much in company with them both.

However, Jane had told her that Sinclair had stayed in Suffolk instead of accompanying her and Maria back to London. And of course, Lord Sinclair had not been invited to this weekend's party. With a sigh of contentment, Charlotte snuggled down into the covers. Only two contenders left.

Oh, no. She came wide awake. Those two were the last men she'd hoped it would be. Alan's reputation alone, however, lent itself to persuading her that he could have done such a thing. Yet, had he had the opportunity? He'd left in the middle of the night the first night of the party. When she saw him, he had been fully dressed and ready to leave. She doubted he'd had time or inclination for a tryst that night or he'd have come to her.

Which left only Nash. Charlotte put her hands over her face, trying to rub away the thought of Nash and Maria. The pieces fit together all too well if one had the wits to look at them properly. Nash wanted a wife. He had spent time with Maria that first weekend and, after Charlotte's refusal, had taken her to bed.

She shook her head. That couldn't be right. If he wouldn't take her to his bed without marriage, why take Maria? If he wanted to marry the girl, why would she be so upset? Did she not want to marry Nash? Was she in love with another man and merely waiting to see if she was increasing before giving Nash an answer?

The room spun and her head ached. Her stomach gave a sickening lurch. That last thought came dangerously close to sounding plausible. Suddenly, the tumbler didn't seem so far away.

She threw back the covers and slid to the ground. Another brandy would help relax her again. Make her forget Nash. Walking carefully, she tottered to the mantelpiece. On the second try, she grasped the glass, then wove her way back to the decanter and added more golden liquid with an unsteady hand.

That should hold her until she fell asleep. She peered at the window. Quite dark out there. It must be time to sleep. She sipped and slid back toward her bed. Well, if Nash had fallen in love with Maria, she would wish them happy. Although really she didn't. She still wanted Nash. Oh, drat. She did still want Nash. A watery little sob escaped her. Charlotte took another drink, only to find the glass empty. When had she drunk all of that? She put the glass on the bedside table, where it immediately toppled over, the crash almost deafening. The last amber drops spilled onto the table.

Charlotte winced and slithered beneath the covers. She closed her eyes and willed the room to stop spinning. The warmth of the fire, the afterglow of the brandy, and her own fatigue finally calmed her. As the spin decreased, lethargy stole over her. Softness enveloped her and she drifted down . . . down . . .

* * *

Charlotte rose toward consciousness, roused by a tickling on her neck. Someone with a stubble of whiskers was kissing her there. Eyes still closed, she smiled and stretched, enjoying the prickly sensation. It sent pleasant gooseflesh all over her. And made her long for more. If only Nash would not tease her so.

She opened her mouth to ask him to reconsider his verdict, but before a word could emerge, his lips covered hers and he slipped his tongue through them to play once more within her. Charlotte sighed and slid her arms around his shoulders, pulling him down to her. She drew in a deep breath through her nose.

The overpowering scent of bergamot filled her nostrils. Her eyes flew open.

Alan.

She reared back against the pillows, trying to disentangle herself from him.

He opened his eyes, then slowly withdrew from her, his tongue lingering in her mouth until the end. He sat up and grinned at her.

"Did I end a particularly pleasant dream? You were smiling in your sleep, so sweetly I couldn't resist." He ran his thumb over her lips. "I wanted that smile to be for me alone."

Charlotte stared back at him, panting, desperately afraid he would know who she had been dreaming of. When he continued to stroke her face and gaze at her with darkened eyes, she relaxed. Thank goodness he thought she'd been dreaming of him.

He leaned toward her and she reared back on the pillow, trying to get away. He'd apparently come with a purpose in mind. But why had he come? She'd told him . . .

Too much drink.

She hadn't been able to talk to him before dinner. Maria

had come instead and she'd drunk too much spirits. He thought she still wanted him.

Needed to tell him. Go away. But she could barely move. Her arms fell from around his shoulders, like weights, onto the bed. Worse, she had to fight to keep her eyes open.

"You've been indulging already, Charlotte?" He righted the overturned tumbler, then sniffed the glass and raised an eyebrow. "Brandy? Did you feel the need to fortify yourself against me and my charms, perhaps?" He chuckled, eyeing the glass thoughtfully. "Well, I believe I can understand that. We've flirted and danced around this long enough. It's time I made good on my wager." He set the tumbler down with a thump that startled her. "I can certainly use a bit of cash now."

Wager? What was he talking about? Charlotte tried to ask the question, but her mouth had gone dry as cotton.

"I've had a standing wager at White's about you since June, my dear." He grinned, and she tried to shrink away from his large red lips. "The chaps have been laying a flutter on when I would make it into your bed. The betting's gone sky high on this weekend, so I need to do my duty. Don't be nervous. I'll make sure you enjoy yourself."

How dare he do something as despicable as bet on her? The wretch! She tried to push him away, but her arms were heavy, as if her bones had turned to lead. The room started to spin again.

"Shall I undress you, my lovely, and ravish you on the spot?" His breath seared her neck, sending chills down her body. He trailed his tongue over her jaw to a spot where her pulse leaped at his touch. Pressing his lips against her skin, he sucked her flesh lightly.

"No." Charlotte finally found her voice, although it came out sounding like a sick frog.

The guttural sound seemed to excite him even more.

His eyes burned into her, his mouth leering. "You don't mean that."

"No, no, no." Maybe if he heard it enough he'd believe it, the conceited wretch.

To her horror, instead of stopping him, her protests spurred him on. He swept the covers away and climbed on top of her, pressing her into the soft mattress. With one hand he pulled her nightgown off her shoulder, then deftly unbuttoned his fall.

Curse the wretch. She couldn't even struggle properly. Too tired, too dizzy.

He set his mouth at the base of her neck, then nuzzled and kissed his way down until he skimmed the top of her breasts.

"Nooo." Her voice wouldn't cooperate. The thin, reedy sound wouldn't carry through the door.

Another nudge of his finger and her breast popped free of her nightgown. She flushed from head to toe, wanting to die of shame.

"No." Her voice was stronger. "Alan, please stop—"

His lips cut off her protest as he thrust his tongue into her mouth.

She tossed her head, trying to dislodge him, but he pressed her harder into the pillow. Damn, she couldn't breathe. Her head spun once more and darkness descended.

Nash banged his knee on the polished cherry sideboard in his hurry to pour a much needed after-dinner drink. He had almost cheered when Lady John had finally risen after an interminable dinner and shepherded the ladies to the drawing room. He'd bolted up out of his seat and headed to the sideboard, splashing a tumbler half full of cognac. Damned fine cognac, he concluded after the first swallow. Charlotte had elevated her store after the last party.

His sour mood stemmed mainly from Charlotte's absence. Jane had made her excuses, but Nash thought something else must be afoot. Her cousin had smiled too broadly and her hands had shaken ever so slightly while telling them of Charlotte's indisposition, a sudden megrim that she hoped would not impede the good spirits of the company tonight. Nash had watched her during dinner; Lady John had eaten no more than he had.

He'd bet his fortune this somehow had to do with that scoundrel Kersey. The man had managed to insert himself into the company again, according to Charlotte. He had to be up to something.

Brack joined him at the sideboard, asking about the situation with the robber gang. He told him as much as he deemed safe. Not that he suspected Brack, of course, but one couldn't be too careful. Pouring another libation, he glanced around the dining room. Lord Kersey was gone.

"Did Kersey go to the necessary?" he asked Brack, giving the question an air of nonchalance. "He promised to tell me where I could get a pair of matched grays."

Brack glanced around and shrugged. "I didn't notice him leave, but I'm sure he won't be gone long."

The hairs on the back of Nash's neck pricked up. In the past, he'd listened to the little voice in his head that accompanied that sensation. It had always served him well. He set his glass down. "Excuse me, Brack. I'll be back shortly." He hurried out of the room and into the hallway.

He could look in the necessary, but something told him Kersey had other business on his mind. Nash started up the main staircase. He had no idea where Charlotte's chamber was, and no evidence that Kersey had gone there. The rake could have simply gone to his own bedroom to attend to his toilette.

Disregarding any qualms, he pressed onward. On the second floor he eased down the corridor on his left with closed doors on either side, his ear cocked for any unusual sounds. He reached the end and had just turned back toward the staircase when muffled voices behind the second door caught his attention.

Braced in the doorway, his ear plastered against the door, he made out a low, deep voice. Then a woman's shrill one.

"No. Alan, please stop—"

Blood hurtled through his body like he'd heard a battle cry. A coppery taste flooded his mouth. He grabbed the handle, but it wouldn't budge. He backed up two steps and kicked the door. It blew inward and rebounded against the wall.

Nash surged in.

Lord Kersey, straddling Charlotte's limp body, raised his head.

A red haze clouded Nash's vision as he grabbed the blackguard's throat and heaved.

"Gawp." Kersey managed the single sound as he flew backward off the end of the mattress.

Nash rounded the bed and dragged the man up from the floor by the front of his disheveled shirt. "When a lady says no, Kersey, a gentleman retreats." Nash reared his arm back. "I suppose that means you're no gentleman." He let fly and his fist crashed into Kersey's nose with a satisfying crunch. Blood spurted over his snowy white shirt, soaking him in a warm shower.

"Waid . . . I cad exsplain." The rake struggled to speak and breathe at the same time.

"Tell someone who gives a damn." Nash hauled off and pounded him again, giving him two quick punches to his eye and cheek. He grabbed the miserable wretch by his shoulders, swung him around the end of the bed, and launched him into the door. Kersey's back hit flat with a bang that rattled the mirror on the wall. He bounced off and fell face first on the floor.

Nash glanced at Charlotte, lying with eyes closed on

the bed, her legs and breasts exposed. With a growl he flipped the coverlet over her. "Charlotte? Charlotte!" He shook her shoulders, his gaze intent on her face. Had the bastard strangled her?

She moaned and frowned but didn't open her eyes.

At least she wasn't dead, thank God.

He turned his attention back to the man groaning on the floor. Nash opened the door, grasped Kersey by the seat of his breeches and the back of his shirt, and threw him out into the corridor, where he slammed into a table across the hall. An ornate vase of flowers crashed to the floor, showering the earl with water, glass, and pink blooms.

Nash grabbed Kersey's shirt again and dragged the man toward the staircase. Much as he'd love to kill him, he'd probably swing for it, even though the rakehell deserved it more than anyone currently in Newgate. Poised at the top of the staircase, Nash pushed Kersey down the stairs. Before he'd rolled halfway down, a crowd of men had gathered at the end of the stairs. By the time Kersey hit the floor, the ladies had joined them. Nash followed him down.

"What's going on, Wrotham?" Lord Brack peered at Lord Kersey's blood-streaked face.

"Oh, dear Lord." Lady John, Georgie, and the rest of the ladies crowded around. "What has happened to Lord Kersey?"

"Jane, shall I send for Mr. Putnam?" Georgie offered, backing away, her face pale.

"Is he conscious?" Fanny asked.

Brack shook the downed man's shoulder and Kersey groaned. "He's alive, at least. Give me a hand, Rob." Brack and St. Just lifted Kersey, whose head lolled and knees buckled. "Why have you beaten him to a pulp, Wrotham?"

"Lord Kersey . . ." Nash paused, unsure what lie to tell. He certainly couldn't tell the truth. "Let us say, Lord Kersey insulted me in a manner I will take from no man.

As dueling is no longer in fashion, I sought satisfaction another way. Fisk."

The butler appeared magically. "Yes, my lord?"

"Have Lord Kersey's carriage brought around. Inform his man that his lordship has decided to return to London and needs his things packed forthwith." Nash flexed his hand, his knuckles suddenly smarting.

"Yes, my lord." Fisk motioned to a footman and headed up stairs.

Keeping an eye on Kersey, who seemed to be coming around, Nash sidled over to Jane. "Can you send Rose to Charlotte? She is in need of assistance."

Jane's eyebrows shot halfway up her forehead. "Is that what this is about?" She turned toward Kersey, and Nash had to grab her arm to keep her from flying at him.

"We don't want to bring Charlotte's name into this," he whispered to her. "Think of some excuse to go upstairs, other than to look in on her, then send her maid to her."

"I can go see about Maria. She was distraught earlier—"

"Alan!" The shrill voice of Maria Wickley pierced the hall.

Nash jerked his gaze to the staircase, where the little widow was running down the steps, clad in a blue dressing gown, her dark plait bouncing on her shoulder.

She ran to Kersey and threw her arms around him. "Alan, who did this to you?"

Kersey groaned, his eyes and nose now puffy and turning dark. "Rutam."

Mrs. Wickley whirled toward him, hands on hips, fire in her eyes. "How dare you lay hands on him? He is an earl, a peer. You had no right to touch him."

"Mrs. Wickley—"

"Don't you dare speak to me. Get away from him." She started toward Nash, hand drawn back.

Nash could only stare at her. It was like being attacked by a hummingbird.

Jane grabbed her just before she swung at Nash, pulling her away from the group of onlookers. "Maria, dear, what are you doing? Here, come with me—"

"No. I must tend to Alan." She jerked her arm out of Jane's hand and ran back to Kersey's side. She looked into his face, tentatively touched beneath his eye.

He flinched and she jumped, then burst into tears.

Jane went forward. "Here, my dear." She thrust a handkerchief into Maria's hand. "Let me send for some water. Bring him into the small reception room while we await the carriage." She led the way, her arm around Maria's shoulders, Kersey following assisted by Brack and St. Just.

While the others were distracted, Nash took the opportunity to run back up the stairs. He stopped a maid in the process of turning down beds and sent for Rose. He wanted to go to Charlotte himself, to make sure she was well, or as well as possible given the scene he'd interrupted, but he'd probably just make matters worse. He dragged his mind back to the business at hand and returned downstairs.

Kersey and Maria were again in the foyer, the front door open.

"Please send my things after me," Maria said, supporting Kersey as they made their way out the door.

"There was no dissuading her," Jane remarked to Nash as they headed toward the drawing room. "She wouldn't even change into proper attire. What the servants at Kersey's London town house will think of her, I shudder to think."

"She is infatuated with Kersey?"

"Something more serious than that, I suspect." Jane shook her head. "I won't talk out of turn, but I believe Maria will shortly become the next Countess of Kersey."

"Then I pity her." Nash clenched his fist, wishing he could pummel the cad again. "I sent for Charlotte's maid. If you would look in on her as well, I would be grateful."

"Of course. I'll go now." She stepped away from the doorway. "Will you wait for word of her?"

"I'll be in the library." He wanted to avoid questions from the rest of the company and God knew he could use a drink. He'd scarcely poured a good three fingers' worth of whiskey when Jane appeared.

"She's asleep. I believe she had a quantity of drink earlier." Jane looked pointedly at the glass in his hand. "I didn't try to waken her."

He clenched his hand around the tumbler and downed the lot. Damn. He longed to know if he'd rescued her before Kersey had . . . He refused to finish the thought. Weariness hit like a wave crashing over him, drowning him with the aftereffects of the fight. Now all he wanted was his own bed and a dreamless night. "Then I'm for home. If you would please send me word in the morning, as soon as she is stirring." He sighed, unwilling to say more. "To let me know how she fares."

"I will, Nash. Thank you." Jane raised herself on tiptoe to place a kiss on his cheek.

"Thank you, Jane." He bowed, then turned on his heel and hurried to the entry hall to find Fisk and ask for his carriage. Worry over Charlotte would not abate until he had spoken to her himself, and even that interview might not put his heart at ease.

Chapter 27

Tick, tick, tick.

The sharp noise sounded in Charlotte's ear with annoying regularity. What the devil was booming like a drum? The ticking continued. Was it the clock over on the mantelpiece? Why on earth did it sound so loud? She twisted on her side to get away from it.

"Owww." Blinding pain as her head exploded with searing streaks of white. Her own moans hurt her ears. She choked them back to a whimper and lay perfectly still. Her stomach protested as well, rolling alarmingly. A burp erupted, filling her mouth with the pungent taste of brandy.

Oh Lord, let me die.

She cracked an eyelid open a slit. The curtains had been pulled around the bed on the far side and the foot, cloaking her in semidarkness. On her side they remained open, as they had last night when . . .

Alan.

Charlotte started up in the bed, twisting toward the door.

"Ahhhhh!" Her scream added scarcely at all to the excruciating pain that shot through her head, wiping away everything else. She grasped her head, pressing it firmly between her hands to prevent it from exploding. Several slow breaths and the stabbing torment receded into a dull ache. Her stomach roiled. Casting up her accounts seemed eminent.

Gingerly, she slid inch by inch over to the edge of the mattress. The handle of the chamber pot poked out from beneath the bed. Too far away. Any downward movement would surely be disastrous. She eased herself onto her back, praying she would settle. How on earth did men drink so much and then act as if nothing was wrong the next day? It wasn't fair.

How much had she drunk? Through the throbbing in her head, a clear image formed of pouring a glass downstairs. One brandy wouldn't have done this, surely? She'd been upset over Maria's predicament, which explained the need to steady her nerves. She must have had several.

An image of Alan's face surfaced. The pounding in her head increased. His body on top of her. Then suffocating darkness. What had the blackguard done to her? Slowly, she shifted on the sheets, trying out her muscles. Looking for soreness where there should be none. Unfortunately, everything hurt.

The door opened and closed with a quiet click. Charlotte dragged her eyelids open, dreading to see anyone.

Jane, a worried frown on her face, tiptoed to the bedside. "Are you awake, dearest?"

Her voice, even low-pitched, created an agony in Charlotte's head.

Her cousin made a *tsking* sound and eased onto the bed.

The dip jostled Charlotte's stomach unmercifully.

"It's almost two o'clock, my dear. The company is assembled for the tour of the estate. I assume I am to give your regrets?" Jane's mouth puckered, but she said no more.

A fiend in cousin's clothing. Charlotte stared at her. If ill will were tangible, Jane would be flattened on the spot. The glare would have to do; it was the only action she could summon and hope to escape the long-expected casting up of accounts.

"I also find I am the bearer of bad or, at least, scandalous tidings, my dear." Jane's teasing manner turned sober.

Charlotte's stomach churned again. What more could go wrong on this ill-fated weekend that had only just begun? Had they all found out about her and Alan last night? Death would seem a mercy right now, if so. Slowly, she peeled her tongue from the roof of her mouth. "What?"

"It's about the altercation last evening. And the aftermath."

Charlotte pressed her hands against her temples. "What altercation?"

"Between Lord Kersey and Lord Wrotham."

Charlotte's heart almost leaped out of her chest. "What?"

Jane rolled her eyes. "I thought you'd certainly know. Nash seemed very concerned about you."

"He was concerned about me?" Dread stole through her. Why would Nash be worried if he didn't know something? Had he seen her?

"Yes. He sent Rose to see to you and then had me come up and look in on you." She grasped Charlotte's hands. "For God's sake, tell me what went on last night."

Writhing as her stomach and head fought over who would make her most miserable, Charlotte clenched her teeth, her gorge rising. "Alan came thinking I desired a tryst."

"But you did not?" Jane cocked her head.

"No. I tried to tell him I had no interest in him before,

in the library, but he left. Then Maria arrived with her dilemma and I didn't remember to tell him not to come. So he appeared here. Oh, Jane." She wanted to cover her face for shame but feared it would have catastrophic effects on her churning stomach. "He saw I was foxed, but he didn't care. He told me he had made a wager at White's about when he would . . . would bed me." Heat rose in her face, making her even more nauseated.

Jane's face paled. "The man's reputation is scathingly deserved." She clutched Charlotte's hands in a painful grip. "Charlotte, please tell me he didn't . . . ?"

"I don't know." Tears started in Charlotte's eyes. "He was on top of me and I swooned. I don't know if he . . . did anything or not."

"My dear. How awful." Jane slid her arms around her.

Thank God for Jane.

"Is that why Nash assaulted Lord Kersey?" Jane sat back.

"What do you mean, assault?"

"He apparently thrashed Kersey for all he was worth, then threw him down the staircase."

"My God." Nash knew. It was the only explanation. Charlotte drew back into the pillows. "Did he throw Alan out the door?"

"No, but there was quite a scene." Jane's face lit with satisfaction and she proceeded to describe the ensuing events, blow by blow. "Considering how easily he trounced the earl, I wouldn't be surprised if Nash has been frequenting Jackson's while in town."

Charlotte rubbed her head against the pillow, trying to ease her unrelenting headache. At least her stomach seemed to have settled. "Did Lord Kersey at least have the good sense to go quietly?" Lord, the *ton* tongues would be wagging in no time.

"Not a bit of it, my dear." She patted Charlotte's hand.

"Just then, Maria rushed down the staircase, screaming like a banshee."

Charlotte listened, amazed, as Jane related the rest of the evening's events. At last she shook her head. "But why would she do that?"

"I'll give you three guesses."

Words stuck in her dry throat. "He is the father of her child?"

"It would seem so." Jane sat back, watching her closely. "They were much in company in Suffolk. I suppose my chaperonage lacked somewhat. But then, she is a widow. Though not for long." She tilted her head. "By the time the carriage arrived, Maria had sent for her bag. She helped him in." Jane sniffed. "I would not be surprised at all if they are married as soon as Kersey can procure a special license."

It wasn't Nash. Overwhelming relief cascaded through her. Not, of course, that it should matter at all to her, but she was glad just the same. "I suppose I was to be Alan's final conquest before he donned the leg-shackle." Charlotte turned her head into the pillow. She would kill the wretch if she ever saw him again.

"Perhaps, although I very much doubt you will be the last." Jane raised her brows. "I'd wager my best horse Lord Kersey will tire of domestic bliss within the year. Unless Maria manages to keep him under the cat's-paw, which I must admit she may. She's a tenacious woman, despite her appearance and manner. Perhaps she will tame the rake after all."

"I'm relieved he won't be pursuing me any longer, but I'm sorry for Maria to be saddled with such a husband. Somehow, I don't believe she'll reform him. No one could." Charlotte closed her eyes. If only she could shut out the world so easily. "So what must I do, Jane?"

Jane smoothed Charlotte's hair back, her touch soothing as always. "I think you need to simply wait and see, my dear. It may be the case that nothing happened at all. Or if it did, nothing will come to pass from it. Of course, there are other options you might pursue if there is a child." She glanced away, staring intently at the still life hung over the bedside table. "You could marry Lord Wrotham."

Charlotte shuddered and slid lower beneath the covers. "I would never do such a thing to Nash." She hardly knew how she would face the man, let alone think about marrying him and foisting the child of another man off on him.

"I do not mean for you to marry him without telling him your plight," Jane said, her lips pinched. "I would never suggest such a dishonorable thing." Her face softened. "Besides, he knows what happened, Charlotte. He loves you. I believe he would marry you still."

He did love her. And she loved him. The ache in her heart deepened. How could she tell him she carried another man's child? If she did. She shook her head so violently pain shot through it once more. "I cannot do that to him, Jane. The child could be his heir."

"It would be his decision to make. Do you think he will stand by and see you disgraced?" Jane sniffed and rose. "He'd publicly announce you carried his child and force you into marriage whether you liked it or not."

Nash would do exactly that. And her father would smile all the way down the aisle. Tears trickled down her cheeks, wetting the coverlet. Soon she'd be a blubbering mess. She wiped her eyes with the back of her hand. Time would tell if there would be anything to regret. Until then, she must keep this secret.

"Then we must be careful not to let him know anything." Charlotte tried to sit up in the bed, in her haste falling back down onto the pillows. "You can make my excuses tonight at dinner and tomorrow. After this weekend I can keep to the Park and live quietly until I know something for certain."

"When did you have your courses last?" Jane's voice continued in its matter-of-fact tone.

"About two weeks ago. But . . ." Charlotte bit her lip.

"But?"

"I am never very regular. Before this last time I hadn't had them since July."

Jane sighed. "That will make it more difficult to ascertain if you are breeding or not. However, if you have seen nothing after three or four months, or if you become ill in the mornings, I would say you are. We will simply have to wait and see."

Not simple at all, but she would find a way to endure the wait.

Her cousin headed toward the door, then turned back, fixing Charlotte with a direct gaze. "Your hiding in here will not serve, you know. Wrotham will suspect something. If you are ill both tonight and for the Harvest Home, I daresay Nash will send for Mr. Putnam. I understand the man carries his leeches in a special porcelain jar."

Charlotte shuddered, torn between the equally real horrors of leeches and humiliation. Jane knew exactly what threats to administer, but this time shame won out. "I cannot meet Nash, Jane. I simply cannot." Charlotte stopped and stared at her. "They all know, don't they? All the guests know what happened." She'd never be able to show her face in society again.

"All they know is that Kersey and Nash became embroiled in a fight," Jane said, offering a glimmer of hope. "Maria's entrance prevented any questions about the reason for it. So I doubt anyone save Rose and I, and the three of you, know anything of your involvement. That, perhaps, will be your saving grace. If the earl doesn't want a more thorough thrashing, he'll keep his mouth shut." She blew out an exasperated breath. "One hopes he would have more sense than to brag to his bride about such things. We can act as if you had nothing to do with the fracas, but only if you put in an appearance tonight and at the festival tomorrow."

Charlotte winced but nodded. Somehow she would find the strength to laugh and talk with Nash as though none of this had happened. All the while chastising herself for not realizing until too late how precious he was to her. A fool indeed.

More carefree than Nash had ever seen her, Charlotte laughed during dinner and tapped her fan on St. Just's arm. Seated this time midway down the table from his hostess, he sipped his wine, puzzled. After last night's events he'd expected a more somber Charlotte, yet here she was, determined to live up to her reputation of the wicked widow. He'd been certain that sobriquet was false; however, with tonight's performance, he wasn't so sure.

After welcoming him, Lady Cavendish had kept her distance, moving away whenever he tried to get close enough for a private word with her. She'd watched him, however.

He'd caught her glancing at him throughout the evening, with a frantic air of gaiety he didn't understand.

Georgina, his dinner partner to his right, played with her wineglass. She glanced from Nash to Charlotte, her small brows puckering. "Has there been any advancement on that front, Nash?"

He shook his head and set his glass back on the table. "I haven't seen her since . . . I went to London." Except for the few minutes last night, when he'd seen all too much. God, but he itched to pound the blighter's face once more. And shake Charlotte until her teeth rattled in her head. She'd said Kersey had invited himself to the party. Didn't she know she couldn't trust him an inch? "She's scarcely spoken to me tonight." Little wonder after that scene. He sighed, a chill of despair washing through him. What could he do when the woman he loved made it clear she did not love him? One of Dante's circles of Hell would be easier to live through than his pursuit of Charlotte.

Georgina peered around, then bent her head toward him. "I believe she's particularly upset tonight. Did you hear about the scandal?" she whispered.

"What scandal?" His blood raced at the word. He'd prayed the fight in Charlotte's room had gone undetected. "Something happened more scandalous than last night's little entertainment?"

"I'm sure you had more than sufficient reason to accost Lord Kersey." Georgie patted his arm. "You really gave him a thorough grubbing. Do you train at Mr. Jackson's?"

"Yes, I have sparred there from time to time."

"I daresay Lord Kersey wishes he had done so as well."

A burst of laughter from the head of the table as Charlotte giggled shamelessly with St. Just.

Nash pressed his lips together so firmly they drew inward. For God's sake, why was the woman flirting with the marquess? He should not have come tonight.

A tug on his coat sleeve brought his attention back to Georgina.

"I heard she is breeding!"

"Charlotte?" His stomach dropped into his shoes.

"Maria Wickley!" she hissed, smacking his arm.

Nash covered his eyes briefly, relief flooding though him, then reached for his wine. "The little mouse?"

"She didn't act very mouse-like last night, if you recall." Georgie glanced at Charlotte. "Sometimes the mouse stands up to the cat."

"Maria certainly did that last night." Nash sipped some more wine. The shy widow had surprised him with her ferocious manner.

"She arrived here yesterday, distraught, and after a conference with Jane and Charlotte, retired to her room." Georgie continued, twirling her glass faster. "She didn't come down for dinner but left abruptly with Lord Kersey. Later, Jane told me, in strictest confidence, Maria suspected she was increasing. But she wouldn't reveal the father's identity." Georgie sat back, an arch smile on her face. "I suppose that is a secret no more. I doubt Lord Kersey would have taken her with him otherwise."

"Indeed." Nash drained his glass. The revelation of Maria's plight, while startling—he'd never for a moment believed that young woman to be so bold—did not weigh heavy on his mind. Kersey had come up to scratch as he ought and Maria would be Lady Kersey well before the child's birth. A common enough occurrence for *ton* progeny to be born less than nine months after its parents' wedding. Society now thought little of it.

Did he need to worry about that circumstance? He thought he'd stopped Kersey in time last night, but he couldn't be sure. Christ. He couldn't very well ask, although the answer would be apparent in three or four months' time. So, the question for him became, could he take a woman to wife who bore another man's child?

He turned his gaze to Charlotte once more and caught her attention. She stopped in midsentence, staring at him. Her deep green eyes suddenly misted. She closed them, seemed to gather strength, and resumed her conversation with Lord St. Just, once more the cheerful hostess.

Nash sighed, blowing away the weight of the decision. He could no more abandon his lady than he could set fire to Wrotham Hall. Much as he would like to deny it, she'd become part and parcel of his life, whether she acknowledged it or not. And if the unfortunate situation came to pass, he would do everything in his power to save her from the *ton*'s censure.

He'd look forward to the outing tomorrow, to the festival. With a little harvest luck, perhaps he could convince Charlotte that no matter the circumstance—her father, Lord Kersey, a possible child, or even her own stubborn nature—he would allow nothing to deter him from marrying her.

Chapter 28

Next morning, Nash timed his arrival at Lyttlefield Park for ten o'clock exactly. The judging of the produce, one of his major duties at the Harvest Home, began at noon. This circumstance gave him plenty of time to collect Charlotte and Georgina, drive out to the festival site, and explore some of the stalls before he had to commence his official duties. He hoped Charlotte would enjoy this rustic celebration as much as he did.

Fisk showed him into a hall that bustled with the gathering company. He nodded to Brack and St. Just, who stood talking just outside the drawing room. Fanny strolled down the stairs toward a waiting Lord Lathbury. Servants ran to and fro fetching hats and cloaks. When he entered the room, Jane, George, and Georgina sat sipping tea, unconcerned with the bedlam that seemed to be increasing out in the corridor. Charlotte was nowhere in sight.

"Wrotham." George hastily set down his teacup and rose to greet Nash. "Good to see you, old chap." He grasped Nash's hand like a drowning man. "Such hubbub going on since I arrived." George lowered his voice. "I'm glad to get out of the house today. A diversion of some sort is the very thing called for. Last night's entertainment went off deucedly odd."

Nash cocked his head. He'd been forced to leave immediately after dinner to coordinate with Mr. Kelliam, the ex-Bow Street Runner he'd hired to secure the properties today. The man had arrived late from London and Nash had worked with him far into the night to assure that the festival would go off without incident. Apparently, he'd missed something significant at Lyttlefield in the process.

"What's happened now, George?" Best to ask and get it out in the open. He wanted no surprises today.

"Nothing actually happened, although our hostess has been acting deucedly strange." George stared longingly at the sideboard, containing a full decanter, then shook his head. "You told me she was a sensible woman."

"Charlotte? Of course she is. Why would you say that?" A sudden rush of dread sent a chill through him.

"Because after you excused yourself and left, the woman forgot to leave the table."

"What?" Nash lowered his voice, though heads turned their way.

"She seemed to sink into her own world." George leaned in to whisper. "At one point Lathbury had to speak her name twice before she acknowledged him, and he was her dinner companion."

"But she did finally rise and retire with the ladies?" Damned strange behavior for Charlotte. Their imbroglio had affected her worse than he'd feared.

"With Lady Georgina's prompting. By then the clock had struck eleven. Never wanted a drink so bad in my life." Poor George sounded so aggrieved, Nash almost felt sorry for him. "I had Mrs. Easton on my right side and she provided little in the way of entertainment, I must say. More engaged with Brack." George's long-suffering look made him want to laugh, but his comments about Charlotte's behavior were sobering.

"Did Charlotte improve later in the evening?" Nash glanced at the doorway, expecting her appearance at any second. They needed to leave soon.

"By the time we joined the ladies, she had retired. Lady Georgina made her excuses. A severe headache." George cut his eyes at Nash. "Same reason for her absence yesterday." He raised his hand as if swiftly downing a glass. "Bit of a tippler, eh? Demned shame, that. Fine figure of a woman." Shaking his head, George caught Jane's pointed stare and hastily joined her on the sofa.

"Hmmm." Nash knit his brows, determined to get to the bottom of this. Charlotte had never drunk to excess as far as he knew. Had she been foxed that night with Kersey?

Charlotte strode into the drawing room, her deep blue cloak already donned and a fetching brown velvet bonnet gracing her head. He stopped, entranced as always by the beauty before him.

"My dears, we must make haste. Lord Wrotham will be here any moment and we will not want to keep him waiting," Charlotte said, going directly to the two women still seated.

Unperturbed, Jane sipped the last of her tea. "You are somewhat behind hand this morning, it seems. He is already come." She nodded toward Nash.

Charlotte whirled about, her cloak swirling around her. She paled a trifle as she focused on his face. "My lord, I beg your pardon. I was not informed that you had arrived." Color rose in her cheeks, dispelling the pallor. She stood silent, simply staring at him, her gaze boring into him with a sadness he did not understand. Finally, she commented, "I am sorry you were called away last evening."

"As was I, my lady." Nash spoke carefully, still unsure of her reaction to him. "An unfortunate necessity, I'm afraid. However, I am quite looking forward to today's festival." He smiled to encourage her. "I hope you will find it as charming as I do."

"I am sure it will be as delightful as the other wonders of Wrotham you've shown us," she said, then blushed and avoided his eyes. "Come, Georgie." She turned toward the sofa. "We don't want to miss a moment of the festivities."

Georgie set down her cup and rose, glancing sheepishly at Nash. "I know you so generously offered to escort both Charlotte and me today." She twisted her hands and hurried on. "However, my brother has requested that I attend with him and Lord St. Just. Would it be too terribly awful of me to renege on my promise?"

Her wheedling tone and the saucy glint in her eyes told Nash he was being given an opportunity to have Charlotte to himself for the day. He beamed at her.

"I completely understand, Georgina." He ignored the icy glare Charlotte shot at her friend. "You haven't seen him since early last month. Of course you would like to catch each other up." Nash winked at her.

Georgina's blush deepened and she cut her eyes over to the doorway, where Brack and St. Just stood. "There is always news to be shared."

Eyes flashing, Charlotte opened her mouth, paused, then seemed to change her mind. "I hope you have a good time, then, Georgie. I expect we will see you there." She peered at Nash and squared her shoulders. "I'm ready."

She was acting damned odd. Better to accept a boon, however, when handed one. If Charlotte would come willingly with him, he'd not question it. "If everyone would assemble at the carriages, we should start now."

The room erupted into a chaos of sound and movement. Jane called for her maid, Brack and St. Just entered

with Mrs. Easton in tow, Fanny and Lathbury appeared
from nowhere. Charlotte stood calmly watching him handle the departure, her eyes fixed on his face. Her scrutiny
unnerved him even more. He'd not forgotten how strongly
her closeness affected him, but it surprised him all the
same.

Thank God he'd left his great coat unbuttoned. The
heat her gaze generated in him made him feel like a small
sun. It would scarcely abate before they reached the
grounds and he'd hate to be perspiring before the day had
begun. Good thing he'd elected to ride. To be enclosed in
the carriage with her would have been his undoing for
sure.

Without another word, he shepherded his flock out to
the waiting carriages. He mounted Minotaur, made sure
there were no stragglers, and set off.

The men rode alongside the carriages, which suited
Nash. By the time they arrived at the Wrotham estate, he
had indeed cooled down. Not that he expected it to last.
This state of affairs with her had to be resolved before he
burst into flames.

The sun hung higher, the day grown a bit warmer
when they crested the rise leading to the south field. Nash
had kept a weather eye peeled for the gang as they rode.
Best to be safe rather than sorry, but no one untoward had
appeared.

The Wrotham Harvest Festival lay spread out before
them, the mix-match of colorful tents and milling people
forming a living tapestry. The largest tent, where meals
and tea would be served, sat in the middle of the field that
a week before had held nothing but stalks of wheat. On
either side of it, stretching in rows, individual stalls had
been erected for a farmer's market, where tenants and
farmers could sell goods or crafts. Other tents had been
set up as well for the produce judging. And in a section of

the field off to the side, the stubble had been cleared to the ground for the afternoon games.

A thrill of satisfaction ran through Nash. A heady feeling indeed, akin to the fulfillment of command he'd experienced aboard ship. These were his people.

He nudged Minotaur and the company headed down the gentle incline toward the festivities.

Shortly, both ladies and gentlemen stood before the main serving tent, gazing around at the bustling scene.

Jane turned to him, a slight smile teasing the corners of her mouth. "Have you instructions for the best way to enjoy the festival, Wrotham? Or are we simply to experience it at our own whim?"

"I believe the latter method will ensure the most pleasure, Lady John." Nash flashed a smile back at her. Such a vivacious woman. No wonder George was smitten with her. "I hope you have brought your purses, for the market is famous for its wares. And," he nodded toward a larger tent where huge casks formed a back wall, "John Micklefield has set up his establishment to serve his special ale."

Grins split the faces of the gentlemen and a hum of voices ensued.

Nash sidled up to Charlotte, whose head leaned close to her cousin's. "Are you ready to accompany me to do my sacred duty, my lady?"

Her head popped up, eyes wide and wary. "What sacred duty is that?"

"The most important activity today, save one. Without it, the festival would be deemed a dismal failure." He hoped his teasing tone would banish that wary look.

Charlotte's eyebrows swooped upward over hazel eyes.

Her eyes were a weathervane to her emotions. Hazel foretold a pleasant disposition; green meant anger or passion. Much as he'd love the passion, he'd be happy to look into the beautiful mingled brown and green flecks for the start of the day.

"I had no idea you held such an important part in the festival, Nash. What is it?"

"I am to judge the produce."

Charlotte broke into a delighted laugh. "You're judging turnips?" Her eyes flashed a lovely shade of mingled brown and green.

"And potatoes, pumpkins, onions, peas, and carrots. It is an essential part of the Harvest Home." He kept his voice light, although his heart stuttered at the gorgeous sound of her laughter.

"Then by all means, let us not keep you from such a vital task. We will meet you later, Jane." Charlotte grasped Nash's arm and began to walk briskly toward a nearby tent.

"I appreciate your enthusiasm, my dear, but you're going the wrong way." Nash chuckled. He readjusted her arm in the crook of his elbow and changed their course, stepping between a stall selling fried pies and one offering plaid woolen scarves. He threaded them through the rows of booths until they came to a large tent on the outskirts of the market.

"Lord Wrotham!" Alfred Smith called from beside a bushel basket of potatoes on the far side of the produce booth.

"This way." Nash started toward the smith, making his way through the heaps of baskets and sacks of vegetables. Despite the cold weather this summer, it looked like there was a bumper crop to judge.

"My lord, my lady." Smith bobbed his head, his florid face already shiny with perspiration. "Lovely day we've got for the ingathering, don't you think? Warming up nicely."

"It is indeed, Mr. Smith. Lady Cavendish, have you met Mr. Smith?"

Charlotte shook her head but smiled and nodded to him. "A pleasure I'm sure, Mr. Smith."

"And mine, m'lady." The smith acknowledged her with another nod of his head, then turned his attention to Nash, his face now sober. "Begging your pardon, your lordship, but there's been some strange men poking around here this morning. I couldn't get a word with them, and I should have come earlier to the manor house to tell you, but I was afraid to leave the women here. I figured I could take care of 'em if the priggers started making a ruckus." Smith flexed his arm, a huge fist at the end of his beefy forearm.

He probably could have put at least two or three intruders out if hard pressed.

"Not to worry, Mr. Smith," Nash hastened to reassure the man. "I should have warned you. I've got men stationed here and at the tenants' homes to guard against the gang. Just a precaution, but one I'm not willing to forgo on such a day. Now . . ." He gazed at the enormous amounts of produce—the farmers proudly standing watch over it—and found them a bit daunting. "Where should I begin? Last year I started with the potatoes. Is that the usual way of it? Or do I start at one end of the tent and work my way down?"

"Potatoes first, then carrots." Smith ticked the vegetables off on his fingers, a litany he supposed the man had learned over forty years of Harvest Homes. "Then peas, pumpkins, turnips, and onions be the last. That be the order of it."

"Right you are." Hell. Onions at the end would be the worst part. As judge, he needed to evaluate each vegetable on shape, color, texture, size, and taste. Eight or nine bites of raw onion, with nothing to follow, would present quite a challenge for his taste buds. What had he done last year? Oh, yes, he'd gone out of order, taking the pumpkin last. Smith had been lenient with him because he had been a novice. This year he'd not escape so easily. The sweet taste of pumpkin had cut the sharp onion admirably, though. Perhaps he'd purchase a pumpkin in order to get that final slice in. No rule against that.

Plastering a smile on his face, Nash nodded and took a deep breath. "Then it's time to start the judging." He turned to Charlotte and discovered sparkling eyes and a strained mouth. "If you wouldn't mind keeping a tally of the points in each category?"

Smith produced a sheet of foolscap and a thick pencil. "If you'd be so kind, m'lady. I'm not the best hand for figuring."

Charlotte nodded and took the pencil and paper. "I would be happy to make my small contribution to the festival." Her merry eyes met his and his hopes soared.

If he disregarded her odd behavior last night, she had been more amiable toward him today than for quite some time. Perhaps the whole affair with Kersey could be put to rest. God, he hoped so. Every time he saw her he wanted nothing but to take her in his arms and . . .

Nash swallowed hard and brought his thoughts firmly back to the task at hand. "So the potatoes first?" He wound his way through the baskets heaped with brown and red root vegetables. "First entry belongs to Adam Thomkins." He glanced at Charlotte, writing the name carefully, using a stray piece of board as a makeshift desk.

He lifted a potato from the basket. It spanned his hand a goodly length and weight, the coating smooth and evenly brown. The earthy smell of it tickled his nose. The perfect aroma for harvest. Nash brushed a little dirt from one end and signaled for a knife. He cut a sliver and bit into it carefully. The fresh taste exploded in his mouth. He'd never have believed a raw potato could taste so delicious. Of course, the first one had last year as well. By the time he'd tasted nine or ten, however, it would be a different story.

"Entry number 1, Lumper. Score fifteen out of twenty."

Charlotte dutifully wrote down the information and they moved on to the next basket. Potatoes, carrots, peas. Nash took only the smallest bites, but raw vegetables were not his favorite food. Tasting became harder and harder. The pumpkins were a blessed relief, but all too short-lived. If he could only get through the onions.

"How are you doing?" Nash asked Charlotte, more to squeeze in a break than anything else.

"I am doing just fine." Her eyes still twinkled at him. "Although I hope luncheon will be served soon. I'm decidedly peckish."

"Witch." He spoke under his breath, but she laughed. "Yes, we'll be able to get something besides raw vegetables, thank God." Her laughter intensified and he continued to the turnips and finally the dreaded onions. Remembering the problems he'd encountered last year, Nash avoided bringing the whole onion close to his face. The paper-thin sliver made it to his mouth without causing tears to flow. That would have been most humiliating. Only two more . . . one . . . done!

Heaving a sigh of relief, Nash called out the final numbers to Charlotte.

She recorded it in her elegant looping script and set down the pencil. "To whom do I give this, Nash? Mr. Smith? He seems to have disappeared."

"Then you need to hold on to it until we can get it to him. Perhaps he's retired to the refreshment tent as well." Nash walked to the washbasin set up for his use. The water had been changed three times due to the grubby nature of the vegetables. After cleaning up, he offered Charlotte his arm and hurried off, glad to shake the dust of this particular tent from his boots.

"Do you have any appetite at all after such an amount of raw produce?" Charlotte's voice held a touch of wry sympathy.

"Well," he began, tucking her arm firmly in his, "if you noticed, I managed to take very tiny bites of everything." He shook his head. "The worst part is, everything begins to taste exactly the same, which makes the judging more difficult. But to answer your question, yes, I do have a bit of an appetite. I'm especially looking forward to Mrs. Campbell's pork pies. They are a treat."

Her return smile warmed him better than the sun that had decided to show itself brilliantly for the first time in days. Perhaps it was a happy omen.

They chatted over lunch, Charlotte relaxed and friendly, asking him about the success of his trip to London and his plans to capture the gang.

"The man who's heading up the detail, a Mr. Kelliam, worked at Bow Street for ten years before retiring. He came highly recommended." Nash took out his pocket watch to consult. He snapped it closed and tucked it back in his waistcoat pocket.

"The games should begin in a quarter of an hour. Would you care to stroll over to the field?" He offered his hand and she nodded and rose. His lady had exceeded his expectations so far. With luck, the rest of the day would do as well. "We can shop along the way, if you like."

She beamed at him, making his knees weak.

"That would be fun, Nash. I'd love to see some of the local wares. We will not, however, be sampling Mr. Micklefield's ale."

He chuckled at the vehemence in her voice. "Agreed. There are plenty of other food booths if you've a mind for tasting."

Nash led her first to Mrs. Faison's stall, with the beautiful plaid shawls and scarves. Charlotte made much over a blue-and-green-patterned scarf, though when he offered to buy it for her, she shook her head.

"Allow me to spend my own money, please, my lord."

The twinkle in her eyes told him she was enjoying herself immensely.

"By all means, my lady." He gestured for her to proceed and she quickly paid for two items, the blue-and-green scarf and a shawl of mingled green and gold. Mrs. Faison wrapped and tied them in brown paper and string and held it out to Nash.

"I'm sure you wouldn't want the lady burdened, my lord," the woman said with a wink.

"You are correct, Mrs. Faison." Nash grabbed the package and followed Charlotte, who had moved to the next stall, where Mr. Tillman had set out all manner of knives.

Booth by booth, they made their way through the bustling crowd toward the playing field. The games must have begun, but he was loath to urge Charlotte to hurry. She seemed the happiest he'd ever seen her, genuinely engaged with the different crafts. She had even begun to exchange pleasantries with the various merchants. He hated to put an end to her pleasure.

As they neared a stall that sold baked goods, Nash spied a booth just beyond. He grabbed Charlotte's hand.

"Nash! What are you doing?"

"You'll see," he said, pulling her along until they stood before Mrs. Hammond's wares.

"What are these?" Charlotte picked up one of the small figures made of strands of wheat.

"Corn dollies, my lady," Mrs. Hammond replied, placing several different designs of the little dolls in front of Charlotte. "They're made from the last sheaf of wheat from last year's harvest and are supposed to bring good luck to the next harvest."

Charlotte smiled delightedly. "Then I must have one, to bring me good luck as well."

"And you must allow me to buy it for you, Charlotte."

Nash pulled some coins out of his pocket. "I insist." He handed them to Mrs. Hammond, who nodded and smiled. "Do you like this design?"

Charlotte turned the little figure this way and that. "Yes. She's the one I want." It had a head and arms and her lower half resembled a skirt. She clutched the corn dolly to her, looking for all the world like a little girl with her first doll. A shy smile crept over her face. "Thank you, Nash. That was very sweet. And I do need all the luck I can get."

He took her arm and they continued toward the games area. "The dollies aren't just for good luck either. They were originally to ensure fertility—"

"What!" Charlotte stopped dead and spun toward him. Her face drained of color until it resembled the cold moon. She thrust the corn dolly from her, staring at it in abject horror, and dropped it, as though it suddenly burned her hands.

Military reflexes still intact, Nash bent and snatched the little figure before it could hit the muddy ground. He held the dolly out to Charlotte. She backed away from him, revulsion frozen on her face. After two steps, she turned and fled over the field, away from the stalls and the games area, making for a stand of trees in the distance.

"Charlotte!" He raced after her, pushing himself because she ran as though hellhounds breathed down her neck. What the devil had gotten into her? He caught up to her just as she reached the woods. His hand shot out and grasped her elbow, spinning her around to face him. "Charlotte!" He grabbed both her arms, afraid she would try to bolt again.

Misery looked out of her haunted eyes.

The horror of it hit him like a punch to the gut. Christ, he was an unthinking fool. She could be carrying Kersey's child and here he was prattling about corn dollies and fertility.

"Don't look at me." She squeezed out of his grasp and shrank away. Her arms stole around her waist as she clutched herself. One hand came up to cover her face and she wept.

His first instinct to comfort, he crept up behind her but hesitated, unsure how she would react to his touch. Her sobbing grew to a steady wail he could not abide for long. Driven to desperation by her keening, he slid his arms around her.

She stiffened, though the sobs did not abate.

"P . . . please don't, N . . . Nash." His name seemed to unleash a greater floodgate. She cried as though her heart had broken. He turned her toward him and she burrowed into his chest, crying in earnest. At a loss, he simply held her fast, willing calm into her body. At last she quieted.

Nash took a deep breath and raised her unhappy face, streaked with tears and blotched with red and white patches. Deep sorrow rimmed her eyes.

She drew a watery breath and said, "Oh, Nash. I'm ruined. I'm completely ruined."

Chapter 29

"What do you mean, Charlotte? Is this about the other night?" Nash peered into her woebegone face, his heart aching. He couldn't help her if she wouldn't allow him to.

She shook her head and shrugged out of his arms. "It doesn't matter anymore." Tucking her head down, she headed once again toward the woods.

"Where are you going?" He ran after her. The woods were still not safe. He had men stationed all around the festival, but if the gang attacked her now, his forces wouldn't arrive in time.

"I don't know. I don't care." She had reached the tree line when he snared her hand and jerked her to a halt.

"Then for God's sake, come with me to see about Kelliam." He gave her hand a comforting squeeze, but he wanted to do so much more. "I need to ride over to Wrotham to see what his runners report. Come with me. The ride will do you good."

"But I can't ride in this gown!" Her scandalized voice sounded stronger. With her mind off her troubles, she reverted to her normal, wonderful, stubborn self. "I'd have to raise my skirts and show my legs."

He laughed. "I assure you, I won't mind."

She slapped his arm and rolled her eyes. "I suspect you wouldn't."

"I have seen them before, if you recall, although a fleeting glimpse only." Her banter encouraged him. If only he could keep her focused on the gang or his patrollers or anything other than her own troubles, whatever they might be, she might return to normal. Perhaps flirtation would help. "I'd appreciate a longer look this time."

"Wretch." Her cheeks reddened and her face lost some of its haunted look. "I am not surprised at all that you'd make advances when I'm so distraught."

"What self-respecting man would not want to save a damsel in distress?" He chuckled, encouraged at the way her eyes had begun to sparkle with their repartee. "And if sweeping you up onto my horse is the only way to do that, what does a little glimpse of leg matter?"

"All right. I'll ride with you to Wrotham. I think it a good idea to see if the gang has showed itself yet. But we will ride in my carriage." She nodded, her jaw set in its familiar determined line.

"As you will, my lady." He offered his arm, but she shook her head. Without another word, she strode off toward the place where the vehicles waited. God, she could be exasperating, but what a magnificent woman.

The ride proved more silent than Nash would have liked. His few conversational gambits produced one-word replies until he gave up. She seemed to brood the rest of the way, her brow puckered as she stared out the window. Likely thinking on what had disturbed her about the corn dolly. He'd tucked the little doll into his pocket in case she wanted it later.

They swept up in front of the manor house as the late-afternoon shadows were beginning to lengthen. He assisted her from the carriage, noting the pronounced lines in the set of her mouth. His intuition whispered if given half the chance she'd bolt for home. He'd listen to that voice. It had saved his neck a time or two. He tucked her arm securely in his and led her inside.

The quiet hall seemed eerie. Acres took their wraps and Nash led Charlotte toward his study, the base for his operation. When he opened the door, Kelliam stood behind his desk, a sheaf of papers in one hand, a single letter in the other.

"What news, Mr. Kelliam? Have they showed themselves yet?" He automatically swept a pile of books off the chair and motioned for Charlotte to sit. She shook her head and followed him as he approached the tall, thin man in a dark gray tweed suit.

Josiah Kelliam, late of Sir Nathaniel Conant's Bow Street Runners, had come highly recommended. An imposing figure, Kelliam had impressed him in their interview in London by refusing the commission due to a conflict with a family gathering. Nash had managed to persuade him of the dire necessity of his presence—by doubling the original fee proposed. The ex-Runner now eyed him with disdain and waved the paper in his face.

"Nothing, Lord Wrotham. Not a speck of trouble either last night or today." The man scowled, his bushy gray eyebrows forming a deep V. "I could have just as well attended my sister-in-law's wedding as come here and saved you the expense."

"Not a word about the gang at all?" Nash plucked the letter from the man's hand and scanned it. Hiram Briggs, also a former Runner, in charge of the men stationed at Lyttlefield, reported that none of his patrollers had seen a thing out of the ordinary. They had ridden the perimeter of the property, crossed the fields and forests, spoken with the men guarding the tenant houses. No sign at all of any gang members. "Something's not right."

"Perhaps they have moved on to another county," Kelliam suggested. "If you've made it too dangerous for them to operate here, the safest thing would be to leave. When did the last attack occur?"

"Almost three weeks ago." Nash looked at Charlotte. "That's right, isn't it?"

She nodded slowly. "Yes, I haven't heard of them showing themselves since they beat Mr. Courtland and stole his horse." She cocked her head. "Has the horse turned up for sale, do you know? I've heard nothing about it."

"No. You're right, it hasn't." Nash eyed her keenly. Was she on to something?

"Well, if they knew better than to try to sell it around here, they'd have to travel a fair way to dispose of it. If it fetched a good-enough price—and it should have; that horse had impeccable blood lines—perhaps they've returned to their homes with the money." Her voice held a note of exasperation. "The price of that animal could have fed and clothed the families of a gang of ten or more through the winter."

Damned if she wasn't right. He'd likely been chasing a ghost and spending a fortune in the process.

"Who is this lady?" Kelliam's curt voice broke in on his thoughts.

"I beg your pardon." Nash recalled his manners. "My lady, may I present Mr. Josiah Kelliam? Mr. Kelliam, this is my neighbor, Lady Cavendish. You're technically working for her as well as me. Both our properties have been vandalized this summer."

"My lady." The Runner nodded, then turned his attention back to Nash. "My lord, it seems you may have no further use of my services. Lady Cavendish's explanation, if her valuation of her cattle is correct, would account for the lack of the gang's presence both today and for the previous weeks. Shame we couldn't have taken them. They'll be back in the spring, I suspect, either here or elsewhere." He pursed his lips. "Rabble always have a way of turning up when least wanted." Kelliam dropped the rest of the reports on the desk. "With your leave, my lord, I'll send runners to the crews, recalling and disbursing them. The men who came with me from London I'll treat to a round of Wrotham ale before we head for home."

Nash sighed. "Thank you, Mr. Kelliam. I'm sorry to have wasted your time, but I did believe the gang would seize this day as a golden opportunity to rob the properties."

"My time and your money, my lord. Well," he picked up his squat, short-brimmed black hat, "I'll give you good day. You as well, my lady." He nodded, plopped his hat on his head, and stalked out of the study.

"You manage to find the most colorful characters, Nash." Charlotte shook her head, a wan smile on her face. She moved to the desk and picked up one of Kelliam's reports. "He's very thorough."

Suddenly in need of a drink, Nash stalked to the makeshift sideboard. He splashed brandy into a tumbler and downed it. He glanced at Charlotte and raised his glass. "Would you like a brandy? Sherry? I find myself in need of fortification after that letdown."

She shuddered and grimaced. "No, thank you. I may never indulge again."

Nash raised his brows. "I'd heard you were indisposed the other night." She hung her head and turned away. He would give anything to know what had caused her to turn to spirits. It must have been dire.

He set down the glass and moved to stand behind her at the desk. "Charlotte, tell me what happened. I know about Kersey." He swallowed. Damn, there was no good way to say this. "I burst into the room after hearing you tell him to stop."

"You were there?" Charlotte gasped, turned bright red, then white.

"I followed him after he left the dining room." He clenched his jaw. "I didn't trust the blighter."

"Oh, God." She sank her head into her hands.

He grasped her shoulders. "I only want to help you, my dear."

She shook her head. "You can't, Nash. I won't let you pay for my mistake."

He turned her until she faced him, her cheeks two pink spots, her eyes leaking tears. "You said before, out in the field, that you were ruined." Best get it out in the open. "Did he . . . hurt you?"

She dragged in a ragged breath. "I . . . don't know."

He pulled her into his arms, wanting to take away her hurts. He longed to put a bullet in Kersey's brain for causing her so much distress. He steered her over to the chair he had cleared and drew up another for him. Taking her hands, he peered into her red-rimmed eyes. "Tell me, love."

Charlotte wanted nothing so much as to vanish into the floor or disappear in a puff of smoke. Nash's expectant gaze seared her to her very soul. How could she admit to him how incredibly stupid she'd been? But he'd not stop until he found out. She'd said too much out in the field. He wouldn't let it go now until she'd made a full confession. Another trek to the top of the clock tower would be a pleasant outing by comparison.

"I feel like the world's biggest fool." She glanced at him. No self-satisfied smile, no archness in his demeanor. He simply squeezed her hands in encouragement. "I never truly desired Lord Kersey. I considered a liaison with him because . . . because I wanted to leave the field open for Georgie, who I believed was in love with you."

He smiled. "I suspected as much after talking to Georgina. But Charlotte—"

"And I was trying to convince myself I didn't care for you."

"Did you succeed?"

Charlotte found that if she stared at their joined hands she could focus on telling her tale. She shook her head. "I was a fool."

Glancing into Nash's face, she found only compassion. "You know about Edward. Did Father tell you about Sir Archibald?"

"No. I only know that you married him shortly after the elopement."

"Father married me off to Sir Archibald as punishment. It was that or the lunatic asylum. And for five years I did my duty to my husband, despite his cruelty to me. I've had no warmth or affection since Edward." Deep breath. "Nor physical consummation."

"My dear!" His eyes widened and he clamped down on her hand as if it were a lifeline. "Oh, Charlotte." He beamed at her.

Her heart clenched as though he squeezed it instead of her hand. "I remained a virgin, until night before last. At least, I don't know now." She couldn't look into his hopeful face any longer. "I was foxed, he got into bed with me, and I fainted."

"So he knew you were foxed and yet he continued?"

Charlotte nodded, then grabbed her handkerchief and scrubbed at the drops trickling down her face.

Nash shot up out of his seat, pacing the room with thudding footsteps, muttering under his breath as he rubbed the back of his neck. A few moments later, he seemed to settle, though he looked longingly at the decanter on the sideboard. Instead, he sat back down and took up her hands again. "I beg your pardon, my dear." His mouth had firmed into a straight, disapproving line. "Please continue."

"That's about all I can say." Charlotte bowed her head and shook it. "Except I don't know if I am increasing or not." What a wonder she could tell him all this. But then, Nash had become so comfortable to be around. Someone you wanted to have with you every day for the rest of your life.

He brushed his thumb across her knuckles, an intimate touch that sent a frisson of warmth up her arm. "You deserve love, Charlotte. You deserve passion. Let me take you into my bed and give you those things as I've longed to do these last months." He lifted her hand and placed a slow, searing kiss on her palm. "And I promise, on my honor, I won't ask you to marry me afterward."

Her heart skipped a beat. The words she'd longed to hear since August, not as welcome as they once would have been. A marriage proposal now would be the sweetest words imaginable. Words of love and passion and commitment had become more appealing than freedom.

He awaited her answer, his thumb stroking over her knuckles.

There was only one she wanted to give. "Yes, Nash," she said as she brought his mouth to hers and kissed him.

Chapter 30

Nash's whole body blazed when she pressed her lips softly to his. His head buzzed like a hive. She was his at last, even if only for the afternoon. Well, if so, he'd damn well make the most of it.

He seized control of the kiss, deepening it, letting his tongue run wild inside her. She would have no doubt that he meant to keep his word, especially about the passion. Perhaps afterward she would desire more. And he would be oh so willing to give it.

Placing his hand on the small of her back, he swept her out of his office and toward the grand staircase. He resisted the urge to pick her up and run with her as he had that day in September, when they had driven each other mad with passion and denial. No such foolish notion stood between them today.

Once in his bedchamber, a fire crackling cozily in the grate, he pulled her to him and stared into her face. The flickering light revealed her beauty, bone-deep, and the emerald green of her eyes, a wonderful sign. Best of all, they shone with trust. His heart soared.

"I have waited so long for this, Charlotte."

She ran her hand down his arm, leaving fire in her wake. "We did not even meet properly until August, Lord Wrotham. That is not so very long."

"I have waited for this moment all my life." He had. The perfect woman in his arms. Even before the title, he'd wanted one woman to cherish and care for and make happy for all his life. What his father and mother had had for too brief a time.

"I'm not worthy of that," she whispered, tears starting from her eyes.

He grasped her chin and forced her to look at him. "You are more than worthy, my lady. You are my vision of happiness and I will not be gainsaid." He seized her head, pressed her lips against his, tilting her face, melding them into one. Hunger erupted in his groin. Appeasement finally to hand, he broke the kiss and made short work of her gown and stays. Her wrap had been abandoned in the office, giving him one less layer to tear through.

At last she stood before him, like the birth of a new Venus. Her pale skin glowed in the firelight, a perfect splash of cream save for her rosy cheeks, the dusky pink of her nipples, and the dark chestnut of the curls above her thighs.

Sight of her created havoc in his breeches.

She glanced down at him and laughed softly. "We must hurry a bit, don't you think? We wouldn't want you to suffer any more than necessary." She drew two pins from her head and the mass of her rich, dark hair cascaded around her shoulders, over her breasts, to curl at her waist.

"No, he has suffered enough at your hands, my lady." Nash tore off his cravat, then began to tug at the buttons of his shirt. Too many of the damned things, to be sure.

He glanced down. Damn, his boots were still on. He plucked them off and dragged his shirt over his head. He dropped his hand to work on his fall.

"Well, let him be soothed by me, then," she said, slipping her hand inside his waistband.

Her long, soft fingers wrapped around his cock.

Dear God. Nash groaned, caught between the ecstasy of her touch and the torture of his need. He wanted to go slow, to pleasure her again and again before taking his ease. That plan would have to be abandoned. They'd be lucky to make it to the bed at this rate.

"Charlotte." He pried her fingers from around him. "Let me see to you first. I want to give you the pleasure you deserve. But if you continue this way, we may end up too fast and frantic."

"Oh." Her face lost some of its joy. "I wanted to—"

"And you will." He bent to nuzzle her neck. "I will beg you to pleasure me." Finally, the blasted breeches and drawers were kicked away. It took all his self-control not to heft her up and impale her immediately on his rock-hard shaft.

Instead, he gathered her to him, pressing his hard heat against her smooth belly. Her gasp turned into a moan that inflamed him that much more. Christ, he would have to hurry. Perhaps their second time could be leisurely.

He raked the covers back, then picked her up and lay her on crisp sheets in the middle of the huge oak bed. Her hair fanned out across the pillows, a dark swath against the stark white. Dear Lord, he hoped she was ready for him.

He climbed up onto the bed, stretching his length alongside her. With a slowness that cost him agonies below, he slid his hand over her breast, watching as first one, then the other dark nipple furled themselves into tight buds. They called to him like sirens. He lowered his head and touched his tongue to the nearest one.

Charlotte sucked in her breath and shifted beneath his hand.

He laved the little peak thoroughly, then blew gently across the moist surface. The skin of her breast pimpled and the nipple contracted even more tightly, jutting up like the tiny stem of his pocket watch. Could he wind her even tighter? He sucked the nipple into his mouth and let his teeth scrape along the hardened tip.

At the same time, he reached her curls. He squeezed the plump flesh and slid one finger inside.

"Owww. That hurt, Nash."

Shame stopped him cold. "I'm so sorry, Charlotte. I must have bit too hard." He peered into her eyes, cursing himself for causing her any pain.

"Not there." She frowned and shifted her bottom. "I didn't think it was supposed to hurt after the first time."

"Hurt where the first time?"

Her cheeks pinked. "Down there."

He smiled. "I haven't done anything *down there* yet, love."

Charlotte frowned. "You have. I can . . ." Her voice lowered, as if someone else could hear. "I can feel you, Nash. It hurts."

What the devil did she mean? "But that's only my . . . I mean, I haven't put myself inside you yet."

"Well, there's something there." Her eyes flashed.

Could she still be sore from lying with Kersey? "Does this hurt?" He wiggled his finger inside her. She did seem awfully tight.

"A little. Not like before."

Perhaps another try. He slid a second finger inside.

"Owww. Yes, yes, that hurts." She stared accusingly at him.

Christ Almighty. Very gently, he removed his fingers and sat up. "Charlotte, do you remember anything about your encounter with Lord Kersey?"

She puckered her brow and bit her lip. "Not much. I was quite foxed."

"Did you feel a hurt, just as now? Were you sore there the next morning?"

"I don't remember feeling anything that night. And the next morning my head hurt so abominably I have no idea if anything else was sore." She looked up at him, sudden hope in her eyes. "So you don't think he . . ."

Nash shook his head and ran a finger down her luscious body, from neck to the silky curls where he had lately trespassed, and delighted in her shiver. "I don't know for certain. But it's beginning to seem doubtful. Was there blood on the sheets the next morning?"

She shook her head. "I have no idea. I was so ill, I didn't think to look. Rose would know. We'll have to ask her when we get to Lyttlefield."

Never letting his gaze leave her face, he stretched out next to her again, running his fingers through those tantalizing curls. Slowly, he pushed her legs apart. "There's another way to find out."

Her eyes grew large before narrowing to slits. "So, if it hurts badly this time and there is blood, then he didn't . . ."

"That's right. He didn't . . . and I'll be your first." God, he hoped that would be true. He cupped her face, caressing her cheek with his thumb. "Will you mind that very much?"

In answer, Charlotte growled in her throat, sending a primal shiver down his spine. She grabbed his shoulders and dragged him over top of her. She pulled his mouth down to hers, pressing her tongue inside. A kiss sweet beyond belief. Made more exciting because she had taken the lead.

His already stiff member swelled to more painful heights.

"Love me, Nash. Love me now."

He'd wanted their first time together to be slow and

pure pleasure; that, now, had changed. Perhaps best to provide some quick pleasure to distract from the pain. He slid his mouth over her nipple, teased it to a point, then nibbled at it.

She moaned and pressed his head against her. Her legs moved restlessly.

Good.

He eased off her and reached again for her opening. Slipping his finger inside, he sighed with relief to find her wet and ready. That would make it somewhat easier when the time came. Gathering some of her essence, he moved to the little button just above and began to massage it.

"Oh, Nash." Charlotte began to moan and writhe the moment he touched that special spot. He smiled against her breast and began to draw on her nipple. She had always responded to his touch magnificently; this time he expected fireworks. As he sucked, he circled around her nub with his finger, coordinating the motions. It shouldn't take her—

"Oh . . . no. Oh . . . Nash. What's . . . what's happening?" Her panted words rose to a high pitch. "Oh, oh, oh. Naaaash." She grasped his head as her body shook with her first climax.

Nash rested against her now lax body, satisfaction akin to orgasm flooding him. He'd given her the ultimate pleasure, the first man to do so. It filled him with joy that he could do this for her after she'd endured so many empty, passionless years. He raised himself so he could see her happiness and found her cheeks wet with tears.

"Charlotte! My dear, did I hurt you?" Christ, that shouldn't have been painful.

She shook her head, tears still streaming, and clutched him anew. "I . . . I never knew . . . that I could feel like this. I thought it must be w . . . wonderful because of what the others hinted at. But I couldn't have imagined this. . . . I'm just so glad it happened with you." She burrowed into his shoulder and his heart lurched so hard she must feel it.

"Shhhh, love. It's all right. I am honored to have been the one to give you such pleasure." He stroked the beautiful head and pulled the covers over them, lest she grow cold.

Charlotte had always overwhelmed him, never more so than now. How could he not be humbled by her confession? He desired nothing more than to love and cherish her for the rest of their lives. Yet now, bound by honor, he could not ask for the privilege. He sighed and held her closer.

"Charlotte." Nash kissed her brow. He couldn't seem to touch her enough.

"Hmmm?"

"There is more, love, if you wish it."

She rolled away from him and ran her hand down his chest. "Yes, there is more." Her hand continued down over his stomach.

He sucked in a breath when she rested it at last on his still-aching cock.

She stared into his eyes, hers two pools of dark desire. "Will you show me?"

She wanted more. Even though she still throbbed with the aftermath of that delightful explosion, yet the ultimate experience still awaited her. With Nash and no other.

A fool. She'd been as bird-witted as any woman seduced by a handsome face and a fast reputation. Only she'd been enticed by a promise of freedom that had ultimately fallen short. Had she a grain of sense, she'd have abandoned her independence and latched onto Nash after their first kiss. She should never have left the library until they were betrothed. Stubborn goose. She really didn't deserve him.

At least her first lover would be one who truly cared for her. She couldn't hope for another offer from him; he'd sworn not to ask. But she had him for now, and there was so much more of him she wanted to experience.

She ran her hand down his hard chest, loving the feel of his smooth skin. Best be bold. Faint heart never won fair gentleman. Continuing down over his taut stomach, she reached his member, jutting stiffly at attention. A stroke along that heated flesh and moisture pooled between her thighs. She gazed into Nash's dark eyes, willing him to see her desire. "Please show me."

He growled and pounced, covering her instantly. His mouth pressed against hers, his tongue driving inside, taking her breath away.

She wrapped her arms around his neck. He continued kissing her until her whole body throbbed with need and she pulled back to ask, "What should I do?"

"Hold on to me."

She tightened her grip as he rose up, his knees between hers.

He spread her thighs and bent her knees, stretching her wide, then pressed his heat against her opening. He breathed deeply and said, "This will hurt."

"I hope it does."

His eyes widened, then softened. "I love you."

Her breath stopped, her head reeled. She couldn't take it in. The pressure between her thighs increased, his outer heat seeking her inner warmth.

He thrust his hips and pain shot through her body, twenty times worse than what she'd expected.

She tried to muffle her moans, but the hurt intensified as he continued forward.

"Charlotte? Is it that bad?" His concern endeared him to her even more.

She nodded, swallowing against a sudden ill feeling. "But that's good, isn't it? It wouldn't feel like this if—"

"No, it wouldn't. Until a moment ago, you were untouched." He kissed her forehead.

So sweet.

"I'm glad." It came out through gritted teeth. She didn't truly feel glad at the moment. It still ached.

"So am I." He smiled and brushed her hair back. "Try to relax, love."

Much easier to give that advice when your insides weren't burning. She let out the breath she'd been holding and the tension eased a trifle. "Nothing has been easy for us, has it?"

"It hasn't at that." He pushed forward a little more.

She tensed, but the hurt didn't increase. When she relaxed, he slid deeper, filling her completely. Without the pain, the fullness inside her and the closeness of their bodies overwhelmed her.

"Is it better yet?"

"Oh, yes."

He gave a little groan and began to move, slowly at first.

The sliding sensation started heat building inside her.

His thrusts picked up speed.

"Push against me, love." The husky tone of his voice sent tingles through her as she lifted her bottom and dug her heels into the mattress. His rhythm steadied as he drove in and out, now deep, now shallow. New tensions began to build within, like the ones before that had given her so much pleasure. She moaned with delight.

"Now that's a sound I love to hear." He seized her mouth again, plunging his tongue into her, even as he did the same below. The movements coincided and the tension rose higher and higher until she exploded once more, moaning into his mouth, squeezing him as she released her pent-up passion.

He continued to stroke into her, pounding so hard she cried out when yet another climax swept through her.

Nash gave one final thrust and a cry as he spilled himself within her. His heart hammered against her chest as he slumped onto her, then rolled away, panting like her team after a long run.

Her own heart gradually slowed to normal. A delicious lethargy stole over her. She rolled toward Nash, a smile on her lips.

He stared back at her, a deep frown over pensive blue eyes.

"What's wrong, Nash?" She must have done something she shouldn't have. But what? Everything he'd told her to do she'd done. Perhaps she should have done something else but hadn't. Because she didn't know to do it. Why hadn't he told her?

"Charlotte." He turned toward her, the distress in his eyes still evident. "I am about to do something dishonorable." He took her hand and kissed it. "Please, forgive me."

She began to tremble all over, as with an ague or illness. What could he do that would dishonor him? Did he intend to abandon her now? A sick dread twisted her stomach and she pushed the thought away. Perhaps he would tell her some confidence now that they were lovers. But what revelation would compromise his honor? Nothing that concerned her, surely. Still, an icy foreboding filled her, so devastating her vision wavered. At long last she had found the love and passion she sought, only to lose it within a span of minutes. She took a deep breath, summoning courage, and tried to smile at him. "What is it, Nash?"

Chapter 31

"I swore I would not do this, but to my mind, circumstances have changed." Nash rolled up onto his side to stare fiercely into her eyes. His jaw firmed and his mouth tensed. "I had no idea until you told me, Charlotte, that you were a virgin. And while it should not make a difference, somehow it does. I swore to you I would not repeat my offer of marriage, but having been the first man in your bed, I would ask to remain the only one."

Her heart hiccupped, then took off like a racehorse.

"I love you, Charlotte." His gaze softened, the blue of his eyes becoming an intense azure. "I want to wake up next to you each morning in this bed. I want to eat breakfast across from your beautiful face every morning. I want to fill this house with the sounds of our children. But I can't do that if you will not marry me." He glanced down and took her hand. "I know you crave your independence, but I will give you as much leave to decide things as is possible given England's laws. We will arrange for you to keep the rights to Lyttlefield to run as you see fit."

Of all the revelations today, that one may have been the most touching.

He looked into her eyes and hung his head. "I know you have been disappointed before and lost a dear love."

She closed her eyes. She didn't want to think of Edward now. She only wanted to think of Nash.

He rubbed her knuckles with his thumb.

Even that small touch set her on fire.

"I know that I could never take the place of that love, but I do think you have a particular regard for me." He gestured to their naked bodies. "I hope it goes beyond this physical expression, although I do find that an excellent argument for marriage." He grinned wickedly. "Think of all the pleasant afternoons we could pass as charmingly employed as we have today."

Her whole body heated. She wanted him so much.

He gathered her into his arms, pressing himself against her once more, stirring her passion in an instant. His body betrayed his interest too as his hard member pushed against her belly. He nuzzled the hollow of her neck, his lips enflaming her as moisture flooded between her legs.

A moan rumbled from within her chest.

"I will break my word of honor, Charlotte, and ask you again, will you make me the happiest man alive and say you will marry me?" He sunk his lips onto her mouth, filling her with his strong essence, pinning her to the bed for what seemed like forever.

At last she shook off his mouth. "I can't, Nash . . ."

The devastation in his eyes twisted her heart.

She hurried on. "If you will not give me the chance to say yes."

He lay stunned, as if flummoxed by her words. "Yes?" A bare whisper.

"Yes." She nodded, her life seeming to click into place as she pulled him toward her. "Freedom means something else entirely to me now. I want the freedom to make decisions, but I also want the security of knowing you will always be there, whenever I need you. I want the right to claim you as mine," she tightened her grip, "and no other woman's for as long as we both shall live."

"Then marry me and never worry about that again."

She hugged him close. "When?"

He laughed. "Tomorrow? Tonight? We've already started the wedding night."

"Wretch." She burrowed further into his chest, loving the clean scent of him. "I would like to have a wedding— a real wedding that I can look forward to. Not a mad dash to Gretna Green, nor a cold ceremony that I dread with all my heart." But there was a fly in the ointment still. "The only thing I regret is giving my father his way once more. He will be smug for the rest of his life over this."

"Would you let him ruin your happiness—our happiness—because of that?" Nash peered into her face.

"No." She tightened her grip on him. "Now that I have you, it will take an act of Parliament to rid you of me." She risked a peek at his face and thrilled to see his tender smile. "I would like to have all our friends and family, and I mean our whole family here at Wrotham."

"The tenants?" His brows rose, but his smile firmed. "I think that's a glorious idea. They would love to be a part of the joining of our two estates."

Charlotte slid her hands down his muscular back and rubbed herself against his shaft. "I believe we should reenact that joining right now, my lord." She seized his lips, thrusting her tongue into him.

After a few moments he eased himself away. "Much as I would love to continue, my love, I fear we have been far too long away from the festival." He nodded toward the window, which showed shadows lengthening where earlier there had been none. "We must hurry back to Lyttlefield so you can change before the supper and the final festivities."

"And what are they, pray tell?" She ran her hand across his taut stomach, trying to tempt him back to their private festivity.

"The crowning of the corn maiden and her joining with the lord of the harvest."

Charlotte sat up, startled by the image of big Michael Thorne coupled with any of the young girls who were vying for the title of corn maiden. "Joining? They don't really . . . join or marry, so they?"

Nash sat up on the side of the bed, and Charlotte reluctantly did the same. No more fun for now.

"A hundred or more years ago I hear they did more than the current symbolic kiss to insure the fields' fertility." He grabbed his breeches from the floor and looked at her over his shoulder. "If the corn maiden got with child, the lord of the harvest married her in the spring to encourage the fields at spring planting."

Charlotte shuddered. Traditions were one thing, but such pagan rituals sat ill with her.

About to don his breeches, Nash glanced down and grunted. "Wait a moment, love." He disappeared behind the screen and she heard water splashing into the bowl. She cocked her head. She supposed she should wash as well. An unpleasant stickiness between her thighs reminded her of their recent lovemaking.

Nash reappeared and she hopped down from the bed. "Do you mind if I . . . ." A sudden embarrassment stopped her words.

"By all means, my dear. And I suppose that puts paid to the question of your virginity." He nodded toward the bed, where a dark stain smeared the white sheet.

Her face heated and she sped behind the screen. Thank goodness she had been with Nash and not that weasel

Kersey. From now on she'd count her blessings every day, the biggest among them being Nash.

She finished quickly, then stuck her head around the screen, suddenly too aware of her naked state. "Can you hand me my clothes, please?"

Fully dressed, he chuckled as he gave them to her. "You must not become shy now, Charlotte. You are glorious au naturel. I will enjoy seeing you thus every night. And devilishly glad we won't have to wait until spring to marry."

She ducked back around the screen. This would really happen. She had agreed to marry him. The misgivings she should have felt didn't materialize. Instead, a calmness spread through her until she could answer back, "So am I. The sooner the better."

"Then name the day, my dear. I will agree to any date that is not too far off."

"Perhaps during the Christmas season? Everyone will be festive already and our joy will compound it." She came around the side of the screen to stand at the end of the bed—their bed soon enough—with her back to him for him to do up her stays.

"It is not yet the middle of October. Don't you think that's too distant?" Instead of taking up the laces, he slipped his arms around her, cupping her breasts, rolling the nipples until they ached with fullness. Charlotte leaned back against him, moaning with new need. "Nash . . ."

He gave her breasts another squeeze, then withdrew and began to tighten her stays.

"Wretch!"

"Lest you begin to have second thoughts, my dear." A laugh and a swat on her backside and he stepped away.

How could he tease her like that? She sighed and scrambled into the rest of her clothes. "Christmas might be too long a time to wait."

He chuckled and led her out of the room.

As they descended the stairs, Nash slipped his arm around her waist, a possessive action she loved. She couldn't wait to get back to Lyttlefield with the news.

They reached the bottom step and she glanced about for her wrap. She didn't want to call the butler and give him ideas about what they'd been doing upstairs together for so long. "Nash, do you know where I put—"

Movement to her right. She wheeled around and found herself face-to-face with a huge bear of a man, retreating from the small reception room, two ornate silver candlesticks in one big paw. He turned, and his dirty gray shirt loomed large at her. A black mask hid his face. In his other hand, a cocked pistol aimed at Nash.

Before she could even scream, Nash had whipped her around behind him, shielding her from the danger and forcing her up the stairs.

No, no, no. He must not put himself in danger because of her. What would she do if . . .

As if by magic, seven other members of the gang converged out of the shadowy corridor, sacks clinking with valuables slung over shoulders or clutched in greasy hands. Charlotte gripped Nash's shoulders.

"Do not worry, my dear," he whispered loudly. "When I distract them, run upstairs and lock yourself in the bedroom. They want goods, not you."

"No," she whispered back, "I won't leave you here with them."

"Charlotte." His voice held the command of a man who would not be gainsaid. "This is not the time to assert your independence. You will obey me—"

"'Ere now, mi'lord." The burly man with the candlesticks waved the pistol at him. "Can't have the lady leaving just when things is gettin' right fun." His eyes behind the mask flickered over her face and she ducked behind Nash. "Them's some nice gewgaws in her ears. Stones'll fetch a right nice price for the Govner."

"'The Govner?' Who's that?" The edge in Nash's tone caught her attention. Why didn't he tell the men to leave? Or call the servants?

"Wouldn't you like to know?" The sneer in the ruffian's voice made Charlotte cringe. "Him's the one's kept us safe all this while. I'm no blab, though. Yer won't get nuffin' out o' me 'bout the Govner."

"I wouldn't be too sure of that. Kelliam!" Nash shouted, and the corridor dripped officers. They materialized from under the staircase, from around the potted plants, out of the receiving room the big thief had vacated. Kelliam himself appeared from behind the long-case clock.

Nash stepped forward, knocking the gun from the thief's hand. Runners grabbed the big man from both sides and wrestled him to the ground. The rest of the stunned gang watched, amazed, as the officers seized and bound them before they could even put up a struggle.

Shocked to her core, Charlotte stared from Nash to Kelliam to the head thief, rolling around on the floor.

"Good work, Lord Wrotham." Mr. Kelliam nodded and consulted his watch. "I hadn't expected you to be at home still. Didn't we agree it would be best if you were not here when the attack occurred? You or Lady Cavendish might have come to harm." He glared at Nash. "And very nearly did."

"I am sorry, Kelliam." Nash caught Charlotte's eye, his twinkling. "Lady Cavendish and I ended up in a spirited discussion about the joining of our estates. We quite lost track of the time."

The wicked man. Charlotte bit her tongue and broke from his gaze. She would make him pay for that little indiscretion.

Nash turned sober. "Have you found out who the informer is?"

"Not yet." Kelliam nodded, and the two Runners holding the thief on the floor pulled him to his feet. "But I'm certain now that I have the cooperation of all these men, I'll know directly. In fact, let us see who we'll be talking to by and by." He reached over and jerked the mask from the man's face.

"Daniel Micklefield!" Nash's face grew dark. "Your uncle won't be able to hold his head up for shame at your treachery."

Charlotte shook her head in sympathy. Poor Mr. Micklefield. There'd be no living this down for him. The scandal might very well ruin his business.

Nash nodded, and the other deputies pulled the masks from the rest of the gang members' faces. "William Bell, Andrew Sharpe, Charles Robinson." His stare became icy. "These are local men. The others I don't know."

"Possibly from London, my lord. We've found many of the soldiers discharged after the war have not been able to find employment and have therefore turned to crime." Kelliam peered into their faces, then turned back to Nash. "We'll take them down to The Bull. Mr. Micklefield gave us permission to hold the blackguards there if we caught them." He cut his eyes toward Daniel. "He's likely to be a mite riled when he finds out one's his nephew."

Nash nodded. "See what you can get out of them. I'm taking Lady Cavendish back to Lyttlefield Park. Keep me informed."

Kelliam nodded, and the whole troop headed out the door.

Charlotte turned to Nash, who blithely placed a finger over her lips. "Shhhh. I'll explain everything in the carriage."

Charlotte gave him one searing look. "My wrap, please."

Once in the carriage, Nash took her hand. She came close to snatching it away, but something deep down stayed her. She'd hear what he had to say for himself.

"I am so sorry to have withheld that little bit from you, Charlotte."

"Little bit!" She pulled at her hand, but he held it fast. "Robbers *and* Runners leaping out at me. I'm surprised I didn't swoon."

"You are made of sterner stuff, as you have proved all summer. I trusted that you would be sensible—"

"And run up the stairs like a ninny and leave you to fight them alone?" He was going from bad to worse.

"Be sensible and stay put." He kissed her hand. "I had to make them believe you were no threat, but I assumed you would refuse to yield your ground. You gave Kelliam a fright, I'm certain. He didn't expect us to be in the house."

"Joining of properties indeed."

"How else would you have me put it?" He grinned at her. "I do beg your pardon, though. I thought we'd enough time to leave before the robbers arrived. They came a bit earlier than expected."

"But why did you expect them at Wrotham? I thought you'd set a watch all over the estates and couldn't find them. And then Mr. Kelliam said—"

"That was part of the plan. We spoke in London about how the gang always seemed to know about my movements here at Wrotham. Kelliam suggested that one of my servants might be an informer for the gang, someone who knew my movements and a great deal of yours as well. There might even be someone passing information about you in your own household." Nash's face hardened and his grip increased.

"Ouch."

"Sorry, my dear." He loosened his grasp and kissed the injured hand. "I believe if we find out who he is, I'll be hard pressed not to throttle him.

"Or her. It could be a woman. Many will do anything for her man." She squeezed his hand. "I know I would."

"So I saw. You acted foolishly, Charlotte, to . . ." He stopped when she put her finger to his lips.

"Let us not waste this night with talk of how foolish we each can be." She smiled and removed her finger. "Else I will have to remark on how terribly foolish you were to try to disarm that robber."

"You do remember I have been in combat—"

She grabbed his face and pressed her lips to his. One way to stop his foolish gabble. A good way, in fact.

They arrived at Lyttlefield Park as the lights were being lit. Charlotte swept into the hall on Nash's arm, eager to find her friends and tell all her news. Lord, what an eventful day!

A babble of excited voices led them toward the drawing room.

"Everyone must have gathered there before heading back for supper and the crowning." She hurried her steps as he led her into the room, crowded with more people, it seemed, than she had ever seen there. She scanned the room, searching the faces. Where was Jane? Everyone seemed clustered around the fireplace. Had it gotten colder? Then, above the din of the room, one voice rose to a crescendo.

"I don't care what she's told you. I tell you, that is my fireplace mantel!"

Charlotte stopped so abruptly that Nash carried onward into the room. He turned, brows raised. But she gave him no sign. There was no disguising that voice.

At last, the bane of her existence had come to call.

"Good evening, Edgar."

Chapter 32

"This is Edgar?" Nash asked, scowling.

"Yes, my stepson." Lord, would the surprises never end this day?

"It's Sir Edgar Cavendish, if you please." The peevish voice rose once more. "And this woman is a blatant thief." He pointed his finger at Charlotte. "I come here to pay my respects to my stepmother only to find she has stolen all my possessions and set them out unashamedly for all the world to see. Even to the Robert Adam mantelpiece."

The company's gaze shifted to the mantelpiece, sleek white marble, with inlaid verd antico flutes in the frieze and jambs.

Jane detached herself from George Abernathy, who seemed to be searching for a drink, and hurried over to Charlotte. "Well, my dear, I think it's time to open your budget."

"I believe you are correct, cousin." She smiled at the company, whose gaze was riveted to her, and moved toward Edgar.

"I fear you are wrong on all accounts, Edgar." She'd

not call him by his title to save her soul. That ought to set up his bristles. "According to the marriage settlements, signed by your father, after his death I was allowed to take any material possessions I brought into the marriage. I have done so."

"But you've taken everything." He spun around, his gaze darting from one piece of furniture to another, until it finally rested on the mantelpiece. "You can't have bought that as well."

"I have copies of my settlement papers and a box full of receipts if you care to peruse them. The document on top is a copy of my grandmother's will, where you will see she bequeathed the mantelpiece to me."

He looked at them with a Friday face. "You've ruined me."

"I think you've done that yourself." Charlotte motioned toward the doorway. "If you've come to collect your furniture, you had best head back to London. Whatever remains belongs to you."

Edgar leaned toward her and she took a step back, almost running into Nash.

"Don't you understand, I'm on the rocks! I've got nothing. Why do you think I came back early from my grand tour? Uncle Gordon wrote and told me my money had run out. But I still had the house and its furnishings."

"You've inherited the house, haven't you?" Nash broke in, impatient. "That should fetch a goodly sum, unless . . ."

"Mortgaged." Edgar spit out the word as if he had a bad taste in his mouth.

Charlotte shook her head. Sir Archibald had always done everything in his power to placate Edgar's every whim. The grand tour had likely depleted his funds completely. Poor Edgar.

Suddenly grasping Charlotte by the hand, Edgar propelled her toward the door.

Before he had gone two steps, he was halted and hoisted up off the floor by Nash's two capable hands, sunk into his black jacket. "Lay hands on her again and I'll draw your cork but good."

"What if I ruin her instead?" Edgar jeered at Nash, who shook him like a terrier with a rat.

"You wouldn't slander a lady. Your own stepmother?" Nash's eyes narrowed.

"He'd do whatever it took to make me give up my possessions." Charlotte sniffed. She'd dealt with Edgar for five years. And the information he thought he held over her was likely scurrilous. "What do you think you know, Edgar?"

"Put me down and let us step back into the hall."

Nash released him immediately with a smothered curse.

Edgar barely caught himself, windmilling his arms to try to keep his balance. He tugged at his coat, rumpled beyond repair, and headed out the doorway. Nash took Charlotte's arm. She sent a speaking look to Jane. *Keep them all here*, she mouthed to her, then followed Edgar out.

"All right, Edgar, what is this scandalous information?" Charlotte had done with his antics. Given the slightest provocation, she'd be happy to turn Nash loose on him. With Edgar's unexpected presence, she'd not even been able to tell Jane the news about her marriage.

"That you've been holding house parties for rakes and rogues and women who are nothing more than lightskirts. How would you like for that to get back to your father, Stepmother?" He sneered triumphantly.

"And who has been spreading this vicious gossip, I wonder?" Charlotte glanced at Nash and gestured, as if she was tossing someone over a balustrade.

"Who indeed, Charlotte?" Nash grinned back at her. "I might venture a guess." He turned his attention back to

Edgar. The smile evaporated. "Are you by chance acquainted with Lord Fernley, Cavendish?"

Edgar paled but nodded.

"Well, let me speak a word in your ear about that gallant. After making improper advances to Lady Cavendish, and likely other ladies of the party, Lord Fernley proceeded to try to balance on the railing of the veranda and fell into the rosebushes. His dignity being somewhat bruised, he left the next day." Nash advanced on Edgar until he had him pressed as flat as possible against the wall.

"Hear me straight, Cavendish. Lady Cavendish has just consented to be my wife. I do not believe you wish to slander the future Countess of Wrotham." Nash thrust his face to within inches of Edgar's. "Both her father and I would be very displeased to hear such tales being repeated."

Edgar opened his mouth to speak when the door knocker boomed. Nash stepped away from his quarry and turned to the door just as Fisk appeared and opened it.

"Lord Wrotham, if you please."

Mr. Kelliam? Charlotte glanced at Nash and shrugged her shoulders. What was he doing here? She came forward as the Runner with another, younger man, strode into the hall. Hands pinioned behind his back, the stranger stared at her in stark terror.

"Kelliam?" Nash came from behind the door. "Thayer?" He addressed the frightened man, whose face now approached the color of new cheese. "What the devil are you doing with my valet?"

"He's your informant, my lord. Daniel Micklefield turned stag almost before we could sit him down at The Bull." Kelliam chuckled. "He told me more than enough about the gang and its movements. Did you know, Lady Cavendish, they've been hiding out all summer in an abandoned barn at Grafton Lodge?"

"Dear Lord." Father would have apoplexy when he found out.

"I popped back over to Wrotham Hall and caught this one," he shook the valet, "with all his belongings just setting out down the road at a trot." Kelliam released the wretched Thayer, who stood before Nash with his head lowered.

Nash's gaze bore into the man, his deepening frown overshadowing his handsome features. At last he spoke one word. "Why?"

Thayer finally raised his head, grimacing. "I had to, my lord. My family in Dorset came on hard times. My father died, you remember, and my mother's still got three little ones at home to feed. I've been sending them almost all my wages, but it hasn't been enough." He took a deep breath, though he still avoided Nash's eyes. "When we were in London in June, my mother wrote that the landlord had threatened to turn them out into the street. I had to do something." Thayer paused, as if trying to gather the strength to continue.

Nash's face remained stony, though a tic made the end of his mouth twitch. "You could have spoken to me if things had become so dire. But continue."

The man sighed. "Happened to mention my predicament to another gentleman's gentleman I'd met at a pub, and he said his gentleman might have a job for me where I could make a good bit of money on the side. So he arranged for me to meet the man. He seemed very pleased you had an estate in Kent. 'That will make it even easier,' he said. When I heard his whole scheme, I tried to say no, my lord. But he gave me a bit of money—enough to keep my mother safe for a while—and the promise of more to come. After that, I couldn't say no."

"Indeed." Nash's cold tone said he didn't care what the circumstances were. "His name, man. The least you can do to redeem yourself is to give us his name."

"Yes, my lord." The poor valet finally looked into Nash's eyes, then a frown creased his brow. He cocked his head, as if bewildered. "But there he is now, my lord." Thayer tried to point, but having no hands to do so motioned with a jerk of his shoulder. "He's in the corner there. Sir Edgar Cavendish."

Charlotte's knees nearly buckled. Edgar had masterminded the robber gang? Impossible. The boy didn't have the brains for such a thing. There must be some mistake. She turned toward the place where Nash had been holding Edgar just as her stepson bolted for the door.

Nash seized him by the back of his collar and hauled him over to Kelliam. "Sir Edgar, you say, Thayer? You are sure?"

"Yes, my lord. The very person. He was supposed to meet the gang later tonight to divide the goods." Thayer stopped abruptly.

"The goods to be stolen from Wrotham Hall?"

"Yes, my lord," the valet mumbled. He looked ready to cry.

Nash shook Edgar and threw him down at Kelliam's feet. "You have one more gang member to secure tonight, then."

"I have never heard a more preposterous thing in my life." Edgar tried to rise and the Runner grasped his hand and helped him to his feet.

"We'll have to see about that, Sir Edgar." Kelliam nodded toward Thayer. "Are you the only one who had contact with him? Do the other members know about him?"

"I know nothing of this gang you speak of." Edgar dusted off his jacket as if highly insulted. Yet his eyes flitted toward the door.

"No, sir. But I have the letters he's sent me with instructions for the gang. He's only ever been here once, to meet with me, not the gang. That was when he came down to get a horse they had stolen."

"My horse!" Charlotte strode over to Edgar, outraged and shaking. "That was my horse you stole, and my estate manager your gang almost murdered." She raised her hand, itching to strike the boy who had helped make her life miserable for so many years. Her hand clenched into a fist, but she let it fall to her side. "I swear, you will pay for that, Edgar. My father will be very interested in this case when I tell him you used his property to hide the gang members."

She glanced at Nash. "I believe it now. When I first married, my father invited Sir Archibald and the two boys down to the hunting lodge. Edgar would have known about an abandoned barn on the property." She glared at him, then said with a sneer, "I don't think it's going to matter much whether you have furniture in your town house or not. I suspect you will not be taking up residence there for some time to come."

"This is an outrage." Edgar's bluster had lost some of its shine. "I demand to be taken to London, where I will be able to explain the situation to a magistrate."

"You can explain it to Wrotham's magistrate in the morning." Nash nodded to Kelliam, who took Edgar's arm none too gently.

"For tonight you'll have to put up with the accommodations at The Bull, Sir Edgar." The Runner pushed the two men toward the door. "A nice locked cellar with the rest of your gang." Fisk, who had stoically witnessed the entire episode, let them out.

Charlotte heaved a sigh and walked into Nash's arms. "Is it over? Is it really over?"

"It is, my love." He kissed her brow and hugged her tight. "Although I am now, unfortunately, in need of a valet."

"I feel so badly for Thayer," Charlotte said, winding her arms around his waist. "He was trying to help his family and ended up duped by my stepson." She peered into his face, his eyes more flinty than she'd ever seen them. Perhaps her best wheedling tone would work. "I know what he did was wrong, but can't we do something for him? Please, Nash?"

He grunted and pulled her back to him. "I'll speak to the magistrate. Ask for leniency. Transportation instead of hanging. That's the most I can do."

"Was he a good valet?"

"I've only ever had the one."

Charlotte laughed. "But until this evening, he did his job well?"

"Yes."

"Then I think you should do something for his family. They will be destitute without him." She gazed into his eyes, willing him to agree. "Please?"

"Well, I suppose a small annuity to keep Mrs. Thayer from destitution might be in order." Nash pulled her head back and smiled down at her. "Will that suffice, my lady?"

"Admirably. Something is always better than nothing, my lord. Haven't you learned that?" And she certainly had something now.

"Charlotte!" Jane's voice echoed in the hall.

She glanced down the hall to find her cousin standing in the doorway to the drawing room. "If you don't come this minute and explain yourself and all these goings on, I shall have to resort to strong spirits to calm my nerves."

"We are coming." Charlotte wound her arm in Nash's and they strolled down the hall. "I've some news for you."

Chapter 33

Moonlight streamed across the fields, dotted with the gaily colored lanterns of the Harvest Festival as Charlotte and Nash walked back toward the carriage. Quite a wonderful day really, despite all the hullabaloo. But she wouldn't have changed a minute of it.

After explanations and wishes of happiness for them, the party had arrived back at the festival just in time for the crowning of the corn maiden. Nora Myers, sixteen and dressed in an enticing pink frock, had received the crown of plaited wheat straw and a decidedly unchaste kiss from Michael Thorne. From her enthusiastic reaction, her parents had best keep an eye on her tonight.

When they reached the carriage, instead of handing her in, Nash glanced around, then grabbed a blanket from within.

"What are you doing?" Although loathe to admit it, Charlotte wanted nothing more than her bed. She'd prefer Nash's bed, of course, but that wouldn't happen for a matter of weeks. Christmas seemed to loom far in the distance. She might want to reconsider that date.

"Shhh." He grinned in the pale light of the moon and

took her hand. "Come on." He led her away from the festivities, still in high gear, toward one of the newly cut fields. On and on, they walked carefully over the uneven ground.

"Nash. What are you doing?"

"Here we are." He spread the carriage blanket on the ground.

Did he want to gaze at the stars? She rubbed her arms. Too chilly out here for that, even with her heavy cloak.

Once he had the blanket spread to his satisfaction, he drew her to him and, without any warning, pulled her mouth up to his. The strains and stresses of the day melted like ice in the sun as he filled her whole world with his presence. He lingered on her lips before slipping his tongue into her mouth, lighting a fire in her belly that the chill air couldn't touch.

He filled his hands with her breasts, pinching her nipples until they ached and tingled. Oh, the blaze he stoked within her would have to be quenched. She only knew one way to do that.

She slipped her hands around his waist, pulling him flush against her, the hard heat of him searing her through their clothes. An ache of need began deep in her core. By the time it emerged, it would be a growl of desire. The next thing she knew, she lay on the blanket, stubble poking her in the back. She ignored it and reached for his waistband.

"Let me do that, love." He knelt above her, fumbling with his breeches, then the chilly air swept over her legs as he raised her skirts above her hips. "We will have our own crowning tonight, Charlotte."

She caught her breath, then thrilled as he entered her. One smooth thrust and he seated himself completely inside her. No pain this time, but a delicious fullness, a sense of oneness. Perfectly right.

He began to move, his slow rhythm quickly giving

way to a fast, hard, frantic pace that drove her into a heated frenzy. This had been the ritual from the beginning of time. Seed to a fertile soil. Their land would be blessed and in the spring . . . She thrust her hips upward, his shaft pounding faster and faster until they both cried out their release to the cold night air.

Nash slumped on top of her and Charlotte lay panting, clinging to him, never wanting to let go. But she must. The heat of their passion cooled and the chill temperature set her to shivering. He rolled off her and pulled her skirt down. The corn maiden gone, she was a lady once more.

He sat up, rearranging his fall. "I'll just be a minute. We'd best get back."

Charlotte sat up, looking all around her. The lights of the festival gleamed suddenly close. "You don't think anyone saw us, do you, Nash?"

He grinned in the slight light. "Only the one who needed to see." He reached above where her head had lain and plucked something from the blanket. In the moonlight, the corn dolly he'd bought her that morning seemed to shine with a light of its own. He handed it to her.

"I really don't see the need to wait for Christmas, do you, love?"

"None at all, my dear." She clutched the little straw doll to her. So precious.

"The banns can be read in two weeks," he said, scrambling up before giving her his hand.

"A special license can be gotten on Monday."

He laughed and kissed her again. "My wicked widow. You need time to prepare for the wedding you never had. I think six weeks will serve." He kissed her again, his lips lingering. "Although I see no need for us to wait for anything except to say our vows. Do you agree, love?"

"I do." The sweetest words to her ears.

Please turn the page for an exciting sneak peek of
WEDDING THE WIDOW
the next installment in Jenna Jaxon's
Widow's Club series
coming soon wherever print and e-books are sold!

Chapter 1

"Here you go, Mrs. Easton." James, Lord Brack, handed her a pint glass of Wrotham ale.

"Thank you, my lord." Shivers of delight coursed through Elizabeth Easton as she accepted the dripping libation and took a long sip, cool and nutty with a pleasant bite. She'd first encountered the brew this past summer, during her friend Charlotte's first house party, at the insistence of her neighbor, Lord Wrotham. Even though ladies weren't supposed to drink it, she'd enjoyed it, and Lord Brack had remembered.

This weekend party had held more pleasurable sensation for her than she'd known since she'd lost her husband over a year before. Much of it because of the Harvest Festival, here in the village of Wrotham. Some of it was sparked by her best friend's announcement an hour before that she and Lord Wrotham were to marry before the New Year.

The bulk of it, she suspected, however, came from the

handsome young man dancing attendance on her, whose arm she now clasped. Lord Brack, or Jemmy, as his sister Georgina called him, had escorted her about the county festival all day, seemingly to their mutual satisfaction. They had enjoyed shopping among the stalls—he'd insisted on buying her one of the sweet little dolls made of stalks of wheat—had a delicious tea, and laughed themselves giddy at the antics of the participants during the various games. With their sizable party, he could easily have changed partners several times during the festivities. Lord Brack, however, had remained at Elizabeth's side all day long. Quite flattering for a widow of six and twenty.

Now they were enjoying a quick pint of ale before the final and, as some had said, most important activity of the day: the crowning of the corn maiden.

She wrinkled her nose at the sharp smell of hops. "I wonder why ladies are not supposed to drink ale. Gentlemen should not be allowed to have all the fun."

"We cannot give up all our best secret pleasures, Mrs. Easton." Lord Brack's sky-blue eyes crinkled as he grinned. He was certainly one of the best-natured gentlemen of her acquaintance.

They strolled away from Mr. Micklefield's temporary stall toward the center of the field, where the games had been played earlier. Even though she'd been sensible and worn her sturdy half boots, the newly mown stubble made her wobble. She clutched Lord Brack's strong arm tighter, the startling warmth of him seeping through his green superfine coat.

"Careful there, Mrs. Easton. We don't want you to come to grief."

Lord, don't let her spill the ale on either one of them.

Lord Brack led them to the edge of the circle that had formed around the hulking Michael Thorne, the harvest lord, and four young women—local girls vying for the honor of being crowned Wrotham's corn maiden.

"They do look pretty," Elizabeth said, motioning to the figures obviously decked out in their finest, most colorful garb, their hair unbound, flowing around their shoulders and spilling over their breasts.

"Yes, they are a bevy of country beauties, aren't they? Mr. Thorne's going to have a difficult time choosing his corn maiden." Lord Brack's eyes sparkled as he sipped more ale. "The three not chosen will be quite disappointed, I fear. Michael Thorne's a very handsome lad."

"Does he choose a girl to marry him?" How scandalous that would be, to be chosen—or not chosen—before all the assembled tenants and members of the village.

"Oh, no. Nothing quite so permanent." Brack's smile flashed again. "He claims a kiss only, said to keep the fields fertile through the winter and into the spring."

"That must be quite a kiss." The four girls preened and giggled as Mr. Thorne walked around them, looking them over with a keen eye.

Lord Brack took another pull at his ale, the torchlight throwing his features into sharp relief. "According to Lord Wrotham, it used to be quite a bit more than just a kiss." He gazed into her face, the gleam in his eyes transforming suddenly into hunger.

"More?" she squeaked. Heat blasted her face, as though she stood too close to the flickering torches. The chilly night became hot as midday.

"Long ago, the harvest lord chose his corn maiden as his bride of the fields. After the toasts and celebration ended, the lord took his bride into the fields and the two spent the night together in a makeshift bridal tent. The next spring, if the corn maiden was increasing, it was considered an auspicious sign for a good crop, and the two married."

"And if there was no child?"

"Then no wedding."

"Oh, dear." Elizabeth clutched her glass of ale, her heart beating furiously. "How . . . pagan." Aware now of her arm through his, she slipped it out and transferred her glass to that hand. "How could the girl's parents allow such a thing?"

Brack shrugged. "It was the custom, Wrotham said. Pagan perhaps," his voice deepened, "but it was considered a great honor for the girl to be chosen." He nodded toward the harvest lord, busy inspecting a harvest bouquet of stalks of wheat and field flowers offered by a very pretty dark-haired maiden on the end. The offering was supposed to be the measure by which the girl was judged, and this one certainly showed hers off to best advantage by holding it in front of her ample bosom. Michael Thorne was getting an eyeful of more than flowers.

Infectious excitement blazed across the girls' faces. Elizabeth's pulse beat faster as Mr. Thorne bent his tall frame to sniff the bouquet. From the tented look of the man's breeches, he was interested in much more than a kiss. A sheer animal heat seemed to leap from him to the girl, their gazes now locked. The power that emanated from them wafted over Elizabeth, making her want to loosen her spencer to cool her body. Lord, she should never drink Wrotham ale again if it made her this fanciful and uncomfortable.

Had the display affected Lord Brack? She sneaked a look at her escort. His cheeks had taken on a reddish hue. He stared at the couple, as enthralled as she.

Too scandalous for their modern time, this pagan performance should be stopped. Yet even in her censure, her gaze inexorably strayed back to the scene unfolding before them inside the ring of torches.

"Has the harvest lord chosen his corn maiden?" Mr.

Smith, the unofficial master of the festival, called from the edge of the circle.

"He has." Michael Thorne spoke, his deep bass voice echoing down Elizabeth's spine.

The power in that voice had her grabbing Lord Brack's arm once more. She needed an anchor if she was to hear this pronouncement.

Lord Brack seemed just as affected as she. Scarcely taking his eyes off the couple, he tossed back the last of his ale, then dropped the thick glass to the ground. His big hand came down and covered hers, heat streaming through her gloves.

She wanted to grasp his hand as well but couldn't think what to do with her own glass. It still contained some ale, which she could not drink, though she was loathe to spill it on the ground. It somehow seemed sacrilegious. Still, she wanted more contact with the strong male protection next to her. So she stepped closer toward him, almost leaning against him.

He plucked the glass from her hands, swallowed almost half in one gulp, then deliberately poured what remained on the ground around their feet.

Protection against the pagan gods or sacrifice to them? Where had these fanciful notions sprung from all of a sudden?

Again the raw animal power of the moment washed over her and she grasped his hand, pressing it to his arm. If she got much hotter, she'd likely steam in the cold air.

"As the seed goes to the fertile ground, so goes the harvest lord to his maiden . . . Nora Myers." Michael Thorne intoned the ages-old chant, then seized the dark-haired Nora, her face alight with joy and triumph, by the hand and pulled her to him.

A jubilant cry went up from the crowd, a wail of lament from the three would-be corn maidens. They scurried out of the circle, arms around one another.

Elizabeth's heart thumped so hard she gasped for breath. Could Lord Brack feel her pulse pounding in the hand he held so tightly?

The harvest lord led his maiden into the center of the circle, grabbed her around the waist, and lifted her above his head, spinning her around. After making a complete circle, he lowered her inch by inch to the ground. As soon as her feet touched the field stubble, he grasped her face— her cheeks red, her eyes snapping with excitement—and lowered his mouth to hers.

A stab of desire jolted Elizabeth, tearing through her like a lightning bolt straight to the apex of her thighs. Her breasts tingled as the harvest lord claimed his corn maiden.

As Thorne deepened the kiss, Nora threw her arms around his neck, pressing herself against the powerful body before her.

Panting, Elizabeth strained forward as well, her hands clasped viselike around Lord Brack's arm. A moan of need began in her throat, but she bit it back. What was happening to her?

She'd not been this aroused in over a year, not since her husband, Richard—or Dickon, she'd called him— had gone away to war. She'd felt his death so sharply, she'd not even thought about love or desire for another man. Not until Charlotte had dragged her to the house party in August. There she'd met Lord Brack, who she'd found very amiable but hadn't thought of as desirable. Well, not exactly. Nor had she paid much attention to his obvious interest in her. Until now.

His arm tensed as he watched the crowning of the corn maiden. From the corner of her eye, she marked his Grecian profile as it stood stark against the flickering torchlight, his gaze fixed on the couple before them. His jaw clenched so tightly she could almost hear it creak. He turned his head to peer down at her, his eyes dark with a desire of his own.

Slipping his arm around her shoulders, he turned them away from the sight of Michael and Nora as applause from the surrounding crowd crashed around them. He led her from the lighted circle, toward a stand of trees at the edge of the field.

Elizabeth had expected her senses would return once she no longer bore witness to the incredible raw sexual power of that kiss. Her body, however, continued to throb, then to ache with the need to feel a man's touch once more.

Lord Brack stopped just at the tree line, well out of the light. He loosed her hands from their grip on his arm, then cupped her face, just as Michael Thorne had done to Nora, and sank his mouth onto hers.

A bolt of fire shot through her, down her arms and legs, through fingers and toes. Her core heated as though a sun burned at the center, and the ache deep inside her, begun while they watched the harvest couple, became a demand she could not ignore.

Brack deepened the kiss, his tongue stealing warm and welcome into her mouth. She arched her neck, opening herself fully. Let him take her here and now.

As if reading her mind, he wrapped his arms around her, pulling her so tightly to him that every muscle in his chest pressed into her, hard as granite yet comforting as a safe harbor against her hurts and fears. Ah, but she had missed that sense of safety so very much.

Still his tongue explored, now her mouth, now her ear, where his rough panting breath sent new shivers down her spine. His lips traveled lower, down her neck. She couldn't repress the moan this time. Her whole body trembled, ached for Dickon to lay her down here on the ground and take her as he had so many times before.

This wasn't Dickon.

Like a spray of cold water shaken from a rowan tree onto her naked body, Elizabeth jumped back from Lord Brack, suddenly very aware of who he was and where they were.

He too stepped back, blinking as if roused from a dream. "Elizabeth?"

Covering her face with one hand, she held the other out as if to fend him off. What had come over her?

He didn't move toward her but looked away, toward the still-lighted circle where Michael and Nora danced wildly with several other couples. "Please forgive me, Mrs. Easton. I'm not sure what came over me."

"No, my lord, I must beg your pardon." Elizabeth didn't quite know where to look. Not at him, not at the dancing couples. She settled for the ground at her feet. Probably best he didn't see her fiery cheeks.

"I am afraid the spectacle of the harvest lord claiming the corn maiden quite carried me away." He sighed deeply. "I think you may have been affected by it as well?"

Elizabeth risked raising her head. "It was . . . most powerful. I believe many pagan rituals are."

"Yes, well, I am sorry I took advantage of you in the moment." He shook his head. "Most unforgiveable."

"I forgive you, my lord." She leaned forward, putting a hand on his arm to reassure him. "I was as much to blame." Heat stole through her palm where she touched his arm. She snatched it back. "One wonders if it is the ritual or the very place itself that channels these feelings."

"You felt it as well?" His eager voice touched that ache deep inside her.

"I must confess I did." She almost whispered the admission. Could she actually be standing here in a field in the middle of the night saying these indelicate things to a man? A particularly nice gentleman too. What *must* he think of her?

He seized her hands, startling her afresh. "Do not be ashamed, Mrs. Easton, I beg of you. I hope you have noticed these last few days of the house party—no, even before that, when first we met—that I have come to have the greatest respect and admiration for you. Gratitude as well, for your friendship with Georgina."

"Lady Georgina is a dear, dear friend. I would do anything within my power for her." The pleasurable tingles where he held her hands had begun anew.

"You are one of the kindest spirits I have ever known." He pulled her a step closer. "I have been waiting for the right moment to tell you just how much I admire you."

His gaze warmed her as much as his words. She could fall into those big blue eyes and be lost forever. Willingly. Oh, dear, was she doing it again?

"Lord Brack." She leaned back, pulling her hands from his and winding them firmly around her reticule. "I fear a sudden headache has come upon me. Likely brought on by that potent Wrotham ale."

"Mrs. Easton—"

She started toward the area where the horses and carriages waited. "Perhaps that is why ladies are seldom supposed to indulge in it." She must get away from this place, before she was truly lost. "Will you please see me to the carriage? I believe it is time I returned to Lyttlefield Park."

"Allow me to escort you back." He fell in step beside her, but didn't offer his arm.

Perceptive man. If she touched him again, she would completely lose control and quite likely abandon herself to him here and now. And while that prospect had a wild appeal to her at that moment and in this place, in the light of day it simply would not do. "Thank you, my lord, for the offer, but I cannot allow you to leave the festivities on

my account." The short drive back to Wrotham Park
alone would give her time to cool this unusual desire for
him. If she remained here, in the wild sensuality of the
night, she might ravish Lord Brack on the spot.

"I believe it has concluded." He swept his hand toward
the now-ragged circle where the locals were milling
about.

Indeed, the festival seemed at an end.

"It would be my greatest pleasure to see you home
safely." He chuckled. "Even though the robbers in the
area are apprehended, a lady at night alone is never a wise
choice."

Although this might be the one exception to that rule.
"Very well, then." Elizabeth resisted a sigh. He'd got
what she called a *stubborn man face* on—Dickon had
shown it to her enough times, she recognized it on other
gentlemen. She would simply have to keep a vigilant distance from this most attractive man. "I thank you for your
kind offer."

His joyful smile did nothing to buoy her confidence.

She steeled herself for the touch of his hand. "Should
we wait for the others, perhaps? They will be needing the
carriage as well." If others accompanied them, surely
she'd be less inclined to think heated thoughts about the
gentleman seated across from her.

"The distance is less than half a mile. We will send it
back directly we arrive." He tapped on the roof and the
coachman started the team. "If you are in distress, we
must get you home for some tea as quickly as possible.

"You are truly kind, my lord." Elizabeth relaxed
against the soft leather seat and smiled at the personable
young man. He would make any woman an excellent
husband in due time. It might even be her, if only she
were ready to give up her love for Dickon.

She firmed her lips into a pleasant smile. Even though
Charlotte and Georgie had been actively advocating a

match between her and Lord Brack, that didn't mean she was ready for it. Such a major change in her life must take more sober consideration than a few days' acquaintance, delightful though the gentleman might be. She had Dickon's children, Colin and Kate, to think of, after all. There was no need to rush into marriage.

Not even to satisfy the hollow ache deep in her core that suddenly yearned to be filled by the man in the carriage.

Connect with

Us

Visit us online at
KensingtonBooks.com
to read more from your favorite authors, see books
by series, view reading group guides, and more.

Join us on social media

for sneak peeks, chances to win books and prize packs,
and to share your thoughts with other readers.

facebook.com/kensingtonpublishing
twitter.com/kensingtonbooks

Tell us what you think!

To share your thoughts, submit a review,
or sign up for our eNewsletters, please visit:
KensingtonBooks.com/TellUs.